Praise for Denis Hamill and

Throwing 7's

"I'll guarantee that you can't read the first chapter of this book and put it aside. . . . It's a sure bet you'll go missing for at least a day after starting *Throwing 7's*."
—*Rocky Mountain News*

"An intriguing tale. . . . Hamill does a good job in coloring his characters. . . . It is a fast-moving tale and has its eye-opening and thoughtful moments."
—*The Pilot* (Southern Pines, North Carolina)

"A crime thriller of shocking proportions. . . . Packs N.Y. action. . . . This is one of those stories that will keep you up reading late into the night."
—*Naples Daily News* (Florida)

"Readers will be as drawn to this complex hero as they are to the compelling plot. . . . Hamill does everything right—a sure bet for any mystery collection."
—*Booklist*

"[*Throwing 7's*] is no gamble. . . . [It's] full of knaves and knights, vendettas, plot twists and hard-boiled action. . . . Hamill knows the city, its neighborhoods and the street lingo."
—*Daily Press* (Newport News, Virginia)

3 Quarters

"Hamill boasts all the shiv-sharp dialogue, flamboyant characters, and hair-trigger action of a Quentin Tarantino film festival."

—*People*

"Hamill knows of what he writes—the city and the good and bad characters that thrive here. . . . As good a tale of New York as it gets."

—*New York Post*

"Denis Hamill gives New York the justice it deserves. *3 Quarters* is a page-turning life on the dark side of this city as only Denis Hamill can portray it."

—Winston Groom, author of *Forrest Gump*

"*3 Quarters* is as scary and breathtaking as a midnight walk across the Brooklyn Bridge. Denis Hamill is one of the true stars of New York."

—Peter Blauner, author of *Slow Motion Riot* and *The Intruder*

"*3 Quarters* is a fast-moving story of corruption and violence in which the cops and wiseguys and lawyers of New York City come vividly to life. Denis Hamill is a writer of talent in the tradition of Richard Price and Jimmy Breslin. He had a good time writing this book and offers one to his readers as well."

—Bob Leuci, author of *The Snitch*

House on Fire

"Urban novel writing at its most intense. . . . Artful. . . . Tough-minded. . . . Hamill offers a sharply etched roster of urban scoundrels and dented heroes lurching through the high-pressure zones of the city."
— *Star-Ledger* (Newark, New Jersey)

"Gritty and hard-hitting."
— *Post-Bulletin* (Rochester, Minnesota)

"[Hamill's] emotionally damaged brothers and the women who love them are real people who react believably. The settings become characters, too, and the Los Angeles fire . . . is particularly riveting."
— *Library Journal*

"Denis Hamill writes with a power and authenticity of which I am envious. *House on Fire* is entirely compelling."
— Robert B. Parker

"Bracing. . . . With brutal clarity, Hamill creates a memorable cast and sets his people on various journeys (literal and psychological) that may or may not end well for everyone here, but do far better for the reader."
— *Kirkus Reviews*

"Denis Hamill knows New York and New Yorkers . . . the same way James T. Farrell knew Chicago."
— Lawrence Block

ALSO BY DENIS HAMILL

STOMPING GROUND

MACHINE

HOUSE ON FIRE

3 QUARTERS

FORK IN THE ROAD

THROWING 7'S

DENIS HAMILL

POCKET STAR BOOKS

New York   London   Toronto   Sydney   Singapore

This book is a work of fiction. Names, characters, places and incidents are products of the author's imagination or are used fictitiously. Any resemblance to actual events or locales or persons, living or dead, is entirely coincidental.

A Pocket Star Book published by
POCKET BOOKS, a division of Simon & Schuster Inc.
1230 Avenue of the Americas, New York, NY 10020

Copyright © 1999 by Denis Hamill

Originally published in hardcover in 1999 by Pocket Books

ISBN: 0-671-02615-1

First Pocket Books paperback printing February 2000

10 9 8 7 6 5 4 3 2 1

POCKET STAR BOOKS and colophon are registered trademarks of Simon & Schuster Inc.

Front cover illustration by Don Brautigam

Printed in the U.S.A.

FOR MY BROTHER JOHN,
for coming marching home again,
and for everything before and since

THROWING
7's

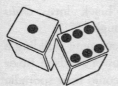

JULY 30

Eddie McCoy heard his wife's muffled scream.

He awoke in a bleary daze in the warm, firm bed, his eyes probing the charcoal darkness. A dull ache pulsed at his temples. *Too much wine with dinner,* he thought. On the night table a digital clock radio with soft blue numerals offered the only light and told McCoy that it was 3:57 AM.

He had fallen asleep listening to a talk radio show where the top state assemblyman and top state senator were debating a legalized-gambling resolution vote looming in the New York State Legislature. The radio host was still gabbing about it at low volume when McCoy heard his wife's strangled whimper again. Then he felt her thrashing as if in seizure.

McCoy said, "Sally, honey, wha' . . ."

He never got to finish the word, as the barrel of a .357 Magnum–Smith & Wesson was jammed into his open mouth, chipping his right front tooth, driving a hot needle into his brain. As his wife whimpered in muzzled panic beside him, McCoy saw two white eyes peering down at him through the holes of a black ski mask. The eyes didn't blink. The cold steel circle of the four-inch pistol barrel triggered McCoy's

gag reflex as it thrust against the back of his throat.
He sucked for air through his nostrils. Only one
worked. He felt his own frantic pulse thumping
against the barrel of the gun. He could smell the
fresh leather of the gunman's new black gloves. *Only
a killer wears gloves in July,* he thought.

From outside his West Side tenement building a
half-block from the banks of the lower Hudson River
in downtown Manhattan, McCoy could hear sporadic
traffic. As the dark river tirelessly emptied into the
harbor he could hear a buoy ding, a ferry horn moan, a
dock dog barking. He gagged again and shifted his
head to the side on the down pillow and looked over at
his wife. Silver duct tape covered Sally's lovely full lips.
Her eyes were wet, deep, smeared with mascara, and
looked to him like little muddy graves. Her left foot
was wrapped in a bloody towel and covered by a plastic bag that was secured by duct tape.

When their eyes met, Sally looked ready to
implode, raging screams leaking from her nostrils like
a puppy's sobs.

Sally was also bound at the wrists and ankles with
duct tape.

"Face China," the gunman whispered to Eddie
McCoy.

The gunman slowly removed the gun from
McCoy's mouth and as McCoy made the turn to his
belly, he lashed out at the intruder with a poorly
thrown right hand. He missed and felt the heavy
thump of the one-pound gun thwack the bone over

his right eye. He felt warm blood lick down his face, saw silver amoebas of light swimming in front of his eyes, thought he might pass out, but struggled for consciousness. For Sally's sake.

"Try that again and I'll violate your wife in a very unpleasant fashion," the gunman said. "And make you watch."

He heard a chilling clash of steel on steel and then saw the gunman opening and closing a pair of heavy-duty cable nippers used by electricians, saw the blue hue of the radio reflect in the shiny blades. The gunman placed the blades under Sally's earlobe and swiftly nicked it, bringing forth a round ruby of blood, which dropped onto the white sheet beneath her.

"Please, no," McCoy said, blotting his bloody eye on his white pillowcase. "Please don't hurt her. Take anything you want. I'll give you my bank card. There's six hundred and fifty-eight bucks in there. The PIN number is eight-two-six-seven. My computer is worth about another eight hundred. My wife's jewelry is a couple of hundred. Please, don't hurt her. Don't hurt us."

"Stop begging," the gunman said. "Begging's for dogs."

The gunman motioned for McCoy to roll onto his belly. He did and the gunman pulled McCoy's arms behind him and snapped a pair of handcuffs on his wrists. McCoy heard them ratchet tight, felt them pinch his skin. He lifted his head as the gunman fastened duct tape over his mouth. His head dropped back on the pillow and he stared at Sally. He winked at her with his good eye, hoping she knew it meant he loved her. Her body was vibrating, spastic in terror.

McCoy continued to stare at his wife, wanted to see as much of her as he could in what he was sure were their last minutes alive. He heard the gunman walk across the apartment, open the door, and drag something loud, hollow, and metallic into the room.

"Lie flat," the gunman whispered in McCoy's ear. "Your foot is gonna feel a pinch and then go numb. Novocaine. To kill the pain. Your wife didn't feel a thing when I did her."

Then McCoy felt the prick of a needle in his left foot, felt it quickly turning fuzzy and numb. McCoy saw the gunman look at his watch, as if counting, and as each second passed his foot became increasingly void of feeling.

After a minute the gunman said, "Just a little snip now."

Eddie McCoy saw him take out the cable nippers again and then felt a sickening pressure on his foot. It wasn't painful as much as it was a humiliating violation.

McCoy watched the gunman wrap his bloody foot in a towel, encase it in a plastic bag, and fasten it with more duct tape.

"There now, all done," he said.

McCoy watched in horror as the gunman trimmed

his second toe like a gourmet butcher, leaving the scraps on the bloody sheet. He placed McCoy's toe into a plastic Ziploc baggie alongside a smaller toe. The red nail polish on that one told him it was his wife's.

If this is a kidnapping and the toes are going to be sent to someone with a ransom demand, we're dead, he thought. He didn't know anyone who could afford a ransom. The only family he had was a sister and she didn't have any money. Sally had no family.

The gunman pulled up a small desk chair. He sat McCoy up in the bed and motioned for him to mount the chair and to climb into the four-by-four-foot wheeled garbage bin that the Chinese landlord used to collect recyclables in their rent-controlled building. It was the last occupied building on Empire Court, which had become a desolate night street in the past couple of years as, one after another, the surrounding dwellings had been abandoned.

McCoy did as he was instructed, hobbling on his bleeding numb foot, almost falling as he climbed into the trash cart.

Now the gunman gently lifted Sally McCoy from the bed and placed her on McCoy's lap in the recycle bin. "Cute," the gunman said. Sally looked at Eddie and buried her head between his left shoulder and his head, leaving smudges of wet mascara on his white T-shirt as she wept. A thin trickle of blood coursed from her nicked ear.

The gunman opened the bedding-chest at the foot of the bed and yanked out a floral patterned down comforter with a flourish and placed it snugly over the McCoys and wheeled them out of the apartment, leaving the door unlocked and ajar behind him.

He rolled the bin to the small waiting elevator, which was jammed open with a broom. The whole snatch had taken less than three minutes. He took the elevator to the basement, the old cables groaning in the pre-WWII shaft. The dank cellar smelled of mold, cats, molting cockroaches, and rodent droppings. The gunman pushed the bin across the basement, to the rear door, which led to the alley where Chung, the landlord, always took out the building's garbage. McCoy could hear the soft meows of a three-week-old kitten and the mother cat that patrolled the basement. Sally usually brought the mother table scraps every day. She had found homes for two of the kittens. She was going to take the last one for herself this week. McCoy felt his beloved Sally sob harder in the dark under the comforter as they passed the meowing kitten.

The air was almost gone and McCoy thrust with his head to move the edge of the blanket. His wounded eye glanced along the inside wall of the bin, leaving a bloody streak. He used his head to nudge Sally's bloody earlobe against the wall so that she would also leave an evidence trail. *It's all we can do*, McCoy thought.

"Be still," the gunman instructed, opening a flap of blanket for air.

McCoy breathed deeply through his one functioning nostril as the gunman shoved the bin out the back door and up the cement incline to the alley. The wheels rolled roughly over the cement of the alley, which ran like a dark, century-old slot canyon between the tenements of Empire Court and the barren warehouses of Ellis Walk. McCoy heard the doors of a vehicle open. He felt the bin shift as it was pushed up a ramp by the grunting gunman into the back of a van. He heard the van doors close and the heavy breathing of the gunman as he climbed into the driver's seat. The engine started and they were soon rumbling through the streets of lower Manhattan.

The trip was eerily brief. *One block, less than a minute*, McCoy thought. *The waterfront. Of course. The terminal. This wasn't a robbery. Or a kidnapping. This wasn't about the apartment. This was about the terminal. This was about untold millions, maybe billions . . .*

McCoy heard the water lapping against the boats of the Harbor Head Marina, nestled almost unnoticed near the tip of the nose of Manhattan Island. He could smell the dirty bay water as the back doors of the van opened and the bin was wheeled out.

"Nice and easy," said the gunman.

The bin jolted over the wooden planks of the dock, and finally, as they came to the end of the deserted pier, the gunman lifted the heavy comforter off the McCoys. He cut the tape fastening Sally's legs and helped her out first. Then Eddie. Stars riveted the night sky and the muted hue of the brightest skyline on Earth bathed the fitful waters near the shore. McCoy sucked in the night air, looked out at the black water, at Empire Island, which lay a half-mile out like a sleeping sea monster. McCoy realized he had indeed been driven a scant block from his home. He could see his own bedroom window from the dock. He should be in there, sleeping, with Sally, waiting for another bright morning.

Instead the masked gunman led McCoy and his wife aboard a twenty-foot Regal boat with fifty-horsepower engine and quickly down into the cabin. He placed the comforter over them.

"It'll get chilly out there," the gunman said.

McCoy watched the gunman climb up on deck, heard him cast off and then the low tremble of the engine coming to life. Within thirty seconds the boat was chugging out into the harbor. McCoy knew where they were going. *Empire Island,* he thought. *Has to be. Coast Guard relocated. Abandoned now. Smack in the middle of the harbor of the richest city on the planet. Real estate bonanza. The mayor called it New York's Monte Carlo. Priceless. And worth killing for . . .*

Sally had stopped crying. She sat in a state of catatonic arrest. When McCoy looked her in the eyes she didn't seem to be there as they bounded over the roiled waters for the next seven or eight minutes.

Then the engine was cut and the boat seemed to drift weightlessly, as if in space, and silence prevailed. Then McCoy felt the mild bump as the Regal met another small dock. He heard the footsteps of the gunman on the upper deck.

Within a minute Eddie and Sally McCoy were led onto Empire Island, in the center of New York Harbor. Behind them the great skyline sparkled. To the left Lady Liberty touched her torch to the starry sky. A Staten Island ferry floated over the water like a giant orange ladybug. Thin traffic glittered on the Brooklyn–Queens Expressway, and laced up the FDR Drive of Manhattan. The downtown bridges fastened the city together like giant clamps. New Jersey lay beyond, etherized in the lunar glow.

As he got his bearings, McCoy heard the low grinding hum of a heavy machine off in the distance, something alive and animated in the stillness. The masked gunman pointed and the McCoys limped on their numbed, injured feet a few hundred yards up a cobblestone pathway. They passed between two large hillocks of gravel and sand, toward a rotating cement mixer, a forty-foot crane, and a backhoe that sat still and ominous around a gaping ten-foot-deep pit that was ten foot square.

McCoy listened to the slow, sloshing revolutions of the cement mixer, the twelve yards of gravel and cement clanking off the steel walls of the big barrel. A dump truck loaded with fifty yards of gravel sat six feet away from it at the edge of the gaping pit. In the upper-right-hand corner of the pit a four-foot-square section was compartmentalized off with timber framing and plyboard. Two fifty-gallon metal oil drums were sunk into that hole like dry wells.

Eddie McCoy looked at the chute of the cement mixer that was pointing directly into the pit. Now he knew how he would die.

The gunman led them between the cement mixer and the dump truck to the edge of the pit. Sally McCoy looked at the cement mixer, the pit, and then at her husband. He winked. Three times, as if to say, *I . . . Love . . . You.* He heard a sound rise from inside her that he didn't know a human being could produce, a high-pitched muffled eruption that he thought might exit through the top of her skull. Most of it came out of her eyes as horror when she looked at her husband.

The gunman urged them closer to the edge of the pit, which looked bottomless in the darkness. Harbor wind blew in circles around them. The gunman gently removed the tape from Eddie's mouth.

"I'll take off her tape too if you want," the gunman said. "As long as she promises not to beg. I hate that, the begging."

"Why are you doing this?" Eddie asked.

"It's what I do," he said.

"It's about the apartment, isn't it?" McCoy said. "The rent-controlled apartment. The landlord, Jimmy Chung, he sent you. So he can sell to Kronk for the terminal . . . Kronk is behind this . . ."

"Look, do you want to kiss your wife goodbye or what?"

Eddie McCoy nodded. "Look, tell Chung we'll move. Tell Kronk he'll never hear a word from me . . . us . . . again. Never. Please . . ."

"No begging," the gunman said, waving a finger.

McCoy knew there would be no reversal, no reprieve. He was going to die. With his Sally.

Now.

This was it.

He leaned close to his wife and whispered in her ear. She sobbed uncontrollably but finally nodded. McCoy looked at the gunman and gave him the cue. The gunman removed the tape from Sally's mouth and before she could scream Eddie placed his mouth over hers, smothering her final wail. As they kissed their final kiss the gunman shoved them into the hole and yanked a lever on the gravel truck, which sent fifty yards of gravel down the chute into the hole on top of them. The screams of the McCoys were fast muffled as the gunman pulled the handle on the cement mixer, which sent twelve yards of wet cement on top of the gravel. He let the foot-deep cement settle and gurgle into a still beige bog. He quickly ran the broad side of a two-by-four over the bubbly top to smooth it out, the summer moon reflecting in the wet surface. Only the four-by-four-foot sectioned-off square remained unfilled.

The gunman shut off the cement mixer and walked back to the boat.

2

Bobby Emmet slapped two turkey burgers on the sizzling grill and promised his fourteen-year-old daughter, Maggie, that they'd be alone for his birthday. His kid was doing eighty-average work at the fancy private school and coming up on finals in two extra-credit summer-school courses and was also scheduled to take her PSATs in a week. If Maggie didn't pull up her grade average and score at least 1,300 in the PSATs, Bobby's ex-wife, Connie, was threatening to cancel her and Bobby's scheduled trip to Florida to visit Bobby's mother when summer school ended.

"Maggie, you could probably give Bill Gates computer lessons," Bobby said as he turned the turkey burgers on the grill. "You have access to all the information ever recorded by human history at your disposal. You were on the honor roll all through grade school and junior high. So what's the problem at school now?"

Maggie shrugged.

They were standing on the deck of *The Fifth Amendment*, the forty-two-foot Silverton boat on which Bobby lived in slip 99A of the Seventy-ninth Street Boat Basin on the Manhattan banks of the Hudson River.

Bobby was shirtless, wearing cutoff jeans and sneakers, the muscles in his six foot two, 210-pound frame rippling after a morning in which he'd done 500 push-ups, 500 sit-ups, and six seven-minute miles, running along the West Side all the way down to Twentieth Street and back uptown to the boatyard. Tomorrow morning he'd hit the free weights at Chelsea Piers and bang the heavy bag for eight rounds. His buddy Max Roth, a columnist for the *Daily News*, was also going to give him another lesson on the rock-climbing wall to build the shoulders and back.

"A shrug's not an answer," Bobby said, turning the burgers.

"My problem is that my mom expects me to cure cancer, write a symphony, and get engaged to Steven Spielberg's son by the time I graduate high school," Maggie said. "I have other plans."

"Okay, so what's your boyfriend's name?" Bobby asked. It was that time in his teenage daughter's life when boys have an impact on everything—clothes, makeup, songs, moods, eating habits, relationship with parents, and especially schoolwork. Bobby thought they should give fourteen-year-old girls a hormone count and factor that into a curve on any PSAT score.

"Not a boyfriend, just a dude I'm talking to," Maggie said, her hands jammed in the front pockets of her faded Gap jeans, her navy and white Air Max Elite sneakers, boys' size six, squeaking on the polished deck of the boat, which lolled in the tame tide.

"So, how old is Dude?" Bobby asked, shoveling a well-done burger onto a sesame bun, handing it to Maggie.

"Name's not Dude, Dad," she said, with a laugh. "It's Cal."

"Calvin . . ."

"Cal. Calvin sounds so herbified. Cal is cool."

"I'm glad Cal is cool," Bobby said, taking his own burger in his two hands now and chomping into it. "But is he smart?"

"I don't hang with dummies. He's a book genius, a computer whiz, a good athlete. But Mom doesn't like him because he's a scholarship kid."

"Say that all over again," Bobby said, taking a slug of club soda mixed with cranberry juice and another big bite of the burger.

"He's from Elmhurst, Queens," Maggie said. "His father is a fireman. But Cal won a scholarship to my snob private prep school."

"Oh," said Bobby. "A working-class kid with brains money can't buy. The nerve of him."

"You got it," Maggie said. "But he's funny, Dad, and cool and nice and . . . *cute*. I don't need a dude with money. I have a mother who owns the third-biggest cosmetics company in America and a step-father who owns the second-biggest one in America. So I don't need a boyfriend to buy me a ticket to my next Leonardo DiCaprio picture."

"You admitted it. You said the magic word."

Maggie picked and nibbled the sesame seeds off

her bun, didn't touch the meat, took a sip of Diet Coke. "What magic word?"

"*Boyfriend*," Bobby said.

"I didn't say *boyfriend*."

"Did too," Bobby said, and then polished off his burger.

"Did not."

"Too."

"Not," she said, a single-strap brace retainer holding together a beautiful smile. "What we need here is some proper proof. Which you'd have if you'd let me take you shopping at the Snoop Shop."

Maggie knew her father had already gotten his pistol carry permit back and that he was committed to at least another year and a half of indentured servitude to a certain sleazy lawyer named Izzy Gleason— who had gotten Bobby out of a murder rap frame the year before. "I want my old man to be a state-of-the-art private eye," she said winking her left eye. "A shamus I won't be ashamed of."

"You read too much Raymond Chandler," he said.

"You gave me his books," she said. "Said he'd be a good change from Jane Austen."

"Touché," he said. "At least the women in *his* books work for a living."

"And I want to help you with your job," she said.

Maggie was determined to buy Bobby gifts at the Snoop Shop, a store in the West Village that sold all those wacky gizmos for surveillance, spying, eavesdropping, and secret recording, so popular with conspiracy freaks, marital paranoids, and assorted degenerates. She'd told Bobby that now that he had officially resigned from the Manhattan District Attorney's detective squad and had a private investigator's license, he should at least have the latest tools of the trade.

"You're a working man," Maggie said. "I'm a spoiled rich kid with too much money for a thousand kids, so at least let me buy my old man some hardware for his birthday."

"Have I ever lied to you, Mag?" Bobby asked, getting back to the boyfriend/schoolwork topic.

"Were the bedtime stories you used to tell me about Sticky the Dog with a magic nose that could smell a lie, true?"

"If you believed in them they were," Bobby said.

"Okay, then you never lied to me," Maggie said. "Never. Not even when you were in jail for the murder of Dorothea. You promised you'd come home and prove you were innocent. And you did."

"Okay," Bobby said. "No lie, you said *boyfriend*. Cal is your boyfriend. Mom disapproves of him because he's working-class."

"*Shanty* is her word of choice," Maggie said. "It sounds dirtier and lower on the food chain."

"You know I wouldn't disapprove of him for coming from people who work with their hands for a living. But I don't automatically approve of him for it, either. I don't care how much money he has, so long as he's nice to you. But if he is distracting you from school, I back your mother—and disapprove, too."

"Cal's so smart he doesn't need to study," she said.

"Good for Cal," Bobby said. "But us mere mortal nerds, we need to study. Maybe it's old fashioned, maybe it's for Herbs, but . . ."

"You're mixing up nerds and Herbs again, old man. A nerd chooses to be a brownnose bore who can't dress. A Herb can't help what he is. He's just born with herbitis."

"I stand corrected. But here's the deal from your old man. I'm just your average, divorced, weekend father. Your mom is your primary custodian. But when you're with me, if you study three hours, you can have three hours with Cal. You read, do your papers, go over vocabulary for the PSATs all Saturday morning, you got Saturday night out with Cal, so long as I know where you're going."

"Cool," Maggie said.

"Plus I gotta meet him."

"*Un*-cool."

"*Un*-cool is *un*-acceptable."

"He doesn't like meeting parents," Maggie said.

"Tell him he has a choice. Me or your mother."

"I'll bring him to meet you next weekend."

"Deal," Bobby said.

"But you gotta shop with me at the Snoop Shop for your birthday," she said. "If you're gonna be a private eye, old man, I'm gonna make sure you're state-of-the-art."

"Okay," Bobby said. "And later we'll see any movie or any show you want and go for a little late din-din at the West Bank."

"I love that place! We saw Winona Ryder there the last time. And Alec Baldwin. Is Bruce Willis really a friend of the owner's?"

"Yep. Steve the owner and Bruce are old elbow-bending buddies."

"Cool."

"I have the cell phone shut off so even your mother can't call to interrupt us. Then tomorrow, you study."

"But you're saying today's just for us?" Maggie said, a coy smile spreading across her tanned face.

"Yep."

"Then I think you might need a pair of those rearview glasses from the Snoop Shop that let you see behind you."

"Huh?"

From behind him on the dock Bobby heard the dreaded voice that sounded like the desperate whine of an airplane engine dying. While on board. Bobby tensed and gripped the boat railing as if it were the arms of the seat on the nosediving plane.

"Christ Almighty, I've been calling all freakin' day!" Izzy Gleason shouted as he came aboard *The Fifth Amendment*, smoking a long cigarette, holding a styrofoam cup in his right hand, his ginger hair gleaming, the big caps on his teeth like a housing tract of igloos. "Your phone's shut off. What the hell's a matter with you? We got us a client with a heartbeat and piece of harbor view property and a real lulu of a case for the newspapers and TV. We'll need your buddy, Roth, from the *News.* '*The Rent Control Murders, featuring Izzy Gleason for the defense.' Bobby Emmet, PI . . . !*"

Izzy Gleason stopped in mid-sentence to stare at two twenty-something women in string bikinis working on early tans on board a Chinese junk named *Armitage* moored in the neighboring slip. "Yoo-hoo, honey pies, if either of you *can't* type I could sure use a secretary," Izzy shouted.

The women were lying belly down on chaise longues, the strings of their tops untied for uniform color. They looked up and smiled. "We'll wait until Bobby's hiring," said Pam, the one with the yellow suit.

"Volunteer us then," said Dot, the one with the white bikini.

"Not today, Izzy," Bobby shouted rushing to the entrance of the boat, waving his arms, blocking Izzy's entrance.

"You think if I started singing 'The Star-Spangled Banner' they'd leap up to attention real fast?" Izzy asked.

"About face, Iz," Bobby said.

"Hey, I got me a Chinaman hiding out, ready to be stir-fried in homicide oil. Out of all the lawyers in our great big city of New York he picked me out of the Yellow Pages," Izzy said. "Funny, huh? A Chinaman using the Yellow Pages. What color you think the phone book is in Peking, anyway?"

"Izzy," Bobby shouted, "I'm having a visitation with my daughter. It's my birthday . . ."

"Happy birthday, Bobby," Pam and Dot sang out in unison.

"Then do I have a birthday gift for you. Your usual ten percent of whatever I get for you to do your Charlie Chan routine, podner . . ."

"I'm *not* your partner," Bobby said.

"You made a deal with me . . ."

"The deal was you get me off the murder charge, I do investigative work for you gratis for two years," Bobby said. "That's called indentured servitude, not partnership."

"And here you are," Izzy said. "Less than a year later, living on my ship, which is part of the deal . . ."

"Boat," Bobby corrected, "not ship . . ."

". . . driving my Jeep, using my office, and my cell phone, which you have turned off—when I need you."

"It's the weekend," Bobby said. "My time with my daughter. I promised her we'd be alone. I might be indentured to you professionally but I am not your goddamned personal slave."

"Dad, if it's a *case*, I don't mind," Maggie said, excited. "As long as I can help you with it."

"See," Izzy said, squeezing past Bobby onto the

deck of *The Fifth Amendment*. He flicked a lit Kent 100 overboard, drained his styrofoam cup, picked up Maggie's untouched turkey burger, and mashed it into his mouth. "Sorry," he mumbled, "is anyone eating this?"

"Yeah, the pet dingo," Bobby said. "Now."

"Is there any un-diet Coke?" Izzy asked, lifting the bun, picking up a salt shaker from the condiment table, and dumping a blizzard of it on the burger. He squeezed on more ketchup, added mayo, mustard, a handful of potato chips, and some bread-and-butter pickles before slapping the bun back on top. He opened his mouth so wide his eyes involuntarily closed as he bear-trapped the burger.

"All we have is diet," Maggie said.

"Thanks, kid, I'll offer it up for the Holy Souls in Burgatory." Maggie smiled and handed him a Diet Coke and a napkin.

"He eats like a blunt head, Dad," Maggie said, giggling.

"Honey, you think you can go play with your dolls while I talk to your old man about big people's things like murder and money?"

"I hope you can swim and eat at the same time," Bobby said, standing and grabbing Izzy by the arm.

"Chill, Pop," Maggie said. "I want to go inside and call Cal, anyway. Izzy's cool. He's . . . *different*. Plus he brought you home to me from jail."

Sometimes she reminded Bobby of things he wished he could forget.

"Bright kid," Izzy said.

Maggie went into the salon of the Silverton and pulled the door closed. Izzy took a long drink of the Diet Coke, pushed the last of the burger in his mouth, belched, and began to pace, like Joe Cocker live in concert. For a man five foot seven and 155 pounds, Izzy Gleason took up more room, could eat more, and made more noise than a hockey team. Since he stepped on board, the Silverton had shrunk to the size of a dinghy.

Izzy wiped his hands on the lining of his light-blue Cerruti suit. His polished white loafers with black leather heels clicked on the wooden deck. He picked at his teeth with the corner of a business card and lit a new cigarette with a disposable lighter.

"You hear the news this morning?" Izzy asked.

"I watched the homicides *du jour* on TV," Bobby said. "When you weren't one of them, I got disappointed and turned it off."

"The Empire Court rent-control couple that disappeared?"

"I saw that, yeah . . ."

"That's my Chinaman."

"The word is 'Chinese,' " Bobby said.

"It's okay I call you an Irishman but I can't call a guy named Chung a Chinaman? Who makes these rules? Japs?"

"Never mind, get on with it," Bobby said.

"The McCoys, the missing couple, they were in a beef with our client," Izzy said.

"*Your* client," Bobby said. "In the immortal words of Sam Goldwyn, include me out of this."

"Jimmy Chung, the landlord . . ."

"Slumlord," Bobby said, "from what I could glean."

"Slumlord, warlord, Lord and Taylor, who gives a rat's ass," Izzy said. "Fact is, when they picked Chung up on suspicion in the disappearance of Eddie and Sally McCoy, he called me. I went down there. And who do you think is there sweatin' him?"

"Charlie Chan," Bobby said. "What is this, charades? Tell me what you want. I have a fourteen-year-old daughter who is suffering through first love, Regents finals, SATs, and a neurotic mother, who just happens to be my ex-wife . . ."

"And not a bad piece of ass-ettes," Izzy said.

"Watch your filthy mouth. That's the mother of my kid."

"Hey, no offense, but I always wondered? What it's like spanking a rich bitch with a cricket paddle?"

"Izzy, I'm warning you."

"Okay, back to Chinese checkers. Anyways, I go down and who do you think has my wily Oriental gentleman under the hot lamp? None other than your steroid—anthropoid—ex-partner, Chris Kringle."

"Noel Christmas?"

"Yeah," said Izzy. "What the fuck kinda handle is that anyway?"

"His mother died giving birth on Christmas Eve and his father had a sense of humor," Bobby said.

"His name might be Noel Christmas but he has a fuckin' face like Good Friday," Izzy said, spitting overboard into the wind. "After Judas's kiss. That no-neck, lamebrain, muscle-bound, lab-primate was at Brooklyn Law School when I was there—twenny years ago, and he's still there, nights! I told them they should give him a fuckin' gold watch instead of a law degree."

"He's tenacious," Bobby said.

"He's *stupid*, is what he is," Izzy said, walking toward the door to the salon. "You have any vodka to kill the taste of this diet shit?"

"It's the afternoon, Izzy. Can't you at least wait till sundown, especially when you're working?"

"I been up since six," Izzy said, pulling out a pack of Goldenberg's Peanut Chews, pushing three chocolate squares into his mouth. "I already did my job. I sprung the shirt-starcher. Now it's your turn to go to work on his alibi and whatever happened to the missing McCoys. Because, personally, I don't think he's gonna be out long before your friend Noel Santa Claus puts another arrest warrant in his stocking. Crime scene apparently looked like Bela Lugosi's lunch. Blood everywhere. Santa put a rush on the blood tests. They found flesh and bone fragments."

"Christmas. His name is Noel Christmas, and he's no friend of mine, either. He was my partner in the Manhattan DA's office for two years, and when I got jammed up he was deafeningly silent. He didn't lift a finger to help me."

"Then here's your chance to pull this Arnold wanna-be's pants down in public and let everyone see what a small metabolic steroid pee-pee he has," Izzy said. "Make my guy walk, send Christmas to hell in his fuckin' toy bag, and collect your ten percent of my fee as my trusty little shamus. Plus ten percent of whatever the building's worth as a bonus. You gonna be a man and earn a few dollars or you gonna let your ex-wife pay your kid's tuition again come September?"

Izzy knew where to hurt Bobby—in his Irish working-class family pride.

"Is your guy innocent?" Bobby asked, coming around.

"How the fuck would I know? I care about that like I lose sleep over the war between Iran and Iraq. You're the fuckin' investigator. I can't understand three words he says. If he was a waiter, I'd order and he'd probably bring me sweet and sour Doberman. That's why I hired me a new girl this morning to translate."

He pointed to the rotunda overlooking the boat basin, where a longhaired young Asian woman leaned over the railing, smoking a cigarette. Izzy waved at her; she waved her cigarette at him in a lazy loop.

"At six this morning, you hired her?"

"She's flexible."

"From where?"

"She's a physical therapist I see for my bad back . . ."

"You hired a chick from a massage parlor as a translator?"

"She's legit, speaks a six-pack of Chinese dialects. She just does shiatsu massages to help pay her way through college."

"Jeez, that's original," Bobby said.

"She rings acupuncture doorbells all over your body. This broad walks on your back, she can translate a slipped disk into a break dance. One visit to The Bamboo Rack and you're a new man. You go in like a totaled Taurus and you come out like a mint Mercedes."

"The Bamboo *Rack?*" Bobby said. "Sounds like a POW camp."

"Anyway, we worked out a barter on the translating gig," Izzy said. "I'm gonna work out a little problem she has."

"Izzy Gleason's Green Card Sweepstakes," Bobby said. "She performs a few illegal acts for you, instead of you paying legal tender, you'll make her a legal resident."

"You have a very dirty mind," Izzy said, grinning.

"Must be the company I'm forced to keep."

Izzy pulled open the salon door, reached into the overhead closet above the sink, removed a bottle of Absolut vodka. He poured the vodka into the opening in the Diet Coke can and placed his thumb over the hole and shook. As the foam rose Izzy covered it with his mouth until his cheeks puffed like a chipmunk's. He swallowed and belched, poured more vodka into the can, and put the bottle away.

"Anyway, I wouldn't let Jimmy Chung answer any

questions," Izzy said. "I told Christmas, charge him or march him."

"Why'd they pick him up?"

"The McCoys had a rent-controlled apartment for like six hundred a month and were always moaning, complaining about silly shit—rodent infestation, no heat in winter, no hot water, ceiling collapses," Izzy said, taking another slug of the cola and vodka.

"Nigglers. How dare they want tickets to the bleacher seats of civilization."

"Chung makes no bones that he wanted them out. Then last night an anonymous caller called 911 from a pay phone, around five AM, said he saw a masked man struggling to load a garbage bin into a white van in the alley behind 22 Empire Court. The license plate he gave was registered to my guy. Cops responded to the building. Did a routine search, knocking on doors. They found the McCoys' apartment door opened. Found blood and flesh and bone fragments on the pillow and sheets. Found similar blood in the recycling bin in the basement. They suspect foul play. The wife has no family. But I hear McCoy has a loudmouth sister who told the cops that her brother and Chung had been at each other's throats for months. So they brought in my guy. Before he could select a plea from Column A or a sentence from Column B, I sprung him."

"That's it?"

"So far. Except my China-client owns the building—which he very generously signed over to me in lieu of an eventual fifty-K retainer," Izzy said, taking another gulp. "This goes to trial, he ups with half a mil or I'll own that building."

"He agreed to that?"

"Like I sez, his English ain't too good," Izzy said. "But he signed his name. Now it's no tickee, no buildee."

"You just got reinstated to the bar last year, Izzy," Bobby said. "You want to get suspended again? Or disbarred this time?"

"Hey, no law or ethics board says I can't pick my price. This is the U.S. of A., as in A good living. I'm a high-priced criminal defense attorney because I'm the fuckin' best there is. This ain't a fuckin' house closing here. They're trying to put my guy in the smokehouse for a double whammy."

"They don't even have a case on him yet," Bobby said. "You don't need me."

"Well, they have motive, they have opportunity, and then there's also the blood they found in Jimmy Chung's van, which if it matches the blood on the pillow and the garbage bin is pretty good circumstantial evidence . . ."

"Okay," Bobby said with a groan. "Where the hell is he?"

"Stashed in my office," Izzy said.

3

Maggie was thoroughly under-standing about Bobby having to do a bit of unpleasant business on his birthday. She said she'd go home to her mother's Trump Tower duplex to study for her PSATs and her finals, which were coming up the next week. They kissed each other goodbye and he promised to see her the next day to go to The Snoop Shop.

Bobby pulled on a pair of dungarees, stuffed his cell phone into the pocket of his black and white Hawaiian shirt, put his .38 into his front pants pocket, made sure his carry license and PI ticket were in his wallet, and left with Izzy.

The boat basin was one of the safest addresses in the big city and Bobby waved goodbye to Doug the dockmaster, the city park worker who took care of all 101 slips, including 99A, the lease for which was in Izzy Gleason's name. The monthly rent was $379, with a fashionable Upper West Side river view.

"This is Beverly," Izzy said, when he introduced the Asian woman in the yellow micro-mini and matching platform heels who had climbed into the backseat of the six-year-old Jeep Cherokee. The Jeep belonged to Izzy and was, like the boat, on indefinite loan to Bobby.

"Betty," the woman corrected.

Bobby drove out of the boat basin garage under the rotunda, up Seventy-ninth Street to West End, and made a right.

"Okay. Betty," Izzy said. "As in Boop-boop-eee-doo."

"Translate, please," said Betty.

"It means you strut a mean spine, Betty Boop," Izzy said.

"Nice to meet you, Betty," Bobby said.

"Happnin'," she said.

Bobby looked in the rearview mirror at the pretty woman in her mid-twenties. She looked nervous as she gnawed the inside of her lower lip, swallowed, stared out the window. She caught Bobby looking at her in the mirror and she put on a pair of big cheap shades. She stuck a cigarette in her cherry-red lips, which made her look suddenly older. And uglier.

"Sorry, no smoking in the car," Bobby said.

"Since fuckin' when?" Izzy shouted.

"Watch your mouth in front of the lady . . ."

"Jesus fuckin' Chrise," Betty said.

Izzy lit his own smoke and Bobby looked in the rearview again as Betty lit hers. Bobby hit the brakes on the corner of Seventy-second and West End. "Out," Bobby said.

"Fuck you talking about, out? This here's my goddamned car!"

"Okay, then I'll get out and you drive," Bobby said, throwing the car into park, turning off the ignition, pulling out the keys, and yanking up the door handle.

"I have no license," Izzy said.

"Then I'll meet you at the office," Bobby said.

Izzy angrily tossed his smoke out the window, nodded for Betty to do the same. She took a last long drag and flipped it out the window and said, "America getting like China."

"Where you from, Betty?" Bobby asked.

"I only know where I going," she said. "I do what I must do."

Bobby parked the Jeep Cherokee in the garage underneath the Empire State Building, where Izzy Gleason kept his office in room B-378, next to the janitor's closet in the basement of the world's most famous skyscraper. When Bobby was working on a case for Izzy he also used the office but, mercifully, hadn't been there in two months.

They climbed the steps to the basement level. Izzy lit a smoke the minute he stopped in front of his office door. So did Betty. The door to room B-378 was already open and a crew of forensic cops was dusting the cluttered office for prints. The room was a wreck from a police toss, and blood was smeared around like an acid head's Rorschach test. Criminalists were putting little pieces of what they thought might be evidence in paper and plastic bags and placing paper tents over what they thought were bloodstains. Others were spraying luminol, a chemical compound that made bloodstains glow under a black light.

"Here they are, the shyster from hell and his dutiful gumshoe," said Noel Christmas, chief Manhattan District Attorney's Office investigator. "What's a matter, Izzy? You knew there was so much blood, you brought help to mop up?"

"Actually, Noel, I'm here to make sure you don't steal the mop," Bobby said.

Christmas stood five eight, weighed about 220, all of it overdeveloped muscle. His pectorals were massive, and his shoulders were as broad as the anchor on a pirate ship. He looked like a suit of armor that had been fitted for a Brooks Brothers three-piece. The knot in his silk tie was a perfect Windsor; his Italian loafers gleamed. He wore no rings on his fingers but sported a gold Tag Heuer watch. He sucked on one Tums tablet after another, and when he spoke, the words came out of his dry white mouth like verbal chalk scribbles.

"Some cases are sad, some boring, some a pain in the ass, some who gives a monkey's fuck," Christmas said. "But this one, shit, I'm gonna have fun puttin' away the sleaziest lawyer in New York."

"Even someone who failed the bar exam for eighteen straight years must have learned that you need a warrant to be in here," Izzy said, grabbing a Tootsie Roll from the candy dish on his own desk, unwrapping it, and biting it into little brown pennies.

Noel Christmas handed Izzy a warrant. "You must miss the joint, Bobby," Christmas said.

Then Christmas looked at Betty, who nervously lit a cigarette.

"I know you get paid for doing the opposite at work, lady, but in my crime scene you better take that fucking butt *out* your mouth," Christmas said. A uniformed cop took it from her.

"When God was giving out class you thought he said 'ass,'" Bobby said. "You don't wear gloves in a crime scene. You walk all over the evidence without shoe covers. You make disparaging, unprofessional remarks to citizens and an officer of the court. You talk while you're eating. And, man, do you smell."

Noel Christmas took the last remark like a punch.

"This is an arrest warrant," Izzy said. "For Jimmy Chung. So arrest him. My meter's running, pally."

Izzy turned to Bobby and shrugged as if to say he had no idea what the hell was going on.

"Our people trailed you and Chung here to this rodent nest after we cut him loose this morning," Christmas said. "The lab techies worked on the blood sample found in the van. Thank God for computers. Pending DNA results, in six hours they made a preliminary match to the blood on the pillowcase, the sheets, the blanket, and Jimmy Chung's garbage bin. We found a judge who gave us the warrant. When we came in here to get him, all we found was this mess. Which looks like another crime scene, and so I sealed it and called in forensic, and now the gang's all here. Except, of course, for Chung."

He pulled out the chair from under the desk. Christmas made a hand signal to a uniformed cop by the door and the overhead lights were doused. Under the black light the luminol spray illuminated glowing blood splatters all over the desk, chairs, and floor. There was one glowing clump of what looked like flesh and possibly cartilage or bone.

"Somebody was butchered in here," Christmas said. He signaled for the overhead light to be put back on. One rod of fluorescent hummed incessantly, like a trapped moth, as it had from the first day Bobby ever entered the office.

"Guess what else had bloodstains all over it?" Christmas said.

"The rag between your legs?" Izzy said.

Christmas removed a sheet of yellow paper from inside a brown paper evidence bag. The document was dotted and smeared with blood. Some of the stains looked like partial fingerprints.

"Recognize it?" Christmas asked.

"Your last bar exam?" Izzy asked. "You slit your wrists when you saw the score was lower than your hat size?"

But Izzy recognized it as a carbon copy of Jimmy Chung's transfer of the deed to 22 Empire Court in lieu of an attorney retainer fee.

"You tell me," Izzy said, knowing he was better off not answering any questions. It was clear to

Bobby that Izzy was now a suspect in the disappearance and possible murder of Jimmy Chung.

"Okay, so Chung gets brought in for questioning
in the disappearance of the McCoys," Christmas said.
"He calls you. You show up in the early hours with
your libido engineer here."

"I not know nothing," Betty said, frightened at
the sight of all the blood.

"Can I ask a hypothetical?" Izzy asked.

"What?" Christmas asked.

"When you pour the steroids on them in the
morning, do those Rice Krispies you call your balls go
snap, crackle, or pop?"

A few of the other cops muffled laughs and bent
lower to the ground to do their work. Noel Christmas
reddened, the veins in his neck rising like cables.

Bobby watched Christmas wave the deed in front
of Izzy's face.

"*Funny*, isn't it, that a couple of people who are
in a battle with their landlord go missing. In steps
Sleazy Izzy Gleason . . ."

"Nobody Beats the Iz," Izzy said.

". . . out of the blue and walks the Chinese gentleman out of my interrogation," Christmas continued.
"He stashes this slumlord in his office here, and with
the help of the same massage-parlor pros-translator
that he brought to my squad room earlier, makes him
sign over the deed to the building in question in lieu of
payment—just in case anything happens to him or he
doesn't pay up. Then when we come here to rearrest

Chung, all we find is blood, flesh, and bone. Just like we found in the McCoy pad."

"Is this leading somewhere, Noel?" Bobby asked.

"Yeah," Christmas said. "Hopefully, to a lethal injection."

"You charging me with something, you creatine cretin?" Izzy asked.

"Not at this juncture," Christmas said. "But I am sending a detailed report to the State Bar Association Ethics Board. And if we can't find Mr. Chung but do prove this is his blood, I'll be looking for you, Mr. Gleason."

"You saying Izzy's a suspect in a homicide?" Bobby asked.

"I'm saying he's a suspect in *three* possible homicides. I think they're all related and can be traced to that bloodstained deed. All I have to do is find the corpus delicti."

"You're out of your fuckin' mind," Izzy said, grabbing another Tootsie Roll from his desk. Christmas clamped his hand on Izzy's.

"Touch that and I'll hold you for tampering with evidence," Christmas said. "Now both of you better remove yourselves and Little Miss Knobjob from my crime scene until we take down the yellow tape."

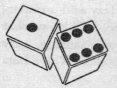

"Okay, my established point is six—as in deep six—and with all these people throwing sevens," Izzy Gleason said, using the gambling term for dying, or crapping out, "I'm gonna wind up with twenny-five to life for hom-two. Or the sayonara syringe for whack-one."

They walked through the parking garage under the Empire State Building, Izzy loading a Snickers bar into his mouth.

"We better check out Chung's building," Bobby said. "Where the McCoys disappeared."

Izzy handed Betty a couple of twenty-dollar bills and asked her to take a cab to his month-to-month apartment in the Chelsea Hotel, on Twenty-third Street.

"When you take care of other thing for me?" she asked.

"Soon," Izzy said. "I don't know if you can grasp this, Bambi, but I have bigger problems right now, like the whole forest is on fire and I'm tied to a fuckin' tree."

"Name Betty, no Bambi, and you make me promise. I did what you ask. You keep your promise."

"Go to the room, rent a few kung fu movies,

order some Chinese takeout, get undressed, and wait for me," Izzy said.

"I don't eat Chinese food."

"Then order a pizza from the ginzo with the dirty windows down the block," Izzy said, exasperated. "Tell Filthy Fredo it's for me, he'll know what to make—extra cheese, pepperoni, sausage, easy on the roach eggs. Save me three slices. Get a bottle of cream soda."

"I get McDonald's, you keep promise," Betty said.

Betty stormed off toward the street exit, passing a woman in her late twenties whose long auburn hair was pulled back tight on her head, fastened with a simple elastic band. She wore little makeup, no earrings, and her face had the unblemished beauty of a life lived clean. She was almost angelic, except for the incongruous icy blue eyes. She wore loose, cuffed jeans, a denim jacket, and plain white sneakers. Her hands were jammed into the jacket pockets as she approached Bobby and Izzy in a steady stride.

Bobby noticed her first, was struck by her streamlined beauty, her savvy body language, her deliberate gait. In the shadowy garage he didn't notice the polar-blue eyes until she was two feet away.

"Izzy Gleason?"

"Esquire," Izzy said, grinning lasciviously. "If you're here about the ad for a secretary, all you need to know is addition, subtraction, silence, and subservience. I'll take your name and number and we can talk over dinner. Tonight's fine. What's your address and what're you cookin'? I don't eat no liver . . ."

"Scumbag," the woman said and threw a perfectly delivered right hand to Izzy's left cheekbone, just below the eye. On impact the roll of quarters in the woman's right fist broke loose, the coins clattering and rolling all over the garage floor.

"Fuck me!" Izzy screamed as he staggered backwards, bouncing off a support column, hands going to his face.

The woman reached in her pocket, came out with her right fist wrapped around another roll of quarters, and went after Izzy again, both hands balled now, hitting him three more punches to the face as Izzy covered his head with his arms.

"Whoa!" Bobby shouted, grabbing her by both arms. It was like trying to hold on to a Jet Ski in stormy chop.

"Let go, you swine, or you're next," the woman shouted.

Izzy stood up straight, a lump immediately forming under his eye. "Hey, you loony twat, what the *fuck*?"

"You walked Jimmy Chung out of that goddamned police station," she shouted, her voice echoing in the underground garage.

"Easy, lady," Bobby said, his arms wrapped around her, his forearms across the tops of her firm breasts, her butt bouncing off him as she bucked in his vise-like grip. Bobby tried not to allow himself to enjoy it. But she was thrilling. She smelled damn good, too. No perfume, no scented soap, no fragrant talc, no fruity hair gunk. She just smelled vibrantly, alluringly, spotlessly clean. In an age of smut, vulgarity, and slutty hype, *clean* was refreshingly sexy. She wasn't hard to look at, either. *You've been too long without a dame,* he thought.

"Your murdering client hurt my brother!" she screamed. "Kidnapped him, and I wanna know where the hell he is!"

"Who's your brother?" Bobby asked.

"Eddie McCoy," she said. "And my sister-in-law, Sally."

"What's your name?" Bobby asked.

"Amy McCoy."

"Mc*Cunt!*" Izzy screamed, cupping his everswelling eye.

"What weight do you fight at?" Bobby asked.

"This is no goddamned joke," she said. "Now let go of me."

"Promise not to throw any more punches?"

"No."

"Then we have a problem."

"You guys have the freakin' problem," she said. "I'm it."

"Let her go," Izzy said, rushing to the Jeep to look at his eye in the side mirror. "Fuck etiquette, I'll punch this bitch's lamps out. Broad gave me a shiner bigger than Petey the dog in *The Little Rascals!* I look like

Vincent Price in *The Fly*. How the fuck do I explain this? I'm supposed to go in front of a judge wearing jive-junkie shades now? 'Good morning, ladies and gents of the jury, José Feliciano for the defense.' Let her go, Bobby. I'll show this psycho snatch what I think of political correctness."

"Yeah, lemme go," she said. "I'll break every bone in your face, you despicable little belly crawler."

"I think she'll kick your ass, Iz," Bobby said, half-amused. "Maybe you better grab a cab home, get some ice on that mouse."

"This ain't a mouse," Izzy said, touching his eye, looking in the mirror. "It's a fuckin' bilge rat!"

"Hey, if the shoe fits," Amy said.

"Izzy, go. I'll deal with the little lady."

"I'll fight you, too, you patronizing, ape-shaped clown," Amy McCoy said. "If you think I'm going to rest while the judicial system ignores my brother and sister-in-law, you're sadly mistaken. I'll punch your face, hound the press, burn down your house, and turn your own dog against you. I won't wait for God to mete out justice while I have a breath left in my earthly body."

"This broad's a wack-job and I'm atta here," Izzy said. "Get her a sandwich board and let her walk up and down fuckin' Broadway like the rest of the end-of-the-world beatniks."

As Bobby held on to Amy McCoy, Izzy Gleason strode out of the underground garage, holding a hankie to his eye. "Bitch Pearl Harbors me while the other cockknocker, Christmas, is trying to nail me for deep-sixin' my own gook client," Izzy mumbled as he passed them. "Great fuckin' day for Izzy Gleason. What ever happened to the luck of the Micks and the brains of the Hebes? Your average legal aid client doesn't have a day like this . . ."

From the cool shadows of the garage Bobby watched Izzy hurry into the bright sun, buy an ice pop from a Good Humor wagon, and place it against his swollen eye. He ripped the wrapper off, took a bite, put it back to his eye, and darted into the middle of Thirty-fourth Street, waving madly for a taxi. A driver wearing a fez crossed two lanes and hung a U-turn in horn-honking traffic to pull up alongside Izzy, who climbed in, giving Amy McCoy the finger.

When he was gone, Bobby let go of Amy McCoy. She turned and swung at Bobby's face. He caught her by the wrist. He squeezed and she dropped the roll of quarters into his other hand.

"Hey," he said, "I ain't the bad guy."

"You work for that bag of garbage?"

"I'm trying to find out what happened to your brother—for his client—which means we're on the same side. Look, Izzy Gleason is a lot of things, most of them pretty unpleasant, but he's no kidnapper, and he's no killer."

"Who the hell are you?"

"A private investigator, which for now sounds better than saying unemployed ex-cop."

"What's your name?" she said. "I'm gonna check you out."

"Bobby Emmet. Let me buy you lunch and I'll save you the trouble. Then you can check my story on a Nexis search. You'll see I did time for killing my fiancée."

"Charmed," she said.

"But I didn't do it."

"You and O.J."

"Izzy got me out of jail. Helped me expose a bunch of corrupt cops who framed me in a police medical-pension racket. I found my fiancée and she was alive. But, in the end, I couldn't save her."

"Reassuring," she said, then softened. "Sorry. Cheap shot."

"It's okay," Bobby said. "So here's the rest of the four-one-one: I'm divorced, and I have a fourteen-year-old daughter who is studying for her PSATs and in love with a guy named Cal who she says is cool. Working for Izzy Gleason is just what I do these days to pay her tuition. For now."

"Okay, now let go of my wrist," she said.

"One more thing," Bobby said. "Since fifth grade, Sister Margaret Timothy, Holy Family School, Brooklyn—I've had this aversion to women smacking me across the face. Since I don't hit women back, I try to stop it before it happens."

"I won't," she said.

He let go and leaned backwards, like Ali from a jab. She didn't throw it and he held out his hand to shake. She looked at it but didn't shake. Instead, she stuffed her hands in her back pockets.

"I'm looking for my brother," she said, "not a friend."

"Fine," Bobby said and fished his keys out of his pocket. He handed her the roll of quarters and walked to the blue Jeep, unlocked the door, and got in and started the engine.

"Hey!" she shouted.

He rolled down the window and said, "What?"

"What about that lunch?"

"Get in."

5

Bobby called Maggie on his cell phone as he drove down Broadway with Amy next to him in the front seat of the Jeep.

"You asked me if you could help," Bobby said.

"Absolutely, Pop," Maggie said.

"Find out whatever you can about the landlord of number 22 Empire Court," he said. "His name is

Jimmy Chung, Chinese born. The Department of Buildings must have his green-card number, and a Social Security number. Use that to get his DMV records. Check his other holdings, his arrest record— here and in China, Taiwan, or Hong Kong, or wherever he's from. See if he has relatives here. Partners. Check out back issues of the English-language Chinese papers."

"I can do better than that," Maggie said. "I can check out the Chinese-language papers, too. I have a language-translation program. It can translate anything from pig Latin to Ebonics. Chinese should be a snap. Then I'll do a worldwide on-line search on Dialog International Services. It's got over three hundred databases, more data than the Library of Congress. It scans two thousand newspapers worldwide."

"Scary," Bobby said, realizing all that information was available to a little girl with braces through a three-pound laptop the size of a box of cigars. "Sounds like a great start."

Bobby unhooked the pine-tree–shaped air freshener that dangled from the rearview mirror and placed it in the glove compartment. He didn't want it interfering with the much better and more exciting fragrance in the car, which bore the name Amy McCoy.

"Why'd you do that?" Amy asked.

"I couldn't smell the forest for the tree," he said.

"They won't let us in the apartment," Amy said. "I was already down there. The cop in charge, Noel

Christmas, he's not very cooperative—even with me, and I'm the relative of the victims. He kept asking me if my brother was having trouble with his Communist friends. He said there was a file on his radical behavior over the years. He's trying to blame the victim."

"I'm not looking to get into your brother's apartment," Bobby said. "Your brother and his wife aren't the only ones missing, leaving behind a trail of blood."

"Who else?"

"Jimmy Chung."

"Good God," Amy said. "He's skipped? He'll disappear into the back alleys of Hong Kong and we'll never find him . . ."

Bobby knew he couldn't yet trust this woman, no matter how good looking she was. But he didn't mind sharing information that would be readily available to her if he thought he could pick her brain about her brother. She could save Bobby a lot of time.

"Noel Christmas seems to think Chung is dead," Bobby said. "And that Izzy Gleason killed him. He found blood in Izzy's office."

"Your sleazy partner . . ."

"Get it straight," Bobby said, stopping for a light at Houston and Broadway as thousands of frantic New Yorkers marched along the downtown shopping street, or headed to chic overpriced restaurants of SoHo or to catch an avant-garde flick at the Angelika. "Izzy isn't my partner. I'm paying off a debt to him in trade."

"Noel Christmas," she said. "What the hell kind of name is that anyway? It sounds blasphemous."

"What did your brother tell you about his beef with Chung?"

"It was your typical landlord-tenant war. My brother has been living there for two years. Chung bought the building last year. It's a rent-controlled building, so you'd need an act of Congress and a wrecking ball to get him out . . ."

"Unless he had him . . ."

"Don't say it, because I have to assume he's just missing and not murdered," Amy said. "Anyway, Chung tried the usual tactics. No heat in the winter, no hot water all year, rodent infestation, no repairs. Eddie reported all this to the city, they took Chung to court, he was fined, ordered to make the repairs, which he never made, and ignored the housing court orders. In the big city he's one of tens of thousands of landlords who hate rent control."

"But no one usually goes this far," Bobby said. "I've heard of threats. A few goons throwing a scare into a tenant to get him to move. But *murder* . . . sorry, I used the word again."

"I guess until I find them I better get used to hearing it."

"I know what that's like," Bobby said, remembering his own search for his missing fiancée. "Did there reach a point where he actually told you he was scared?"

"About a month ago," she said. "He started

telling me that Chung didn't want to just raise his
rent, he wanted him out. He offered Eddie ten
thousand dollars. Eddie said no. Then he offered
twenty. Then thirty. We had dinner three weeks ago
and he said Chung's offer had gone up to fifty thousand dollars. Eddie turned him down. Then, my
brother was down in Puerto Rico for a long weekend, and when he returned he found that the
upstairs tenant had moved out without even taking
his furniture. Another tenant moved when Eddie
went to Atlantic City for a weekend."

"Chung was buying them out?"

"Eddie wasn't sure," Amy said. "He never heard
from them again. No forwarding addresses. No new
phone numbers. Just . . . *gone.*"

"Your brother and his wife were the last hold-
outs?"

"Yeah," she said. "But my brother began to
develop some theory. It sounded far-fetched, so I
didn't pay much attention at the time. My brother
was always into conspiracies. He said the city wanted
the land to build a new terminal or something, a
whole big parcel of downtown land. He said it
involved Sam Kronk—you know, the big real estate
developer and Atlantic City casino king."

"Yeah, 'course I know who he is. But there's
already a ferry terminal and three heliports. What did
he mean, 'terminal'?"

"I'm not sure," she said. "Maybe I just have more
faith than most, but I told him I refused to believe, as

corrupt as the city is, that they'd send goons around harassing or kidnapping citizens to build new buildings."

"What did . . . does your brother do for a living?"

"He's a freelance writer," she said. "His wife is an artist."

"What kind of stuff does he write?"

"He's older than me," she said. "Forty. So he grew up in the paranoid sixties, early seventies. He still believes the whole world is corrupt, that all big money is involved in a global conspiracy to exploit the working class and the poor. So he writes mostly for left-wing periodicals—you know, about plots between the government and big business. He spent time in South and Central America, he exposed corporate America's rape of the rain forest, and he wrote about the child-labor mills that make clothes for major American corporations with celebrity names, like that total phony with the talk show. Lately he's been writing about the prospect of casino gambling in the city and how the working classes will be robbed by Sam Kronk. He spent time in casinos in Puerto Rico and Atlantic City, investigating Kronk."

"I remember reading some of your brother's stuff. He used to write for the *Village Voice*, no?"

"That's right," she said.

"Kronk is one very big enemy."

"Eddie considers Kronk one of the worst exploiters in the city—the world. He talked about how Kronk took gambling money from working people to support political campaigns of politicians he could manipulate. He thinks Kronk has Mayor Brady in his pocket."

"Yeah, well, he's not alone there."

"He says because of term limits, Kronk is going to bankroll the mayor's run for the Senate, the way he did with Senator Arena. Then he would handpick the next mayor after Brady, and own two U.S. senators and a governor. My brother thinks Kronk wants to own every major politician from both major parties in New York and New Jersey. He once called Kronk 'the epitome of egomania and money and corruption gone mad.' "

"Your brother is a dying breed," Bobby said, as they rumbled past Canal Street, which Bobby thought of as the city's last tool shed, a ten-block casbah of sidewalk displays of electronic gadgets, mechanical doodads, tools, hardware, plumbing supplies. "The days of the radical muckraker are pretty much gone—replaced by an overload of gossip columnists. Too bad, I'd rather see a thousand guys like Eddie McCoy than one more item about Sam Kronk's latest bimbo on his newest yacht. There isn't a more self-absorbed man alive than Kronk. He lives for headlines. He pays paparazzi to follow him."

"Yeah, well, in spite of the thousands of words my brother has written about him, I don't think Kronk even knows he exists."

"Never know," Bobby said, glancing into her blue eyes, which had thawed to a sweet azure. "Guys like Kronk usually know about every dime they own and every word written about them. He's petty, like the mayor—a grievance collector."

By 1:15 PM Bobby and Amy were in the alley behind 22 Empire Court. Morning news stories had attracted a few lunchtime gawkers, the sort of people Bobby always suspected were responsible for 99 percent of rubbernecking traffic jams in New York. Uniformed cops were standing sentry outside the front doors, blocking anyone from entering the crime scene. The anonymous 911 caller had said the masked man loaded the heavy recycling bin into the white van here in the alley.

"Which means he wheeled it in from the cellar," Bobby said. "Come on, there're no cops at the back door."

Bobby walked down the ramp, pulled open the door and entered the dim cellar first. He held out his hand for Amy McCoy and she took it. Her hand was small and coarse, the unpampered hand of a woman who had worked most of her life. *Clean and hardworking.* He found that sexy, too. He realized he hadn't even asked her what she did for a living.

"Eddie's a writer," Bobby said. "What do *you* do?"

"Right now, a lot of praying," she said.

A wild-eyed black and white cat appeared before them, hissed, its hair on end, and then ran to protect her kitten.

"Smells like the catacombs," Amy said. "This place isn't fit for that kitten."

"Safe bet Sam Kronk didn't spend many nights down here," Bobby said, walking directly to the Bell Atlantic telephone junction box mounted on the wall. He opened the panel and looked inside, grabbing several telephone wires, deftly pulling them apart for deliberate inspection, trying to trace their course from the box.

"Something isn't kosher," he said, tracing two lines from the junction box, seeing that they extended along the ceiling toward the rear of the massive cellar.

"Maybe your brother had reason to be paranoid," Bobby said.

"Why?" Amy said. "What are we looking for?"

"I'm not sure," Bobby said. "You said your brother and his wife were the last tenants in the building. But there's two phone lines. If Jimmy Chung owned the place, I'm betting he had some kind of equipment room and office he used here. A janitor's hideout. A place he kept his tools, pipes, brooms, shovels, and odds and ends. A TV and a phone of his own. But it also looks to me like an extension running from your brother's phone was spliced right out of the junction box with a simple two-dollar Radio Shack jack. The wire runs parallel to a second phone line, to the back of the cellar."

"You mean like Chung had his own line and ran a tap off my brother's?" Amy asked.

"Yeah," Bobby said.

They moved deeper into the cavernous cellar,

past the rusted oil tank of the heating system. The parallel phone lines were looped through dangling BX cables and exposed, overhead hot-water risers and waste pipes.

"If you see plaster fall, hold your breath," Bobby said. "This joint has to be a toxic asbestos waste dump. I bet the last time this cellar was painted it was with molten lead."

The cellar bottlenecked and they moved down a passageway too narrow to walk two abreast. The walls were damp and moldy with seepage from the nearby harbor, scaly algae and moss clinging to old bare granite stones that had probably been quarried from the lower-Manhattan bedrock over a century ago. A single dim incandescent bulb burned forty feet ahead. As they walked down the corridor, they passed small barren rooms, once known as woodbins. A few of the rooms were stacked with boxes and old carriages, carcasses of long-forgotten bicycles, discarded sinks, bathtubs, and toilet bowls. A rat scurried past, its red eyes like two lit cigarette embers in the half-gloom.

"Jesus, Mary, and Joseph the carpenter," Amy shouted, clutching Bobby's big biceps. He liked the way it felt. Their eyes met in the palpable gloom. She smiled, abashed, the tough façade fading in the spooky dark.

"That rat hasn't gotten his eviction notice yet," Bobby said.

When they reached the end of the corridor,

Bobby saw that the phone wires ran into a square wooden box of a room, twelve by twelve, sitting on top of a raised cement foundation. The box was studded out with two-by-fours and hammered together with plyboard, with the pink, hairy stubble of fiberglass insulation showing at the bottom like a fallen hem. A wooden door was snugly fitted into a frame, secured by a sturdy steel hasp and heavy padlock. Bobby lifted the lock, saw that it was a Medeco, knew it was unpickable. He walked back down the dim corridor, went into one of the small dirty woodbin rooms, rummaged around until he found the frame of an old bicycle. He carried the rust- and mold-encrusted frame to the clearing, jammed one arm of the front wheel fork in behind the hasp, and yanked the bike backward. The hasp tore free from the wooden frame in a splintery gouge.

Bobby placed the bike on the floor, brushed the crud off his hands, and went into the room. Amy followed. The light switch was on the wall to the left and when he flicked it on an exhaust fan whirred in the ceiling and an overhead ersatz Tiffany lamp shone down on a teak desk, swivel chair, small couch, tiny refrigerator, Mr. Coffee. A twelve-inch TV sat on top of the refrigerator. On the desk, bottles of Glenlivet scotch, Boodles gin, and Stolichnaya vodka were stacked on a serving tray with four polished rocks glasses. A thick-pile, woven area rug covered the floor.

Bobby traced the two phone wires to an ordinary

old-fashioned telephone sitting on the desk. Next to it, a multi-phone-jack-connector hitched together a ten-hour Panasonic tape recorder with a VOX automatic telephone recording device and a TT Systems caller-ID box. The tape from the recorder was missing. Bobby examined the simple operation as Amy looked around at her feet for more rats.

"What the hell is all of this?" she asked.

"In-house phone tap," Bobby said, fingering the phone wire that was linked to the VOX box, the caller-ID box, and the tape recorder. "This wire is spliced into your brother's telephone line at the junction box and runs back here. Every call he makes is recorded. Gotta tell you, Miss McCoy . . ."

"Amy," she insisted.

". . . that if someone thought enough to tap your brother's phone, it means he worried somebody. Posed a threat. Maybe they did read his stuff. Maybe it was about the land and this terminal you're talking about. I dunno. But you don't illegally tap a man's phone unless he's screwing your wife or bad for business."

"Oh, sweet Jesus . . ."

"This setup would make no clicking sounds because it was voice-activated by this VOX box, which costs about twenty-five bucks in an electronics store. The VOX box triggers the tape recorder to start taping as soon as someone starts talking on the line upstairs. This had a ten-hour microcassette, usually more than enough for a day. And the caller-ID box told Chung the name and number of who it was who was calling."

Bobby pressed the caller-ID replay button. There were only two numbers on it. He was startled that he recognized one of them as Max Roth's, his columnist friend at the *Daily News*. "Do you know this number?" Bobby asked, pointing to the other one.

"It's mine," she said. "I don't know the other one."

He didn't tell her that he did; he wanted to talk to Roth first.

As he held the caller-ID box in his hand he noticed that on the underside was a sticker bearing the name of the retailer where it had been purchased. Hing How Electronics, 5157-A Eighth Avenue, Brooklyn. He looked under the tape recorder, same retail sticker. Ditto for the VOX box.

Amy picked up the bottle of scotch. "I could use a belt," she said and poured herself an inch and shot it back.

"Join me?" she asked, as she poured a second shooter.

"Booze makes me dumb," Bobby said. "And slow. Which is okay for mindless vacations, but not when I'm working."

Bobby looked at the back of the bottle, under the label he saw another retail sticker. Ho Luck's Liquors, also with an Eighth Avenue address in Sunset Park, Brooklyn.

Bobby erased both numbers from the caller-ID box.

"I know where we're going for lunch," he said.

Bobby swung open the cellar door leading to the alley. Standing there was Noel Christmas and two uniformed cops who had their guns drawn. Another man wearing a light trench coat and rose-tinted RayBans looked startled when he saw Bobby, who recognized him immediately as U.S. Attorney Sean Dunne of the Eastern District, which covered Brooklyn, Queens, and Long Island. He was out of his turf. Amy came out of the cellar behind him, carrying a calico kitten in her arms. Sean Dunne hadn't seen them yet but when he spotted Bobby and Amy he turned away immediately and hurried to a black Chrysler that he drove himself.

Bobby also found it odd that a U.S. attorney did not have an armed Justice-agent driver with him.

Bobby watched the Chrysler disappear as Christmas popped two Tums in his mouth, pursed his lips and said, "What the hell do you think you're doing? This whole building is a crime scene."

"Well . . ."

"I asked him to bring me here to get the kitten," Amy said. "My brother's wife took care of it. In their absence, I'm doing the humane thing. Problem, Detective?"

"How the hell did you hook up with *him?*" Christmas demanded.

"I'm considering hiring him," she said.

Fast on her feet, Bobby thought.

"That's a conflict of interest," Christmas said, pushing a third Tums into his mouth, his muscles bunching under his suit. "His boss is defending a suspect in your brother's disappearance."

"Yeah, but you said Izzy is now a suspect in Chung's disappearance," Bobby said. "So, I'm also looking for Chung. So is she. I think this makes it an ethical push."

"I thought you edited the word 'ethics' from your vocabulary when you hooked up with Izzy Gleason," Christmas said.

"Yeah," Bobby said. "But he also edited a fifteen-to-life sentence to not guilty and freedom. Something you never tried to help me get, even though you were my partner, Noel."

The kitten meowed in Amy's arms.

"He touch anything else down there?" Christmas asked her.

"No," she said. "But I can tell you, I'm pretty handy around mechanical things, and I think you better look at my brother's phone line. It looks like it might be tapped."

"That a fact?" Christmas said.

"Yeah," Amy said.

"Why didn't you tell me?" Bobby asked.

"You were too busy playing with the kitten," she said.

"And you figured all this out by yourself?"

"Yep," she said.

"Get the hell out of my crime scene," Christmas said.

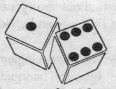

6

"Maybe Christmas is right," Amy said, shaking some soy sauce into her wonton soup. "Maybe I shouldn't be talking to you."

"Then don't," Bobby said, stripping clean his fifth spare rib and picking up another. "You didn't tell me anything my daughter couldn't find out about your brother with a simple computer search. She's so good she could find out the name of the guy who delivered the rice you're gonna eat for dinner."

They were sitting in a red Naugahyde booth in the rear dining room of the three-story Golden Pagoda restaurant on Eighth Avenue in Brooklyn's bustling new Sunset Park Chinatown, where over a hundred thousand Asians had settled in the past ten years, replacing many of the older Norwegian and Irish, who had died or relocated to the suburbs.

Bobby chose the place because it was two blocks from the Hing How Electronics shop where Jimmy Chung had bought his phone-tapping equipment. Also because Bobby knew the owner of the restaurant, a young first-generation Chinese-American named Ben Lee, from when they were both students at Brooklyn College. Lee owned two of the biggest Chinese restaurants in Brooklyn, this one and another on Avenue U, which also had a burgeoning Asian population.

Lee was the president of the Brooklyn Chinese Merchants Association, a member of the local Democratic Club, and knew just about everyone there was to know in the Chinese business and civic communities of Brooklyn.

When Bobby and Amy entered the huge, elegant restaurant, which boasted three upstairs banquet rooms and seating for over a thousand, they passed the 200-gallon tank of live carp, lobster, jumbo shrimp, crawfish, trout, octopus, and sea bass that bathed the entrance with a soothing aquatic glow. Amy gaped in awe at the aquarium. "This an exotic pet store or a restaurant?" she asked

Bobby asked the maitre d' if Ben Lee was around and was told he was en route from his other restaurant and would be there soon. Bicycle deliverymen dressed in white linen suits rushed in and out of the restaurant. A hungry lunch crowd packed the main dining room. Bobby asked for a corner booth.

"Maggie's mother, Connie, was sitting where you're sitting now fifteen years ago," Bobby said.

"Should I feel honored?" Amy asked. "This where you take all your hot dates?"

"I proposed and she said yes," Bobby said. "Ben Lee's father ran the place then, so we used to eat cheap, before the old man went back to Hong Kong to retire. Jesus, time just evaporates. I dropped out of college, joined the cops, and one of my first assignments was to bodyguard the daughter of a famous cosmetics baron who the intelligence unit had learned was the target of a kidnapping plot."

"And naturally, out of courtesy, respect, and professionalism, you slept with her," Amy said.

"She asked *me* out, asked me to take her to Brooklyn," he said.

"Rich girl slumming with boy-toy cop," Amy said.

"Maybe," he said, shrugging. "The only place I could afford was here. We ate here ten times. On the eleventh I proposed. I fell in love with a woman but I married a millionaire. After we had Maggie, we tried to make two socioeconomic backgrounds work under the same Brooklyn roof. We couldn't. The divorce was amicable but sad."

"Yeah, that *is* sad," Amy said. "Still friends?"

"I get along better with her new husband than I do with her, but I still like Connie."

He didn't tell her that Maggie had helped both of them through it by continuing to love and forgive them both.

"Why'd you tell me all this?"

"Because if I'm gonna keep asking you personal questions, you deserve to know something about who's asking," he said.

"Noble of you."

"Yeah, well, Brooklyn is also known as Kings County."

Bobby and Amy ordered lunch from a tall Asian waiter in his fifties, who said his name was George and who had an irritating tic in his right eye. He used no memo pad and suggested ribs, soup, crispy bass, lamb with garlic and broccoli, and lemon chicken. They agreed to everything.

George the waiter brought the drinks and appetizers quickly. Bobby couldn't stop staring into Amy's big blue eyes.

"I don't even know you and I'm telling you my brother's life story," she said.

"So tell me about yours," Bobby said.

"My life has nothing to do with any of this," she said. "Nobody cares what I do."

"Try me," Bobby said.

"I teach."

"Where?"

"A Catholic school in Queens."

A busboy came and cleared away the rib bones and the soup bowls, and the waiter with the tic slid the main dishes onto the table. Bobby thanked him and they dug in.

"God, I haven't eaten since yesterday," she said.

Bobby looked at her naked fingers. "You live alone?"

"No," she said. "Soon, maybe."

"Live with your folks?"

"Dead," she said, swallowing some lamb. "God, I wonder if Eddie and Sally are being fed."

"Sorry. I was prying."

"You sure were."

He figured she was busting up with a guy, and the last person Bobby wanted to get *involved* with was a confused, emotionally short-circuited lady on the rebound. All she'd talk about and compare him to was the last boyfriend. Add to that the cargo of grief that would consume her if her brother and his wife turned up murdered, and Amy would be one very messed-up woman. No matter how pretty, how sexy, how clever, how tough she was, this dame wasn't for him.

She has as much baggage as I do, he thought.

"Between us we could open a luggage store," he said, without realizing he was thinking out loud.

"Huh?"

They were interrupted by Ben Lee, who walked directly to their table, big smile on his handsome face, his black suit and tie a full generational evolution from the sneakers and jeans of college.

"Bobby, babes!" Ben Lee said. "How's my main round-eye?"

Bobby stood and he and Lee embraced.

"You running for office or coming from a funeral?" Bobby asked.

"Is there a difference?" Lee asked.

"We gotta talk."

"Don't I get to meet the lady?" he asked. "That's why I wear this penguin suit, to meet beautiful women. Hi, I'm Ben Lee."

Amy shook his hand as Bobby said, "Sorry, Ben, this is Amy."

Lee held on to her hand and bowed formally.

"You have a beautiful place," she said.

"Not as beautiful as the company Bobby's keeping," Lee said.

"The food is amazing," Amy said, embarrassed. "I can't get over that fish tank."

"Bring your bathing suit next time," Lee said.

"We really need to talk, Ben," Bobby said.

"So talk."

"It's about a guy named Jimmy Chung."

"Oh." Lee's smile melted, and he looked around to see if anyone was listening. A few waiters looked Bobby's way. George, the one with the eye tic, glanced over as he took an order at another table. His tic seemed to accelerate at the mention of Jimmy Chung's name.

Bobby nodded, motioning for a quiet corner near the front of the restaurant. Away from Amy.

"Sure," Lee said.

"Excuse me," Bobby said to Amy.

"Don't let me interfere with *men's* talk," she said, the coldness returning to her blue eyes as she dropped her chopsticks onto the plate and leaned back in the booth.

Bobby and Lee walked toward the front of the restaurant, passed a gushing fountain and a backlit waterfall, crossed a bamboo footbridge under which golden carp swam through the lily pads in a brightly lit pond. They stopped in front of the gurgling fish tank.

"Jimmy Chung is one bad fucking dude, Bobby," Lee said.

"Who is he?"

Lee went suddenly quiet as he looked around the restaurant, at his own maitre d', his staff of waiters, busboys, and deliverymen, other Chinese patrons. George the waiter brought a bill and a credit card to the register.

"We should go up to my office to talk," Lee said.

He turned to George and barked, *"George, wo bu yao gei dadaianhua, bu darao."* Telling him he wanted no phone calls or disruptions.

"Mei wenti," said George, meaning "No problem."

Bobby followed Lee past the cash register, a carved-wood dragon, an overfed ceramic Buddha, and up a flight of red-carpeted steps. The walls of the stairwell were covered in gold-veined mirrors stenciled with dragons, pagodas, and various Chinese symbols and characters.

"Hey, the whole neighborhood is jumping these days," Lee said. "The brownstone yuppies of Park Slope have discovered us big time. Stockbrokers dropping C-notes like confetti. I'm thinking of renaming the place the Dow Wow Dow."

Bobby smiled and followed him to an office at the rear of the second floor. Once inside, Lee double-locked the door, snicked on the TV to New York One, the all-news station, and turned the volume up loud. He wheeled his leather swivel chair from behind his cluttered oak desk and positioned it two feet from another chair and motioned for Bobby to sit. He did.

Lee sat and leaned close to Bobby as the TV anchor gave the next day's weather forecast, which was going to be sunny and mild.

"Ask," Lee said, just louder than a whisper.

"Who is Jimmy Chung and why would he wiretap and then kill a couple of people over a rent-controlled apartment?" Bobby asked.

"He's from Hong Kong," Lee said. "Came about ten years ago. He had gambling money when he came. He worked in Chinatown for a few years, ran a couple of gambling parlors on Grand Street, Division Street. But he got caught in the middle of a turf war. Fucking Young tong Turks against the old ponytails. The *dai lo dai*, or boss, of the Ghost Shadows, and his *sai mas*, all Young Turks, were gonna whack Chung, but he bought his way out of getting murdered. See, Chung knew people from the Italian mob on Mulberry and Thompson Street. That's why he was chased out of Chinatown. The Young Chinese Turks thought he was giving kick-backs to the Italians, to buy his way into a piece of their gambling operations. He wanted to form a coalition. I heard he paid a hundred grand to the Young Turks to get the contract off his head. He promised not to open any more gambling parlors in Manhattan that would compete with theirs. As far as I know he hasn't."

"What did he do then?" Bobby asked as the TV reporter showed a clip of Sam Kronk at a Mayor Tom Brady fundraiser at the Water Club. The anchor said Brady would soon be announcing that he was throwing his hat into the ring for the United States Senate race.

"Chung took most of his money and put it in real estate," Lee said. "Did okay, too. The fucking prices are through the roof these days all over town. He has some here in Brooklyn. Some in Queens. He owned a noodle shop for a while here on the avenue, a front for a numbers book, trying to build his bank back up. A little bit of the same shit in Queens. He closed the noodle-numbers joints a few years ago. The local cops who were taking the payoffs to look the other way said the DA's office was getting suspicious. I could never prove this, but then I heard he became what they call a *snakehead*, helped smuggle in a couple of boatloads of illegals from Mainland China."

"I thought they cracked down on that after the *Golden Venture* ran aground on Rockaway back in the early nineties," Bobby said.

"All they did was alter their routes," Ben Lee said. "Instead of sailing straight here they sail to

Guatemala or the Caribbean. Stay in a safe house for a week. Then smuggle the illegals across the border into the U.S. and fly them up to New York. It's become very expensive, the going rate is forty-five thousand dollars a head. That's a quarter of a million dollars for a family of five. A lot of them sell themselves into indentured servitude to get here."

"They're willing to give up their freedom to come here? What's the point?"

"They don't believe the horror stories they hear back home," Lee said. "They think it's just their relatives who don't want them here competing for the same jobs. They still have grandiose ideas about America, the land of opportunity. But those who can't afford the full fare become what're called 'piglets,' indentured servants in sweat-shops, massage parlors, on slave-labor farms in Long Island and New Jersey. They have no papers, can't speak English, and they're afraid if they go to the police there'll be recriminations against their families back in Fujian, Zhejian, Sandong."

"They're also terrified of the INS deporting them," Bobby said.

"Of course," Lee said. "So they work off their debt for years. For the chicks in the massage parlors it can be as much as seven or eight years, to pay off forty-five thousand dollars 'transportation fee' plus a rolling thirty-percent interest. Some of the piglets are just sold to people who own the farms where violent enforcers beat them and make them work like slaves.

The enforcers themselves are usually working off their own indenture. It's a shameful, brazen, vicious fucking circle, Bobby."

"Why don't they just run, go to another city?" Bobby asked.

"Like I said, the snakehead who brings them here always has the names of all their relatives back home in China. Any of them cross him here, he has paid cutthroats back in China who will kill their relatives. Or put those relatives on a blacklist so they can never get smuggled in. So the ones here try to keep on the good side of a snakehead prick like Jimmy Chung, or whoever he sells their debt to, until they work off the money they owe. Bad news dude."

"How prevalent is this slave-labor racket?"

"Anyone who gives you a real answer is a liar," Lee said. "But it's huge. Bobby, right here in this Brooklyn neighborhood alone there's probably five hundred sweatshops. In the cellars of private homes, apartment buildings, in apartments, in factories, storefronts, garages, women and kids sewing day and night. They close one down, another two open. The cops bust at least ten whorehouses a year where these poor chicks, most still teenagers, are held against their will. Then another one opens. It's bad. As far as I know, Chung sells his piglets to brothel owners and restaurateurs, farm owners. But I hear he keeps a piece of a few of them. He likes having his piglet chicks for rainy nights. He's really small potatoes when you compare him to the really big snakeheads. But I hear he got into snakeheading through the back door. Gambling is his first love. When people got so deep in debt to him he would own them and he would sell their debt to others. When he got run out of gambling he became a snakehead. But he wants to get back to his first love, which has always been gambling."

"So he isn't making really big money out of it?"

"Well, he has to spread what he makes around," Lee said. "He also smuggles in these exotic fish called Arowana, from Cambodia, which collectors will pay like six grand apiece for. But no matter how he got it, gambling, snakeheading, smuggling, a few sweatshops, massage parlors, a labor farm, Chung had seed money again. Then, three years ago, he bought some real estate here in Brooklyn, a building on this block in fact, and a building in Manhattan. Surprised me, because it was rent-controlled. Pain in the ass. No money in it. And he's not allowed to run a gambling joint in Manhattan again or he gets whacked by the *dai lo dai* of Mott Street and his *sai mas*, the crazy-assed Young Chinese Turks."

"So he's gone legit?"

"Well," Lee said. "Depends on what you call legit. I don't think he ever took more than a few small-time gambling busts in all his time here. He's very clever, very elusive, stretches the law."

"So why would he harass rent-control tenants?" Bobby asked.

"I don't want this to sound like political sour grapes," Lee said. "But Chung also started dabbling in politics. He always seems to be for the guy I'm against. He contributes money, uses what influence he still has with other people to get people elected. A local assemblyman, state senator, councilman."

On the TV a female reporter was now interviewing the State Assembly leader, Carl Pinto, who was announcing that a legalized gambling resolution, which had been passed by both houses of the state legislature in the last session, had to be approved a second time in two consecutive legislatures before it could go to a public referendum. "This time, if it passes both houses on August sixth it will go to a vote of the people as a referendum on the November sixth ballot," Pinto said on the tube. "The polls are about fifty-fifty statewide now. I'm for it. But it's anyone's guess if we get legalized gambling in the state."

Bobby noticed that Lee was listening intently to this item on the news. "I supported this guy," Lee said. "Chung didn't because Pinto is for legalized gambling. But Chung, who wants to get back into illegal gambling someday, doesn't want gambling to be legal. So he funneled soft money to Stan Lebelski, majority leader of the State Senate, who's on the fence."

"Seems Chung supports candidates the mayor touts," Bobby said.

"Yep," Lee said.

"Chung have enough money to make a difference in an election?"

"Not of his own," Lee said. "But he knows how to launder other people's. How to take big people's money and make it look like it's coming in small donations from a thousand little people. You get two, three, four hundred people to contribute a few grand each, it becomes a cool mil."

"He uses the people in the sweatshops?"

"Right," Lee said. "Even the legal ones. Gives them a C-note for themselves, has them sign their name to a post-office money order made out to a politician. Of course they'll do it."

"In a local race, that can make a big difference," Bobby said.

"Bet your ass," Lee said. "And then he cashes in the favors. A zoning variance here, housing violation overlooked there."

"Which people's money? Sam Kronk's?"

"I'm not sure," Lee said. "I can ask around a little bit. But I see where Izzy Gleason is defending Chung. Just be careful, Bobby. Chung is dirty. Don't let him contaminate you."

"You haven't heard yet, then?"

"What?"

Bobby told him about Jimmy Chung now being missing, leaving blood all over Izzy's office, making Izzy the main suspect in his disappearance, which the head prosecutor believed was murder. And linked to the disappearance of the McCoy couple.

"That's some fuckin' pu pu platter," Lee said.

"Please, I've had my fill of Chinese jokes today."

"How long is a Chinaman's name," Lee said.

"I give up. How long?"

"No, dummy, that's his name, *How Long*."

"Ho ho," Bobby said.

Lee shut off the TV and they left the office, laughing, and went down the stairs.

"Chung operates out of this neighborhood now, so I'll find out whatever else I can," Lee said. "His family comes from Hong Kong. Mine too. I'll see what they can find out about him over there. He's a treacherous fuck, but I'll shake the trees."

"Thanks, Ben."

"So who's the dame? She's a real looker."

He told her who she was.

"Nothing is ever what it seems with you," Lee said. "I'm surprised she trusts you."

"Who says I trust *her*?" Bobby said.

"That sounds like a marriage in the making," Lee said. "Me, I'm still looking for the right one."

"You don't know what work is until you've been married."

When they reached the entrance Bobby saw Noel Christmas standing by the big fish tank. The register man and the deliverymen were shouting to each other in Chinese, checking bills and addresses on outgoing bicycle orders.

"You following me?" Bobby asked Christmas.

"Nah," Christmas said. "What are you doing here?"

"Eating lunch with a lady," Bobby said. Christmas

stared at Ben Lee, munched his antacid tablet with his front teeth.

"Who are you?" Christmas asked Ben Lee, flashing his badge.

"I am my humble father's number-one son," Lee said. "I've been dying to say that all my life. Me, I own this joint."

Bobby looked past Christmas and saw that the booth where he had been sitting with Amy McCoy was empty. He spotted his waiter, George, and asked where she was.

"Lady pay bill and leave, yeah," George the waiter said. "Soon as you go upstairs."

"She must have read her fortune cookie," Christmas said. "Saw there wasn't much of a future with you."

"But I'm always at least one step ahead of you, Noel."

"Think of it now as my being right on your heels," Christmas said. "This was Jimmy Chung's neighborhood. So why wasn't I surprised when I saw your car parked out front? With pussy waiting for ya."

"You still paying your wife to tie your shoes, Noel?" Bobby asked.

Bobby said goodbye to Ben Lee and went out to his Jeep. He didn't see Amy McCoy anywhere as he climbed into the front seat and started the engine. He heard the rustle from the backseat. The hair on the back of his neck stood up. He drove another block and then swiftly yanked the Jeep to a stop in a bus stop and spun with his .38 pointing at the stowaway in the backseat. The orange and black kitten looked up at him from the floor and meowed.

"Oh, Christ," Bobby said.

7

Bobby checked the clock on the Jeep's dash: 2:30 PM. He looked at his caller ID on the car phone and saw that Maggie had called. He got her on the phone and she said she was doing the database search on Chung and already had some interesting stuff she wanted to show him. "Tomorrow. We'll have lunch at the West Bank," he said.

"They make slammin' chicken," she said. "Pick me up."

Bobby promised he would and then drove downtown along Eighth Avenue toward Thirty-sixth Street, where he would go left to Third Avenue, then down to Hamilton Avenue, to the Brooklyn Battery Tunnel to Manhattan. As he drove through Brooklyn's Chinatown, he was thinking about Amy McCoy just up and splitting on him.

Probably got insulted, he thought.

But he couldn't risk sharing vital information with her about Chung. He didn't know Amy McCoy well enough yet. He was still feeling her out, picking her brain. For all he knew, *she* could have killed her brother and his wife. Maybe there was an insurance policy. A will. He doubted it. Freelance left-wing journalists who live in roachy rent-controlled pads usually didn't leave huge estates. But he had to be cautious. Plus, Amy was impulsive. She could get herself killed trying to act on important information, or at least screw up his investigation.

He drove past the double-parked trucks that delivered fresh fish, meats, and produce to the scores of Chinese stores along Eighth Avenue. Dozens of bicycle deliverymen from various restaurants and grocery stores whizzed past him, ignoring traffic lights, weaving in and out of horn-honking traffic like fleeing bandits. They all dressed in white linen outfits, as if they all used the same laundry.

The neighborhood was like a great cultural transplant. In the finger snap of a single decade this amazing patch of Asia had been swatched and sewn into the crazy quilt of New York.

As soon as Bobby hung up with Maggie, the phone rang again. Not many people had his cellphone number. Unfortunately, Herbie Rabinowitz was one of them. Actually, Herbie had saved Bobby's ass on more than one occasion. Standing six foot six, with muscles in his eyebrows, Herbie could toss full-backs the way others his size tossed dwarfs. There was absolutely no reason on Earth that a man his size ever needed a black belt in jujitsu, but he had one. When Bobby had asked him if he took martial arts for the Zen philosophy of inner peace and tranquility, Herbie had said, "Fuck that noise, I took it to kick better ass." Herbie was also an inveterate gambler who spent his life cursing and dodging "cops and wops," but probably his greatest misfortune was being Izzy Gleason's first cousin, and being indebted to the shady lawyer for keeping him out of the joint and cement shoes. In addition to his being loyal and dependable muscle, Herbie was also a gourmet cook, schooled at the Culinary Institute of America in upstate New York.

"Bobby, it's Herbie," he said.

"I have no money to lend you, Herbie."

"I'm calling because I know about my cousin Izzy being in a pickle," Herbie says. "I'm working for a guy . . ."

"That's encouraging."

"Morris Daggart."

"Moe Daggart?" Bobby said. "Jesus Christ, Herbie. I thought you didn't like people like him. His real name is D'Aguardia, as in Lou D'Aguardia, also spelled M-O-B."

"Yeah, well, he don't come off like no mutz-a-rel wop and I'm sort of working off a gambling debt,"

Herbie said. "And doing a mitzvah for my rabbi at the same time. Besides, Mr. Daggart's mother was Jewish, so that makes him one of my tribe."

"Herbie, why are you calling me?"

"Mr. Daggart wants to see you. He's legit now," Herbie said. "Even the gambling debt I owe him, it's from one of his legal gambling boats."

"Before the mayor dry-docked him," Bobby said, making a right onto Ninth Avenue, where he would get quicker access to Thirty-sixth Street, looping around the bus yard, the train tracks of the above-ground BMT subway line, and the high fences of Greenwood Cemetery.

Bobby knew that Daggart was involved with several legit businesses over the years and was even running a legal offshore gambling boat out of the Java Street Pier in downtown Brooklyn for a while before Mayor Tom Brady enlisted the political help of U.S. Attorney Sean Dunne of the Southern District to enforce a little-known federal smuggling law that required the gambling boats to go twelve miles out instead of three, which made the operation unprofitable. Brady cited the danger of mob infiltration but most newspaper pundits said the mayor had really killed the gambling boats in deference to Sam Kronk, whose Atlantic City casinos were being hurt by New York gambling. Daggart had taken the city and the feds to court and the case was pending.

"Okay, so you're working for Daggart," Bobby

said as he stopped for a light before making the winding turn along the cemetery. "Who's the rabbi?"

"Rabbi Simon Berg," Herbie said.

"I hear he's a good guy," Bobby said of the cleric who did great work with the kids of Brooklyn, trying to bridge the racially troubled waters in places like Crown Heights. His philosophy was that if you kept kids on basketball courts you kept them out of criminal courts. "My brother Patrick works closely with Rabbi Berg through the Police Athletic League. Rabbi Berg is in cahoots with Moe Daggart?"

"Yep," Herbie said. "So is Father Jack Dooley and Reverend Gaston Greene."

"Jesus Christ," Bobby said. "'The Three Wise Men and One Wise Guy.' Sounds like a *New York Post* headline."

"I crapped out for twenny-seven K on one of Mr. Daggart's cruises before he was dry-docked," Herbie said. "He's letting me work off the marker in trade as security."

"Herbie, what the hell are the three most progressive, maverick clergymen in the city doing in bed with Moe Daggart?" Bobby asked as he made the left from Ninth Avenue onto Thirty-sixth Street, a barren stretch sandwiched between the fence of the graveyard and the train tracks.

"That's what they asked me to call you about," Herbie said. "They want to hire you."

"I don't do God's work, Herbie," Bobby said.

"Tell them I'm a happily guilt-ridden retired Catholic."

"But they say it's tied into cousin Izzy's problem with the McCoy couple and the missing landlord, Jimmy Chung."

"I'm impressed that you're keeping up with current events, Herbie," Bobby said. "But I can't see how that unlikely crew fits in with the case I'm working . . ."

"I told them I could get you to at least come listen. I told them you were my . . . *friend.*"

"Look, I'm busy right now, Herbie. I have to talk to a few people," Bobby said. "Call me tomorrow . . ."

"I knew you'd come through for me."

"But tell them I'm *not for hire,*" Bobby said. "I won't take Daggart's scummy money. And I couldn't take money from men of the cloth and look Saint Peter in the eye on Judgment Day. So, if I find time, I'll listen to what they have to say. But that's it."

"Shalom," Herbie said.

"Peace, Herbie," Bobby said just as a bicyclist appeared in front of his right fender. Bobby slammed the brakes, dropped the phone. He heard metal on metal and a thud, saw the Chinese deliveryman dressed in a white linen outfit disappear from view in front of his Jeep. The bicycle clattered to the street, the front wheel spinning. Bobby threw the car in park on the barren street alongside the cemetery.

Bobby jumped out of the car, as Herbie shouted

over the cell phone, "Bobby, you okay? You okay, baby? Talk to me, Bobby . . ."

Bobby rushed around the front of his Jeep to attend to the fallen deliveryman who lay on the ground in a fetal ball, his white linen outfit smudged with dirt.

"Hey, buddy, you okay?" Bobby asked as he squatted over the injured man who rocked and moaned in pain. "I'll call an ambulance."

Before Bobby could stand, the fallen man shot out a blinding kick that caught Bobby on the chin. He hadn't been hit this hard since he boxed against a fellow cop named Forrest Morgan for the NYPD heavyweight championship over ten years before. Now Bobby heard a vehicle screech to a halt, heard the voices of other young men.

Control, Bobby thought, remembering the mantra that kept him alive as a cop in the joint. *Think and you will control the situation. Get up . . .*

He staggered to his feet and was quickly punched in the left ear from the side, another blow from yet a third man hit him in the belly, a fourth attacker dressed in white linen rammed a punch into Bobby's kidney. "Mind your own fuckin' business, asshole," said a Chinese guy with a Brooklyn accent. "Forget Jimmy Chung!" another yelled.

Both guys in front of him threw more punches at Bobby's face. He dodged under one and caught the second on the top of his skull, making the man howl in pain. Bobby buried a left hook to his ribs, felt them crack like balsa.

"Mudda-fuckuh!" shouted the man, his English as Brooklyn as murder in the afternoon.

The guy behind Bobby threw a second punch to his other kidney but Bobby reached behind him, caught his fist, whipped him around in front of him, skull-butted his small nose, and shot-putted him into the other two attackers. He pulled the guy back by the hand like a returning yo-yo, pried open his small fist and bent his index and middle finger backward until he heard the bones crackle and the fingers stood up perpendicular to his knuckles. The guy on the ground leapt up and threw another karate kick. This time Bobby ducked under it, grabbed his ankle, pulled off his sneaker, broke the man's big toe like a hard pretzel, and as he held him spread-legged, punched him square in the balls. The little man issued a long high-pitched hiss like a truck tire going flat. Bobby dropped him and the man started belly-crawling toward the white van that was parked with its motor running.

"No," he heard one of his attackers shout at another. "*Bu guang!* No guns, man! The man said *bu guang.*"

But Bobby heard the slide of an automatic pistol. He dove behind the Jeep and yanked his own .38 from his pants pocket.

"This big fuck hurt me," shouted the one with the gun.

As the two others shouted frantically in Chinese, a spray of four bullets whizzed over Bobby's head, pinging and ricocheting off the metal cemetery fence and chipping a headstone behind him. Bobby rolled to the front of the car, still concealed behind the wheel, and fired from the ground at the shooter. The slug tore into his right shoulder, sending an instant crimson stain across the starched white linen jacket. The shooter screamed and spun, his automatic firing recklessly before he dropped it. Two of the others rushed to him, collected the gun, and dragged their buddy into the rear of the waiting white van. The one who had faked the bicycle accident now sat behind the wheel, grimacing in pain. He squealed away, zigzagging the wrong way down the one-way street.

Bobby took note of the license plate: New Jersey—VQR-749.

He kicked the bicycle and the abandoned sneaker out of his way and when he slid into the front seat of the Jeep, Bobby could still hear Herbie Rabinowitz screaming into the cell phone. "Bobby, Bobby, pick up the fuckin' phone! Are you okay, pal?"

"Herbie," Bobby said. "I think I'm gonna need you around. When can I meet with Daggart and these holy rollers?"

"They're all here right now," Herbie said, excited. "What's the address?"

8

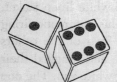

The Metro Tech Center was the new economic pacemaker of downtown Brooklyn, a five-million-square-foot development of high-rise office towers, reno-vated buildings, five colleges, a gleaming new Marriott Hotel, all surrounded by a tree-shaded commons sit-uated on five square blocks of what was until the late 1980s a tableau of urban despair and decay.

After parking the Jeep in an underground lot—where he left the kitten with a small torn-open carton of milk, and the windows cracked for air—Bobby crossed the busy commons, where workers and stu-dents ate lunch, read books and newspapers, did homework, sunbathed, made out, or talked in cheer-ful knots. It looked like a snapshot of civilization. He entered the lobby of a copper-topped tower, rising twenty stories above this municipal, judicial, and com-mercial hub of the city's most populated borough. After downtown and midtown Manhattan, Metro Tech had transformed downtown Brooklyn into the city's third-largest commercial center. With the Dow booming, this complex was now a Brooklyn annex to Wall Street, home to offices for Bear Stearns, Goldman Sachs, Morgan Stanley, Chase Manhattan. It also rented space to some of the highest-priced of

Brooklyn's infamous Court Street lawyers and the new high-powered Brooklyn entrepreneurs who led the charge for the borough's sixty thousand commercial enterprises that had for too long been stigmatized with the "dese, dem, and dose" identity pinned on it by Hollywood.

Bobby stepped off the elevator on the nineteenth floor, impressed that Moe Daggart could afford the tariff. The name of his company—NUCENT VENTURES INC., MORRIS DAGGART, CEO—was raised on his polished oak door. Bobby rang the buzzer on an intercom panel and a woman's voice crackled, asking who it was. He told her and was buzzed in.

The large, oval reception-office was decorated in a rich, dark-wood paneling, with soft fluorescent panels shining from the ten-foot ceiling and inlaid, deep-pile, royal-blue carpeting underfoot. A sexy receptionist wearing a telephone headset sat behind a bulletproof glass wall that separated the outer office from the suite of offices within. Two muscular young men dressed in neat blue business suits and wearing Clark Kent hairdos stood in square-jawed silence on the other side of the wall near the steel security door. Bobby noticed two security cameras peering at him.

"Hello, Mr. Emmet," the receptionist said, smiling in an effusive gush, all blue eyes, white teeth, and blond curls. "Mister Daggart is expecting you."

She reached under her desk, pushed a security buzzer, and one of the young suits pulled open the door for him with a polite preppie nod. Bobby stepped through the door and instantly heard the piercing whine of a metal detector. The taller of the preppie security guards immediately began patting Bobby down.

"You better whisper 'I love you' in my ear when you feel me up, honey," Bobby said, grabbing the man by the wrists, staring into his eyes. Bobby heard the slide of an automatic pistol behind him and without turning brought the heel of his boot down on the second guard's big toe. That one screamed while the first one, unable to break Bobby's grip, attempted to head-butt Bobby. Bobby suddenly freed his wrists, stepped to the side, and let the first guard lurch under his own power headfirst into the door jamb.

"Oh my God!" said the receptionist, with a short gasp. Her eyes widened and she looked like she was about to laugh.

Bobby winked at her, turned to the second one, snatched the Beretta 9-mm Parabellum from his loosened grip, quickly ejected the live round from the chamber, and disengaged the clip from the gun. He buried the loose bullet in the soil of a nearby potted palm.

Herbie Rabinowitz appeared from a corridor of the inner office, wearing a rumpled tan suit that fit his six foot six frame like a drop cloth with sleeves, his size-fourteen Timberland ankle boots too big for the tapered legs of his pants. His yarmulke was bobby-pinned to an overgrown mess of dark curly hair that looked like a pile of black fusilli. Herbie noticed the big blond guy holding his head where he'd given himself a bump, and the other one who was trying to walk off the pain in his big toe.

"Everything hunky fuckin' dory here, Willie?" Herbie asked the big blond.

"The old sports were just showing me the ropes of NuCent Ventures Inc.," Bobby said. "From head to toe."

"Hope they didn't bother you," Herbie said.

"Nah," Bobby said. "We're all in the security business. Just talking a little shop."

Herbie looked the two suits up and down. "Hah-vid," Herbie said. "They row boats."

"How are things on the Charles, guys?" Bobby asked.

"Wet," said Willie, the big blond, checking the bump with his hankie for blood. There wasn't any.

"Like I says," Herbie said. "Educated. Their old man spends a quarter-mil to educate them in that Beantown windmill and they wind up working under *me* here in Brooklyn. Go figure."

"I'm not educated enough," Bobby said. He handed back the gun to the one with the broken toe. He stuffed the bullet clip into his breast pocket. "Thanks," Bobby said, patting his own pistol in his front right pants pocket, "but I think I'll stick to my S&W .38 Police Special."

"Bobby, I love you like a new uncle for what you are doing for me," Herbie said leading Bobby into the suite of offices.

"I'm not doing anything for you," Bobby said. "And if you feel the need to be nephewed, stick to Uncle Sam. Leave me out. But what are you doing working on shabbos?"

"Special dispensation from my rabbi because we're doing God's work," Herbie said.

"He pay minimum wage?"

Bobby followed Herbie down a long corridor, past a few small offices, where college-age men and women ticked away at computer keyboards. They passed a few more young security men dressed in the same blue suits as the two by the door.

"Everything cool, Mr. Rabinowitz?" asked one who walked like a robot.

"Why the fuck wouldn't it be, numb nuts?" Herbie said and kept walking.

"*Mister* Rabinowitz?" Bobby said.

"Usually only judges call me that," Herbie said.

"During sentencing," Bobby said.

"But Mr. Daggart, he respects me. He's letting me pay off the gambling debt and gives me a salary to eat at the same time. I still put a few bucks down on the games. The wops here in Brooklyn don't know me too good, yet. Plus, there's an OTB over on Montague Street where I met a great tout . . ."

"Why so much horse flesh in here?" Bobby asked, skeptical of the whole setup.

"I run security for a special operation," he said. "Lots of cash flow. Purring like a cathouse, too. But, sorry, it's a mum freeze secret."

"Sounds like this God's work ain't too kosher to me, Herbie," Bobby said.

"You trying to say it's wopped-up mob money?" Herbie asked.

"Is a pig's pecker pork?"

"I know Mr. Daggart is half Ital, but he don't surround himself with your average Guido geeps."

"Nah, he uses class help, like you, Herbie."

Herbie squinted, didn't know if it was a compliment or not, and said, "Matter fact, the cops and the wops both look the other way on this one."

"What's the operation called? Grand Theft City?"

"It's a very socially redeeming operation," Herbie said. "Mr. Daggart says we're doing yeoman work here, actually giving back what City Hall has stolen from the people. A mitzvah. A little daily good deed."

"Daggart has always been known for wearing a heart on his sleeve," Bobby said. "After he rips it out of somebody's chest."

They reached the door of an office at the far end of the plush corridor. Herbie knocked. A deep-timbred voice said, "Bring him in, Herbie."

Herbie held open the door for Bobby, who stepped into the thirty-by-forty-foot office, the whole front wall of which was glass, looking out over the great port, a panorama of the Brooklyn waterfront, the downtown bridges, the Manhattan skyline. Bobby could see all the way up to the Empire State and Chrysler buildings. It was like a ringside seat to the greatest show on Earth.

The walls of Daggart's office were decorated with images of the New York harbor—lithographs of fighting ships of the Revolutionary War, sepia photographs of the Brooklyn Bridge in various stages of construction, modern paintings depicting Operation Sail, posters of the visit of the Tall Ships, and photographs of the fireworks display over the harbor marking the one-hundredth anniversary of New York.

Moe Daggart stood, gently placed a framed eight-by-ten picture facedown on his glass-topped desk, and circled around with his right hand outstretched to Bobby. Bobby figured Daggart had started on his deep Caribbean tan sometime in midwinter.

"Greetings," Daggart said.

Bobby limply shook hands with Daggart, who was an elegant six feet two, with the trim, long-muscled body of a swimmer. He moved with the graceful confident strides of a man with money in the bank and an educated plan in his head. Bobby knew that intelligence was something that was detectable without more than a word being spoken. It came out in attitude. Daggart was smart, looked it, and knew it.

Three men who were seated in white leather armchairs also rose. Bobby shook hands with Father Jack Dooley, Rabbi Simon Berg, and Reverend Gaston Greene, baby-boomer clerics who were no strangers to civic activism, some of it bordering on the outright political, overstepping the separation of church and state. Bobby's brother, Patrick, a cop who ran the Police Athletic League in Brooklyn, had worked closely with each of these clerics and had often told Bobby about their good work.

Father Dooley, who had black-Irish movie-star good looks, was notorious for packing his pews with giggling teenage girls and swooning housewives. On Saturday afternoons, randy widows, single women, and adulterous wives lined up outside of Father Dooley's confessional booth to unload their sins of lust to the handsome priest. The guys in St. Brian's Parish were always scheming about bugging Dooley's confessional, to find out who was banging whom.

The forty-five-year-old priest was often in hot holy water with the Brooklyn Diocese because of rumors of his broken celibacy and for his pitched battles with City Hall, which often involved picketing and preaching, urging letter-writing campaigns to protest funding cuts for social programs. But the bottom line showed that he was a good earner. His collection baskets were always overflowing with perfume-scented donation envelopes, he successfully solicited generous endowments from private and corporate sources into church coffers, and so he was begrudgingly tolerated by what he called "the unctuous mummies" of the church hierarchy. "Just once I'd love to see a fat white bishop play midnight B-ball in the hood" was a sound bite that almost got him defrocked.

Reverend Gaston Greene, an eloquent, honey-voiced orator, was no shrill charismatic grandstander like Al Sharpton. Instead, he had a popular church in

Flatbush that had been converted from an abandoned movie palace, and he used it for weekly TV and radio broadcasts on the social issues that plagued the children of the inner city. Greene was a Vietnam veteran who came home after the Tet offensive with a Bronze Star and a Purple Heart to find his fellow vets and their kids destroyed by drugs and poverty and divided from the rest of the city by racial barriers. He decided the real war was here at home, and over the past thirty-odd years—playing election-year poker with City Hall behind the scenes—he'd probably done more at the grassroots level to combat drug abuse and integrate white and black teenagers than any man in the city. On more than one occasion Reverend Greene had taken a baseball bat to local drug and gun dealers who dared to desecrate his churchyard. In his part of Brooklyn, Reverend Greene was bad for bad-business.

All the newspapers had documented Rabbi Simon Berg's background. When he was just twenty-seven years old, Berg had been one of the top show-business lawyers in New York, representing music, movie, and sports stars, hot directors, rich producers, and flamboyant promoters. He'd made millions, lived large, been crowned king of the yuppie scum. Then, in one tragic day, his life had forever changed when his beloved wife, Shirley, a childhood sweetheart from Midwood, Brooklyn, whom he'd met at Edward R. Murrow High, was murdered by a gang of malevolent teens as she jogged from their million-dollar Park Slope mansion through Prospect Park. After her death, Berg found solace only in God, chucked the career, went to Israel, joined a kibbutz, studied and became a rabbi, came back to Brooklyn, and ever since dedicated himself and his small fortune to working with the youth of the city. Friends called him nuts, an ideologue, a dreamer. *Killers are killers*, they'd said. *You can't change them.* Berg thought differently and had been working with kids of all races and religions in the streets, playgrounds, and alleys for over ten years.

Berg couldn't walk through Crown Heights, Midwood, Bed Stuy, Boro Park, East New York, Bensonhurst, Fort Greene without being mobbed by young people who wanted to participate in one of his arts programs—theater, dance, music, film. He even had his own TV program on the Brooklyn public-access channel, where kids aired their own films and plays, created their own talk shows, played music.

What the hell were these good guys doing with a bad-news asshole like Daggart? Bobby asked himself.

"Bobby, we're all pleased you found time to come," Daggart said.

"The man I'm doing some work for is in trouble," Bobby said. "He helped me when I was in trouble. Herbie said you guys wanted to talk to me about his trouble. It's part of my job to be here. No thanks are in order."

Daggart made a flourish for everyone to sit and the five men formed a semicircle. The receptionist came in with a tray of coffee and mineral water.

"Thanks, Cindy," Daggart said.

"Wel-come," she sang as she high-heeled it out of the room, leaving lusty little impressions in the rug, like a tantalizing trail of doe tracks.

In front of the clerics, Bobby felt slightly awkward watching Cindy in her tight skirt, revealing blouse, and high heels. When he turned to look at them instead, he saw all three watching her leave. *Women are right*, he thought. *Men are all dogs. Some pedigree, some mutts, but all bow-wows.*

"Cindy is a woman of many talents," Daggart said.

"Nice setup," Bobby said, addressing Daggart, whom he'd always thought of as a mutt. "Must be tough making the nut on this place with your gambling boat in dry dock."

"It's a setback," Daggart said. "But I anticipated problems from City Hall and so I built the legal fees into the initial start-up costs. After all, Mayor Brady is a Sam Kronk puppet. Kronk sees my little six-million-a-year off-shore gambling boat as a threat to his billion-dollar casino empire, so he used Brady to sic Sean Dunne, the federal prosecutor from Brooklyn's Eastern District . . ."

"I know who he is," Bobby said. "I worked with him when I was at the Manhattan DA's office, on joint county and federal prosecutions. He's smart, savvy, and sneaky. Also dealt with his twin brother, the FBI guy, Donald Dunne, aka Dum Dum Dunne."

"Ah, but Donald no longer works for the FBI," Daggart said with a knowing smile. "These days, he happens to be Sam Kronk's deputy chief for security in Atlantic City. Actually for his whole operation."

"Convenient," Bobby said.

"Yes," Daggart said. "Anyway, Brady got Sean Dunne to use an old federal smuggling law to make me sail twelve miles out instead of three. They know that was an untenable situation. It takes too long. It costs too much on fuel. It pisses off the gamblers, who can just as easily drive to Atlantic City. So I've taken the city and the feds to court. I'm waiting for a date."

"Tough fight," Bobby said.

"Tough fight I can live with," Daggart said. "But then to bury me, Mayor Brady and Sean Dunne . . ."

"Not to be confused with his brother Dum Dum Dunne," Bobby said.

". . . decide to change the rules," said Daggart. "If I win on the smuggling law, they intend to have my license to operate lifted by the City Gambling Commission, on grounds of moral turpitude, citing organized-crime affiliations."

"Nooooo," Bobby said, feigning incredulity. "You, Daggart, the former D'Aguardia, son of Alfonse D'Aguardia, once boss of the third most powerful mob family in New York, before he was rubbed out."

Bobby was trying to ruffle Daggart's wrinkle-free demeanor. It didn't work.

"I don't deny what my father was," Daggart said.

"But it's small-minded, unfair, and lazy to blame me for the sins of my father. I've never been arrested or indicted in my life. I've been investigated. Even by you, Bobby, when you worked for the Manhattan District Attorney's office. And like all the other witch hunters before you, you came up with bupkis!"

When Bobby was in the DA's office he was part of a team that investigated some of Daggart's companies, an electronics chain and a fast-food chain, both of which they suspected were mob laundries. Eighteen months of undercover investigations couldn't make a case for anything more than Daggart's store managers hiring a few illegals with fake green cards, which were violations but not crimes. Bobby suspected Daggart was dirty, but he had to admit that they never turned up any proof.

"That part is true," Bobby said, nodding to the clerics. "Fair's fair."

"I've had legitimate companies on the stock exchange and got SEC clearance," Daggart said. "I have a degree from NYU and an MBA from Harvard Business School. I'm a member of the Brooklyn Chamber of Commerce. I've done business with the biggest banks in New York. But now, all of a sudden, because I want to run a little offshore floating crap game, I don't meet the moral standards of the city because my father, who was killed when I was nineteen, was a member of organized crime. This is un-American. It might take me two or three years, all the way to the Supreme Court, to beat them. By that time my gambling-boat idea will be old hat, the competition will be prohibitive, and I'll be bankrupt from legal bills, but I'll clear my name."

"This is why we agreed to Moe's idea," said Father Dooley.

"We have a common enemy, brother Emmet," said Reverend Greene.

"The ever-odious Mayor Tom Brady," said Rabbi Berg.

"The Un-Holy Trinity," Bobby said. "Three heads talking as one. Okay, so what's Moe's idea?"

"Before we tell you what it is, we want to hire you so you can't break the confidence," Father Dooley said.

"First of all, I'm not here to work for you," Bobby said. "I put money in poor boxes, I don't take it out. And I won't work for him."

He pointed to Daggart.

"You don't have to trust me," Daggart said, with a smile and shrug. "But I'm prepared to trust you. The reason I trust you is that when you investigated me, you didn't fabricate evidence. You didn't manufacture lies. You could have, but you didn't frame me. You came, you snooped, you found nothing, you closed the case."

"And I wrote my report," Bobby said. "That's what you're supposed to do."

"You're honest," Daggart said. "And right now I have nothing left to lose. When you see our operation, I think you'll agree it's for the public good."

"Please, don't tell me you're running a charity here, Daggart," Bobby said. "They don't teach philanthropy at Harvard Business."

"Sure, I'm getting compensated," he said. "But I'm willing to let you in on what we're doing anyway. I figure that if you expose me, you'll also expose these good gentlemen, who most certainly practice the philanthropy they preach. I think I know enough about Bobby Emmet's background to believe he won't do anything to get in the way of that. Besides, I think what you'll find out, if you dig as deep as I know only you can dig, is that this Kronk-Brady-Dunne business is all tied in to the problems Izzy Gleason is having."

"Okay, Daggart," Bobby said. "Tell you what. If you trust me, why don't you give me a minute alone with God's little helpers here to discuss it?"

"Fine," Daggart said without hesitation. "I have to use the john anyway. I'll be back in five. It won't take longer than that for them to explain it."

Bobby watched Daggart stride out of the office with the sure-footed poise of a man with nothing to hide. *Maybe I'm wrong about this guy*, Bobby thought.

As soon as Daggart was gone Bobby stood and strolled to the great wall of windows, peered out at the frantic city, a pulsating, undulating metropolis run by an ambitious mayor with delusions that someday he might live in the White House.

"Before you tell me what you're doing with Daggart," Bobby said, "maybe you should tell me *why*." He turned and looked at Daggart's neat desk, upon which rested a leather appointment book, a photograph of Daggart's mother, a picture of Daggart as a young man on the New Utrecht High swimming team, and the picture Daggart had placed face-down when Bobby entered the office.

"You see," Reverend Greene said, sitting on the edge of his chair and leaning toward Bobby, "Mayor Brady might be a great law-and-order guy who cut crime . . ."

"Can't knock him for that," Bobby said, flopping into Daggart's leather desk chair and swiveling.

"No," Dooley said, "but at the same time he also cut things like most funds for day-care centers, senior-citizen centers, food pantries, battered-women's shelters, after-school programs, summer-jobs programs, youth-sports programs . . ."

"My brother Patrick complains to me all the time about that stuff," Bobby said, leaning forward on Daggart's desk now. "But what the hell does that have to do with you guys going into business with Daggart?"

"We need money for those programs, Bobby," Rabbi Berg said. "If there are no jobs for kids, no after-school programs in the next school year, no place for people to get help, the city is gonna be hit with a backlash from the underclass like it's never seen before."

"We've tapped out everyone," Greene said. "No one who gives a damn has any money left. Juvenile delinquency is up in the city, across the country. There aren't enough jails for kids. Gangs are on an upswing because they're offering a structure the kids aren't getting in their broken homes or from any of the canceled social programs. If we ignore these kids, let them run wild again, this city is gonna explode. If not this summer, then next year for sure. I can feel it, Bobby Emmet, I can hear it, I can smell it like blood on the wind. I don't want to see all the good work we've been involved with be undone. If we don't fill the gap for these kids, the drug dealers and the gang leaders will."

"So we decided to raise some serious money of our own," Father Dooley said. "We think that if we raise fifty to seventy-five million dollars we can build an all-purpose United Churches social-services, sports, and artistic center for the needs of these kids."

"A refuge for our youth, that they can go to to keep them from getting sent to the youth house," Berg said. "A criminal prevention center, as opposed to a criminal detention center. One that could be a national model, the kind of success story that could shame the city into duplicating it. A place with ballfields, basketball courts, boxing rings, a homeless family shelter, a social-services building, an after-school tutoring center, a state-of-the-art computer building, a film and theater arts studio, an adult jobs training center. It's been a dream of ours for the past ten years. And now we have the land all picked out in Coney Island, a place people always thought of as the last stop on the subway. But we want to call the place First Stop, the place where the train leaves the station, loaded with kids prepared for the workplace and the world. We think with Moe Daggart's help, and your input, we can make this dream of ours come true."

"Fifty to seventy-five million!" Bobby said, lifting the face-down picture frame on Daggart's desk. His heart did a double-thump when he saw the photo of Zelda Savarese, the gorgeous tennis star, in her little white dress, with long, tanned legs that could make a sensible man act foolish. Zelda Savarese was kissing *Moe Daggart*, who was also in tennis whites. The inscription on the photo read: *To Moe, All my love, always, Zelda.*

Bobby couldn't believe it. *What the hell was a gorgeous champion like Zelda Savarese doing with a lowlife like Moe Daggart? Kissing him! On the lips!*

"Well, that's getting into the why," Rabbi Berg said. "Excuse us a sec, Bobby."

The three clerics huddled together, whispering amongst themselves as Bobby sat staring wide-eyed at the picture of Zelda Savarese. Like half the men in the world, Bobby had been in love with Zelda Savarese from afar since the first day he ever saw her on a tennis court at Forest Hills about eight years before. He'd been infatuated by her entire essence, her thick gleaming black hair floating behind her, the muscles in the long legs bunching as she charged the net, the cute little butt peeking from under the teeny white skirt as she fiercely aced a serve, the sweat glistening on her high cheekbones like the patina on a Da Vinci bronze, the passion in her fervent dark eyes when she backhanded a winning shot.

Her brilliant, panting smile in victory. A pure champion. A pure male fantasy. A pure dream girl. Kissing a pure nightmare like Moe Daggart.

"We all agree that we should *show* you instead of *telling* you," said Father Dooley.

"Huh?" Bobby said, lost in reverie.

"You asked how we intended to raise so much money," Berg said. "We'd like to show you the fundraising operation instead of just telling you about it. So that you can see for yourself that this is no pipe dream—prove that we can actually pull this off. Then you decide if you want to help us."

Bobby placed the picture facedown on the desk, got up, and walked toward the clergymen. "Look, guys, I don't have time for communion breakfasts, bake sales, or church bazaars. I'm busy. I have three missing people I'm looking for. All of them maybe murdered. For which my client is the prime suspect. I was told this was all somehow connected to that, but . . ."

"If what Moe Daggart says is true, it is," said Dooley.

Daggart now knocked on his own door, peeked his head in, smiled, and said, "May I?"

Bobby nodded. Daggart entered and the clerics told him they'd decided to take Bobby on a tour of

the operation. Daggart shrugged and nodded. "Fine,"
he said. "Great."

"And you're telling me this has to do with Izzy
Gleason's legal problems?" Bobby said.

"I promise you," Daggart said. "It has everything
to do with the jackpot your lawyer friend is in right
now. And then some."

"Okay, when?"

"Tonight is Saturday, a good night," said Berg.
"Agreed?"

The others nodded.

Bobby was also still damned curious about why a
tennis queen like Zelda Savarese would want anything to do with Moe Daggart. And why he would put
such a flattering photograph face-down on his desk
when Bobby walked in. It wasn't important, but it
bothered him, like a light he'd left on at home. That
question alone was enough to make him want to
know more about Moe Daggart.

"I don't expect the truth from Morris D'Aguardia
Daggart," Bobby said, turning to the clerics, looking
each one in the eye. "But for you guys—hey, if God is
your witness, and he's not copping the Fifth, then
show me the promised land."

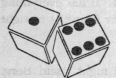 "Money up the yin yang," Herbie said.

Bobby had counted four Mercedeses and six Lexuses in the past ten minutes. Now a BMW. And a Lincoln Town Car. Maybe a dozen new Cadillacs. They all pulled through the gates of the parking lot of St. Brian's Roman Catholic Church in Dyker Heights, a mostly Italian neighborhood of one- and two-family homes in southwestern Brooklyn, just ten minutes by car from the poverty and squalor of the Coney Island projects.

Dyker was a great neighborhood for disposable income.

Bobby sat behind the wheel of his Jeep, Herbie beside him in the passenger seat. Bobby was alternately looking in his sideview mirror for a dark, late-model Lumina he could have sworn had tailed him from the underground garage of Metro Tech. But he couldn't see it now. *Probably just paranoia*, he thought.

He watched men in expensive suits and ties and women in designer evening wear stepping out of the fancy cars and handing their keys to valet parkers. More limos pulled up, dropping off well-dressed middle-aged couples. The people drifted toward the basement steps of the big church on the quiet avenue.

"Who's getting married?" Bobby asked.

"Their money and our wallets," Herbie said. "Come on, I gotta go to work to make sure these fuckin' Hah-vid hooples we call security don't let the loot get legs. Leave the car here for a fast getaway."

Herbie yanked his way out of the Jeep, still wearing the same rumpled tan suit. He adjusted his yarmulke on his head and lurched toward the church. Bobby climbed out, checked once again for the dark Lumina, and didn't see it. He followed Herbie across the avenue to the lot where the valet parking kids were clammy with summer sweat. The churchyard was now full and they were parking the cars in a nearby supermarket lot under a big Brooklyn sky that was jittery with stars.

"I always feel funny walkin' into a Cat'lick church wearing my yarmulke," Herbie said. "I look okay?"

"Aside from your suit having more wrinkles than Einstein's brain, you look fine, Herbie," Bobby said. "Like a sinner. Just what they want in church. Penance means money."

"Everything goin' good?" Herbie asked the main valet parker, a kid in his twenties with dark, Italian features.

"Over a hundred cars so far, Mr. R.," said the valet.

"Cops cool?"

"No problem," the kid said.

"One comes, you get me on the honker, hear?" Herbie said, taking a hand radio from his suit jacket pocket.

"You bet, Mr. R.," said the valet parker as members of his team took the wheels of several newly arrived cars—a Camry, a Land Cruiser, another Lexus. Bobby was beginning to catch on.

They were all here to visit Our Lady of the Losers, otherwise known as Lady Luck.

These people all had that hungry, manic, near-degenerate look of insatiable gamblers. A look that said the answer to all their problems was always just one wager away. As each couple descended the steps to the church basement entrance, Bobby noticed Willie, the big blond guy from NuCent Ventures Inc., greeting them with a courteous nod, holding open the door. Loud music blared from the basement every time the door opened.

"The floating crap game has washed ashore, eh, Herbie?" Bobby asked as he followed the big man down the steps. Willie grimaced when he saw Bobby approach.

"Everything okay, Willie?" Herbie asked.

"Exceptional," Willie said, avoiding Bobby's line of sight.

The bump on Willie's forehead had been properly iced and covered with makeup. He looked fine. Herbie hurried into the crowded basement as Bobby paused beside Willie, clapping his hand on the big man's shoulder. "No hard feelings, huh?"

"On your part, perhaps," Willie said. "Not mine. Life is long and you'll get yours, asshole. We'll see each other again, alone."

"You finally get to use your head for more than a hat rack and you still don't learn basic manners," Bobby said, wagging a scolding finger. "I guess when you flunk everything, the only job left is flunky."

Bobby clapped Willie's shoulder again and walked into the church basement. Live music played and the room was thick with shouting, laughter, cigarette and cigar smoke. And money—this was no nickel-and-dime church bazaar. This was big money. Money was everywhere. He heard the dinging and gonging of computerized slot machines; the chiming of silver dollars rattling into metal bowls; the rat-a-tat-tat of the roulette wheel; the loud din of gamblers at their desperate work; croupiers calling cards; crap-shooters screaming at the little red cubes skipping across the fast green felt. And everyone seemed to be shouting about money, above the efforts of a not-bad girl lounge singer who played her own piano on a small stage.

Attractive professional waitresses, dressed in form-fitting tuxedos, dispensed cocktails and hors d'oeuvres to the crowd. Bobby recognized several off-duty cops in the room, three of them brass, and certainly a few gangsters. He thought he recognized at least one local machine pol, a sitting supreme court judge, and a retired surrogate judge. He'd noticed a few MDs on license plates outside. He recognized a few of the shadier-looking guys in this room as low-level wise guys he'd pinched on Super Bowl Weekend gambling sweeps over the years in the DA's office.

The room was still filling with people. A line had formed at the cashier's booth to buy chips. Bobby looked around in amazement, started counting—eight blackjack tables, five craps, two roulettes, one baccarat, and two dozen slots. If they'd had the space, they could have jammed people around a dozen more tables.

Bobby saw Father Jack Dooley walking his way, and except for the collar, he looked like a star at a Hollywood premiere party.

"I'm impressed, Padre," Bobby said. "But fifty, seventy-five mil? From a little Vegas night?"

Dooley chuckled.

"This is just one small piece of the operation," he said. "A casino in the neighborhood, close to home, where it's safe, where people can gamble, where they don't have to pay taxes that our mayor wants to spend to build a billion-dollar baseball stadium for a multi-millionaire owner so that millionaire professional ballplayers can play a kid's game while the same mayor cuts funding for little leagues and midnight basketball for kids in places like Brooklyn."

"Touché," Bobby said. "Priorities do seem a little out of whack."

Bobby watched Herbie lead two uniformed armored-car drivers to the cashier's booth, where he made them sign a receipt for bags of cash, and watched them carry the swag out a back door, accompanied by a red-haired, preppie NuCent security guard.

"This is a match made in heaven," Dooley said. "Daggart can do what we can't do. We can do what he can't do. After all, who is going to come into a church or a synagogue and arrest people for wagering money at a little fundraiser?"

"I've seen bingo halls raided for taking line bets," Bobby said.

"With police brass and judges in the room?"

"Actually, no," Bobby said, smiling.

"Do you object?"

"No," Bobby said. "Not to what you're using the money for. But who knows what Daggart will do with his take."

An attractive woman in her early forties, wearing a low-cut dress and too much mascara and lipstick, walked up to Father Dooley carrying a tray of gambling chips. She handed him a drink. "Scotch, rocks, a splash, like you like it, Father Hunk," she said. "Do me a favor, will ya, do your abracadabra routine over my chips so I can go home a loser."

Father Dooley made a mock blessing of the woman's poker chips. "See, if I lose, I'm gonna be sick," she said. "And you still make bedside sick calls at night, don'tcha, Father Hunk?"

"Don't worry, you'll be a winner tonight, Rose," he said. She winked and shook her ass all the way back to a blackjack table.

Bobby smiled, said nothing, looked around as the

priest sipped his scotch. He saw Herbie leading a muscle-bound young guy with a ring in his nose out the back door.

Bobby excused himself from Father Dooley and followed Herbie outside into the churchyard, where he had the muscle-bound guy lifted off his feet and pinned to the rectory wall. He also saw the red-haired preppie and two uniformed guards loading sacks of cash into an armored truck.

"I seen you trying to pick that poor fat bastard's pocket at the craps table," Herbie said. "Think this is a fuckin' joke here? You rob that fat bastard, you're robbin' *God*, you know that? Since Moses, you rob God, you get the shit kicked atta ya."

"I didn't think about it like that," the muscle-bound guy said.

"God sent that fat bastard here to lose his money so the church can give it to poor dumb fucks like you to play ball and lift weights," Herbie said. "I'm all dressed up and now you're gonna make me break your hands with a greasy wrench."

Bobby watched the armored truck pull away.

"No, man, please, I'm sorry, man," the guy said. "Sorry, it won't happen again . . ."

Herbie looked toward Bobby, who shook his head. Herbie dropped the guy to his feet. "On the arches," he said and hopped the guy in the ass as he hurried away.

"I wasn't gonna hurt him," Herbie said. "Not on Cat'lick property."

"Herbie, an armored truck just pulled away," Bobby said, pointing.

"Yeah, we gotta follow it," Herbie said.

Ten minutes later, Bobby was driving toward Boro Park, where Rabbi Simon Berg had opened his Reform temple. He braked for a red light and saw a dark car that looked like a Lumina stop a block back, where there was no stoplight. The car parallel parked and Bobby's angst ebbed. He drove on, checking for the tail. Nothing. He turned onto Fourteenth Avenue and approached Berg's Reform temple.

"I feel more at home here with my own tribe," Herbie said as Bobby parked across the street from the temple. Young guys wearing yarmulkes were parking cars in the synagogue lot, and also using the lot of a funeral parlor down the avenue.

As Bobby killed the ignition he noticed the same uniformed guards carrying sacks of cash from the back of the temple to the armored truck. One of the NuCent Inc. preppie security guards accompanied them and seemed to be waiting for someone before they left. Bobby checked his side mirror again, thought he saw a Lumina cross Fourteenth Avenue at a crawl before speeding down the side street.

"Where do they take all the money?" Bobby asked.

"First it's brought down to the counting room at

NuCent Inc.," Herbie said. "The girl geniuses Daggart hires from Harvard Business School count it. Actually they use machines, keep records, bundle it, all while the guards wait."

"Where the hell do they take it *then?*" Bobby asked. "You can't bank that kind of cash without accounting for where it came from."

"Alls I know is it's taken to a special location that only Mister Daggart and the Three Wise Men know about," Herbie said.

Bobby and Herbie got out of the Jeep and walked across to the parking lot, which was jammed with fancy cars. Herbie walked to the armored guards and the NuCent preppie.

"What's the shekel count?" Herbie asked.

"One and a quarter," the preppie said.

Herbie looked down into the eyes of the shorter armored-truck guard. The guard nodded. Herbie opened a receipt book and made the guard sign it.

"See you in Flatbush," Herbie said.

The guard nodded and he and his partner climbed into the back of the truck, signaled their driver, and drove off into the night.

"Come on, I'll give you the two-cents tour," Herbie said. "Then I gotta take you to the next one."

The basement of Rabbi Berg's Reform Temple for a United Brooklyn was just as crowded as the one in Father Dooley's St. Brian's. The doctors and nurses from nearby Maimonides Hospital crowded around the tables, shooting craps and playing blackjack. The older, blue-haired ladies were dropping twenties, fifties, and C-notes on mah-jongg.

"When the old dolls find out the old man is bangin' some young piece of ass on the side, they get even by gambling his fuckin' burial fund," Herbie said.

"Herbie, you're cursing in temple."

"Like I says, I got a special fuckin' dispensation from my rabbi," Herbie said, speaking out of the corner of his mouth, Buddy Hacket–style.

Bobby followed Herbie through the busy casino.

"Look around," Herbie said as he patrolled the loud room. "You got more dentists in here per square dishonest inch than the Hamptons on Labor Day Weekend. If you're gonna pick a place to have a heart attack, do it here. Wall-to-wall sawbones—surgeons, dermatologists, gynecologists, dickologists, ass-cancer-ologists, medical suppliers, pharmaceutical-company drug dealers, local real estate bandits, every kind of fuckin' nursing-home and Medicaid swindler they make. The Syrians, these miserable pricks, they wake up in the mornin' with a piss hard-on and oil gushes out, and they play high-stakes roulette and baccarat like it was fuckin' Parcheesi. Then, over there, at the blackjack tables, you have your fuckin' diamond merchants, dressed like stumblebums but, oy, they gamble on blind cards like the Messiah was arriving on the 6:15 outta Babylon in the AM. We take wheelbarrows of swag outta here every Saturday and Sunday night. Wednesday we do half the business, but, hey, we can scrimp on the food during the week, too. And believe me, Bobby, my tribe ain't bashful around an oat bag. They eat like your people drink. Every weekend is like a bar mitzvah for Aaron Spelling's kids here. But you know what? Most of them know where the money's goin'. They don't know all the details, but with Rabbi Berg involved, they know it's something for the youth, a mitzvah, so they don't mind so much losing. They figure it's a down payment on the airfare and a time share in a ground-floor condo in heaven. A lot of them'd come even if they knew the tables were rigged. Contrary to what your average greaseball might say about us, my people have hearts as big as their appetites."

"You should do PR for the Anti-Defamation League, Herbie," Bobby said, looking around at the chips rattling on the tables, wheels spinning, dice tumbling—and the money changing hands. So much cash he couldn't believe it.

This casino had twice as many tables as the one in St. Brian's. Bobby thought he recognized a few yuppie stockbrokers, a trio of shady Court Street lawyers, and a couple of writers from Park Slope mixed in with the Boro Park and Bensonhurst crowd. People were gambling so heavily, with such reckless abandon, Bobby thought the place might go into a collective seizure.

Herbie walked around with an imposing authority, carrying his walkie-talkie, snatching shrimp, bagel chips, lox, chicken fingers from the trays carried by circulating waitresses. He signaled to the band-leader to up the tempo of the music and the quartet launched into an instrumental rendition of "Brown Sugar," by the Rolling Stones. Herbie stopped to supervise a few plainclothes NuCent security guards as they moved from one croupier to another, collecting chips, bringing them back to the cashier, who sold them again.

"So, this is the *how*," Rabbi Berg said as he sidled up to Bobby.

"It's more than I would have expected, Rabbi," Bobby said. "But then illegal gambling in the city is estimated at over three billion a year. So why should it be?"

"I know you have reservations about Daggart," Berg said. "So do I. But one of the things I learned in my years in show business is that there is no such thing as permanent enemies, only permanent interests. Daggart has the same interests as us. Beating our mayor at his own mean-spirited power game. As a Brooklyn kid from a working-class Jewish family who made good with a free, open-admissions CUNY education, I find it repulsive to watch this turn into a two-tiered city of the rich and the poor. Ever since my wife died the way she did, I realized I had spent too much time looking at the city from the penthouse. I needed to get back down to the street to make sense of Shirley's death. When I did, I found good kids who had gone bad, some maybe because they couldn't find another way to go."

"Liberal knee-jerk socio-babble," Bobby said. "If you know right from wrong, you go right—or pay the penalty for going wrong."

"We had parents who taught us," Rabbi Berg said. "Some of these kids have parents who were kids themselves when they were born from teenage pregnancies, prostitutes, crackheads, junkies, or just institutionalized zombies. I want to change a few of them before they kill another Shirley, and before they ruin their own lives. This administration isn't doing that, Bobby. In fact, Brady's cut what little funding we had. And now the new yuppies, like I used to be, march through the working-class neighborhoods, glomming all the property, paying three times the rent your average blue-collar worker can afford. The working and middle classes are fleeing to the suburbs again because they can't afford to live in the city. That leaves just the rich and the poor."

"And bad things waiting to happen," Bobby said, nodding.

"We're trying to give at least some of these kids a shot, take care of some of the old-timers, too, and hope we can embarrass the next mayor to make some changes in this town," Berg said. "So we made a deal with Daggart, who has his own reasons to hate the mayor. He had this plan. It's working. What can I say? But I'm not a fool. I know Daggart has his own agenda."

"If Daggart turns on you, promise to let me know first," Bobby said.

Rabbi Berg smiled and shook Bobby's hand. "Thanks. I will."

Herbie walked over and told Bobby they had to move on.

They drove straight across the center of nightside Brooklyn, passing Ocean Parkway and Coney Island Avenue. At Bedford Avenue Bobby caught a red light and looked up and saw the dark Lumina in his rearview mirror. He turned in his seat, and the driver behind him put on his brights.

"You okay?" Herbie asked.

"We're being tailed," Bobby said.

Herbie twisted in his seat and saw the Lumina behind them back up and make a quick U-turn. The traffic light turned green.

"Bobby," Herbie said. "I gotta get to my next stop. No time."

Bobby drove on, crossed Nostrand Avenue, and finally parked on busy Flatbush Avenue, across from an old art-deco movie palace where Bobby remembered seeing *Jaws* as a teenager. The marquee now proclaimed: THE THEATER OF HEAVEN CHURCH—STARRING JESUS CHRIST! Rev. Gaston Greene, Director. Adult Prayer Meeting Tonight!

The big crowd under the marquee was well dressed and orderly. There were middle-aged couples, young singles, some old-timers dressed in their best summer clothes, all waiting on line to get through the front doors, handing in tickets to a black NuCent Inc.

security guard. Bobby watched as a police car slithered by—the cops checking out the crowd—and kept going. A team of black valet parkers wearing red vests took the wheels of the fancy cars that pulled up in front of the church and drove them around the corner to the lot in the rear. Bobby watched a familiar-looking armored car parked in the same lot. He left the Jeep parked on Flatbush Avenue and he and Herbie tried to cross the street. Dollar vans—private, multiseat vehicles that transport the people of inner-Brooklyn around their neighborhoods for the flat fare of a buck—kamikazied by, screeching to abrupt stops to pick up fares.

Flatbush Avenue was a throbbing artery of new Caribbean, Asian, and Hispanic energy, a prospering neon blur of late-night discount stores, loud music, fast-food restaurants, and idle, homegrown teenagers who gathered in ominous clumps at each street corner, wearing macho attitudes like fashion statements.

"Wasn't for the Rev, this neighborhood would be in flames," Herbie said.

"Reverend Greene does good work but I think the cops have a lot to do with keeping the crime down," Bobby said.

"Don't talk to me about cops," Herbie said. "I know what those fucks do to me when they get me in the station house. I shit square blocks thinking what they do to the poor shvartzes. I mean, look what they did to that kid with a plunger . . ."

"You can't paint the whole PD with the same toilet brush, Herbie," Bobby said.

"The way you got treated as a cop in the joint," Herbie said. "That's the way cops treat the black kids every day."

"*Some* cops, Herbie."

"Sometimes you're closed-minded, Bobby," Herbie said.

Herbie made the armored-car guard sign for the five duffel bags of cash that they carried from the rear of the huge church.

"Two jumbos?" Herbie asked one of two black NuCent security guards who helped the uniformed guards carry the money to the truck.

"Two jumbo and forty large," said the guard.

"Let's boogie," Herbie said.

"You're way too hip for me these days, Herbie," Bobby said. "Those guys are taking out a quarter-mil?"

"It's Saturday night, man," Herbie said.

"How long has this been going on?" Bobby asked.

"Isn't that a song?" Herbie asked.

"*Brother* Rabinowitz," Bobby said. "How long—and if you tell me that's a Chinaman's name, I'll use your yarmulke for a Frisbee."

"*'Chinese,'* Herbie said. "*'Chinaman'* is derogatory."

"Herbie, tell me how long Daggart and the Three Wise Men have been holding these Vegas nights?"

"Since April, since Mr. Daggart was put in dry dock," Herbie said.

"And you've been getting crowds like this, money like this, every weekend?"

"Yep," Herbie said.

Herbie led Bobby through a rear fire exit into the massive lobby that still had the same art-deco design Bobby remembered from over twenty years ago. The giant chandeliers still dangled from the high vaulted ceilings, but a busy bar had replaced the old candy counter, and gamblers were being served champagne and mixed drinks.

The walls of the lobby were lined with computerized slot machines, and two dozen gaming tables were set up across the plushy carpeted floor. Over-and-under games with twenty-dollar minimums were located on each of the landings leading up to the balcony, attended by gorgeous, smiling black women in evening gowns. Bobby made a mental note not to ever bring Izzy Gleason here without an attending undertaker to help clean up the mess.

The lobby of the sprawling balcony was crowded with hundreds of gamblers, betting at two dozen gaming tables. As Herbie checked with his security team and the house bank, Bobby walked to the balcony railing and looked down into the crowded theater. Busy slot machines lined the walls of the outside aisles. A gospel group of girl-singers was on the stage, singing a song with a catchy refrain *Jesus was a gambler, and He bet His life to save our souls . . .*

Herbie escorted Reverend Gaston Greene through the crowd to greet Bobby. They shook hands.

"Have you seen enough yet?" he asked.

"There's more?"

Reverend Greene leaned against the railing. "Bobby, we've got this operation tickin' like a Rolex."

"Connected to a time bomb," Bobby said.

"We've got these Vegas nights in our own three churches and temple every weekend. Plus we get another church or synagogue in each borough to hold a Vegas night a week. Next week, for example, there's gonna be a United Jewish Organizations banquet, at a four-star hotel in Manhattan, fifteen hundred people. Once those banquet doors close, the whole place turns into a casino. They got two regular churches in Manhattan where them UN diplomats— the ones who can park anywhere—and pro athletes and movie stars come to gamble. Rabbi Berg has all his old show-biz pals going to his games instead of Atlantic City and Vegas. They televise the big closed-circuit fights, ball games, horse races on a big-screen TV. Mr. Daggart has organized this so well that anyone who wants to gamble doesn't have to leave the city, or his own neighborhood."

"The cops don't bother you?"

"The cops don't much like the mayor, either," Greene said. "They cut crime in half and he reneged on their pay raise. He's gone hard-line on them, too. Cops in this precinct see we're making their job easier. We put kids to work, we keep others off the street in night sports programs. They know we go after drugs and gun dealers. They know the money has to come from somewhere. Besides, a few come in here to bet a few dollars. Plus, Mr. Daggart has taken care of a few people at certain levels of high command. We're doing what we have to do, Bobby. This is my neighborhood. It's dying under this guy Brady. I've never said this about a mayor before, but I don't think he likes black people. He certainly doesn't like poor people—or even working people. He goes after hospital workers, cab drivers, hot-dog vendors. He needs an old-fashioned bully's ass-whuppin'. I can't do that, but I have an obligation to do *something*. Daggart is no saint, but he ain't the devil, either. The devil lives in City Hall these days, so I implore you to listen to what Daggart is saying about the mayor. Maybe if he can connect him to Kronk, who might be involved in these murders, he'll have to step down and we'll get a new mayor with a little bit of humanity in there."

"I'll listen to him, Reverend, but I still don't understand how the wise guys let Daggart get away with all this," Bobby said. "What's his take? And what does it all have to do with Izzy Gleason?"

"Now that you've seen the operation," Herbie said, tapping his watch, "I'm supposed to take you to meet Mr. Daggart. He'll explain."

"Where we meeting him?" Bobby asked as he waved goodbye to Reverend Greene.

10

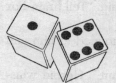 Bobby pulled his Jeep up behind Moe Daggart's Mercedes limousine, which was parked down the block from 22 Empire Court. He checked again in the rearview to be sure he wasn't being tailed. He wasn't. The dark Lumina had disappeared.

As Herbie led Bobby to Daggart's limo, he saw the yellow crime-scene tape billowing in the night breeze off the harbor. A police car was parked outside the old empty building. A procession of cars filled with ghoulish rubberneckers crawled past the building. One car with Jersey plates double-parked and a couple jumped out to take Polaroids of each other in front of the building, posing and smiling for the camera. The cops made them move along.

"They'll be selling T-shirts with forensics photos by the morning," Bobby said.

"Who?" Herbie said. "How much? I'd like to get one. Sleeveless, a guinea T . . ."

"I was speaking rhetorically, Herbie," Bobby said.

Humidity hung in the city like the exhaust from a giant launderette. Herbie adjusted his yarmulke, wiped sweat from his brow, and tapped on the back window of the Mercedes limo. The power window rolled down.

Moe Daggart sat in the backseat; Willie, the NuCent goon, was behind the wheel.

"Come in and have a seat, Bobby," Daggart said.

"Want me to check him for wire?" Willie asked.

"If we're gonna talk," Bobby said. "Tell brain-box to scram."

Willie glared at Bobby. Moe nodded to him and he exited on the street side.

"I'll break his nose if you want," Herbie whispered to Bobby.

"Nah," Bobby said. "Wait till it rains and we're both bored."

"You got it," Herbie said.

Bobby climbed in. As he closed the door he saw Herbie grab Willie by the tie and pull him close to his face, like a puppy who had just soiled the rug.

"What do you think of my operation?" Daggart asked as Bobby settled into a leather seat facing him, the cool air engulfing him.

Daggart opened a small refrigerator in the back of the limo where beer, soda, mineral water, and splits of champagne were stocked. He handed Bobby a bottle of Poland Spring. Bobby held the bottle to his ear as he cracked it open, making certain the seal hadn't been tampered with. It hadn't. He took a slug. It was cold and good.

"I think it's highly illegal," Bobby said.

"Ah, but it's okay for churches to run fundraisers," Daggart said.

"I know from working in the DA's office you need

special licenses to run those kinds of Vegas nights," Bobby said.

"So maybe they push the collection envelope a little . . ."

". . . but like you say, who's gonna crack down on a church or a temple? A match made in heaven. Blah, blah, blah . . ."

"You sound unimpressed," Daggart said.

"No, I *am* impressed," Bobby said. "Lots of cash money. They might actually raise a third of the number they're talking about."

"Your math is good," Daggart said. "But that money is just being used as a bank."

"For what?"

"Put it this way, who's going to tap a church or synagogue phones?" Daggart asked, grinning.

"So you're taking sports action too?" Bobby said. "Using the Vegas nights' money as the bank, you could double your money by the end of the baseball season. And then football . . . "

"We've almost made it there already," Daggart said.

Bobby nodded, looked at Daggart with near admiration. He still thought Daggart was shady. But if the holy rollers get their money, a lot of kids who only had the option of jail or the cemetery before age twenty-five might make it out of places like Coney Island.

"What's your angle, Daggart?" Bobby said. "We both know you couldn't give two shits never mind two bits about a big social-services complex for poor senior citizens and inner-city kids. You're going to hell in the next life, so why would you be doing God's work with the padres in this one? Unless there was a major grubstake in all of this for you."

Daggart laughed. He took a long drink of water. He swallowed in moderate, even portions, with controlled grace, as if he'd even studied that at Harvard. He made a refreshed smack of his lips and looked Bobby in the eye. "The thing I love about you, Emmet, is that you might live on a Silverton on the Hudson but you never lose your Brooklyn bluntness. I like a man who cuts through the bullshit and makes his point."

"Then make yours, pal," Bobby said.

"Okay, I want to get even with Kronk and Brady for what they're doing to me," he said. "This operation is siphoning three, maybe four times the money from Kronk that my little gambling boat would have. He's hurting—a little—and the city doesn't get a dime in taxes. I'm taking twenty-five percent of the take to operate it. As you saw, there is overhead—staff, entertainment, rent, armored trucks, a few greased police palms. And, of course, we also have to give the *fellas* a piece . . ."

"How much you giving the mob for letting it go on?"

"Fifteen percent goes into the elbow for them," Daggart said. "That leaves sixty percent for the padres."

"The wise guys are letting you run Vegas nights and a sports book for a measly fifteen cut? Why?"

"Just like the clergymen, the racket guys have their own vendetta to settle with Brady," Daggart said. "Just like Brady shut down all the social programs, dried up all the money for youth programs, he's also stepped on the mob's neck everywhere they move. He clamped down on the Fulton Fish Market, which hurt them bad. Also put a lot of ordinary working guys out of work because they couldn't pass moral turpitude tests. He did the same thing at the Convention Center, the Meat Market, the Hunts Point Produce Market, the Garment Center."

"He's the mayor, they're gangsters, that's what he's supposed to do," Bobby said with a dry chuckle.

"But Christ, if anyone driving a hi-lo in any of those places had a criminal record, they were fired," Daggart said. "You did time. So you tell me, where else does a guy with a record who is trying to go straight go for an honest job?"

"Hold the violins," Bobby said. "A lot of those same guys had no-show jobs because they were made-mobsters or did after-work leg breaking for the wisenheimers."

"Perhaps," Daggart said. "But he fired almost everyone whose name ended in a vowel."

"That's right, not many of them were parishioners at Reverend Greene's church, were they, Moe? They weren't exactly into affirmative action, hiring minorities. It was all closed union jobs and everyone kicked back a piece to the wise guys, whether it was an Italian at the Fish Market or an Irish carpenter at the Convention Center."

"Okay," Daggart said. "They took care of their own. But not all the people the mayor canned were mobbed up. People lost houses, families busted up, guys strapped on the iron and did stickups to pay their kids' medical bills. Italians hate Brady, Bobby. He even had the temerity to clamp down on the Italian feast in Little Italy. He won't even let them celebrate July Fourth with fireworks in their own neighborhood in Ozone Park. I'm not saying they're angels. I'm just trying to answer your question as to why they are letting us operate. One of the reasons is because we *can get away with it*. They'd rather take fifteen percent of our operation for doing nothing than risk more RICO busts. They're letting us operate, because the mayor has made their lives miserable."

"Bighearted of them," Bobby said.

"But the main reason they have a personal hatred for Mayor Brady is because they think he's a hypocrite," Daggart said. "If he was really Mr. Clean like he pretends to be, that would be fine. That would be business. But he's just as dirty as they are. Only he does his deals with big legitimate money like Sam Kronk's. So they have a personal hatred for Brady. They won't whack him, or Kronk, because they know that would just bring more heat on them. So I made them an offer they couldn't refuse."

"You offered the mob a Don Corleone deal?" Bobby said. "Whose head did you promise?"

"Mayor Brady's," Daggart said.

"Ambitious," Bobby said, "and nuts. This is the most vindictive mayor we've had in fifty years. How the hell do you expect to deliver Brady for them?"

"With your help," Daggart said.

"Oh," Bobby said. "Nice. Thanks, but I really don't have the time to do any more *time*. I'd sort of like to be there when my kid graduates high school, college, gets married, has kids. Besides, I'm already busy working on a case."

"Ah, but like I've told you, we're involved in the same case," Daggart said.

"I've been waiting all day to hear this," Bobby said. "How?"

"First we wanted to let you know what was at stake," Daggart said. "Both morally and financially."

"Lessons on morality I take from my mother, thanks," Bobby said.

"Okay, so let's walk and I'll show you politically," Daggart said.

They stepped out of the limo and Bobby gazed up Empire Court at the determined huddle of press and gawkers gathered outside number 22. A few feet away, Willie slumped on the fender of Bobby's Jeep, Herbie wagging a finger at him. Bobby walked abreast of Moe Daggart as he strolled the one block to the waterfront. A uniformed cop with half-moons of sweat under his pale blue uniform shirt was directing traffic away from Empire Court. Bobby and Daggart crossed the street and leaned on the railing overlooking the harbor. The glow of the skyline, which could be seen by astronauts from space, reflected on the wavy black water. Bobby never lost track that he lived in the capital of the world.

A half-block south was the entrance to the Harbor Head Marina, where a collection of customized yachts and sailboats owned by the rich yuppies from the financial district were moored. A few smaller boats lolled on the night tide. Daggart leaned his back on the guard rail of the seawall and looked at the row of tenements, most over a century old, standing like stubborn rotting teeth at the mouth of the city.

"What do you see?" Daggart asked.

"Murder," Bobby said.

"I'm sure you're right," Daggart said. "And you're also looking at your motive."

Daggart dramatically swept his hand over the dirty red-brick buildings of Empire Court, then glided it across the tenements along the avenue leading to Ellis Walk, which was the next street over. He kept gliding his open hand—sweeping past the harried uniformed traffic cop—until it seemed to bless the Harbor Head Marina. And then with the same hand he pointed out at Empire Island, in the center of the harbor.

"And there's what you might call opportunity," he

said. "The greatest, most lucrative business opportunity this city has seen since Peter Minuit swindled the Indians out of the piece of real estate we're standing on for twenty-four bucks worth of trinkets."

Bobby followed Daggart's finger to the darkened Empire Island, sitting in the middle of the great harbor like a neglected stepchild of Manhattan.

"Empire Island," Bobby said. "The abandoned Coast Guard base? Yeah, so? What about it?"

"If the legislature passes the resolution to legalize gambling on August sixth," Daggart explained, "it will go on the ballot as a referendum in November. The people are split fifty-fifty right now. But the momentum is moving toward approval."

"Yeah, I've heard that," Bobby said. "And you think if it passes, gambling in New York City will be on Empire Island?"

"Big time," said Daggart. "Because in the legislation, the lawmakers can make it site-specific, borough by borough, neighborhood by neighborhood—street by street, if they want."

"You mean they can say it's okay to have gambling on, say, Twenty-third Street but not Forty-second Street? In Manhattan but not Brooklyn? In Times Square but not the Village? Like that?"

"Correct," Daggart said. "And most legislators, like their constituents, are okay with legalized gambling so long as it doesn't come into their neighborhoods. They want the revenue it will bring the city, the jobs and the tourism and the commerce. But they don't want the traffic, the hookers, the mobsters, the general riffraff that gambling attracts, in their neighborhoods. So, what I know from my spies inside Albany is that the one specific site in the city everyone in the State Assembly and State Senate can agree on, if it's legalized, is Empire Island. Where it wouldn't disturb anyone."

"It makes sense," Bobby said. "Like a little resort inside the city. They could build great hotels there. I know from having been there on a military murder case once that there's already a golf course. Casinos, nightclubs, discos, and restaurants could stay open all night. Good idea."

"It's a *great* idea," Daggart said. "But there's a hitch. How would everyone get there?"

"I guess they'd have to build a new ferry terminal . . ."

Bobby nodded, fell silent. He looked at the ground under his feet. He assessed the land to his left, and his right, the little marina, and the buildings across the street, which included 22 Empire Court.

"Is this where music swells and I go 'Ah ha'?" Bobby asked.

"The reason they killed the McCoys and the reason this Jimmy Chung is also probably dead is because someone needs that property. To build that terminal. To make unimaginable billions."

"And you're saying that that someone is Sam Kronk?"

"Get your friend Max Roth to check the clips and

you'll see that Sam Kronk has already toured Empire Island with Mayor Brady as a possible casino mecca," Daggart said. "Brady has been encouraging him for years to make plans to transplant his Atlantic City casino empire to New York once we get legalized gambling here. He's offering tax abatements, zoning variances, a complete cakewalk through the bureaucratic red tape. Millions of the gamblers in Atlantic City still come from New York. Same with Vegas—why do you think they built a place called 'New York, New York' out there? City Hall had the Economic Development Corporation do its own report on the impact of gambling in this city."

"I *bet* it's a win-win doozy," Bobby said.

"Bobby, the stats speak for themselves: the New York metropolitan area has thirteen million people aged twenty-five and older with a median annual income of over thirty-eight thousand dollars, twenty-seven percent over the national average. New Yorkers made eleven million out of state casino visits last year, making us the largest casino feeder market in the nation. New Yorkers made five million visits to Atlantic City alone. Four million to Vegas. Another million and a half visits to the Indian reservation in Foxwoods. New Yorkers travel to New Orleans, Canada, the Caribbean, to gamble. Bobby, think of it, Atlantic City's casino revenues last year were over four billion dollars. In New York, with our tourist trade, it would be triple that. The city estimates that one single seventy-thousand-square-foot casino in midtown would generate two hundred and sixty million dollars in revenues and create twenty-five hundred new permanent jobs. *One* casino!"

"What about Empire Island?"

"The report says that a resort scenario like the one they can build on Empire Island would generate five *billion* dollars a year! That's why Kronk knows if gambling is legalized here, it will kill him in Atlantic City. That's why he has always been publicly against legalized gambling in New York. That's why the banks in New Jersey always contribute money to the campaigns of New York State legislators, to buy their anti-gambling votes."

"But now, with term limits, the permanent government is coming apart," Bobby said.

"The tide is changing," Daggart said. "New Yorkers want it. Our little church-basement operation proves that. Even my little cruise-to-nowhere boat did six million a year in revenues. The bigger boats do a hundred mil. Legal gambling is coming to New York. It's like trying to hold back the Mississippi."

"And Kronk knows it," Bobby said.

"Right," said Daggart. "So he's starting to make his move. He can't officially say he's in favor of legalized gambling in New York because the New Jersey banks who hold the paper on his Atlantic City casinos would go nuts, call in his notes. So he has to be sneaky about it, lobby through the back door, behind the scenes."

"Using his buddy Mayor Brady."

"Right," Daggart said. "Brady is a lame duck.

He's relying on Kronk's money to help him run for the U.S. Senate. In return, in his final months as mayor, he'll let Kronk shave the dice and mark the deck before gambling is even legal here. See, Kronk won't be satisfied to just own the first casino on Empire Island. He knows the other outfits—MGM, Bally's, Trump, Resorts, Caesars—will all follow. But the one place where he simply cannot lose, where he'll have a monopoly, is right here—under our feet."

"The terminal," Bobby said.

"He'll make money on everyone who passes through this terminal," Daggart said. "He'll have a hotel here for overspill, restaurants, a heliport to the airport, parking lot, a limo service, a pleasure-craft marina, souvenir shops, camera stores, one-hour photos, pretzel carts, hot dog wagons. You name it, he'll cash in on it. Kronk wants to own the gateway to Empire Island, which is like owning the keys to the next century."

"But first he needs the land," Bobby said.

"Some of that land became available when the McCoys went missing," Daggart said.

"That's a lot to accuse someone of," Bobby said. "It's even harder to prove."

"Yes it is," Daggart said. "Kronk surrounds himself with the best lawyers money can buy and completely insulates himself with a security force of over a hundred, all of them retired federal agents. Run by a guy named Ralph Paragon—and his second in command, Donald Dunne."

"Dum Dum Dunne," Bobby said, rotating his arm like a wheel as he repeated a familiar spiel. "Brother of Sean Dunne, the U.S. Attorney for the Eastern District, who is the one Mayor Brady used to invoke the old smuggling law to shut your boat down."

"See what I mean?"

"Sure, but you have a big problem."

"The problem isn't just mine," Daggart said. "That's where you and me have the same goal. See, I have a feeling you're going to have to prove the same thing in order to clear Izzy Gleason once they arrest him for Jimmy Chung's murder. Because in order to prove Izzy is innocent, I think you're going to have to prove Kronk is behind it. And Mayor Brady is behind *him*."

Bobby looked at Daggart and then out at Empire Island and across the street to Empire Court. He thought about Amy McCoy, and her paranoid older brother who had been hounding Sam Kronk, following him to his casinos in Puerto Rico and Atlantic City. Writing his stories that no one read for the paranoid fringe press—no one except maybe Kronk and Brady, who were afraid, in this day of the Internet and a voracious cable news furnace, that the story would be picked up by the legit press.

Bobby was now certain that Amy McCoy would never see her brother or his wife again. It made his blood boil that some rich, smug prick like Kronk thought he could get away with just knocking off a couple of what real estate baroness Leona Helmsley once called "little people," because they were in the way of his future billions. A rich prick who thought he was immune because he surrounded himself with layers of ex-feds, oily lawyers, and crooked politicians. And it steamed Bobby that Izzy wound up holding the bloody bag. Izzy was a grubby little shyster, but the only one he'd ever hurt was himself. Bobby couldn't let him take the fall for a scummer like Sam Kronk.

Bobby knew he was going to have to postpone his trip with Maggie down to Florida to see his mother. That really pissed him off, because he would disappoint his kid, and his mother. And send Connie into a war dance. He knew he'd be dueling with Noel Christmas, the Dunne brothers, Sam Kronk, Mayor Brady . . . and whoever the hell was driving that goddamned blue Lumina that again appeared, whispering along the avenue, like a dark apparition in the night.

The Lumina stopped, its tinted windows closed. Bobby stared but said nothing. He couldn't see a license plate from this side view. And he didn't want Daggart knowing anything until he checked it out first. The sweaty uniformed cop strode angrily toward the Lumina and shooed it away as he did to all the gawkers who wanted to get a glimpse of the building the press was calling the site of "the rent-control murders."

Bobby watched the Lumina turn up a darkened

side street. He knew he had an awful lot of work to do. He didn't know if he could trust this snake-oil salesman, Daggart, but he did know he needed some allies. And you couldn't go after a guy like Kronk without some operating expenses.

He looked up at the Twin Towers that stretched 110 stories above the granite footrest of Manhattan. "You know that taking on Kronk and Brady is gonna be like trying to knock those suckers down," Bobby said.

"Kronk builds those babies for sport," Daggart said.

"You want to do this just to get even over your gambling boat?" Bobby said.

"That's part of it," Daggart said. "But I started that boat knowing that one day soon gambling was coming to the city. I wanted to build a nest egg so that maybe I could own a small casino of my own one day. Sure, I'm ambitious. I'm an American. I'm a New Yorker. I'm a businessman. I want *mine*. I believe in capitalism."

"So did your old man," Bobby said.

"He was cruder than I am, from another age," Daggart said, with an ironic smile. "He was more like a robber baron."

"Yeah, he killed people," Bobby said. "For money."

"But he was up-front," Daggart said. "He was a racketeer. His people killed each other, up close and personal—usually one on one. Sam Kronk kills people in rent-controlled apartments from his penthouse. He kills strangers he never met. My old man never killed anyone for a fucking rent-controlled apartment. Neither have I. I come from my father, sure, Bobby. I can't change my gene pool. But I am my *own* man, not my *old* man. I try to live a legitimate life, and Mayor Brady and Sam Kronk paint me as a mobster. They don't want me to have a life. If they get away with branding me as a mobster, they steal my future, my dignity. So it's about more than one little gambling boat. I want to prove that these hypocrites are the *real* gangsters. And the padres and I are willing to donate whatever funds you need to help us do it. At the same time, you clear your buddy's name."

"I have to think all this over, consult with my client."

"Let me know," Daggart said as they walked back to their cars. Willie held open the back door of the Mercedes limo for Daggart. The preppie blond gave Bobby a dead eye as he climbed into the driver's seat. Herbie got in the front passenger seat, winking at Bobby.

Bobby walked back to the Jeep and saw the Lumina reappear at the corner, one block east. He climbed in, started the engine, pulled out, drove west, and made a right at the corner. He made a quick U-turn, facing the oncoming traffic. He sat there for thirty seconds and now here came the Lumina, hanging a right. Bobby saw the sweaty uniformed cop storming his way, incredulous.

"Yo! Are you on fuckin' glue?" the cop yelled.

But Bobby wasn't paying any attention to the cop. He popped on his brights and studied the pale blue license plate of the dark blue Lumina before it leapt into reverse. Other cars began to honk. The cop pulled out his ticket book as he approached. Bobby memorized the New Jersey plate number: SN2-78K.

The Lumina made a left on the avenue as the cop neared Bobby's window. "Pull this piece of shit to the fucking curb!" the cop barked. Bobby took out his wallet, showed him a facsimile of his old police detective shield and his old NYPD ID card.

"Retired from the job," Bobby said.

"Jesus Christ, guy, you gotta get the fuck atta here. I got a sergeant with me and he's in no fuckin' mood."

"Thanks," Bobby said, and made a quick U-turn.

11

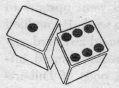

As Bobby headed up West Street, his cell phone rang and he looked at the caller-ID read-out. It was the same number that had been his for almost seven years when he was a Manhattan District Attorney's investigator. The number now belonged to Noel Christmas.

"Yeah, Noel, what is it?" Bobby asked.

"I thought about what you said today about me never offering you any help," Noel Christmas said. "So as a professional courtesy, I'm gonna let you come down to the office to see something before you see it on a witness stand."

Bobby was exhausted. "Can it wait till tomorrow?" Bobby asked.

"I'm gonna ask you to surrender Izzy Gleason tomorrow," Christmas said. "Because if I have to issue an APB and go searching for him, I can't be responsible what happens to him if he's picked up as armed and dangerous by some gung-ho cop looking for a Captain Courageous collar. And if I have to break a sweat and wrinkle my shoes finding him myself, I can't be responsible if he gets lost for a week in the system. So I think you owe it to your client to come down here for a preview of what we have on Gleason."

Bobby crossed Chambers Street to One Hogan Place, the offices of the Manhattan District Attorney's office. He parked the car, jammed an NYPD parking pass his brother Patrick had gotten for him into the dashboard, and went upstairs to the squad room where he used to work. He nodded to a few old cop friends, who seemed awkward saying hello to him. The room was freshly painted, off-white, and was subdivided with pods of Dilbert-style cubicles, making it look more like an insurance firm than the old-fashioned cop shop he remembered.

Noel Christmas, sans jacket, walked up to him carrying a file folder. With his big muscles straining against his damp white shirt he looked like a sack of cannonballs with legs.

"Like I say, Bobby, professional courtesy," Christmas said, tapping Bobby's shoulder with the file folder. "First, the blood in Gleason's office matches a sample they have in Chung's file at the INS. It's his blood. Come on, I want you to listen to what Elizabeth Wang has to say."

"Elizabeth Wang?"

He led Bobby to the prisoner interrogation room, where he stood with Christmas on the viewing side of a two-way mirror. Betty, Izzy's Chinese translator, whose real name was Elizabeth Wang, was sitting at a table, wearing a conservative blue pants suit and low heels, chatting with a female detective. Christmas buzzed the detective. She picked up a telephone.

Christmas told her to start from the top. The detective nodded, hung up, and looked at Betty.

"Let's go through it one more time," the detective said.

"How many time say same thing?"

". . . so you were turning a trick when Izzy Gleason got the beep," the cop said.

"No," Betty said. "I told you I was giving him legit massage. Izzy likes you to walk on his back. He a little crazy. *Fuza*. Regular customer. He say his spine is his most sensitive erogenous zone. Anyway, I walk on his back, he gets a beep, he makes a call on cell phone. He's trying to communicate with someone speaking Chinese. He asks can I translate for him; he say five hundred dollar for me. I say sure."

"Then what did you do?"

"I went down here with him," she said. "You know what happen here. I translate. Izzy tell Jimmy Chung to be quiet, that he'd get him out. Which he does."

"Then what happened?"

"Then me, Chung, and Izzy go back to Izzy office at the Empire State Building," she said. "I already tell you this three time . . ."

"One more time," the cop said. "Then you can go."

"So, I go back to his office," Betty said. "Izzy tell me that if this guy Chung want Izzy to be his lawyer he has to put up fifty grand as retainer or sign lien on his property at 22 Empire Court. Izzy has form for this, like he does it a lot."

Christmas looked at Bobby and offered him a Tums. "My stomach's fine," Christmas said. "How about yours?"

"No thanks," Bobby said and looked back in at Betty Wang and the female detective. "Then what happened?" the detective asked.

"Jimmy Chung sign the paper," Betty said. "Then Chung ask me how much would it cost for trial. I ask Izzy. Izzy say it could cost like a quarter of a million dollars or more for a full trial defense. That fifty thousand just a retainer. That he would take the property if Chung had no money. I translate and Chung got piss off. Chung say he wanted to get a different lawyer now. Izzy said fine, but you already signed a fifty-thousand-dollar retainer. Chung stand up and start yelling in Chinese that Izzy was a thief. I couldn't believe my eyes. Izzy Gleason just walk to counter, pick up knife, yeah, and stuck it in Jimmy Chung neck. Kill him."

Betty shrugged and lit a cigarette.

"What utter bullshit," Bobby said.

"Maybe, but I have me an eyewitness," Christmas said. "And we found the bloody knife with Gleason's prints in the building garbage chute. We had a video surveillance unit track Izzy Gleason, Elizabeth Wang, and Jimmy Chung from here that night, to Gleason's office. We wanted to make sure we knew where Chung was if we got a blood match on the van or if we found the McCoy bodies. Anyway, Bobby, we have proof Izzy Gleason went to his office with Chung. Proof that this girl was also in that office. Proof that the blood we found there and on the knife was Jimmy Chung's. Now she's telling us what happened in there."

He paused as the female detective began questioning Betty again.

"What happened to the body?" she asked.

"Not sure," Betty said. "Izzy tell me to go upstairs and wait for him in lobby. He say he call some friends who could get rid of body through the underground garage. He say if I keep my mouth shut there is seven grand in it for me."

"This seven thousand dollars?" the female cop asked, tapping a stack of cash with a pencil.

"Yes," Betty said.

"I was scared," Betty said. "I was confuse. Izzy say we both be quiet or both get arrested. I go with Izzy to see that Bobby Emmet guy. Izzy said Emmet could make things right. We came back to the office, pretending like nothing ever happen. Izzy say that Bobby Emmet take care of everything."

"Nice," Bobby said. "Now I'm a janitor in a drum."

"And we find cops there, blood everywhere, but body gone," Betty Wang said. "I was too scare to say anything then. But now that I think it over, I not gonna take no fall. All I did was walk on a guy's back, translate for him Chinese. Izzy Gleason killed Jimmy Chung. He got rid of body. Not me."

Christmas showed Bobby a written statement

Betty had made, and the knife, which was in an evidence bag. "We're preparing the arrest warrant now. We called his hotel, checked some of his haunts. Can't find him. As a courtesy I'm giving you till 3 PM tomorrow to surrender him before I put out an APB."

"Without a body this is still a piss-poor circumstantial case. Anyone could have smeared blood on his knife. A hooker witness."

"Yeah," said Christmas. "So maybe with the right judge Gleason gets bail at night court. Otherwise he's gonna go through the system. He's a little light in the ass for that. Do your buddy a favor, Bobby, and send him in on his own. It'll look better for him."

"You don't believe this hooker, do you?" Bobby asked.

"All I know is I have a missing couple, I get a suspect, and the suspect walks with Gleason," Christmas said. "Then I find a bloody scene in Gleason's office, and a broad who says she saw Gleason kill Chung, his own client, after he signed over his building to him. Bobby, even if I liked Gleason—which I do not—I got no choice but to arrest him and let the courts sort it out."

"Aren't you gonna hold her?" Bobby asked, pointing at Betty Wang. "As a material witness?"

"She's a cooperating witness. She came in on her own, turned over seven grand in evidence. On what grounds do I hold her?"

"You mean she showed up in a fit of conscience?" Bobby asked.

"That's right," he said. "We didn't have to pick her up or sweat her or flip her. We can't exactly lock her up now."

"Christ, what a horseshit story this is. Somebody must be paying this hooker to testify against Gleason."

"Now who would do something like that, Bobby?"

"Probably whoever snatched or killed the McCoys," Bobby said.

"Then I suggest you find out who that is," Christmas said. "Right now I have me a collar waiting to happen."

12

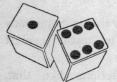 Bobby called Izzy. Got his machine. Left a message. He beeped him and called him again. No answer; no reply. He couldn't find Izzy anywhere. He left messages with the desk at the Chelsea to contact him as soon as possible.

He called Maggie on the cell phone, apologized again for not being able to make dinner. She said, "It's cool, old man, as long as we meet for your birthday tomorrow," she said.

Bobby promised.

"Did you cram for your history final?" he asked, trying to juggle fatherhood with murder.

"Cal called and helped," she said.

"You studied on the phone?"

"Sure. And by e-mail. He asked me questions. I e-mailed the answers. He corrected the ones I got wrong. I know I'm ready for the test now. He got a hundred on the same Regents final two years ago."

"Two years ago? How old is Cal?"

"Old enough to get a hundred in history, old man," she said.

"We're gonna have to talk about that."

"How was your day, Pop?" Maggie asked, changing the subject.

"Busy," he said.

He didn't tell her about the blood in Izzy's office, Jimmy Chung being missing, Amy McCoy giving Izzy a black eye, the phone tap on Eddie McCoy's line at 22 Empire Court, the confrontation with the Chinese deliverymen in Sunset Park, Moe Daggart and the Three Wise Men and their gambling operation, Betty Wang claiming she saw Izzy murder Jimmy Chung, and the very good possibility that Sam Kronk and the mayor of New York City might be behind three homicides.

Instead, he looked at the calico kitten sleeping in the box on the seat beside him and said, "And I have a surprise for you."

"No, the surprise is supposed to be for you. I'm taking you shopping tomorrow at the Snoop Shop, whether you like it or not."

"First we'll eat lunch," Bobby said.

"Good," she said. "Because I downloaded and printed a bunch of stuff about that guy Jimmy Chung for you."

"Great," Bobby said. "One more thing. I need you to check a couple of license plates for me. I'd ask Patrick, but he's still down in Florida with your granny."

"Done deal, old man," Maggie said.

He gave Maggie the plate numbers of the Lumina and the van driven by the Chinese guys who attacked him. He didn't tell her why. "I'll pick you up at eleven," he said.

"Cool, old-timer," she said.

"You getting too old to pick a star?" he asked, referring to a practice they'd started when he got divorced from her mother when Maggie was eight. Each of them would pick the brightest star in the night sky and wink at it before going to bed, and in this way they would feel like they were still under the same roof. Winking at a star for his kid also kept Bobby sane when he was in jail.

"Never too old to pick a star for you, Pop," she said. "Got one. The wink's coming your way. Good night. Love ya."

"You too."

By the time he got on board *The Fifth Amendment*, Bobby was brain numb and exhausted. He held the kitten in his left hand as he opened the salon door and knew instantly that something was amiss. The pillows on the couch had been straightened, the dishes in the sink were in the drying rack, the door of the bedroom was ajar.

He pulled the .38 from his right pants pocket, still holding the kitten in his left hand.

He saw the sleeping form in his bed. Knew it wasn't Maggie. Smelled too good to be Izzy Gleason. He tiptoed across the room, put the kitten on the foot of the bed, aimed the barrel of the gun an inch from the intruder's nose, and turned on the light.

"God Almighty," said Amy McCoy, blinking into the barrel.

"You came an inch from meeting him," Bobby said.

"Sorry."

"Looking for this?" he asked, lifting the kitten and dropping it on her chest.

"I wanted to apologize," she said. "For running out on you."

"Hey, you paid the bill," Bobby said. He clacked the gun on the night table, unbuttoned his shirt, sat on the edge of the bed, and pulled off his boots.

"You're not getting undressed, are you?"

"Amy," Bobby said. "I know you're distraught. I'd be, too, if my brother was missing. But I've had a full day at the races. If I don't sleep, tomorrow will be a waste and I won't be of any use to myself or my client. Or you."

He stood up, unbuckled his belt, opened his top pants button and pulled down the zipper of his dungarees. Amy watched in nervous fascination as Bobby stood in his navy-blue Jockeys. Bare-chested.

"You act like you never saw a man get undressed before."

"Well . . ."

"Look, here's the deal," Bobby said. "I guess I trust you because I just put the gun on the night stand. I don't think someone drops by, washes the dishes, straightens out the living room, takes a nap, and then blows the host's brains out. It's late. You've had a tough day, too. I think you're about as good-looking a woman as a man might ever find sleeping in his bed. Especially under circumstances like this."

"You do?" she said, almost childlike.

"Well, yeah," Bobby said. "If you don't believe me, there's a mirror in the bathroom. You'll recognize yourself. You're the one with the gorgeous blue eyes, the one who's so beautiful she doesn't need makeup."

"Get lost," she said, abashed.

"So anyway . . . where was I? Oh, yeah. So it's late, I'm going to bed. You're more than welcome to climb right in with me. But if you're gonna say no to where that leads, say it now and I'll take it for an answer, before anything starts. But please don't get into the sack with me if you intend to frustrate me any further. If no's the answer, you can park your cute behind on the couch or hit the road and I'll see you around."

"You always this straightforward with women?"

"Just when they do B&Es into the place where I live."

"What's a 'B&E'?" she said. "It sounds disgusting!"

"Breaking and entering," Bobby said.

"Oh . . . but you'd sleep with me just like that?" She snapped her fingers.

"Amy, I'm a practicing heterosexual. You're a very attractive woman. So . . . yeah. I would—in a heartbeat. I'm single, you said you're single, or breaking up, or something. Unless you've got health problems . . ."

"No! Of course not!" she said.

"Jesus, take it easy. I mean what the hell are you

doing here, anyway? How did you know where to find me?"

"You told me."

"Oh, yeah, right. See, I'm brain-dead."

"I came because I can't get any answers from Detective Christmas about Eddie. They're treating me like a suspect."

"They should," Bobby said, walking closer to her, smelling her clean fragrance again.

"I didn't want to go home and sit by the phone like a helpless little girl," she said, looking in his eyes, down at his Jockeys, a tremor starting in her hands.

"If I was still on the force, I'd treat you the same way," Bobby said, stepping closer, until he stood a head above her. "But since I'm not, I'm trying to seduce you instead. So that I can pick your brain in naked, vulnerable, disarmed, postcoital bliss. Amazing the stuff you can get away with without the ethics of a badge."

"Please don't take this the wrong way," she said, swallowing, searching for words. "You're a very . . . attractive man."

He kissed her softly on the lips and she froze. He then pressed his lips firmly against hers. Her teeth remained shut. He put his hand on the back of her neck and massaged her; her lips slowly parted, she opened her mouth, and he kissed her deeply. She didn't seem to know what to do at first. But then she sighed and quickly fell into the rhythm. Bobby felt her thawing in his arms. She groaned as he pressed himself against her; felt himself growing aroused. She wrapped her arms around his bare back, her unpainted nails tracing softly on his flesh. Bobby's right hand drifted down her back, touching her buttocks. She yelped, her nails digging, her tongue probing deeper into his mouth. He kneaded her firm, small left breast. She touched his tailbone, pulled him closer to her, felt him hard against her.

Score, he thought. *I'm gonna score . . .*

And then in one urgent thrust Amy pushed herself away from Bobby, her prayer-steepled hands going to her mouth. "God forgive me and have mercy," she said.

Bobby stood in shock, at full arousal, not knowing what to do with his hands that only seconds before had been all over her.

"No cigar," he said.

"I'm sorry . . . I shouldn't have . . . I didn't mean to . . ."

"Don't worry. Blue balls are just what the doctor ordered. Dr. Kervorkian. Do me a favor, Amy. Please go home. Call your old boyfriend. Drive *him* nuts, but leave me alone. Leave your phone number. If I find out anything about your brother, I'll call you. Promise."

"I'm sorry . . ."

"It's okay. It's an occupational hazard. Bye-bye."

He turned, pulled back the top sheet of his bed, punched the down pillow to a head contour.

"I came to tell you that when I left the Chinese

restaurant today, I went into a teahouse across the street to call myself a car service," she said. "As I waited, I sat in a window seat and ordered a cup of tea and a piece of pastry. I saw Noel Christmas arrive. I saw you leave, but I was mad at you, so I didn't go after you. Then I saw Noel Christmas leave. Then I saw that other guy arrive and your friend, Ben Lee, got into the car with him and they drove off together."

Bobby turned to her, intrigued.

"What other guy?"

"The one that was with Noel Christmas today in the alley."

"Sean Dunne?" Bobby said. "The U.S. attorney?"

"Yeah," she said. "Him and Ben Lee, they were laughing, very chummy-chummy. And looked like they were in a rush."

Maybe Daggart was on the level, Bobby thought. *These guys were all in cahoots. But Ben Lee?*

His old college pal? The mayor of Brooklyn's Chinatown, in bed with a U.S. attorney, who was in bed with Mayor Brady, who was sleeping with Sam Kronk? Who was maybe somehow connected to three murders? Including Jimmy Chung's? Making Izzy Gleason the prime suspect.

Maybe, he thought.

"That's all I came for. I'm sorry about doing . . . *that* to you."

She glanced at the pup tent in his drawers.

"Oh, that happens all the time," he said. "So if

you ever want to go *all the way,* drop by. Meanwhile, good night, Amy."

Amy McCoy looked him up and down again, swallowed, exhaled deeply, and hurried out of the salon. Bobby heard her running down the walkway to the dock and then heard her footfalls disappear in the night.

They say when a fighter hits the canvas face first he's not getting up before the full count. Bobby hit the bed without putting his hands in front of him to break the fall.

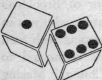

13

JULY 31

Bobby awakened to the sound of a whining blender and Izzy Gleason screaming.

"Kill that fuckin' prick!" Bobby heard Izzy shouting. "Yeah, yeah! Destroy that fuckin' fag bird, Wiley . . ."

Bobby staggered into the salon of the Silverton to find Izzy wearing a blindingly white Versace suit, sporting a pair of Ray-Bans, a white straw Panama Jack hat, and white mesh summer shoes. Bobby just blinked silently as he watched Izzy mixing Stolichnaya vodka and Meyers rum into a blender with a package of banana-flavored Carnation Instant Breakfast mix, some skim milk, two bananas, a Hershey bar, and a handful of ice. He hit the puree button but forgot to put the lid on the blender. A slop of the mix erupted from the blender onto the counter. Izzy yawned and placed his hand over the top of the blender to keep it from lapping out.

"I'm gonna shove your hand into that if you don't turn it off," Bobby said, knuckling sleep from his eyes. "We need to talk . . ."

Izzy hit the off button and took the blender pitcher off the whirring machine and drank from the spout. He licked the beige mustache from his upper lip, sucked the mess off his hand, and pointed excitedly at the TV, where Wile E. Coyote was chopping Roadrunner's head off with a meat cleaver.

"Finally!" Gleason screamed. "Justice! He finally got that arrogant little prick. Check it out, now Wiley's deep-frying this pain-in-the-balls bird and eatin' him. Roadrunner drumsticks. Roadrunner wings. Use fuckin' hot sauce, Wiley!"

Bobby looked at the crude rip-off of the popular RoadRunner cartoon that was playing on his VCR.

"Izzy, what are you doing here?" Bobby asked, looking at his watch. It was 6:17 AM. The seagulls were crying in the sky and misty Sunday morning was spreading like gray-haired gossip over the Seventy-ninth Street Boat Basin.

"I'm defending a true artist who's bootleggin' these underground Roadrunner snuff cartoons," he said.

"Maybe I'll turn on my video camera and we can make one of our own when they strap you in," Bobby said.

"I'm no First Amendment expert, but a spoof's a spoof," Izzy said, ignoring Bobby. "Southern-fried Roadrunner is a political statement, legitimate satire protected by the Founding Fathers . . ."

"Izzy, we gotta talk."

"It's saying that there's nowhere to run. That we're all trapped. Doomed. My client is an NYU film student, an animator. He just wants Disney or Dreamworks to notice him and give him a job. I told him we'd get him some major pub."

"Izzy, they have an eyewitness against you . . ."

"He doesn't expect to win, he just wants the publicity," Izzy said, taking another slug of his drink. "Before they order a cease-and-desist he's gonna sell millions of copies. He's gonna give me profit points. It's the hottest bootleg item on the Internet. I told him we'd get him on network TV, maybe even try the case on Court TV. Ten points on the sales of this could mean millions, Bobby."

"Izzy," Bobby said, "they're going to snuff you if you don't listen to me and pay more attention to your *own* case."

"That's why I'm here," he said. "To see how I'm doin'."

"No, you're here rooting for the bad guy again and drinking that fucking King Kong cocktail."

"It's called a banana sunrise," Izzy said. "Great eye-opener. Get all your vitamins, minerals, and hair-of-the-dogables you need in one blast of the magic blender. Presto, you're ready for another wonderful fuckin' day in the neighborhood."

Bobby yanked off Izzy's glasses and looked at the Amy McCoy shiner, which resembled a soft plum. "You need an eye-opener all right," Bobby said. "But you might want to close both of them, maybe for good, after I tell you what's gong on. Didn't you get any of my beeps? My messages?"

"I was at a party with my NYU client all night. They threw the party for the *underground* film in an abandoned subway station. Get it? Phones and beepers don't work down there. What's up?"

"You better sit down while I tell you what's up," Bobby said. "But first, use a fuckin' *glass!*"

Over the next half-hour, as Izzy drank two glasses of banana sunrise, Bobby told him everything that had happened the day before. Ending with the news that Betty Wang was testifying against him.

"That's what I get for being a fucking nice guy to broads," Izzy said.

"What are you gonna do?" Bobby asked as he shouted to Izzy from the shower.

"Without a body they got cock," Izzy said. "At trial, without a corpus delicti, and a massage-parlor witness, I can beat this faster than a Boy Scout in a peep show. I also don't have bail collateral—except maybe this boat, which ain't enough. Besides, my ex-wife has a lien on it. And they're gonna ask for, and get, high bail, because the judges don't exactly have me high on any bar mitzvah or Christmas card lists. As it stands right now, I'm looking at eight to ten."

"If they convict you, Izzy," Bobby said, stepping out of the shower, toweling off, "it'll be more than eight to ten."

"I'm talking inches in my Hershey Highway *tonight* if they send me to Rikers in this fuckin' white suit! First things first. I'm goin' shoppin' for a Yiddle school uniform. I'm gonna shave my head and my eyebrows, leave the sideburns, and with this shiner, if anyone—straight, gay, or Norwegian—can get a chub lookin' at me, they belong in a fuckin' straitjacket instead of jail."

"So what do you want me to do about the proposal from Daggart and the clergymen?" Bobby asked.

"Do you have a fuckin' high school diploma? Of course take it. They got God on their side—as in In God We Trust. Cash money. The dirtier the better. I'm gonna need some of that to make bail. Make that part of the deal. I don't care if they have to put up Moses' menorah or the Pope's hat, they better bail me outta night court before they transport me to the rock where some very large non-Jewish inmate will turn me into a Maytag on a perpetual spin cycle. And tell them you want my cousin Herbie working for us.

If they don't give me bail, I want Herbie in the court-room to coldcock a court officer so he goes to Rikers with me for protection."

"I'll tell them you'll take the deal," Bobby said.

"Abso-fuckin'-lutely," Izzy said. "Full expenses. Plus whatever else we need. Maybe this Daggart has a few broads worth cultivating? Preferably soft women. Wallflower types. Maybe forty-something and suddenly abandoned by Harv-the-hubby for Heide-the-Finnish-nanny? Like that. Emotionally needy women with a lot of sad chapters in their books. I need a secretary like that to handle the phones. *Yo hablo inglés* is optional."

"Izzy, you're facing a homicide rap, and you're thinking with your little head again. Why is this Betty dame doing this to you?"

"You tell me," Izzy said, pouring the last of the banana sunrise into his glass.

"Did you really give her seven thousand dollars?" Bobby asked.

"Yeah," Izzy said. "It was part of the deal."

"What deal?"

"I needed a translator in a hurry and Berlitz was closed," Izzy said. "So I asked this Beverly broad . . ."

"Betty," Bobby said.

"Whatever, and she said she'd do it if I took care of a small problem she had."

"The green card?"

"Green card my blue balls," Izzy said, taking a slug of his drink. "I wish. I could get her one of them

from a pimply beaner for fifteen hundred and a cold
Corona. No, her problem was that she had tits like
two dimes on an ironing board. She said she's been
trying to save for implants. But every time she saves,
The Bamboo Rack gets raided by vice and she has to
pay fines. So I agreed to buy her the implants if she
came with me to get Jimmy Chung out of stir and
then worked for me for three months."

"You were paying a translator with breast
implants?"

"Actually, it was supposed to be fifteen grand,
but I worked out a barter deal with the plastic surgeon," Izzy said. "I'm representing him on a malprac-
tice suit. Chick went in for breast implants and he got
the files switched and did a reduction instead. She
wanted to look like Dolly Parton and came out like
Rod Stewart—could pick a fuckin' lock with her. She
sued. He hired me to defend him and was gonna do
Becky's implants half-price for me. I was just hoping
he didn't implant them on her ass. Anyway, now I
hope he does."

"How the hell do you get involved with people
like this?"

"I figured she'd be a major addition to my practice," Izzy said. "With her on my staff, with a pair of
new jugs, I figured I could advertise in the Chinese
papers with her picture in the ad, and half of
Flushing would come stampeding like a fuckin'
Chinese fire drill to my door for me to defend
them."

"Instead she's testifying against you, Izzy," Bobby said, exasperated. "Murder two . . ."

"Take Daggart's money," Izzy said, draining the last of his banana sunrise. "And find Jimmy Chung. That bastard is alive."

"I refuse to take a salary from Daggart."

"Good. Then they can pay *me* for your services, as a loaner."

"Up yours," Bobby said. "You aren't collecting a paycheck for me keeping you out of jail. Uh-uh. I'll take expenses. They can post your bail. That's it."

"I better go get ready to go through the system," Izzy said.

"One more thing," Bobby said. "I'm also gonna try to help Amy McCoy find her brother and his wife."

"Great," Izzy said, ripping off his glasses. "Why don't you ask her if I can borrow a pair of her thong panties to wear to the joint while you're at it."

"I told her you weren't the enemy," Bobby said.

"Suddenly I can empathize with the poor fuckin' Roadrunner," he said as he hurried off the boat.

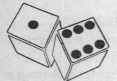

14

Bobby arrived at Chelsea Piers at eight, worked out on the free weights for thirty minutes, hit the heavy bag for six rounds, and then met Max Roth, the *Daily News* columnist, at nine, on the racquetball court.

Roth was five eight, a pain-in-the-ass vegetarian, in perfect health. He had been Bobby's friend since they both went to Brooklyn College together. They had used each other professionally ever since. Since Roth's phone number was the last one registered on the caller-ID box rigged to the illegal tap on Eddie McCoy's phone in Jimmy Chung's room in the basement of 22 Empire Court, he was hoping he might have some information for him.

Bobby let Max beat him in the racquetball game. He knew, as a student of human behavior, that winners were always more loquacious and giving than losers. After the game they walked around the indoor track, drank some water, and Bobby told Roth what he knew. He asked him what he and Eddie McCoy had talked about.

"Poor Eddie told me he thought his phone was tapped," Max Roth said. "But he's been telling me that since Reagan was in office. Since I first met him, back when we worked together on the *Village Voice*, about twelve years ago. This time he told me it was tapped by Sam Kronk and a cabal of crooked pols, including Mayor Tom Brady, Assembly Speaker Carl Pinto, Senate Majority Leader Stan Lebelski. Oh, and the governor. I told him the only thing all those people could agree on was that oxygen was necessary to sustain life on planet Earth. Eddie used to write me letters in code, only he never gave me the key. Or he'd talk cryptically on the answering tape, sounding like a schizo. Sometimes he'd run from his apartment to call me back from a pay phone. And then he'd be afraid *my* phone was tapped. He was always paranoid."

"I think he had reason to be this time, Max."

"Maybe you're right. When I first heard he was missing, I thought maybe it was a publicity stunt. A way for him to get people interested in his wild story. But when it came over the wires late yesterday that this Jimmy Chung was also missing, leaving a pool of blood in your sleaze-ball attorney's office, I figured something serious was going on and that I'd be hearing from you soon."

"Why didn't you call to let me know you'd talked to McCoy?" Bobby asked.

"He was a source and what he said was confidential, Bobby. He might be a paranoid, but if he asks me not to tell anybody we spoke, I abide by that. Plus, when I saw Gleason was involved I wanted nothing to do with it. I mean, he's representing a goddamned slumlord. A slumlord suspected of killing a guy I used to work with. A guy I liked. I knew you were indebted to Gleason. I didn't want to cross swords with you in print, so I stayed away from the story."

"What specifically did McCoy talk about?"

"Bobby, do you really think something's happened to him?"

"Yes. Something bad."

"Then I guess I should tell you what he said," Roth said. "I was going to avoid this story, but if you think somebody might have killed Eddie McCoy, I should be on it."

"What did he say, Max?"

"You gonna give me whatever you dig up first?"

"Only if you hold it until I say it's okay to print."

"The regular agreement," Roth said. "Okay, Eddie said the real reason they were trying to get him out of the building was because they—Kronk and Brady—wanted to build something big down there. He didn't say what. He said other tenants had moved out, without a trace. It sounded nuts. He said he needed to see me in person to discuss it. I told him I couldn't meet him until Monday. That I was busy yesterday covering the Brady fundraiser for his Senate race. He is right about Brady being beholden to Kronk. He's his biggest campaign contributor. But even he can only legally give so much."

"He can filter it through little people, no?"

"Sure," Roth said. "Through individuals, dummy

corporations, as soft money to PACs. But you have to be able to prove that it's all coming from one source. Hard to do when it's cash, and spread around by bagmen."

"I think Jimmy Chung might have been a political go-between bagman like that," Bobby said.

"For who?"

"Kronk to Brady, maybe," Bobby said. "I doubt he ever met with Kronk, but probably with his people. Used sweatshop workers to mail in contributions."

"Good story, if you can prove it."

"Max, you remember Ben Lee?"

"Sure," said Roth. "Nice guy, old man had a good restaurant where we used to freeload. President of the Asian American Club at Brooklyn College when we were all there. I see his name on press releases all the time. He's like the mayor of Brooklyn's Chinatown now. Big in Asian immigrants' rights. Did he know Jimmy Chung?"

"Yeah," Bobby said. "He says they were political enemies. But then I found out he might be close to Sean Dunne, who is a Brady butt boy, which could also put him in Kronk's corner. Listen, can you discreetly find out which political circles Ben really runs in these days? Who his friends are? His ambitions? Whether he's on a friend or enemy list at City Hall."

"You don't want me to talk to him?"

"No. Just sniff around the edges. Ask the reporters down in room nine at City Hall. Ask your federal contacts. Maybe check the Board of Elections and see which campaigns he gives to."

"I'll find out what there is to know," Roth said.

"And you have more contacts than I do inside the Manhattan DA's office these days," Bobby said.

"I do?"

"Don't bullshit me, Max," Bobby said. "You didn't get that Queensboro Bridge bid-rigging contract story last month out of the Queens DA's office. It came from my old office. I could smell it."

"Okay, so I know a certain clerk who shares my fondness for watercress and endive salads," Roth said, with a proud little smile. "We happen to bump into each other during lunch in the same downtown health-food restaurant now and then. What do you want to know?"

"What Noel Christmas has been working on lately," Bobby said. "Especially anything with cross jurisdictions to Sean Dunne's U.S. attorney's office in the Eastern District."

"Sean Dunne involved in this, too?"

"Yeah, but I don't know how."

He didn't tell Roth about Amy McCoy seeing Ben Lee getting into a car with Sean Dunne or anything about Daggart and the clerics. Some things were better kept close to the vest until he understood them better himself first. But he'd whet Roth's appetite enough to know that the tenacious reporter would switch to his ferret mode, burrowing through the bureaucracy, picking the brains of old pols, machine hacks, beat reporters, cynical flatfoots, hungry young prosecutors, anonymous clerks, gossipy sources, and the readers of the *Daily News*. When Max Roth wrote one column, often some anonymous reader called with a new piece of vital information, leading to a second and third and fourth, until an exposé led to an indictment. Accessing Max Roth and his column was sometimes like setting off an underground chain reaction in the city.

"Anything else? Maybe a foot massage and a backrub?"

"Maybe you can keep your ear to the ground about how that legalized-gambling resolution in the legislature is going," Bobby said. "What the infighting is like. Who stands to win and lose."

"Come to think of it, Eddie McCoy said something about Kronk and legalized gambling in New York. That what this is about?"

"I'm not sure," Bobby said.

"This could take a few days."

"That's fine."

"Bobby," Max said, "if Izzy Gleason goes down, don't hold on to his ankles. I don't want to write that story."

"This time the dirty little runt is clean," Bobby said. "That much I'm sure of. And I owe him."

"That you do," Roth said. "But I don't. I won't let him taint me, understand?"

"Perfectly."

"One more thing," Max Roth said.

"What?"

"Happy birthday," he said.

Bobby looked at his watch: 10:15. He had forty-five minutes to shower and get uptown for Maggie.

15

"That child has been looking forward to that trip to Florida all year," Connie Matthews Sawyer shouted as Bobby stood in the foyer of her penthouse apartment in the Trump Tower on Fifth Avenue.

Bobby looked at his ex-wife and knew exactly why he'd married her all those years ago. She was smart and ruthless, still easy to look at, tall and long-legged, tanned and almost as ravishing in her chic designer clothes as he remembered her the first time he saw her naked. And try as she might to be a tough rich bitch, Connie's eyes were always a hair-trigger away from a beaming smile. She was also secretly generous and a helluva good mother. And she liked men.

"Maybe this'll soothe the savage beast," Bobby said, handing her an envelope. She snatched it from him with a hand that was almost wrinkle-free, the nails perfect. She opened the envelope and took out five one-hundred-dollar bills.

"What the hell is this?"

"Child support," Bobby said.

She looked at him and tried to stifle the laugh but couldn't hold it. "Great," she said. "I'll get Maggie new sandals."

Bobby smiled and winked.

"Don't you wink at me, ass-face," she said. "I don't want goddamned child support from you. I told you when we were getting divorced I was willing to give *you* alimony. But no, not you, not Bobby 'Tool-belt' Emmet."

"Gunbelt," Bobby corrected.

"Macho bullshit."

"Five hundred every two weeks," Bobby said. "A thousand a month. That was the deal."

"I'll save it for the doorman's Christmas tip," she said.

"They hiring here?"

"Stop the nonsense," she said. "I read about your mutt mouthpiece being in trouble. I hope they put him in a cage filled with his ex-clients."

"He's innocent," Bobby said.

"That swine might not be guilty of what they're gonna charge him with," Connie said. "But he was born with horns and cleft feet. So, puh-leeze, don't tell me Izzy Gleason is *innocent*. It's like saying Hugh Hefner is a virgin."

"I take your point," Bobby said. "Now can I see Maggie?"

"She's in her room," Connie said.

"Can you draw me a map?" Bobby asked.

"You're a real wit," she said, walking closer, diamond earrings clicking, her breasts moving freely under her sheer white Versace blouse, the dead-tight designer jeans still fitting her teenage-narrow hips. "You know, I was planning to take the Lear down to surprise you guys. Wanted to bring you, Maggie, your mom, everyone over to the Palm Beach house for a weekend."

She unbuttoned a third button on Bobby's shirt, to reveal more of his muscular chest. "Happy birthday," she whispered, glancing down the corridor to be sure they were alone, then gazing at him with smoky eyes, wearing the Opium perfume that he knew that she knew used to drive him nuts.

"My mom would have liked meeting Trevor," Bobby said.

Connie rolled her eyes. "He was gonna be in France," she said. "Launching some new goddamned line of wrinkle cream. I thought it might be nice, for old times' sake, if all of us were together as a family for a weekend. Me and you could have gone for a late dinner, alone, to discuss Maggie's future. Stone crabs, cold beer, a midnight swim . . ."

"Jeez, Con," Bobby said. "Maybe next time we go down we could all bunk in my mom's senior-citizens condo in Marco Island, to make it even more cozy.

They have a pool. And we could all play shuffleboard together, and bingo and canasta."

"You'd piss in Cinderella's shoe," she said, pointing down a long hall. "Go down there, make a left at the Matisse, and go two rights until you come to a small Monet. Maggie's is the wing overlooking the park."

"If I get lost I'll ask a guard," Bobby said as he strolled down the hall that looked like it was carpeted with the pelts of a thousand white Persian cats. It was like walking through the halls of a museum, decorated with framed art, some of it modern, Boteros, Warhols, Picassos. Some of it from old Impressionist masters like Cezanne, Manet, Degas, Pissarro. Bobby became momentarily lost in the maze of rooms, alcoves, and hallways. He rang a buzzer on one door, hoping it was Maggie's. Trevor Sawyer answered the door, wearing khaki shorts and smoking a Cuban cigar. His eyes widened and he smiled with genuine pleasure.

"Hey, Bobby," he said. "Good to see ya, fella."

They shook hands. "Sorry, I was looking for Maggie," Bobby said, backing away politely.

"Come in a minute," Trevor said, looking furtively down the corridor to be sure they were alone. He led Bobby into his oak-paneled study that was lined with bookcases. There was no TV, no radio, no CD player, no personal computer, no phone. Just a large desk, comfortable lounge chairs with matching ottomans, overstuffed sofas, excellent reading lamps, a big illuminated globe. Bobby was struck that there was zero street noise. Even the sound of the helicopters that often buzzed above the skyscrapers of the city could not be heard in here. Trevor closed the door, which made a cushioned sigh as it fit snugly into the jamb, like a lid settling onto Tupperware. The office was like a womb.

"Soundproof," Trevor said. "I need one place in the world with no phone, no voices, no women, nothing but me and a cigar and my thoughts. This is where I figure out who's trying to fuck me. And my wife."

"When I want that kind of solitude these days I go out to sea and drop anchor," Bobby said.

"What I wouldn't give for your life," Trevor said.

"It's not much but it's not for sale," Bobby said.

"I see your lawyer friend is in a bit of a jam," Trevor said.

"Yeah," Bobby said. "I'm obliged to help."

"You should," Trevor said. "He did right by you. Loyalty and reciprocation are important in this lousy world."

"I think so."

"He was straight up with me," Trevor said. "But when Connie found out I used him to post your bail that time, she hit the roof. She didn't mind bailing you out, but she hates Izzy Gleason."

"It takes a certain type of woman to feel affection for Izzy."

Trevor chuckled and said, "Well, I don't think he's capable of murder. Maybe he is, but I couldn't see it in him. So if there's anything I can do, you let me know. I can't write a check because everything is in a joint account now. But if I can do anything else, please, I'd like to help."

"Trevor, what can you tell me about Sam Kronk that I haven't already read in the gossips?"

"He's a sidewinder," Trevor said. "He swindled me twice on investment deals. One time on a building in Times Square. The other on a hotel in Puerto Rico. My own fault—as Voltaire said, 'Once a fool, twice a pervert.'"

"You think you can listen to the tom-toms in your circles about his plans if legalized gambling is approved in New York?"

"Sure," Trevor said. "I'm sure there's talk. Do you think Kronk might be involved in this nasty bit of business that Izzy Gleason is caught up in?"

"Maybe," Bobby said. "Kronk and the mayor."

"Of course," Trevor said. "They're joined at the hip. I'll keep my ear out. As a matter of fact, I think Connie knows a thing or two about Kronk herself. She's not a fan of his, either."

"Thanks," Bobby said as Trevor led him out the door and pointed the way to Maggie's wing. They shook hands.

"So what did Connie give you for your birthday?" he asked.

"A hard time," Bobby said, smiling.

"I'm sure that's what she'd like from you," Trevor said. "I'm not a particularly jealous man. I have everything a guy could want. I'm not even jealous of Connie. I don't think she fools around . . ."

"She's all talk," Bobby said. "Always was."

"I know," he said. "With everyone else. But I don't think she'll ever quite get over you. With you, I think she would . . ."

"Trevor, that's just not in the cards," Bobby said.

"For that, I owe you one," Trevor said.

"No, you don't. For being so good to my kid, I owe *you*."

When he finally found Maggie's room she was standing at her laser printer, as pages zipped out at a speed of thirty per minute.

"Hey, old man," she said, rushing to him and giving him a discreet hug.

She kissed his cheek. Once she reaches puberty a daughter stops embracing her father the same way she did as a child. Her hands lasso his neck, she stands at a discreet angle so her breasts won't touch him, and the old kiss on the lips moves east to the cheek. That's called grown-up. *And as they grow up, you grow old,* Bobby thought. Bobby missed her being a little kid he could wrestle with, fling in the air, and tickle to near seizure. But the rewards of a teenage Maggie were great. The kiss and the hug were different, but now his kid could do research and run license plates and call him Old Man instead of Daddy.

Bobby looked around the room, thirty by forty

feet, with a king-size canopy bed. There was enough state-of-the-art computer equipment to run the local branch of the FBI—desktop PCs, laptops in various colors, notebooks, printers, assorted terminals for photographs, graphics, and computer games.

But some things never changed. The place was a teenage mess, with dirty clothes piled high, the bed unmade, discarded McDonald's and Pizza Hut boxes on the night table and the floor. The bedroom opened to a big vanity, a dressing room, and a huge private lounge, furnished with a pool table, Ping-Pong table, a jukebox, an entertainment center with big-screen TV, stereo sound system, and an ice cream soda fountain.

"What are the business hours?" Bobby asked.

"I'd rather hang out in Joe's Pizzeria on Prospect Avenue in Brooklyn any day of the year," she said.

Bobby walked to the big windows and looked out over the shimmering emerald of Central Park.

"Nice little back yard," he said as he watched a condor sail from the park to the high cornice of a skyscraper on Fifty-seventh Street, where the big birds were known to nest, feeding on rats and squirrels from the park.

"I'd rather have Prospect Park and Coney Island, Pop."

"So when you're old enough, go get an apartment in Brooklyn."

"Don't think I won't," she said.

She handed him a manila envelope filled with

printed material on Jimmy Chung. She also read from a single sheet of paper.

"The blue Lumina is registered to a guy named Raphael Paragon," Maggie said. "Lives in Bay Head, New Jersey. Here's the address."

She handed him the information. He recognized the name as a former FBI agent who Moe Daggart said headed security for Sam Kronk.

"Can you do a bio search on him, too?"

"Right now?" she asked. "It could take time."

"Later's okay. What about the white van?"

"That's registered to something called Lucky Eight Farm in Farley, New Jersey," she said. "I have to do a corporation search to find out the names of the human beings involved."

"You can do that later," he said. "You ready to go to lunch?"

"Sure, but first we're gonna hook you up to the new century."

She took Bobby by the hand and led him through the penthouse to the main living room. Connie and Trevor now sat on facing suede couches.

"Trevor tells me you're looking into the amazing Mr. Kronk?"

"I just mentioned it in passing," Trevor said.

"Well, yeah, I'm trying to get a touchstone on him," Bobby said. "Beyond what the gossips tell you."

"I know a few people who have known him," Connie said. "Quite intimately. They can tell you some bone-chilling stories."

"I'd love to hear them," Bobby said. "It could be important."

"I'll let you know," she said. "But I'm doing it for you, for Maggie's father, not that waterbug you work for."

"Thanks," Bobby said. "Oh, sorry to bother you, Con, but there's one more thing you can do for me."

"What is it?" she asked, looking from her husband to her ex-husband.

"You think you could write me a receipt for the child support?" Bobby asked.

"I'll tell my accountant," she said, dead-eyed.

"Thanks," he said and left with Maggie.

16

Maggie stood with Bobby at the glass counter of the Snoop Shop on Hudson Street in Greenwich Village. The place was a haven for paranoids and Peeping Toms.

Ever since the celebrated "nanny murder trial" in Massachusetts, couples with young children flocked to the Snoop Shop to buy hidden video cameras. Business executives also bought surveillance equipment here to trap thieving employees. Some bosses wanted to discover if their premises were bugged by rival companies and would hire the Snoop Shop people to do a bug sweep of their offices. Married people bugged their home phones, trying to catch each other cheating. Or put trackers on a spouse's car to tail him to a rendezvous with an extracurricular lover.

Maggie pointed to a bank of video screens showing their images from different angles. She pointed to an overhead image of herself and Bobby on one monitor.

"Where's that camera?" asked Maggie.

The white-haired man behind the counter introduced himself as Leonard and pointed to the smoke alarm positioned high above their heads. Bobby shook his hand. He knew the guy was an ex-cop just by the skeptical look in his eye. Maggie then asked where the camera projecting the low-angle image was hidden and he pointed to a phone jack on the baseboard. There was another camera in a wall thermostat. Still others in a desktop telephone, in a loose-leaf binder, in a clock radio, a lamp, a Bible.

"The whole world's a stage," Bobby said.

He and Maggie laughed and made funny faces.

"What are you looking for?" Leonard asked.

"What do you have for detecting bugs?" Bobby asked. Leonard reached into the showcase and removed a ballpoint pen.

"This is the cheapest and most portable gizmo," he said. "See this red light on the bottom of the pen?

It lights up when you're in the presence of a bug, body mike, or other listening devices. Or if you're afraid the light will attract attention, you can set it to vibrate in your shirt pocket. It has a microwave head that picks up the frequency range of all transmitting devices."

"Phat!" said Maggie.

"Sorry, they don't come any slimmer," Leonard said.

"She means cool," Bobby said. "Phat, with a *ph* . . . never mind."

"I don't know from fat with a *ph*, but the pen picks up RFs, or radio-frequency waves," Leonard said. "Cell phones and walkie-talkies use RFs, between one hundred hertz and 1.5 gigahertz. They travel in sound waves, and they vibrate. Anyway, when someone is using a hidden mike, this pen picks up the RF vibrations and the red light goes on."

"Can you sweep a car with it too?" Bobby asked.

"Sure, but you might want something a little more sophisticated for your home or office," Leonard said and reached under the counter and pulled out something called the Boomerang Non-Linear Junction Detector, a long-handled mechanical device that looked like an electric ice scraper for a car windshield.

"This baby can locate covert devices even when they're not operating," said Leonard. "Tape recorders, radio transmitters, amplifier mikes. In walls, furniture, plants, ceilings, floors. The second and third harmonic sensitivity differentiates between semiconductor junctions and dissimilar metals."

"Oh," said Bobby, who actually knew from experience about most of what Leonard was saying. "You mean if John Gotti had bought one of these he'd be a free man today?"

"Probably," said Leonard.

"How much is it?"

"Twenty-six thou . . ."

"It isn't polite to ask the price of gifts, Pop."

"She's buying it?" Leonard said. "Stick with the pen, kid."

"I'm a spoiled rich kid," she said. "So show us some more expensive stuff."

Leonard looked at Bobby, blinked, smiled, and said, "If you're ever putting her up for adoption, let me know."

Leonard proceeded to show Bobby an array of surveillance and countersurveillance gadgetry— night-vision scopes, miniature spy cameras, wrist-watch cameras, belt-buckle cameras, a simple device that you plug into a phone jack to detect a tap, tracking bugs that could be planted on vehicles, parabolic directional microphones to pick up distant conversations, telephone voice-changing transmitters, tie-clip video cameras, a pair of sunglasses with built-in microphone and video camera, sunglasses with rearview mirrors that enabled you to "watch your back," V-neck upper-body armor that could be worn under a regular shirt.

Bobby was familiar with a lot of undercover gadgetry but he had never used half this stuff when he worked for the DA's office. There they had other tools—like legal wiretaps, search warrants, and subpoenas.

"This stuff is great," Leonard said placing a spray can and a portable battery-operated ultraviolet light on the countertop. "Fluorescent tracing powder. You just spray this stuff on any surface and it leaves an invisible residue that when you touch it, it glows on your hands under the UV lamp."

"Liar's powder," Maggie said.

"That's a good name for it, kid," Leonard said. "Gotta use that in my next catalogue. This stuff will tell you whose hand has been in the cookie jar, all right."

Bobby would only let Maggie buy him the bug detector pen. She made him wait outside while she paid the bill.

Bobby took his gift outside, and in less than a minute, the glowing red top on the new bug-detector pen helped him locate the transmitter on the Jeep. It was the cap on the radio antenna.

The Jeep Cherokee's antenna is designed so that it can be screwed off at night or when you put the vehicle through a car wash. Someone had obviously replaced Bobby's old antenna with a new one, only the nickel-plated screw head was now actually an XLF-3 Tracker that operated on two 392 silver-oxide batteries, which were concealed under the O-ring at the base of the antenna. The tracker did not interfere with his radio but when used in conjunction with a

Mini-10 Tracker Receiver, mounted in the dark blue Lumina, it was easy to track Bobby around town.

Bobby screwed off the antenna and put it in a trash barrel. The Lumina would probably track the garbage truck to the Staten Island landfill by late afternoon.

His cell phone rang. It was Izzy Gleason. "I talked to the DA and Noel Christmas," Izzy said. "I'm surrendering at One Hogan Place this afternoon at four. The DA promises to let me make night court. Tell Herbie to come post my bail—he's family, and this way no one questions it or traces it to anyone else. And tell that fucking buttonhead to be there on time with the cash. I'm betting a quarter-mil, but tell him to bring a half-mil, just in case. They'll get it back when the trial is over."

"You okay, Iz?"

"Yeah," he said softly.

"What's wrong? You've been jailed for contempt before."

"That was different," he said. "I called my kids at school in Maryland. They never called back."

"They're probably out, Izzy," Bobby said.

"Yeah, out of my fuckin' life," he said. "I think I might have embarrassed them for good this time. Suspended for conduct unbecoming is one thing. Murder for profit is another."

"You're gonna beat this and look like a hero," Bobby said.

"You really think so?"

"Yeah," Bobby said, sensing Izzy's spirits lifting.

"Broads love heroes," he said. "They'll be lining up to work for Izzy the hero. And I got a hero for them right here . . ."

"Goodbye, Izzy," Bobby said. "Call me when you get out."

He hung up. Maggie came out of the store smiling.

"How much you spend?"

"You're the detective," she said.

"Wiseass," he said.

They had brunch at the West Bank Cafe, on Forty-second Street, where they got to choose from a buffet of eggs. French toast, pancakes, bacon, sausage, potatoes, lox and bagels, fresh turkey, salad, fruit salad. It was top quality, plentiful, and reasonably priced—about ten dollars for all you could eat.

Steve Olsen, the popular owner, lost money on Bobby who had a little bit of everything except turkey (he didn't want the tryptophan in the fowl to make him sleepy and slow). Maggie balanced the scales by eating just a bowl of fruit salad.

"Not hungry?"

"Cal hates fat girls," Maggie said.

"He said that?"

"No, I can just tell," she said. "He only talks to thin girls."

Uh-oh, he thought.

"He's missing out on some of the best conversations in the world," Bobby said. "I bet his mother put on weight when she was pregnant with him."

Maggie giggled, an inadvertent piece of the little girl she used to be escaping from the wannabe adult. "I'll tell him that."

"Tell you what, today we're celebrating *my* birthday, not Cal's, so do me a favor and have something to eat with me," he said. "Please."

"If you put it that way . . ."

She got up and returned with a plate piled high with French toast, scrambled eggs, and bacon and ate like a kid after a swim meet. Bobby winked at her and took out the printed material on Jimmy Chung.

"What are you looking for specifically?" Maggie asked.

"I dunno," he said. "Anything connecting him to gambling, or the mayor, or Sam Kronk . . ."

"I already read most of it," Maggie said, taking the stack of papers from Bobby. "The guy was born in Hong Kong, had no arrests listed on his INS application for a green card, came to work in the U.S. twelve years ago, listing his occupation as a botanist. Plant scientist. That's why they gave him a work visa, because he had a special skill. But there's no record of him ever working in that field here. He worked in various places in Chinatown, restaurants, a noodle factory, an import-export business. He got involved in local politics. There is one picture of him there posing with the mayor and Sam Kronk at the groundbreaking for the Asian Arms Hotel in Chinatown about five years ago."

Maggie sifted through the papers and found a printout of the old Chinese newspaper clip. Stapled to the clipping was the computerized English translation of the caption. It identified Mayor Brady, and Sam Kronk as the builder. Jimmy Chung was listed as the real estate agent who had brokered the deal. There were members of the local Democratic Club, merchants association, and some dumpy white guy with bug-eyes who was not identified.

"So he has a history with Kronk," Bobby said, sifting through the rest of the stack. "Nothing on gambling?"

"Not that I remember. Most of it is about squabbles with rent-control tenants in some of his properties. He managed a lot of buildings, including that one at 22 Empire Court."

"No," Bobby said. "He owned the building."

"That's not what it says in the Chinese papers," Maggie said, shuffling through the printouts, finally locating the one she was looking for. "There was a rent strike there about three years ago, when other tenants lived there. A reporter covered the story for the Chinese paper. It's all kinda boring, Pop."

Bobby read the translation; it said Jimmy Chung was in fact the manager of 22 Empire Court, which was owned by a corporation named Waterfront Holdings Inc.

"Who owns Waterfront Holdings Inc.?" he wondered aloud.

"I ran that through the computer and it says that it's owned by something called Rapa Properties Inc. A sub-something . . ."

"Subsidiary," Bobby said. "A dummy corporation."

"It got confusing, so I printed it out for you to look at. It's worse than reading about fifteenth-century European expansionism."

Bobby looked at the address for Rapa properties. It was a post-office box in Louisville, Kentucky. Izzy Gleason was holding a deed to a building signed over to him in lieu of legal fees by Jimmy Chung, a piece of property he might not even own. In his greedy race to get his hands on a piece of real estate, Izzy had hired a massage-parlor translator who probably didn't understand the difference between manager and owner. Chung would have signed his vital organs over to Izzy to get away from Noel Christmas.

On the other hand, maybe he did own Waterfront Holdings Inc. and Rapa Properties, of Louisville, Kentucky.

"There's no name of a CEO," Bobby said.

"I know," Maggie said. "Since Mom and Trevor both have that title, I looked for a name. But not here. There's an 800 number, but all you get is an answering machine telling you to leave a message."

"Think you can find out who pays the phone bill?" Bobby said. "What bank the check is drawn on? Where they mail it from? The same goes for real estate taxes to the city. Just available databases, Maggie. No hacking."

"Me? Hack? The phone company is on-line, Pop," she said. "I'll see what data they have available."

"You all set for the history test tomorrow?"

"Hope so," she said.

"Got time for a movie?" he asked, sipping some coffee.

"I better go cram, Pop," she said. "I'm gonna study with Cal."

It was starting to happen, he thought. That time in a father's life when his daughter wants to spend more time with her boyfriend than her dad. He knew it was irrational and immature, but he was feeling just a trifle jealous. He also had a nagging resentment toward this kid Cal.

"I got stuff to do anyway," Bobby said.

He dropped Maggie back at the Trump Tower. She promised to do the computer searches he'd asked for after she finished her history test in the morning. She kissed him on the cheek and promised she'd pick a star.

As Bobby drove slowly back uptown to the Boat Basin he called Daggart on the cell phone, told him Izzy wanted to join forces, so long as they provided bail, expenses, Herbie Rabinowitz's services, and whatever other unforeseeable resources they might need.

Daggart said everything would be taken care of.

"I'm glad you're on board," Daggart said.

"We might be sailing side by side," Bobby said. "But I'm not on board anybody's ship. I sail alone."

"Aye aye, sir," Daggart said.

"I'll be in touch," Bobby said and hung up.

17

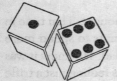

It was 4:15 PM by the time Bobby got back to the Boat Basin.

He walked down the floating wooden walkway to slip 99A. Connie was sitting on deck wearing a white floppy sun hat and a skin-tight white pants suit, red high-heeled sandals. Three other beautiful women dressed in skimpy summer attire were sitting on deck chairs. All of them were sipping screwdrivers.

Bobby strode up the walkway to his boat and Pam and Dot, the two women from the neighboring *Armitage*, looked at him over the tops of their sunglasses.

"Hi, Bobby," Pam sang.

"Happy birthday, Bobby," said Dot.

Bobby nodded, smiled, gave them a thumbs-up, and climbed on board *The Fifth Amendment*. The door to the salon was open and he saw a collection of plain white boxes stacked in the middle of the floor. Various bottles of liquor and orange juice were on the kitchen counter.

"You always liked a pad with a nice view," Connie said, pushing her sunglasses down on her nose to peer at Pam and Dot in their string bikinis.

"Just your average girls next door," Bobby said. "Aren't you going to introduce me to your friends?"

Connie introduced Marjorie, a tall, leggy all-American natural blonde; Priscilla, a near-anorexic blue-eyed brunette; and Giselle, a dark-eyed, full-bodied Latina. All of them were in their twenties. None of them wore wedding rings. All stared warily at Bobby through sunglasses. Bobby and the women exchanged hellos.

"You wanted to know about our friend Mr. Kronk?" Connie said. "These ladies have a tale to tell. It can't be repeated, because they've all signed confidentiality agreements with Kronk and they're afraid of being sued. Or worse. They've already been treated badly enough by him. They're afraid of any reprisals."

"The quality control of your employees has skyrocketed, Con," he said.

"They work under contract for my company," Connie said. "My girls tell me everything. I told them I wanted them to tell you about Kronk. I also promised them that you'd never let him know they spoke to you."

"Of course not," Bobby said. "In fact let's go inside."

They followed Bobby into the salon, where the women took seats on the couches. Bobby looked at the white boxes.

"Trevor sent that stuff for your birthday," Connie said. "Actually, it's from both of us. If you're going to insist on paying child support, you might as well earn some decent money."

Bobby opened the flap of the top box and saw the Boomerang bug sweeper, night-vision scope, telephone-rigging devices, automobile-tracking gizmos, cameras, the "liar" powder, and body armor.

"Maggie called from the Snoop Shop?" he said, remembering that she had asked him to wait outside while she paid for the bug-detector pen.

"Yeah," Connie said. "She told Trevor about all the stuff. He ordered it and had it delivered."

"I can't accept this," Bobby said. "This stuff must have cost Trevor a fortune."

"Don't worry, we have two fortunes," she said. "Trevor likes you. Besides, someday I'm sure he's going to ask you to do a piece of work for him. Probably following me around. I *wish.*"

The women all laughed and sipped their drinks. Bobby didn't know which one to look at first, his eyes skipping from one pretty face to the next.

"You divorced *him?*" Priscilla asked.

"You need glasses, mama," said Giselle.

"He's as good as he looks, too," said Connie. "Except he thinks money is for paying utility bills and the mortgage. He actually believes all you need is *enough.*"

"Oh," said Marjorie. "That explains it then."

The women laughed again and Bobby folded his arms and leaned against the kitchen counter.

"I'm also boring," Bobby said. "So tell me about the exciting world of Sam Kronk."

The laughter seemed to skid to an abrupt stop.

"Each of them were known as Kronkettes," Connie said.

"Sounds like recruits," Bobby said.

"Glorified mistresses," said Giselle, the most eager to talk.

"Actually we *were* recruited," said Marjorie, in a Texas drawl. "Sam'd see us on the runways during Fashion Week in Bryant Park."

"Or in my case I was a lounge singer in a small casino in Atlantic City," said Priscilla, in a flat Middle-American twang.

"I was auditioning to be a Knicks City Dancer," said Giselle.

"How did he recruit you guys?" Bobby asked.

"He always sends his number-two security guy," said Giselle. "Mr. Dunne, Donald Dunne, he comes up to you, shows you a card that says he's the vice president of security for Kronk Enterprises. He tells you he works directly for Sam Kronk. He asks your age. If you're engaged, married, going steady, or living with a guy. You tell him no. Like me, you're from Bushwick. You can't believe it when this guy tells you that Sam Kronk, the famous billionaire, admires *you*. That he'd like to meet *you*. Have dinner with *you*. You think of this rich guy who can have anyone and he wants to date *you!* So, naturally, you say, Yeah, sure."

"And when you say 'Yeah, sure,' this guy Dunne takes you in his limousine," said Priscilla. "There's a fashion expert in the limo who takes you to the best boutiques in New York, he helps you buy whatever you want for your date with the great Sam Kronk. Then they take you to a beauty salon on Madison Avenue where all these amazing makeup people and haircutters do an assessment of how they're going to make you look like a queen."

"Sounds more like a dream come true than a nightmare," Bobby said.

"Yeah, but then they take you to Kronk Castle Hotel in Atlantic City," Giselle said. "He has one whole private floor, the thirteenth, which is not accessible to the public. Casinos never use the thirteenth floor, anyway, because it's a bad-luck number. The main elevators don't even stop there. He has a special entrance in the lobby, to the left of the concierge desk, a plain black unmarked door. You put your computerized key card in the slot to open it, then you use the card to get the elevator, and it takes you up to the thirteenth floor. The computer code to the key card is changed every day."

"He has his own private world up there," said Marjorie. "Movie theater, restaurant, bowling alley, game room, gambling room, a health clinic, swimming pool, sauna, gym. He has bodyguards and security cameras everywhere."

"Man's entitled to a little luxury," Bobby said. "He's a billionaire."

"When Don Dunne takes you there, the first person you meet is a lawyer, Barry Polo," Priscilla said. "He's real nice and explains to you that because Mr. Kronk is adamant about his privacy he wants you to

sign a confidentiality document about everything you
see or hear or do in this place. If you don't sign it
you're asked to leave. He also offers you a job as a
Kronkette for seventy-five thousand a year. All you
have to do is look pretty and occasionally be seen in
public with Mr. Kronk. They also say that because
Mr. Kronk is often subjected to frivolous lawsuits, he
needs you to sign another document that indemnifies
him from legal action in the event your employment
is severed for any reason. I think he was sued by a
woman for sexual harassment or something once."

"Paternity, I heard," said Giselle. "She was the
first Kronkette. Name was Smith or Jones, probably a
fake name. Anyway, Sam won, of course, but ever
since he takes precautions against it ever happening
again. He protects himself."

"They also offer you a room, meals, and career
counseling," Marjorie said. "It all sounds so irresistible.
A seventy-five-thousand-dollar salary, health insurance, free shows, a room on the private thirteenth
floor of a famous casino hotel, and all you have to do is
look pretty and smile when you appear in public as an
escort with Mr. Kronk or one of his rich friends."

"What's the catch?" Bobby asked. "Is this a private harem?"

"You could call it that," Giselle said. "Next, they
make you take a physical exam."

"That's normal in any big company," Bobby said.
"To make sure you're not a junkie or sick. The insurance companies insist on it."

"But the real reason he asks for the physical is to check to see if you have HIV, herpes, syphilis, or any other sexually transmittable diseases," Priscilla said.

"Because once you become a Kronkette, they don't let you go out with any other guy while you work for him or else you're immediately terminated," said Marjorie. "And you have to stay in shape. Part of your job is to stick to a low-fat diet, and work out in the gym. If you get overweight, you have a week to lose it or you're terminated."

"You agreed to all that?" Bobby said. "The weight, and not going out with other guys?"

"It's not spelled out in the contract," said Giselle. "But if they see you with another guy they call it a breach of security. They keep an eye on you at all times. The eye in the sky watches you when you leave the thirteenth floor. Or a security guy goes with you if you leave the hotel. If you so much as kiss another man they terminate you. They let you keep the money but just try getting hired somewhere else in show business once he dumps you. He knows all the fashion designers, the other casino owners, the modeling agencies, studio heads, producers, casting directors, gossip columnists. This guy Don Dunne goes around spreading nasty stories about you. That you have AIDS, the clap, that you're a thief, a junkie, that you leak stories to supermarket tabloids, that you can't be trusted. You get on Kronk's shit list, you can't prove it, but you're blacklisted in all the places a model, actress, dancer, singer wants to work. Lucky you get a job working a topless club."

"So you do what he says," Bobby said.

The three women looked at one another. "Hey, we're not the first young girls willing to sleep with a billionaire like Kronk," said Giselle. "He's not *that* bad looking. I mean he wears a wig, a special girdle T-shirt to hold in his gut, lifts in his shoes . . ."

"He even wears lifts in his tennis sneakers," said Priscilla, and they all laughed.

"But one on one, he treats you nice," said Giselle. "He might be a little kinky, but he isn't mean. He has like a dozen Kronkettes living on the thirteenth floor at the same time. But they come and go. When we left, new ones arrived. Dunne recruits them all over the place for Kronk. Waitresses. Showgirls. Models. Dancers. Singers. Beauty contestants. Struggling actresses. Ring card girls. Once you're hired, they wait six weeks, keeping you under surveillance, and then they ask for a second blood test to make sure you're clean. If you are, then Kronk is ready for you. He has a vasectomy and he doesn't like to use rubbers, so he makes sure all his girls are clean and disease-free. And makes sure they stay that way."

"He sleeps with a different one each time," said Marjorie. "Sometimes two at a time, if you know what I mean. In the year I spent there, I was with him six or seven times."

"It was always consensual?"

"Yeah," said Priscilla. "He never forces himself on any of us. He doesn't have to. And we're all of legal age. He makes sure of that. Kronk is forty-seven years old. His trophy girls must be no more than half his age."

"That means when he's sixty he'll be with thirty and unders," Bobby said. "Whatever happened to the French formula of half a man's age plus seven?"

"It died with cloning," Connie said.

"Of course he publicly dates women older than the Kronkettes," said Marjorie. "The celebrities he's always '*itemed*' with in the gossip columns, the ones he goes to big public functions with. The ones he brings to his penthouse suite instead of the thirteenth floor. So he dates older women in public, but his Kronkettes are his private fantasy girls."

"His actual girlfriends don't know about the Kronkettes?" Bobby asked.

"Once they hear rumors of other chicks they usually hit the road," Priscilla said. "But he just uses most of them, too. He lays 'em and betrays 'em. I've heard him complain that with those chicks he has to use a rubber, because he's afraid of diseases and he can't control who they've been with. That's why he keeps the Kronkettes."

"And after a year as Kronkettes, all of you were too old for him?" Bobby asked.

"Yeah," said Giselle. "Or he becomes bored, or afraid we'd stray. Whatever the reason, after a year, he wants you replaced with fresh blood. I think it's his way of trying to stop his own biological clock. Or forming emotional attachments. Of course this prick never did anything for our careers except let people see us on his arm around the hotel. He just terminated us. Gone. No flowers, no kiss goodbye, no thank-you, no nothing. Like he never knew us."

"Our computerized key cards were deactivated," said Marjorie. "Our clothes were packed. We were given a month's severance. And a promise of a good reference if we ever needed one. The same as he's been doing since the beginning."

"It's a megalomaniacal operation," Bobby said. "But if you were twenty-one and you signed the contract there isn't much you can do. He never forced himself on you or specifically asked for sex for money. You probably can be sued if you violate the confidentiality clause."

"The other thing that he does to ensure he doesn't get sued is videotape all the sexual encounters to prove they were consensual," Giselle said, taking a sip of her drink and uncrossing and crossing her legs. "The room has hidden cameras and he always makes you come fully dressed into his room, which is like a house of horror. You are told in advance that he likes you to undress him. Then yourself. He makes you initiate it. Christ, this is embarrassing."

"It's okay," Bobby said. "We all do things we regret in life. Don't we, Con?"

"Yeah, we sure do," she said.

"He has hundreds of videotapes of all the chicks he's slept with on the thirteenth floor," Giselle said. "Keeps them in the big safe up there. Just in case you're not afraid of getting sued by him, Don Dunne shows you one of the tapes. Only it has a blue dot over Kronk's face but you're right there, doing what you do. *Everything.* He tells you he'll send copies to your parents, your friends, your boss wherever you work. If you ever get married, he'll show your husband and your kids. That it will wind up on the Internet. These people don't fuck around. And if that doesn't work, he tells you that it's sad how many people die in car accidents every year. You think about how much money he has, how many people he has working for him, and so you believe he can do whatever he wants to anybody. Honey, I grew up in Bushwick where I knew some bad dudes with switchblades and machine guns, but these fuckin' people know how to scare the shit out of a girl with a smile, a bankbook, and a promise."

"What do you mean his bedroom is a house of horrors?" Bobby asked.

"His weird bone collection," Priscilla said.

"Bones?" Bobby said.

"He collects skulls and bones," Marjorie said. "Like a sicko."

"What kind of bones? Dinosaur?"

"Some animal, some reptile, some human," Priscilla said. "Cabinets filled with them. Whole skeletons. Showcases filled with them. Some are framed. Some on shelves like freaking knickknacks."

"Human bones?" Bobby said.

"Yeah," Giselle said. "It's legal. He has all kinds of skulls from giraffes, hippos, elephants, cats, dogs.

And people's skulls. Skulls that are hundreds of years old. Some newer ones. I don't know if he does it as a warning, like he will make you part of his collection if you cross him, or if he's just a wacky bone freak. But he collects bones. He showed me catalogues. There's a few stores right here in the city that sell the stuff. Legally."

Bobby had read of a few of these stores in the *Times*, with names like Queequeg's, Armature, Evolution, and he knew there were another fifty places like them around the country.

"Some people have too much money," Bobby said.

"Most of it was mail-order stuff from overseas," Giselle said. "He had clipping from the newspapers about it, the new craze. People get arrested for selling certain stuff like fetuses, ashtrays made from gorilla hands, stools made from elephant feet, shit like that. But he just likes the rare bones. I know he wanted some special bones but they were illegal, endangered species or some shit like that. I asked him once why he collected that stuff, and he said that there was only so much art you could collect. He said, 'Anybody can own a Picasso but only one person can own the skull where all that art came from.' That's a sick fuck."

"So he collects beautiful live women and the bones of the dead," Bobby said.

"Men are worse than dogs," Connie said. "At least dogs bury their goddamned bones."

"Sam Kronk buries his bone," said Giselle.

"What little of it there is," said Priscilla.

The women laughed, but Bobby thought there was a lingering sadness locked inside the mirth.

"Connie, I told you, the rich aren't just different," Bobby said. "They're a moral subspecies."

"Don't you lump that macabre mutant in with me," Connie said. "He sounds more like the kind of ghoul your partner Gleason would go robbing graves with. Now, if there's nothing else you need to know, my girls would like to enjoy the rest of their Sunday afternoon. I don't like the way Kronk treated them, or Trevor, so I figured I'd help you out."

"Thanks, ladies," Bobby said. "Connie."

"If you ever need to get in touch with me, you can call me," Giselle said.

"He'll call *me* if he needs to speak to you," Connie said, nudging Giselle and the other girls out of the salon.

"*Now* who's the control freak?" Bobby said

"Go chase bad guys across a roof," Connie said.

The women laughed as they left *The Fifth Amendment* with Connie. Bobby smiled. In the morning, there were a few people he would be chasing.

18

AUGUST 1

Izzy was released on $350,000 bail a few minutes past three AM. He rattled Bobby from sleep at five with a phone call.

"Wait'll I find this bamboo bimbo," he said.

Bobby warned Izzy to stay away from Betty Wang or else he'd be charged with witness tampering.

"After a night in a cage with every kind of white-trash mutant and non-Caucasian madman they make, it would have been nice to come home and visit my new pair of business investments," Izzy said. "I give her seven G's honest cash for a pair of new lung warts and she drops a counterfeit dime on me."

"Izzy, you have to concentrate on *why* she did it, not just that she did."

"That's what I have you for. I don't walk around with a magnifying glass and a curved pipe. You're the fuckin' Sherlock."

"Then go lay low and let me find out," Bobby said and hung up.

Herbie Rabinowitz, who was once an A-plus student at the Culinary Institute of America until he was caught selling school food to local stores to pay off mob bookmakers, appeared on board *The Fifth*

Amendment by 6:30 AM, carrying two paper bags. Bobby swallowed a handful of pills—C, B-12, E, DHEA, ginkgo biloba, zinc, a multivitamin, and an aspirin for the heart.

He called his younger brother, Patrick, in Florida at seven and asked him to head back home. He told him that he was going to need him and his legal gun and badge up in New York.

"I'll catch a noon flight," Patrick said.

Bobby did his push-ups and sit-ups as Herbie told him about a shaved-headed, eyebrowless, black-eyed Izzy appearing in front of the judge "in his bar mitzvah suit." In the kitchen, Herbie also prepared a couple of perfect lox-and-onion omelets with bakery-fresh onion rye toast, crispy hashbrowned potatoes, arugula salad with goat cheese, strips of red and yellow peppers, and wedges of luscious Israeli tomatoes. He served it with big, steaming mugs of strong Kona coffee and tall glasses of fresh-squeezed grapefruit juice served over ice cubes with straws.

"If we're gonna kick ass, take names, and leave red stains on white shirts, we gotta eat," Herbie said.

Bobby devoured the food, the best breakfast he could ever remember eating.

After a quick shower, Bobby dressed in black jeans, polished black loafers, a black-collared polo shirt, and a small reversible windbreaker, tan side out. Into one suitcase he packed a gray sports jacket, black dress pants, black jeans, blue jeans, various shirts, sneakers, steel-toed Timberland boots, socks, underwear, toiletries, vitamins. In a separate suitcase he packed some of the Snoop Shop equipment.

He placed both bags into the back of the Jeep. He made sure he had his wallet, cell phone, passport, and his .38. There was already a heavy, black, nylon rope and a grappling hook, climbing boots, belt, and gloves in a box in the back of the Jeep. His toolbox was equipped with pinch bars, screwdrivers, ratchet sets, pliers, Vaseline, fishing tackle, glass cutters, suction cups, channel locks, and hammers. In the glove compartment was a lock-picking set.

"You bringing any luggage?" Bobby asked.

Herbie lifted a large crumpled paper bag, reached in, pulled out a .44 Magnum Colt Anaconda, a toothbrush, Afro pick, three yarmulkes—white, black, and royal blue—and five wrapped stacks of $100 bills. "Mr. Daggart sent fifty grand for expenses," Herbie said. "Says if we need more, I should call."

"No offense, Herbie," Bobby said, "but you've been wearing that same suit since the day before the clap of Creation. It has more stains than Baby Huey's bib. And you smell like night court."

"Been busy, Bobby."

"First expense money we're gonna spend is on some new clothes for you," Bobby said. "And you gotta lose the skypiece, amigo."

"I gotta wear my beanie, Bobby," he said. "Even cousin Izzy says my yid lid is the only thing that keeps my brains from popping out like a jack-in-the-box. As long as I wear this, God won't let no mob wop or mick cop put one behind my ear, no offense to your own ethnic persuasion, Bobby."

"If you can break legs for God, I'm sure Rabbi Berg will give a special dispensation to go without it for a few days," Bobby said. "The yarmulke might stand out where we're going, Herbie."

Herbie touched his yarmulke and worry creased his face.

"And remember, you have no license for that gun," Bobby said.

The first stop was the office of U.S. Attorney Sean Dunne at Cadman Plaza, Brooklyn, a few blocks from the Fulton Shopping Mall and Moe Daggart's NuCent offices in Metro Tech.

"Leave your gun here and go buy a suit and have the one you're wearing dry-cleaned and burned," Bobby said. "Buy some casual, dark-colored clothes to last you for a few days. Shirts, socks and underwear, and a reversible jacket, tan on one side, dark on the other, with a hood. And get a jumbo can of Right Guard, a razor, aftershave, Listerine. Then meet me back here in a half-hour."

Herbie walked off toward Fulton Street.

Sean Dunne saw Bobby right away. He offered him a seat, which he didn't take, preferring to pace instead. Through the office window Bobby could see the

Brooklyn waterfront and the Manhattan skyline, the same vista as from Moe Daggart's plush offices.

"I expected you but not so soon," Dunne said.

"Why?"

"Because you saw me in the alley with Noel Christmas," Dunne said. "And you're probably wondering why I'd be in Manhattan, which is not my district."

"That occurred to me," Bobby said. "But of course Jimmy Chung lived in Brooklyn."

"Right."

"But that's not the reason you were there, was it?"

"I can't discuss this with you, Bobby," Dunne said. "It's an ongoing investigation. You should know that."

"But the investigation isn't just about Jimmy Chung, is it?"

"How do you mean?"

"The newspaper clips tell me Chung worked for big people," Bobby said. "Friends of yours. The mayor, for example. He helped get him Asian votes in both his elections. In the Chinatowns of Brooklyn, Queens, Manhattan."

"That's hardly a federal offense," Dunne said.

"Unless he carried bags of campaign money across state lines," Bobby said. "Like from Jersey, just across the George Washington Bridge or through the Lincoln Tunnel, and it wound up on Eighth Avenue in Sunset Park, where Chung lived, and where little old seamstresses with no English sent in thousand-dollar money orders to local pols. If my career taught me anything, Sean, it was that not all politics is local. Just dirty politics."

"And you think this Jimmy Chung was doing this?"

"Maybe. By the way, your brother works in Jersey, doesn't he?"

"Yeah . . ."

"For Sam Kronk, no?"

"Look, my brother Donald and I rarely speak about business."

"I know about the sibling rivalry. Twins are known to either adore or hate each other. Especially when one outdoes the other. You both started at Quantico together. You both climbed the ladder quickly. Except *you* became a bureau chief, and then a U.S. attorney. And *he* got marooned in Cleveland, where he took an early retirement a few years back. I remember him as one tenacious but brutal field fed, a loose cannon. But you were slicker, the polished pol, the loyal company man, going to the right dinners, working on the right campaigns, getting appointments, like this one."

"Donald doesn't blame me for how his career went," Dunne said, checking his watch. "Our career paths took us different ways. This is no secret. I hope you didn't come here to rehash old gossip about me and my brother, Bobby, because I have nothing to add. I might not always see eye to eye with Donald, but he is my blood. And if you think Chung was a bag man for Kronk, show me some evidence, I'll look into it. Meanwhile, I have to be in court in ten minutes on an entirely different matter. The world really is bigger than you, Jimmy Chung, and Izzy Gleason."

"Chung might have been part of something bigger."

"Like what?"

Bobby took out a pack of peppermint Tic Tacs and rattled the box in front of Dunne. "Do me a favor, will ya," he said, fanning Dunne's breath. Dunne self-consciously held out his hand and Bobby tapped a few mints into his palm. Dunne slapped them into his open mouth, sucked on them vigorously. Bobby turned his back on Dunne, walked to the window, pointed at Moe Daggart's gambling boat, which lay in dry dock at the Brooklyn pier. "Why'd you go after Daggart and his boat, Sean?"

"*Please*," Dunne said, "the guy's dirtier than a pigpen. We can't have him tooting around like Mark Twain on a Mississippi gambling boat off the coast of New York."

"The pundits seem to think it was a blatant favor to the mayor. Who was doing it for Sam Kronk. Who is your brother's boss."

"I've been friendly with the mayor for twenty years," Dunne said, "since he had this job. But I'm not beholden to him. He's the mayor of the city. My job is federal. I just agreed with him that it looked awful having Moe Daggart running legal gambling out of the city. I found a legitimate law and I enforced it. Period."

Bobby didn't mention that Amy McCoy had seen him get into a car with Ben Lee two days before, at the Golden Pagoda. Some things were better left unsaid until he knew more himself. Max Roth was checking out Ben Lee and he might give Bobby some better ammo to fire at Sean Dunne the next time they met.

"So as far as you know," Bobby said, "Jimmy Chung is just a guy from Brooklyn who maybe got murdered in Manhattan, and so you went to see Noel Christmas at the crime scene to check it out?"

"Like I said, I can't talk about ongoing investigations," Dunne said, munching the Tic Tacs now.

"So there's more to it, then?" Bobby said.

"I didn't say that," Dunne said.

"You didn't deny it, either," Bobby said, stepping toward him, cocking his head. "Look, I gotta tell you, Sean, my client just got bailed out of night court on three-fifty large for the murder of Jimmy Chung. Christmas had hauled Chung's ass in for killing the McCoy couple only two days ago. Then he hauls Gleason's ass in for killing Chung yesterday. This stinks from the head. I know that you know more than you're saying, but so do I, pal. And I promise, before this is over I'll be hauling in a few more jail-addressed asses myself. I am not going to sit around and let my guy get framed for a crime both me, you, and Christmas know he didn't commit. You can stonewall me all you want. You can threaten me, too. I've been there before."

"Sounds like you're threatening *me*, Bobby," Dunne said, drawing his lips taut. "So, I'll remind you, I am a United States attorney."

"I don't give a rat's ass what you call yourself," Bobby said. "You're just another crummy pol on the make. Me and you never liked each other, Sean, even when we had to work on cross-jurisdictional cases together. But I always cooperated with you because you were a fed and because my boss was a politician. But get this straight—I don't have a boss anymore. I answer to me."

Bobby stepped closer, popped a Tic Tac in his mouth, and leaned his face an inch from the prosecutor's. "So fuck you, Fed. Fuck your brother. Fuck the mayor. Fuck Sam Kronk. I've eaten bigger and gamier fish than you for lunch."

Dunne stood, staring back, anger venting. Bobby fanned the air again, stuffed the pack of Tic Tacs in U.S. Attorney Sean Dunne's breast pocket, and left.

19

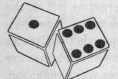 "You're losing your marbles," Herbie said after they pulled over at a rest stop to get gas on the way to Atlantic City.

"Maybe it is a coincidence," Bobby said, checking his car for bugs again with the pen-shaped bug detector. "But I'm telling you, that red Dodge Durango has been no more than five car lengths behind us since we left Brooklyn."

"There's a *nun* driving the Durango," Herbie said. "I went and checked it like you said. And it's a *nun.*"

"Priests, rabbis, ministers—why not a nun? Start a choir."

"Who do you think dresses funnier? Cat'lick nuns or your average Hasid with white socks and everything else black?"

Bobby finished sweeping the car for bugs. There weren't any.

"Both of them probably look at Hare Krishnas like they're oddballs," Bobby said. "I could never quite understand making fashion statements to an entity that delivers us naked into the world. But if it helps get you through the night, God bless 'em one and all."

"Are nuns like priests? I mean are they allowed to, you know, bury the baloney?" Herbie asked.

"Nuns are celibate just like priests and brothers," Bobby said. "They refrain from sex because they're married to God. When I was in Catholic grammar school, the joke was that they were called nuns because they didn't get none."

"None what?"

Bobby looked at Herbie and blinked, twice. "Never mind."

"Oh!" said Herbie as the joke clicked. He laughed. "I get it. Okay, then that solves it! Nuns are weirder than Hasids. I mean, a Hasid might dress like it's thirty below zero on the Fourth of July but at least he gets to bang out a full accounting firm of kids when he takes the costume off at night. That settles that then, once and for all. Nuns are definitely weirder than Hasids."

"You're a regular theologian, Herbie."

They drove out of the gas station, passing the red Durango. Bobby slowed and saw the back of the nun's habit as she rummaged on her front seat. Bobby shrugged and kept driving for Atlantic City.

Herbie went to the front desk to check in under his name.

Bobby stood with the suitcases and reconnoitered the lobby and the casino of the tacky Kronk Castle. Kronk had a standing reputation for cutting corners and using shoddy, sub-code materials and bent-nose contractors in his construction. This monument to himself was no different. Hyped as the jewel

in the tiara of Atlantic City, once made famous by the
Steel Pier, Miss America, and the Monopoly board
game, the Kronk Castle was built more like a tenement on Baltic Avenue than a Boardwalk hotel. Once
you got past the shimmering mirage of its exterior,
the Castle resembled a glorified Motel 6. Bobby
knocked on a wall, heard the hollow echo, saw the
mismatched seams of the chintzy, glittering wallpaper
covering the Sheetrock. Herbie drifted over while
the clerk clicked at a computer keyboard. Bobby
pointed to the carpet on the floor, a third-rate synthetic in blinding Day-Glo green with a scattering of
forest-green dollar signs. "I've seen better rugs on
game-show hosts," Bobby said.

The support columns were covered with cheap
mirrors to promote the illusion of more space than
there really was. But the reflections were distorted,
like TV screens with weak picture tubes. The furniture in the lobby was durable but gaudy.

"I dunno, Bobby, lots a people think it's got
style," Herbie said.

"Yeah," Bobby said. "It's called Postmodern
American Shit."

Bobby drifted into the loud casino, where the
blinking computerized slot machines and the rattle
of money mixed together in a pulsating assault on
the senses. It was designed to keep gamblers from
concentrating. Euro-trash, Asian millionaires, jive
rappers, Oklahoma oil dudes, working stiffs, and
yuppie suits jammed around the fifty-two blackjack

tables, twenty-four craps tables, fourteen roulette tables, thirty-five keno seats, shouting at the cards and the dice and the spinning wheels. Waitresses in their thirties—too old to be Kronkettes—wearing minidresses and tight Kronk Castle T-shirts delivered drinks to the gamblers.

Middle-American retired couples and the proverbial little old ladies in tennis sneakers played the 1,900 slot machines, some of them sitting on bar stools, leaning on walkers, clutching cups of coins. Some of the slot machines were situated at eye level for the handicapped in wheelchairs. *Every last quarter*, Bobby thought.

Retired heavyweight boxers, has-been tennis pros, once-popular football and basketball and baseball players, and entertainers who were famous for just shy of fifteen minutes in the seventies or eighties drifted through the casino, signing autographs, greeting people, schmoozing. They were paid to talk to people about what they used to be or almost had been. They had the yellowed, crinkled look of their old newspaper clippings and Bobby thought there was something terribly sad and desperate about it all. The standing Os and the roar of the crowd mournfully reduced to a handshake and idle chitchat with tourists. Bobby passed the all-night restaurant where burgers were twelve bucks, and a couple of upscale restaurants where entrees started at thirty. He looked into a barbershop, a beauty salon, a few boutiques. He stopped and gazed out a big window at the immense swimming pool area, where hundreds of people sat broiling themselves on deck chairs and where whole families splashed together in the noon sun. Overweight women insisted on wearing bikinis. Men with hairy beer guts cultivated over losing football seasons drank more beer in the ocean breeze. There was an I-don't-give-a-shit-if-I-croak mentality that pervaded the behavior of gamblers on vacation. They were here to eat, drink, smoke, get laid, gamble hard-earned money. Bobby envied their cavalier attitude. It was a high-wire act, life without a net, and it took a certain amount of balls. They gambled their health along with the mortgage, and if they threw an early seven, they'd probably die happy.

He saw a surge of sunbathers rush to the fenced-in tennis court, peering through the partly camou-flaged cage. The men were ogling and the women were oohing and aahing. Bobby couldn't see who was on the court. Probably a couple of celebrities, here for a fundraising tournament.

As he strode through the casino and circled back to the lobby, he noticed that Kronk Castle security was everywhere. Uniformed square-badge rent-a-cops patrolled, stern-faced but professionally pleas-ant, their uniforms as crisp as the tablecloths in a four-star restaurant. But Bobby also immediately spotted the plainclothes security men, middle-aged guys with earpieces, carrying corresponding hand radios. They strutted the lobby, every one of them wearing identical gray sports jackets with a tiny gold KC on the left lapel and black patent-leather thick-rubber-soled shoes. They tried their best to look casual, but with tight ties and starched collars in mid-summer they were about as subtle as feds at a mob funeral.

Most of them were in their mid-forties and in good shape. But the security guy in charge, wearing a navy-blue blazer, was a plump balding man with bug eyes. He wore a sneer like a decal of authority. Bobby thought he looked vaguely familiar but couldn't remember where he'd seen him before.

Bobby watched a gray-jacket escort a pretty young woman past the concierge's desk, and open a plain black door with a computerized key card.

Bobby stopped, pulled a handful of quarters from his pants pocket, fed them into a slot machine, and watched in the wiggly mirror of a support column as the gray-jacket led the woman through the plain black door. Bobby knew immediately that was the door leading to the private elevator that went to Sam Kronk's exclusive thirteenth floor, where his secret harem of Kronkettes was housed.

Bobby lost a buck and a half in quarters, and when the black door closed, he walked back to the front desk.

Herbie handed him his room key as a bellman came over to grab their bags, which included Bobby's two suitcases and three shopping bags containing Herbie's new clothes. Herbie clutched the bellman's wrist. "I look like one of Jerry Lewis's kids to you?" Herbie asked the bellman. "I carry my own bags."

"Thanks, anyway," Bobby said to the bellman, handing him ten of Moe Daggart's bucks for his efforts. "I'll carry mine, too."

Bobby walked toward the main elevators, pausing to watch two more beautiful young women in their early twenties being quickly ushered toward the plain black door by another security man, this one dressed in a maroon blazer. Bobby recognized him immediately. Donald "Dum Dum" Dunne carried an unlit cigar in one hand and a hand radio in the other, and wore the corresponding earpiece. He stopped to give frantic directions to three gray-jacketed security men, pointing with the big cigar and dispensing orders. The three men separated and moved with alacrity on their assigned missions.

Dum Dum Dunne was the identical twin of his brother, Sean, but he walked with more swagger, his eyes more calculating. He jammed the unlit cigar into his mouth, held the door for the two Kronkettes, one a long-haired flaming redhead, the other a short-haired platinum blonde, and shooed them in. They breezed past Dum Dum in their youthful splendor. *Kids,* Bobby thought, *just kids, six or seven years older than Maggie, and this vile prick Kronk is using them as human party favors. Little sex slaves, in a private fuck-parlor decorated with human skulls. If ever someone needed an old-fashioned general-principle asskicking it was Samuel Kronk.*

Once the two Kronkettes were safely inside, Dum Dum Dunne slammed the black door and scrutinized the lobby, spoke urgently into his radio. Suddenly a commotion erupted at the front doors of the hotel, sending a shiver through the crowd.

Bobby saw a flying wedge of uniformed and plainclothes security men marching from the front doors into the lobby like Secret Servicemen escorting a president. In the pocket of the flying wedge was Sam Kronk, sweaty in tennis shorts and shirt, tinted shades, custom-made white tennis sneakers. He had a perfect tan and he waved with his racquet to the people who stared at him as he passed. On his arm was a gorgeous dark-haired woman, also gleaming with a healthy sheen of perspiration, wearing tennis whites. When he saw her, Bobby's heart began to thump.

Zelda Savarese looked as beautiful as she had that day when he'd first seen her on the court at Forest Hills seven years ago. Up close, in person, the famous beauty mark on her high right cheekbone still made Bobby want to reach out and touch her. She had a hypnotic, magnetic quality that was almost spooky. She turned cynics into swooning groupies. Although she'd had a stormy relationship with the press in the past couple of years, she looked like she was *supposed* to be famous.

Bobby saw the guard in the blue blazer signal to Dum Dum, who in turn motioned to a gray-jacket who held a phalanx of paparazzi penned behind a silk rope. The gray-jacket unhooked the rope, setting loose the herd of photographers, who circled Kronk and Zelda Savarese, strobes popping. Bobby's racing heart hit a speed bump when he saw Sam Kronk kiss Zelda Savarese on the lips.

It was a prearranged photo-op for the next day's tabloid gossip pages. Zelda looped her arm around Kronk's waist, leaned her head against his shoulder. Then they kissed again, a deep, lingering one this time.

"Are there any wedding plans in the works, Sam?" shouted a tabloid hack with an Australian accent.

"We're taking it one step at a time," Kronk said.

"Are you in love, Zelda?" asked another reporter.

"Right now you can say I'm in-*volved*," Zelda said, flashing a gleaming smile, her sweaty hair stabbing down in long black spikes. "We're not ruling anything out."

The security men surrounded the couple and moved them through the crowd, past Bobby and Herbie, toward a private penthouse-suite elevator. This was the elevator he took with the women in his public life.

"One smack and this guy shatters like a wine-glass," Herbie said.

As they passed, Bobby stared at Kronk's face, covered in waterproof makeup for the cameras, his perfect toupee like a crash helmet, the lifts in his custom-made tennis shoes tilting him forward at a slight angle, the special belly-bulge T-shirt girdling him into his white shorts, the whole performance making him glow with a shabby halo of money. Bobby thought Kronk looked like a man who truly believed he held the deed to the universe. *I'd love to foreclose on it*, Bobby thought.

Bobby stared at Zelda Savarese, just feet away from him, her celebrated face a few tiny lines older than her publicity photographs. Still, a truly fabulous-looking woman.

But something is wrong with this picture, he thought as he momentarily caught Kronk's eye. Kronk nodded as if Bobby were just another supplicant with his nose pressed to the bulletproof glass of the rich. Bobby stared back with unblinking eyes and Kronk looked quickly away. Kronk *paid* people to look at strangers.

Now Bobby caught Zelda Savarese's eye and she seemed to half-smile. He remembered the photo of her kissing Moe Daggart and thought there was something wrong with that picture, too. *Maybe it's just that I'm not the guy in either picture*, he thought. *Silly immature jealousy*.

But he thought there was something else amiss here. It all just didn't fit together. Bobby and Zelda held the eye-contact for several seconds, long enough for Kronk to notice. He followed her stare to Bobby.

Bobby looked at Kronk, imagined him without the rug, the girdle, and the lifts and broke up laughing. His laughter flustered Kronk.

Zelda smiled at Bobby and the moment was broken when a surge of fans reached out with autograph books or simply to touch the magic couple for superstitious gambler's luck. Kronk shook a few hands. Zelda scribbled in several autograph books. Bobby saw a frazzled Dum Dum glancing in his direction and turned his head. It had been five or six years since they'd last met but Bobby didn't want Dum Dum to recognize him. Yet.

Kronk whispered into Dum Dum's ear. He nodded and turned toward his boss, the one wearing the blue jacket, the one Bobby thought looked vaguely familiar.

"Ralph," Dum Dum said, "he says make sure we keep the twos and threes away."

Bobby knew "twos and threes" was copspeak for blacks and Hispanics. On police arrest forms the multiple choice boxes denoting race were usually stacked in a uniform order: 1)white, 2)black, 3)Hispanic, 4)Asian, 5)other. Thus "twos and threes" were law-enforcement code words for "niggers and spics."

"Got that, Ralph?" Dum Dum said.

"Roger," said the dumpy bug-eyed one named Ralph.

Bobby now knew he was Ralph Paragon, head of Kronk security. Ralph Paragon was also the name of the owner of the dark Lumina that had been tailing him. Bobby stared at him, narrowing his eyes, thinking harder, and now he remembered where he'd seen his face before. In that five-year-old photo Maggie had printed, the one where Kronk, Mayor Brady, and

Jimmy Chung were breaking ground for the hotel in Chinatown in Manhattan.

If this was Ralph Paragon, Bobby suspected he was somehow a player in all of this, a man with ties to the principals of this treacherous alliance.

Paragon testily beckoned Dum Dum to his side and said, "In front of my guys, you call me *Chief,* not Ralph."

"Sure, Chief," Dum Dum said, twirling his unlit cigar.

Dum Dum returned to Kronk's side. Bobby watched Paragon whisper directions to another security man, who relayed it to the others. Soon all the security people were pushing the minority fans away from Kronk and Savarese, who finally made it into the private elevator. Then, through the crowd, standing and watching, like an incongruous apparition, Bobby saw a nun. She wore large dark glasses and she seemed to be staring at Kronk, her hands jammed in the loose puffy sleeves of her opposite arms.

Bobby thought she looked vaguely familiar, wondered if it was the same nun from the red Durango. He was distracted by Dum Dum Dunne, who followed Kronk and Zelda into the private elevator. The door slammed shut and Ralph Paragon directed two uniformed guards to stand sentry outside it.

Bobby looked back toward the nun. She was gone.

The press hurried away to file their pictures and gossip items. The gaping crowd in the lobby dispersed in excited chatter. Some compared autographs; some commented on what a great couple "Sam and Zelda" made, as if they were family members. Bobby could understand their adulation of Zelda Savarese, who in addition to her natural beauty was a great sports talent, a champion. But how could anyone admire a man just because he had made a lot of money? Much of it dishonest money, lifted from the paychecks of working people like themselves.

"I shook Sam Kronk's hand," one southern man said, holding up his right hand like an icon of worship. "Now I'm gonna roll dice with this here hand that shook the hand of *The Man*."

Bobby heard the bell for the public elevator gong. He and Herbie entered and he pressed number fourteen.

They checked into their separate but adjoining rooms. Bobby's had a queen-size bed with a polyester bedspread, dull-gray shag rugs, matching canvas drapes, an oil painting of sailboats on the Atlantic— screwed into the wall—and a little desk and chair. Bobby found the room safe in the bottom of his closet, placed his gun and passport in it, punched in Maggie's birthday as the security code, and locked it. He opened the door that adjoined his room to Herbie's and knocked on his door. Herbie opened it. Bobby showed him how to lock his gun and most of the cash in the safe.

"Fucking safe is so small I could tear it outta the floor and wear it for a beeper," Herbie said. "Besides, I wanna carry my gun."

Bobby convinced him it was a bad idea. For now. And he put forty grand in the safe and gave Bobby most of the other ten.

"You gamble five," Bobby said. "I'll carry the rest."

Herbie walked to the window and opened the drapes.

"Great view," Herbie said, opening a sliding door and stepping out onto a small balcony. "I come to Atlantic City and all I get to look at is the parking lot."

Bobby leaned over the railing and saw that the next balcony was two floors down. Floor number thirteen didn't have any balconies. There didn't seem to be any windows, just air conditioners built into the brick. He traced the line of air conditioners to the end of the building and noticed a lone bay window on the far end of the thirteenth floor. *Probably Kronk's bedroom,* Bobby thought.

He told Herbie as little as possible about what he knew so far. He figured the less Herbie knew the less he could inadvertently blab.

Bobby stepped out into the hall and hurried down the corridor. He determined that the room above the thirteenth-floor bay window was the fourteenth-floor linen supply room. He tried the door. Locked.

He went back to his room, making a mental note of a glass panel with a fire ax and an extinguisher.

"Herbie," Bobby said, as a loose end nagged him. "That nun in the red Dodge Durango . . ."

"Bobby, this is A.C., there's a million broads, they

wear price tags around their necks, and you're interested in a *nun*?"

"Did you get a good look at her?"

"I looked at her, yeah."

"What did she look like?"

"Look like? Fuck kinda question is that? I couldn't
pick a Hasid out of a lineup if he killed my Aunt Ruth,
and I'm a Jew. You expect me to remember what a
Cat'lick nun looks like? She looked like a maitre d'
with a hood. I don't mean no disrespect, Bobby, but
when you see a nun, you don't, like, check her out,
know what I'm sayin'?"

"Young, old, black, white, yellow?"

"I guess she was youngish," Herbie said, scratching
his head. "Nuns, you don't see the face, you see the
cloth. Like cops. Me, I see a nun wearing the prayer
beads and that cross with Jesus nailed to it, I look away
like Dracula. I see a cop, I walk the other way."

"Was she wearing sunglasses?"

Herbie thought for a moment. "Now that you
mention it, maybe," Herbie said. "But, ya know, like
Jackie O glasses. Big. For driving, I guess. It's sunny
out, Bobby. Funny, but you never see a Hasid wearing shades. If Moses was leading a Hasid across the
Sinai and offered him a pair of Ray-Bans, he'd stick
with his reading glasses."

Bobby knew he wasn't going to get any more
details. "Let's go gamble Moe's money," Bobby said.

Herbie's eyes widened like a kid's going to an
amusement park.

20

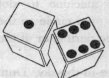

Bobby watched Herbie drop twelve hundred at a blackjack table as rapidly as a guy paying for a fast-food lunch.

"If I could wear my sky piece I'd be winning," he whispered to Bobby. "Without it I'm just another mope drawing cards. With my yarmulke, God knows I'm one of his chosen people."

"Just choose a card, Herbie. I'm gonna circulate."

"Hit me," Herbie said to the croupier. "Before I hit you."

The croupier looked at Herbie in astonishment, then at his pit boss, who nodded to a gray-jacket. The croupier gave him a card. "Over," the croupier said, scooping up Herbie's chips.

Bobby drifted into the crowd, checking out the security men, glancing at the eye-in-the-sky security camera that scanned the floor for card counters, people working signal routines, pickpockets, and assorted other scam artists. Bobby finally spotted Ralph Paragon. Bobby turned his back to him, put on his Snoop Shop rearview glasses, and plugged some silver dollars into a slot machine. Bobby saw Paragon speak to two of his security guards, giving them casual orders, sending them on their rounds.

Paragon was soon joined by Dum Dum Dunne,

who was clearly Paragon's number two. The pair strode through the casino, whispering to subordinates, checking on the climate. A cop on the beat would call it "taking the temperature of the situation." Bobby hopped from slot machine to slot machine, and finally saw the two men circle to the rear of one of the three bars on the perimeter of the main casino.

Outside the scope of the eye-in-the-sky, Dum Dum and Ralph entered a back door to a half-busy bar called the Straight Flush Saloon, which was decorated in an unimaginative western motif with hitching posts, saddle-scooped stools, brass spittoons, a player piano. Paintings of saloon-girl dancers, Annie Oakley, Wyatt Earp, and Doc Holliday hung on the walls above about a dozen Japanese tourists, who sat at old-fashioned card tables, sipping whiskey. The fortyish bartender was dressed in jeans with a big western belt buckle, garish western shirt, and a lariat instead of a tie. When he saw Dum Dum and Ralph enter the back room he made two quick drinks and carried them through a pair of saloon-style swinging doors at the service entrance from the bar.

Bobby passed the back door the two security men had entered, furtively peered through the diamond-shaped window, saw the room was furnished with plush rawhide-covered booths and upholstered snugs and faux kerosene lamps that were wired with low-light bulbs to promote intimacy. Dum Dum and Ralph were seated at a booth, sipping their drinks. Dunne was talking on a plain, black desktop hard-wired phone. Ralph was making entries in a log book. Bobby walked to a strategically located slot machine, and started playing quarters, keeping an eye on the back door to the private room. After fifteen minutes he saw the two men leave.

He waited two minutes after they had disappeared back into the casino, put away the rearview glasses, and took a seat at the bar. There were only two other customers seated at the bar. A cocktail waitress stood idly by, waiting for the Japanese at the tables to buy another round.

Bobby ordered a cranberry juice with soda from the bartender, who wore a name tag that identified him as Gerry, and paid for it with a hundred-dollar chip.

"Keep the change," Bobby said.

"Hey, thanks, buddy," the barman said, slipping the chip into his shirt pocket and snapping the pearl button closed.

"On a streak. Hey, you know, I could have sworn I recognized one of those guys who just left the back room."

Gerry looked surprised. "Them?"

"Yeah, I'm from New York. I'm here with a few buddies from the Bureau for a few days, chilling out after a big case."

"Bureau? FBI?"

"Don't broadcast it," Bobby said, smiling, looking around cautiously. "Yeah, I could have sworn I used to work with one of those guys. Ralph, Ralph Paragon?"

"Yeah, that's him," the bartender said. "He's the security bigwig here. You could probably contact him in his office. You can get it through the switchboard. It's up on the second floor, room 233, I think."

"I don't want to disturb them when they're on duty."

"Ralph and Mr. Don Dunne, his deputy . . ."

"Not *the* Donald Dunne?" Bobby said, feigning shock. "Jesus, I thought he looked familiar too. He's a legend in the Bureau."

"Really? He works right under Ralph Paragon. Good guy. Takes shit from nobody."

"Sounds like him," Bobby said. "Usually catch them here?"

"They clock long hours, man. They usually work noon to ten or even midnight," Gerry said. "And they come by here for lunch at four and after that for their ten-minute breaks every two hours on the hour, have a coffee, or a cocktail, a smoke, shoot the breeze, make a call on a hard phone because they're always afraid their cellular phones and hand radios are being monitored. It's like their private office away from the office back there. This place is off-limits to the other security guys. Once a week, on a Wednesday, Mr. Dunne even interviews new greeter girls back there."

"The dirty dog," Bobby said with a smile. He felt the buzz of his beeper, which was set to vibrate, and he checked the number. Maggie was calling him.

"You gotta see some of the broads he finds," Gerry said, shaking his hand as if it were on fire. "I'd like to have his job for one day. Chicks from little tank towns all over the country, from Europe, some from New York and Philly. All on the make."

"And he makes them all."

"Actually he says he doesn't touch the private stock."

"Private stock?"

"He interviews them for Uncle Sam," Gerry said. "Mr. Kronk has always been fond of the young ladies."

"Dunne just gets to interview them?"

"Yeah," Gerry said. "Your pal Ralph interviews the male help. I kid him that his wife arranged it that way. Dunne's single, so he has no problem."

"What kind of guys does Ralph interview?"

"Almost all of them are like you, from the Bureau. Actually Don screens them and Ralph approves them. He's too busy with nuts and bolts to deal with hiring and firing. Why, looking for a job?"

"Nah," Bobby said. "Not yet. Got another ten till retirement. But I'll talk to them about it anyway."

"Wanna give me your name and room number? I'll have Ralph call ya," Gerry said.

"It's okay," Bobby said, getting up. "Don't mention I was even asking. I'd like to surprise him, okay?"

"Sure," Gerry said, tapping the hundred-dollar chip in his shirt pocket. "Thanks again, pal."

Bobby passed Herbie on the way out of the casino, noticed that he now had a stack of chips in front of him that was beginning to resemble the New York skyline. He also noticed that Herbie was wearing a Mets cap. Bobby stopped.

"A lucky run," Bobby said.

"I was down thirty-five large. I went up and put on a yarmulke, put the Mets hat on top of it. I was you, I'd convert, 'cause I haven't pulled a bad card since."

"You *are* a card, Herbie," Bobby said. "I have some calls to make. Don't maim anyone while I'm gone."

"Sure, Bobby," Herbie said, raising his bet by five hundred dollars and then looking at the croupier. "Hit me, mother-jumper."

When he got to his room, Bobby called Maggie.

"Hi, Daddy," she said faintly.

There was a crack in her voice that sent a chasm through his heart. "What's wrong, baby?"

"Nothin'," Maggie said.

"Hey, what about our deal? Remember? No lies, all truth, even when it hurts, because a lie always hurts more?"

There was a long silence and then Maggie said, "Cal."

Rage filled Bobby's head like a poison gas. "Did he touch you, baby? Did he hurt you?"

"Nothing like that, Daddy," she said.

He felt minor relief. But his kid was in pain. He knew she must have been ripped apart inside to be calling him *Daddy*. She hadn't called him that since she turned fourteen. "What did Cal do to you, Maggie?"

"I discovered his password and hacked into his PC," she said. "I got suspicious when he sent an e-mail to my address but it was to a girl named Wanda. I wanted to get into his PC to see what he and Wanda were up to . . ."

"Sometimes you're better off not knowing," Bobby said. "There's an old saying, 'Beware of what you wish for.'"

"I wish for Cal to burn in hell," she said. "I tried all the usual AOL passwords. His middle name, his mother's maiden name, the last four digits of his Social Security number, his dog's name. Then I remembered that Cal and his friends were always talking about something called 'sebab.' Like it was some kind of code. And they'd laugh. So I tried it, and sure enough S-E-B-A-B was his password. And when I got into his messages, there was all this e-mail between him and Wanda. And a million other girls, some at school, girls in other schools, older girls. Then I figured out that 'sebab' was 'babes' spelled backwards. Mom's right, all men are dogs."

"Hey," Bobby said.

"Except you," she said.

And so now he had a kid with her first broken heart.

"Sometimes when you snoop you find what you don't want to know," Bobby said. "Believe me, I know. It's what I do. And so many people are disappointing."

"It sucks," she said. "It's like a physical pain."

"It's worse than physical pain," Bobby said. "Don't worry that it hurts. It's supposed to. But you'll learn not to trust guys so much. Especially when they're older than you."

"I don't want to tell Mom, because she hated Cal without ever meeting him," Maggie said. "She'll say it was because he was a shanty scholarship kid."

"Wait until you catch a rich-kid two-timer and *then* tell Mom."

Maggie laughed, which made Bobby feel better.

"What should I do, Pop?"

"Did you tell this Cal creep what you know, yet?" Bobby asked.

"No," Maggie said.

"Then say nothing," Bobby said. "Just go to the wall on him. Pretend he doesn't exist. Like you've matured beyond him. A guy who uses 'babes' backwards as a password has an ego-gratification problem. So hit him in his ego. Make him feel inadequate. Small. Beneath your dignity. Not because of his financial status, or his looks, or anything superficial like that. No, make him and everyone else think he's *boring*. Nothing hurts a male ego more than a girl saying he's a snooze.

When he tries to talk to you, just pretend to snore. Then keep walking, head high. Spread that wire on him to the other girls at school, too. Say you broke up with him because you were bored to tears. See how much e-mail he gets then."

"Old man, you are the best!" she said. "I'll hit the snooze button and drop an e-mail bomb on him."

"You'll be having too much fun watching him squirm to think about your broken heart, kiddo," Bobby said.

"Cool," she said. "Oh, by the way, I got that information for you. About that guy Ralph Paragon, like you asked."

"Great," Bobby said.

"I did that search of Rapa Properties and I found out that the phone bill is paid every month by none other than Ralph Paragon."

"Rapa, the first two initials of each of his names," Bobby said. "So Paragon owns 22 Empire Court?"

"Sort of, but it's complicated," she said. "I looked for other properties owned by Rapa, and all the other buildings in that two-block area that have been abandoned over the past few years have been bought up by Waterfront Holdings, which is the sub-whatever-you-call-it of Rapa Properties."

"Subsidiary," Bobby said. "You found this out from the Buildings Department?"

"Yep," she said. "They're on-line. And then I traced how they became abandoned. One building on Ellis Walk was evacuated on account of a flood fifteen months ago. Another on that same block burned seventeen months ago. Nine months ago on Empire Court there was one building that just collapsed. There was a gas explosion in another one six months ago. After they were all abandoned, Waterfront Holdings bought them for Rapa Properties."

"Maggie, there's a bureaucracy called the New York State Division of Corporations and State Records," Bobby said.

"I checked it," she said. "But that's New York State. Rapa is actually incorporated in New Jersey with the Kentucky mailing address. So I opened up my copy of *How to Investigate by Computer* by Ralph D. Thomas and it suggested I access Dun and Bradstreet's On-Line, which I did through Dialog Business Connection."

"I believe you, Mag. Cut to the paper chase."

"Dun On-Line lists 1.4 million businesses. I typed in Rapa Properties and it gave me the same Louisville address, the same phone number, and yearly sales, which was zero. *And* the owners and officers. The owner of Rapa is listed as Ralph Paragon. The officers are Toni S. Paragon—Toni with an *i*, the girl's way—and George S. Paragon."

"What do you want to bet Toni and George Paragon are his wife and son?"

"No bet," Maggie said. "I checked with the Jersey Matrimony Bureau. You're right. They were married four years ago. This any help?"

"Lots, kiddo," he said.

"One more thing. Rapa Properties has two other subsidiaries. One named Lucky Eight Inc., which owns a farm in New Jersey."

"Which you traced the license plate of the white van to."

"Guess who the manager of Lucky Eight Farm is?"

"Jimmy Chung," Bobby said.

"Right. And the other subsidiary is something called Bamboo Therapeutics Inc., which is really a massage parlor in lower Manhattan called . . ."

"The Bamboo Rack, also probably managed by Jimmy Chung."

"Correcto," she said.

"You're a cyber queen," Bobby said. "I want you to print that information out and fax it to me here at my room. And, Mag—thanks."

"Thank *you*, old man," Maggie said. "For your advice."

Back to old man, he thought. *Progress. She's going to be okay*. "Just remember, when it comes to Cal, snooze is the word."

Maggie faked a snore. "Gotta go spread it around. Love ya."

"Ditto, kiddo," he said.

He gave her the fax number and in less than ten minutes the transmission began. Bobby was going to give the information to Max Roth to use in his column. He could imagine the headline: KRONK AIDE TIED TO MISSING COUPLE.

But he was going to wait until the time was right.

Paragon had a wife and kid. He wanted to be sure he was right before he had a whole family smeared in print. He folded the papers and put them in his back pocket.

Bobby opened his suitcase that was filled with the equipment from the Snoop Shop. He chose a three-inch-square voice-activated micro telephone tape recorder with a three-hour tape. It would activate immediately when a phone was picked up and stop when it was hung up. He covered the small tape recorder with double-backed duct tape. He thought of using an FM transmitter microphone to bug normal conversation, but instead chose another tiny VOX tape recorder because they could not be detected with a bug detector since they did not transmit radio waves. Gerry the barman had already said both Paragon and Dum Dum were slightly paranoid about eavesdroppers.

He quickly changed into dark jeans, pulled on a dark T-shirt, reversed his jacket to the navy side, and tied on a pair of white sneakers.

Now he donned a high-quality medium-length dirty-blond wig made of yak hair—which was closest to human hair—with long bushy sideburns and matching goatee that he had bought months ago from Incognito, a disguise store in Manhattan that served the movie and theater industry. He knew from undercover experience in the past that the best way to wear a wig was under a hat, so that no one could see the weave line. He tugged a Yankees cap over the wig, and put on the pair of rearview shades. He looked in the mirror and nodded hello to a stranger.

Down in the casino he stood at Herbie's table long enough to be sure not even Herbie recognized him. Herbie's once towering Manhattan skyline of chips was slowly starting to resemble Newark. Bobby saw Herbie take a slug of straight scotch. It made Bobby shudder to think of Herbie with a nasty drunk on.

He crossed the casino to the bar area and checked his watch. It was 3:46. In fourteen minutes Dum Dum and Ralph Paragon would be coming by for their lunch. Bobby watched the half-empty bar for five minutes until he saw a party of guys all stumble from the casino into bar stools, shouting war-whoops and counting their chips.

As they ordered a round from Gerry the bartender, Bobby walked to the side door. He had to act quickly. He stepped inside, his sneakers silent on the wooden floor, and hurried directly to the booth where he'd seen Dum Dum and Ralph sitting earlier. He took one of the small recorders and affixed it to the underside of the table with the double-backed duct tape, careful not to make it visible or obtrusive in case one of them crossed his legs and accidentally kicked it. His shoulder hit the table and the phone on top rattled in its cradle, making the bell ping faintly.

He froze.

Then Bobby heard Gerry coming his way and he scurried behind the booth. The barman peeked in, looked around curiously, then heard his new customers calling for their drinks. Gerry went back to serving his customers.

Bobby traced the hard-wire phone to a wall jack located behind a fake potted plant near a men's room. He unplugged the phone from the jack, plugged it into a double-jack adapter, and then plugged in the user-activated, three-hour micro tape recorder. He hid the recorder in the green styrofoam gravel of the potted plant.

Bobby heard the swinging door from the bar open again. He checked his watch: 3:57 PM.

"Don? Mr. Paragon? You in there?" Gerry asked.

Bobby remained hidden behind the fake plant. He saw the top leaves shivering slightly and he held his breath. Gerry took two steps into the back room.

"How long I gotta wait for that gah-damn stinger, fella?" shouted a half-drunk bar patron.

Bobby's lungs were ready to burst when he heard the bartender going back to his bar. "I'm coming, I'm coming," he intoned as the swinging doors flapped behind him.

Bobby exhaled and crawled toward the side door on his hands and knees. He was at the door when he suddenly realized he'd forgotten to activate both recorders to a standby automatic VOX mode. He rushed back to the booth table, snicked the switch. He scrambled back to the machine in the potted plant and activated that one.

His watch told him it was 3:59.

He got up and walked as quickly as he could to the side door, opened it, and slinked out. Then he heard the swinging doors and Gerry's voice from inside.

"Don? Mr. Paragon? . . . Jesus Christ, I'm fuckin' hearing things."

Bobby walked to the nearest slot machine and pushed in some quarters.

At exactly 4:01 PM, Dum Dum Dunne and Ralph Paragon circled in from their casino rounds and furtively ducked into the back room of the Straight Flush Saloon. Bobby saw Gerry the bartender open the swinging doors to greet them, pantomiming a big hello to Dum Dum and Paragon.

21

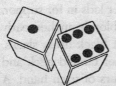

Bobby went back to his room, put on his sports jacket, dark chinos, white shirt, tie, and polished loafers. He kept on the same disguise, only this time he stopped by the gift shop in the lobby and bought a Panama Jack straw hat to wear on top of the wig. He couldn't do business with a Yankee cap on.

He drove forty-five minutes north, to the Bay Head address Maggie had gotten from the New Jersey DMV for the dark-blue Lumina registered to Ralph Paragon.

Bobby sat in his Jeep in the immaculate suburban community of single-family homes on generous, half-acre plots. He stared up at the large Colonial house on a small hillock above the quiet street for twenty minutes. White Corinthian pillars, white picket fence, white mailbox with black and gold letters that spelled PARAGON. He could see a Mainship 47 motor yacht tied to a private dock on the inlet behind the house.

A brand-new silver Mercedes 450 SL was parked in the driveway. The Lumina was nowhere in sight. Probably in the employees' parking lot at Kronk Castle. *He takes the wind wagon to work to look modest and honest*, Bobby thought. *He leaves the Mercedes at home, where he lives large and dirty*.

He saw a boy of about nine in a wet bathing suit come tear-assing from around the back pool-area of the house, a playful cocker spaniel chasing him across the big green lawn. Then Bobby saw Toni Paragon step out of the front door to call her kids in for supper. She was a tall, stunning-looking blonde in her early thirties, dressed in heels and tight black dress slacks. She wore strings of gold around her tanned neck and large-gemmed rings on three fingers of each hand. A small apron was fastened around her thin waist and she held a wooden stirring spoon in her right hand stained red with tomato sauce. Mrs. Paragon looked like the kind of wife a man would risk a speeding ticket to get home to at night. Especially if she said *she* was in the mood. She also looked like the kind of high-maintenance young wife a middle-aged gnome like Paragon would beg, borrow, and steal to hang on to.

"Come on, Georgie," she shouted, a big white smile gleaming against the deep tan that Bobby figured she'd gotten lying poolside out back. She holstered the spoon in her apron pocket, pounded her chest, and made ape noises. "Uh-uh-uh," she mimicked, pointing to her open mouth, and then pounded again on her chest like Mighty Joe Young. Her son laughed. The dog barked and ran in berserk circles. Bobby laughed aloud from the vantage of his car. The lady was funny.

The kid ran past his mother into the house as she tousled his hair and playfully slapped the wooden spoon off his bottom. He already knew a lot about her. She cooks, she keeps an immaculate house, she stays in fabulous shape, she loves her kid, she manages to keep a smile on her beautiful face.

Some guys have all the luck, Bobby thought. *And it still isn't enough.*

Paragon runs security for Kronk, top salary maybe $100,000, $125,000 a year. No way he can afford the mortgage on this house plus a new Benz, a brand-new Mainship 47. And the wife's jewelry and a second car.

One word came to Bobby's mind—*dirty.*

Bobby was certain Paragon was more than a

floor-walking card-counter cop. *Why the hell else would he have been following me around in his Lumina all over New York? He had to be balls deep in this McCoy-Chung-Kronk mess.*

He drove to the next corner, made a right, parked on a side street, out of view of Paragon's house. He waited five more minutes until he knew the kid would be served his dinner and then he'd catch her at that most vulnerable moment. He walked up the street to the pathway to the house, rang the doorbell. Toni Paragon answered with a polite, inquisitive smile.

"Hi, help ya?"

She was even prettier up close, big hazel eyes, not a red line in them. Her tight tanned skin was fuzzed with a platinum down by the temples and on her bare arms. She looked around for Bobby's car but didn't see it. That seemed to make her uneasy.

"Mrs. Paragon? Toni S. Paragon?"

"Yes?"

"I was wondering if you drive a dark-blue Lumina," Bobby said. "Plate number SN2-78K?"

"Is something wrong?" she asked, suddenly concerned.

"No," Bobby said, looking past her into the expensively furnished home, a chandelier in the foyer, a formal dining room with a table big enough to sign the Magna Carta, big fireplace in the living room, overstuffed sofas and lounge chairs.

"I'm from radio station WKGB and we spotted

the license-plate number driving in Manhattan on Saturday night. We're having a sweepstakes contest. Your phone is unlisted, so I'm here to tell you in person that Ralph Paragon is one of ten finalists whose names have been entered into a drawing for a trip to Las Vegas."

"Oh . . . that's . . . nice," she said, regaining her composure. "Very nice. Thanks. I thought maybe something horrible had happened."

"Is your husband home, ma'am?"

"He's on the way," she said, trying to close the door. "Any minute now. Thanks for stopping by. Now I have to go."

"Don't you want to know about the second and third prizes?" he asked.

"Oh, knowing Ralph the way I do, he wouldn't be interested in second or third prize," she said. "And I doubt he'd even want a trip to Las Vegas. He doesn't gamble, doesn't like the nightlife. He's a homebody, a family man."

"Well, you don't mind if we keep in touch, do you?"

"Look, I have to get back to making dinner," she said. "Sorry, I have no time. Drop us a note. You obviously have the address. Bye, sorry, bye now, gotta go."

She gently closed the door. He heard her lock it and fasten a chain.

Ralph Paragon was a thieving asshole, and she was a beautiful, dedicated wife, dutifully waiting for him to come home for his dinner, Bobby thought. She had been so concerned when she thought something had happened to him. She wasn't going to take it very well when he packed his toothbrush and kissed her goodbye before he left for a long life in jail. If he was lucky. Because like New Jersey, New York now had a death penalty.

Herbie reluctantly left the blackjack table at 6:45 PM, down by almost four thousand dollars. Bobby had shed his disguise and led Herbie through the casino toward the Straight Flush Saloon. He told Herbie to take a seat at the bar, order a drink, and then start an argument.

"No problem," Herbie said. "I'm in a foul mood anyway. Who you want me to lip off to?"

"The bartender, a customer, I don't care," Bobby said. "Pick a face you don't like. I need the bartender distracted for a few minutes."

"I could body slam him onto a baccarat table if you want," Herbie said.

"That would be excessive," Bobby said.

"Not really, I'm pissed pi-squared about dropping four grand of Mr. Daggart's money."

"Just tell the bartender that he makes a shitty, watered-down drink," Bobby said. "A distraction, not a disaster, Herbie."

Herbie approached the bar and Bobby took his spot by the slot machine nearest the back door. Herbie took a seat at the crowded bar, his Mets hat on backward now, revealing a piece of the yarmulke underneath it.

"Yo, beernuts, gimme a Manhattan," Herbie said,

snapping his fingers loudly. "And make it taste like Brooklyn."

A clearly tired Gerry looked through the crowd toward the arrogant big man demanding a drink. He nodded and turned to make the drink. Bobby walked directly into the back door, disengaged the micro recorder from under the table of the booth.

"Yo, shit-for-brains," Bobby heard Herbie shout. "I asked for a fuckin' Manhattan. This tastes like a Long Island Iced Tea. I look like a stooge from the burbs to you, beernuts?"

"I don't have to take this," shouted the bartender. "You're a nasty guy, so I'm not serving you at all."

Bobby hurried to the potted plant and unplugged the other tape recorder and the double-jack adapter. He plugged the hard phone line into the regular jack.

"When I say a Manhattan, I mean Manhattan, home of the Rangers, not the fuckin' Islanders, understand?" Herbie said.

"Hey, Frankenstein, you're outta line," Bobby heard another guy scream.

Bobby slipped out the back door, the tape recorders safely in his pockets.

As Bobby saw two uniformed security guards rush to the scene, he caught Herbie's eye and signaled for him to cool it. Herbie did.

"Sorry," Herbie said meekly, handing Gerry two hundred-dollar poker chips. "Sorry, pally."

The uniformed guards approached, each wielding a baton.

"We have a problem here?" the younger of the two guards asked.

"No," Gerry said, securing the two poker chips in his shirt pocket. "Just a minor misunderstanding."

"I was just leaving," Herbie said.

"Good idea," said the older guard. "We've had a few complaints about you, now. You were abusive with a croupier earlier."

Bobby motioned for Herbie to meet him upstairs. Herbie brushed by the uniformed guards and walked across the casino toward the elevators.

Bobby sent Herbie to his room for a shower and then locked himself in his own room, where he listened to the tapes for the next hour. He listened first to the one recorded at the table. Mostly mundane, banal banter, two guys talking shop. They talked about a boxing weigh-in and press conference that would take place on the Boardwalk in front of Kronk Castle at 8:00 PM. Two top heavyweight contenders would be fighting the next night, the victor getting a title shot here at Kronk Castle in December.

"... millions of twos and threes around for that," said Dum Dum. "He bringing the Savarese chick with him?" Paragon asked.

"Yeah," Dum Dum said.

"Why you think he hates the coloreds so much?" Paragon asked.

"I don't think he hates them so much as he's afraid of them. Me, I think they remind him of his nannies," Dunne said. "Remind him that he was raised by the help instead of a mother and father. The spics he don't mind too much. He loves Spanish broads."

"He loves all kinds of broads," Paragon said. "I couldn't handle that kind of life."

"You really like the faithful little missus at home, huh?" Dunne said.

"Yeah," Paragon said. "Matter of fact I do. Something to be said for it. There's never an extra dollar in the house but I'm happy. She also works her butt off to bring in extra cash."

What a bullshit artist, Bobby thought. He tried to tabulate the value of Paragon's controlling interest on all the Rapa properties that would be used for the Empire Island Terminal. He thought of the Mercedes in his driveway. The Mainship yacht. The big house. The high-maintenance wife. Even a farm somewhere here in Jersey. Paragon wasn't fronting for Kronk for nothing. He was going to get his reward. But what Bobby found odd as he listened to the rest of the tape was that Dunne seemed to be in the dark. There was no mention of anything to do with Empire Island Terminal, the McCoys, Izzy Gleason, Mayor Brady, the gambling bill in the New York State Legislature.

"Better get back," Paragon said. "I want you to make sure the guys are careful out there on the Boardwalk. It's an unprotected environment. Outdoors. The public."

"*I'll handle it,*" Dum Dum said. "*Don't worry about me.*"

Then Bobby heard a long silence as if the two of them had left together. In the silence the machine clicked off. Then he heard it activate again as if they had reentered. This time there were no bantering voices. He heard someone dialing a telephone but all he could hear was mumbles, as if the man's hand were cupped over his mouth and the mouthpiece of the phone as he spoke. Bobby couldn't tell which one it was, Dunne or Paragon. Christ, it could have been Gerry the bartender for all he knew.

Bobby quickly changed to the telephone tape. Only a brief piece of the tape was used. He heard two rings and then heard someone using a voice changer answer with a mechanical hello.

Whoever was at the phone in the rear of the Straight Flush Saloon also used a voice changer. It sounded like two people speaking underwater.

"*Number One?*"

"*Yes,*" answered the person on the other end.

"*This is Number Two.*"

"*Any news?*" asked Number One.

"*Everything is fine,*" said Number Two.

"*I'm getting nervous,*" said Number One.

"*Don't,*" said Number Two. "*After August sixth, it's history waiting to happen.*"

"*What if they don't get the votes in Albany?*" asked Number One.

"*We're all going to Puerto Rico on the private jet*

tomorrow afternoon," said Number Two. "To make sure we do. It'll all be sorted out down there where no one will be recognized."

"Good, then I want all the players there," said Number One.

"Including you?"

"Maybe," said Number One. "Maybe not."

"It's risky. But you're the boss."

"Everything must go smoothly. I've put too much time, too many years, into this for it to go wrong. What about the other businesses in New York?"

"That's going the way it's supposed to go," said Number Two. "The right people are following the breadcrumb trail to the Big Bad Wolf."

"Good," said Number One. "I have to go."

The tape went silent and the machine automatically clicked off. Bobby lay on the big bed, digesting all he'd heard. He listened to it again. Three times.

He picked up the hotel phone and then thought better of it and used his own cell phone. He called information, got the number for American Airlines, dialed the airline, and was put on hold. He paced the room, walked to the window, distractedly peered out at the parking lot as he listened to the Muzak. Twilight descended on Atlantic City. And then in the mystical light he saw her.

The nun.

Getting out of the red Dodge Durango and walking toward the back entrance of the lobby. She walked like a woman on a mission. *What the hell was a nun doing . . .*

"Thank you for calling American Airlines," the cheerful operator said. "May I help you?"

"Yes," Bobby said. "I'd like to book a seat to San Juan tomorrow morning, please. Yes, coach—no, someone else is paying. Let's make that first class."

The nun was gone and after a few minutes the operator confirmed a seat to San Juan. He thought about checking into the Kronk Caribbean. Instead, he booked himself a room in the Caribe Hilton, on the same glorious stretch of beach, a great hotel where he'd stayed a few years before when he'd gone to retrieve a prisoner from Puerto Rico on a fugitive warrant for a New York murder.

Bobby checked his messages at his 800 number. Izzy had called, wanting a progress report. "I could use a few bucks from Daggart's expense money myself," Izzy said. "My fucking spine needs walking on something terrible after sitting in lockup all night. And what about the soft women I asked about? Oh, and what about my murder charge? Call me."

Bobby's brother Patrick had also left a message saying he was back in town like Bobby had asked, waiting for his call. The last message was from Ben Lee. "Bobby . . . Ben . . . we gotta talk," he said, sounding urgent. "It's very important. About who and what we talked about when you were here. Something I found out from Hong Kong. Plus, I have something else about the girl witness. You know who I mean. I can't talk on the phone. Come see me at the restaurant tomorrow, a little after midnight. We'll be closed. We really need to talk. Call me if you can't make it, otherwise I'll expect you then. Ciao."

Herbie banged on his adjoining door. Bobby opened it.

"The front desk just called me," Herbie said. "They want me out of the hotel. Giving me to eight o'clock tonight or they'll have the cops up here."

"Not surprised," Bobby said. "You're a troublemaker, Herbie. And a sore loser. But don't worry, theologians throughout history have been misunderstood."

"I know," he said. "Look what happened to Kahane. So what're we gonna do?"

"We leave," Bobby said.

"But they ain't givin' me a chance to win Mr. Daggart's money back."

"Pack," Bobby said. "I want to catch a press conference before we leave."

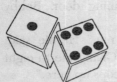

22

After checking out, Herbie and Bobby loaded their suitcases into the Jeep and set the alarm. Bobby saw the red Durango parked near the stairs leading up to the Boardwalk and this time he took down the license plate number—New York KY3-67J.

"We get the bum's rush and you're still chasing nuns?" Herbie said. "You're getting worse than Cousin Izzy."

They climbed the stairs where Bobby saw bubbling neon and digital billboards dazzling the Boardwalk under an immense starry sky. A steady breeze blew in off the Atlantic. A giddy anticipatory crowd had formed outside Kronk Castle, where an ersatz boxing ring had been set up to hold the weigh-in and to promote the following night's heavyweight brawl.

The fighters had not yet arrived, but already different factions of supporters in the crowd were shouting out the name of their man. A ragtag crew of print reporters, perhaps the worst-dressed white-collar professionals in the universe, stood around comparing notes and exchanging jokes. TV news crews from ESPN, Sports Channel, and a few of the networks had set up their cameras. Klieg lights bathed the mock ring, where Boxing Commission officials gathered around an imposing scale, waiting for the fighters to arrive for the weigh-in.

A bunch of once-famous sports and entertainment greeters milled through the crowd, each one escorted by a Kronkette and a gray-jacket, each one stopping to pose for pictures for grubby paparazzi.

The crowd on the Boardwalk began to swell when the fighters finally emerged from separate doors of the hotel and walked up opposing ramps to the ring, surrounded by uniformed guards and handlers. The chanting of the crowd grew louder, almost feverish.

Strobes flashed and videotape rolled. The fighters climbed through the loose ropes and pranced around with their arms aloft. Now and then, when they converged, they paused to eyeball and trash-talk each other. Reporters jotted down every word, cameras taped it all. The fighters went nose to nose, feigning violence, but were separated by their handlers.

All at once the paparazzi and the crowd turned away from the fighters and the ring toward the hotel. The strobes popped and the floodlights blazed.

Bobby turned and saw the flying wedge of gray-jackets and uniformed square-badges cutting through the crowd to make way for Sam Kronk and Zelda Savarese. Kronk wore a tuxedo and Zelda looked splendid in a simple tight white minidress, showing off her deep tan and stunning figure.

"This guy's life is an infomercial," Herbie said.

Bobby followed their approach. Zelda Savarese

seemed frightened by the clawing crowd. She flinched, cowered, appeared trapped. Bobby read her lips as she said, "I hate this shit."

She scanned the crowd, searching. She met Bobby's eyes. She half-smiled—again—the way she had in the hotel lobby earlier in the day. She rolled her eyes as if to express her displeasure with the situation. *She's looking right at me,* Bobby thought. *Why me? God, don't stop . . .*

As the flying wedge pushed through the crowd toward the ring, Zelda kept looking at Bobby, the smile becoming more sly, the eyes so dark, so beautiful. *And still looking at me,* he thought.

"She's lookin' at you, Bobby," Herbie said.

Kronk was beaming for the cameras, waving to the crowd, but when he turned to look at Zelda, he noticed that she was staring at Bobby. Bobby felt Kronk's glare and looked him straight in the eye. The rich man blinked, trying to place Bobby's face. He glanced back at Zelda, saw she was still staring at Bobby. Kronk leaned close to her ear and Bobby could see him mouth the words, "Who's he?" She shrugged and kept her eyes on Bobby, who didn't break the connection. Until something out the corner of his eye—a black blur—stole his attention.

He broke eye contact with Zelda Savarese. Glanced toward the distraction. *The nun.*

She was angling through the crowd, head bent, making her way toward Kronk and Zelda Savarese. The cowl shielded her face.

Her hands were again buried in the opposite puffy sleeves of her loose habit.

She's out of a different picture, Bobby thought.

Completely out of place. She half-turned. He saw her big sunglasses—at night. Adrenaline pumped in him.

He looked back at Zelda Savarese. She had followed his eyes to the nun. Zelda seemed suddenly alarmed. The crowd was chanting her name. *"Zel-da! Zel-da! Zel-da!"*

"Zelda, what's a class act like you doing with an asshole like Kronk?" shouted a fan in the crowd. He was quickly surrounded by uniformed security guards and hustled across the Boardwalk. The man broke loose and punched one security guard, knocking him to the Boardwalk. Another man from the crowd rushed to his side and began brawling with the security guards. A blood thirst bubbled in the air as the security men beat the men with blackjacks and hand radios. A sweaty shiver rocked the crowd.

Autograph hounds, paparazzi, worshipful fans turned from a trapped Zelda to watch the furious melee. Zelda looked at Bobby, as if for help. He looked into her eyes. Then back at the nun—who was now four feet from Kronk and Zelda.

Bobby saw the nun's hands suddenly emerge from their opposite sleeves. He saw the right hand swish into sight, a TV light glinting on the small Sauer Pocket .25-caliber automatic. Bobby pushed through the distracted crowd. He looked at a bewildered Kronk. Then

at Dum Dum Dunne and Ralph Paragon, who were
excitedly elbowing fans out of the way, oblivious of the
danger, trying only to get to the brawl.

"Sorry, Sister," said Dum Dum as he brushed by
the nun.

Ralph Paragon even made room for her.

Her gun hand came up waist high, the barrel
pointed at Kronk. Zelda saw the gun, her eyes grew
wide, looking at Bobby.

Bobby snatched the pistol from the nun. Then
grabbed her wrist with his free hand and spun her
around. He stashed the gun in his pocket and held
the nun's wrist amid the shouting and the screams
and the pushing and swaying of the crowd. His grip
immediately loosened when he saw a part of her
cowled face. *Jesus Christ, she looks like Amy McCoy*,
he thought.

"Yo, let go of the sister, bro!" shouted a man who
grabbed at Bobby's hand. No one else but Zelda had
seen her raise the gun.

"*Amy?*" Bobby said, but her face was covered in
sunglasses, shrouded in shadow and the habit as she
bowed her head.

The nun abruptly slapped his face, pushing away
into the pulsating crowd, which parted to let her pass.

"Oh, shit," yelled a fight fan. "My man got hisself
smacked and double dissed by a sob-sister!"

Bobby stood in shock.

"Bobby, you fuckin' nuts?" Herbie said. "Grabbin'
a nun!"

Bobby looked back at an astonished Zelda Savarese who kept staring at him even as she was rushed toward the ring, mouthing the question: *"Who are you?"* Bobby looked at her as Kronk stepped through the ropes to mixed cheers and jeers. He held out his hand for Zelda but she hesitated, and she and Kronk exchanged words.

Bobby knew he could always find Zelda Savarese so he went after the nun, pushing through the reluctant crowd.

"Hey, don't be fuckin' pushin' me, man," one guy said, pushing Bobby.

Herbie yanked the man toward him like he was on wheels. "You don't like gettin' pushed?" Herbie said. "Then hows about I pull your fuckin' arm off?"

"Chill, Herbie," Bobby said and then put Herbie between himself and the crowd, which he parted like a snowplow. Bobby sprinted to the parking lot. Just in time for the red Dodge Durango to race past him, heading north, toward New York. He decided not to chase her; he already had the plate number.

He waited for Herbie to catch up and then climbed into the Jeep.

"What the hell was that all about?" Herbie asked.

"I've been getting smacked by nuns all my life," Bobby said.

"It looked like the same nun from the gas station on the way down," Herbie said. "You think she followed us?"

Bobby wasn't sure, but the less he told anyone,

the better, until he figured out how all the pieces fit together. He started the car.

"I have things to do and people to see back in New York," Bobby said. He never mentioned the planned trip to Puerto Rico.

Bobby drove slowly toward the exit of the parking lot. A woman dressed in white stepped in front of the Jeep. It was Zelda Savarese, waving for him to stop. He did.

"Bobby, that's . . ."

"I know," he said.

Zelda walked to his window. "Can I buy you a drink?"

"Sure," Bobby said. "Where?"

"Anywhere but this dump," she said, climbing into the backseat.

They sat in a small corner booth in the bar of Trump's Taj Mahal hotel, farther down the Boardwalk. Herbie was in the casino shooting craps.

"How did you know she had a gun?" Zelda asked.

"I didn't," Bobby said. "*She* just didn't belong."

"You watch people," she said. "I noticed you this afternoon in the lobby. You watched everything, everyone."

"If you noticed me then you must be observant yourself," he said.

"You don't like Sam Kronk, do you?"

"I never met the man," he said.

"I could tell by the way you looked at him," she

said. "Like he was beneath your contempt. I don't like him either."

"You don't like him, but you're with him?"

"No, he's with me," she said. "There's a difference."

"You let him be with you."

Zelda slid closer to Bobby in the booth, looked him in the eyes, searching for answers. She smelled like a fashion show, the perfume expensive and plentiful. She almost made him nervous. *Don't be disarmed by her fame, her talent, her beauty,* he thought. *This chick sleeps with Sam Kronk.*

"Who *are* you?" she asked.

He was tempted to mention the photograph of her and Moe Daggart but he had to control himself. It was a hole card. He wanted to know more about her, get her to tell him about Kronk first. He'd mine her for information about Daggart later.

"I'm just a guy you asked out for a drink," he said. "I'm also a fan. I saw you play at Forest Hills about eight years ago."

"Am I really that old?" she said.

"You were twenty then."

"God, I remember it as another lifetime," Zelda said, sighing.

"You didn't notice me in the crowd then."

She smiled that fabulous smile and his heart leapt. She was even sexier to look at here in the soft candlelight, across a cocktail table, than she was in the little white dress on the court.

"I think you're some kind of cop," she said. "You're too polite to be a reporter. No way you work for Sam. He'd never have anyone as good-looking or as confident as you working for him. It would bring out his own shortcomings."

"If you're trying to use flattery to win my heart it won't work," he said. "You already won it a long time ago."

"Now I'm flattered," she said.

She had seen his Jeep, she wasn't stupid, she could remember a plate number. He knew she could trace the plates to Izzy Gleason, who owned it, and find out who he was. Any one of Kronk's ex-feds could figure out who he was in a half-hour.

"I *was* a cop," Bobby said. "I'm retired."

"And now you work for who?"

"For myself. But I also do some work for a lawyer," he said. "It's a long story."

"Married? I don't see a ring."

"Retired from that, too."

"I'm single."

"I know, but you're spoken for. It's in the papers, Zelda. Every day."

She nodded, her eyes dancing with reflections of the candle flame. She stirred her white wine spritzer.

"I'm also in a bind," she said.

Christ, he thought, *everybody wants to hire me.*

"I don't work for people on first dates," he said.

"Sam Kronk has something I want," she said.

"And how many billion would that be?"

She gave him a wounded look, nodded, and waved for the waiter to bring her a check.

"I guess I picked the wrong guy," she said, still insulted. "Again . . ."

"Sorry, that was uncalled for."

"Look, I don't want his money," she said. "He has something that belongs to me."

Bobby thought about the vault where Giselle said Kronk kept the raunchy videotapes of the Kronkettes.

"Is he blackmailing you?"

"Not exactly," she said. "I mean he doesn't extort money from me. He doesn't want to marry me. He just wants me to *be* with him."

Bobby took a long sip of his ginger ale with lime.

"You mean he blackmails you into appearing with him in public?"

"That's right."

"You're saying nothing happens when you go up to his penthouse? Trying to say maybe he's gay, uses you as a beard?"

"No, he isn't gay," she said. "I wish. Sam is, well, this *bastard* says I'm too fucking *old* for him to have a sexual relationship with. Not that I'm interested, mind you, because I find him gross and revolting. But he does want me to go through a whole public charade of dating, courting, maybe even get engaged. Announce a wedding date . . ."

"A year of cheesy publicity on the arm of a sports queen," Bobby said. "And then the bust-up and on to the next victim."

"I knew you were as smart as you look."

"And you figured all this about me by watching me take a gun off a little nun?" Bobby said.

The waiter brought the check. Bobby reached for it. She put her warm hand on top of his. Clasped it. Looked at him and whispered, "I invited you." She took a wallet out of her small bag, placed a credit card on the check. In an ID window of the opened wallet Bobby saw her New York driver's license with one of the most prestigious addresses in Manhattan, the Dakota, the apartment building at Seventy-second Street and Central Park West. He knew it well. John Lennon had been murdered on the sidewalk outside of it.

"I'm going back to the city tonight," she said. "I'm not scheduled to 'appear' with Sam again until tomorrow. He wanted me here for this silly boxing promotion."

"Thanks for the drink," Bobby said.

"That's it?"

"Was there something else?"

"Actually, I want to hire you to get back what Kronk has that belongs to me," she said and wrote down her phone number with a 212 area code.

"There are a thousand private eyes, lawyers, leg breakers, other people who might be better at this than I am," Bobby said.

"I want someone who's not afraid of him," she said. "You're not. I could tell this afternoon by the way you looked at him. I saw the way he looked at you and couldn't hold your stare. A guy like you scares Sam

Kronk because you don't fear him and you don't look like you're for sale."

"But you want me to work for you?"

"I just want to *rent* you," she said.

"What exactly is it that he has of yours?"

"I'll tell you when you tell me you're working for me," she said.

"Drugs, smuggled diamonds, art treasures, human skulls, anything like that?"

"Nothing like that," she said.

"Could I get arrested for being in possession of whatever it is you want back from him?"

"No."

"Good."

"That means you'll work for me?"

"I'll let you know."

"I better go," she said, standing, shaking his hand. "Thanks for stopping something very ugly from happening out there tonight. You don't even like Sam and yet you saved his life. Maybe mine too."

"You don't have to sing for the Kronk choir to stop someone from shooting him," Bobby said.

"I like a man who still believes in right and wrong."

"Jesus, let's not get corny," he said. "Sometimes I work for bad people. Even people who root against the Roadrunner."

"Sometimes bad can be very good, too," she said.

Bobby stood. "I'll drop you off."

"No," she said. "I shouldn't be seen with you if I can help it. I'll take a Boardwalk trolley."

She looked him in the eyes again. Some women just know when they drive a guy nuts no matter how hard he tries to hide it.

"Oh, by the way," she said, "since you're not a cop anymore, are you allowed to mix business with pleasure?"

"Who's gonna stop me?"

"See what I mean?" she said. "I like your attitude. Bye."

She walked out of the lounge, the muscles in her long athletic legs bunching as she strolled through the lobby of the Trump Casino toward the Boardwalk exit.

Gorgeous, he thought.

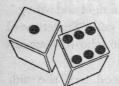

On the drive home from Atlantic City, Herbie fell asleep in the back of the Jeep. Bobby called Maggie and asked her to run the plates on the red Durango. She said she would, Bobby said he'd call her in the morning, and they each said they'd pick a star.

He also called his brother Patrick and asked

him to meet him at the West Bank Cafe for a late dinner.

Bobby dropped Herbie off at his house, where he lived with his elderly Aunt Ruth in Bay Terrace, Queens. Herbie gave the rest of the expense money to Bobby.

At the West Bank, Bobby ordered a garden salad and the linguini with shrimp in a light tomato crab sauce. Patrick ordered a steak and fries. Patrick was almost a decade younger than Bobby and had his mother's pale-blue eyes and his father's high cheekbones. With his short blond hair and cheerful demeanor, he looked more like the ice cream man than a sergeant in the NYPD. Patrick ran the PAL in the borough of Brooklyn, which gave him free reign to move around, from neighborhood to neighborhood, wherever city kids needed a ball and an adult to show them a few of life's little rules, like *Shoot hoops, not each other*.

They had already exchanged pleasantries, and as they ate Bobby avoided asking about their mother in Florida because he was feeling guilty about not making it down to visit her. Again. He knew she was sick with Parkinson's disease. Medical science had developed some great new drugs and would probably come up with a miracle cure early in the new century, but most of the new drugs worked only if the insidious disease was caught in the early stages. Mrs. Mary McClelland Emmet had missed that boat by about ten years. The doctors said her condition was now irreversible. Bobby didn't want to hear more bad news before dinner, especially about his mother.

Bobby had filled Patrick in on most of what was going on in the case.

"So you think Izzy was set up by these people with a bogus deed?" Patrick said. "To deflect attention from this guy Ralph Paragon, who is fronting for Sam Kronk to get the property for this Empire Island Terminal?"

"Eddie McCoy was a holdout tenant," Bobby said. "There was no way of getting him out of a rent-controlled apartment. More than that, he was a reporter. And he was on to Kronk. So these people needed to get him out and silence him permanently before someone started to listen. He only wrote for lefty rags, but Christ, the whole Paula Jones case started with a story in some right-wing rag that got picked up by the mainstream press. It was only a matter of time before someone from the legitimate press picked up McCoy's story."

"Someone like Max Roth," Patrick said.

"Exactly," Bobby said. "And so they got this Jimmy Chung to whack the McCoys. Had him sign over a bogus deed to Izzy in lieu of a retainer."

"I'd give a week's pay to hear Plato and Izzy debate ethics."

"In front of a jury he's the best there is," Bobby said. "Contract law and real estate aren't his strong suits. Greed is. So I'm convinced the hooker, Betty Wang, also knew this. She knew Izzy well enough to know he'd run in the middle of the night for a hot client with a piece of property."

"Sounds like our Sleazy Izzy," Patrick said. "So these two set Izzy up?"

"I think what's happening here is that Jimmy Chung went along with being arrested to throw suspicions off someone else," Bobby said. "My bet is he had an alibi but it would come out later, after the trail of the real killer was cold, proving he was somewhere else when the McCoys disappeared. Then, whoever set this all up whacked Jimmy Chung—and left Izzy to take the fall. And paid Betty Wang to testify against Izzy."

"And you think that someone might be Ralph Paragon?" Patrick said.

"He's the one the property reverts back to," Bobby said. "McCoy is out of the building, silenced for good, and the property is free and clear. Whether he did it himself or used subordinates, I don't know. I'm still trying to figure that out. But I'm supposed to meet Ben Lee tomorrow night to see what he knows. He said he had news from Hong Kong about Chung and something else about a witness. I'm guessing he means this Betty Wang."

"And all of this is tied into the vote in the legislature?" Patrick said, as the waitress brought fresh sodas to the table. Bobby asked her for the check. She nodded and walked off.

"In order for a gambling law to go on a public ballot as a *referendum,* a *resolution* must pass both the State Assembly and the State Senate in two consecutive legislatures," Bobby said. "It's already passed once. They vote again on August sixth."

"That's four days from now," Patrick said.

"I know," Bobby said. "That's why they're getting desperate. This whole thing has to come to a boil before then. If it passes next week in the legislature, the citizens get to vote for it on November sixth."

"Which gives them three months to get all their ducks in a row to start building the terminal and the first casino on Empire Island," Patrick said. "Which will be owned by Sam Kronk."

"Which will mean untold millions, billions," Bobby said.

"But if it goes down in flames on August sixth, everyone is shit out of luck," Patrick said.

"That's right," Bobby said, mopping up the remaining sauce from his bowl with crispy bread.

"So this Paragon, you think he's Kronk's bag man?" Patrick said, biting into the last of his well-done steak, picking up a few of the delicious shoestring fries with his fingers.

"I'm starting to think that, yeah," he said. "And if anything goes wrong, using Dum Dum Dunne as the guy who will eventually take the fall. Dum Dum isn't exactly subtle. He can't get out of his own way. He got his nickname about five years ago for using hollow-point dum dum bullets at a kidnap-hostage situation. He shot at the kidnapper who used the hostage as a human shield. The bullet hit the hostage in the shoulder. Which might have been just a flesh wound if he was using regular ammunition. But because it was the dum dum it expanded on impact through the soft tissue and severed a major artery. Killed him. Problem was, he literally jumped the gun while the negotiating team was close to resolving the situation. They transferred Dum Dum to Wisconsin, Cleveland, Idaho. Finally they offered him early retirement and he took it. He wound up going to work for Kronk, under Paragon."

"You think his brother Sean is gonna stand by and let Kronk set him up for a fall?" Patrick asked.

"Sean and Donald Dunne might be twins but they aren't the closest of kin," Bobby said.

"But, Bobby, Jesus Christ, they're still brothers," Patrick said. "Like us. Cain might have killed Abel himself, but I don't think he would have let someone else whack him."

"You might be right," Bobby said. "But Mayor Brady owns Sean Dunne. And Kronk owns Brady. Ultimately, it's Kronk's call. If I'm right, and this is all still very fluid right now, human sacrifice isn't beyond Kronk's capabilities. Everything about the disappearance of the McCoys and Jimmy Chung points to him. Kronk wants Empire Terminal and he'll do what he has to do to get it."

"So what do you want me to do?" Patrick asked.

"Sit on Ralph Paragon," Bobby said. "If I'm right, tomorrow afternoon he'll get on Kronk's private jet to Puerto Rico. There's some kind of summit there about the gambling resolution in the legislature. I want to know who else he sees up here before he gets on that plane. All the players are supposed to meet down there. I'm going down on the third. I don't want anyone to know where I am."

"You want to know who he sees, what he does, where he goes, until he leaves," Patrick said.

"Yeah," said Bobby as the waitress brought the check.

"What about Dum Dum Dunne?"

"They'll be together a lot," Bobby said. "So get details of what he does, too. But stay on Paragon like a bad rash."

He gave Patrick five thousand dollars for a room, a rental car, meals, and to gamble.

"Stakeouts suck," Patrick said.

"Get the local newspaper, circle some houses in the Paragons' area, if anyone stops you, tell them you're house hunting in Bay Head," Bobby said. "Getting a lay of the land."

"Good idea," Patrick said.

Bobby took another gulp of soda. There was a long, awkward, aching silence.

Finally Bobby said, "How's Mom?"

"Older every day," Patrick said. "She misses you. Bad."

Bobby looked pained. "I had every intention of getting down there, with Maggie," Patrick said. "I feel like shit."

"She understands," Patrick said. "But the Parkinson's is getting worse, Bobby. She shakes more.

You can really see it when she holds her teacup and saucer. It sounds like castanets."

"I'm going down as soon as this is over," Bobby said, anger building in him now that this case—these greedy bastards—had gotten in the way of him seeing his ailing mother. Prevented him from bringing Maggie to bask in her grandmother's modest, kind, eloquent goodness—something she didn't see a lot of in Trump Tower.

"I told Mom that, too," Patrick said.

"One way or the other," Bobby said, "I'll see her before the summer is done."

"Good idea," Patrick said. "I don't know how many more she has left."

The two brothers looked at each other, their silence crackling with shared memories of a dead father, a decorated hero cop and first-rate father who had died in a shootout during a third-rate check-cashing robbery stakeout. Memories of a sick mother, of happy family years together, summers in the Coney Island surf, winters sledding on Monument Hill in Prospect Park, years of unqualified love and devotion from a mother who always, *always*, always had time for her kids. And now Bobby couldn't find the time to see her. It made him want to break things—hurt people—especially the ones in his way.

"I better go," Bobby said, smacking some bills on top of the tab. "Gotta get this dirty show on the road."

Patrick nodded and they left the restaurant together.

"Be careful," Patrick said.

"You too, squirt," Bobby said and messed up his kid brother's hair as they parted and walked along West Forty-second Street to their cars. Bobby turned to him one last time and said, "Just in case, bring your gun."

24

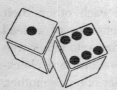

AUGUST 2

He slept fitfully, dreaming of his mother, awakening in a sweaty tangle in the sheets at three AM. He got up and urinated. Something was bothering him about the case but he couldn't figure it out. Something the person who called himself "Number Two" had said on the phone tape: *The right people are following the breadcrumb trail to the Big Bad Wolf.*

Bobby saw the case as a series of calculated chess moves. The pawns were people he knew: Izzy; Noel Christmas; Sean Dunne, whom he knew only professionally; Dum Dum, whom he'd crossed paths with a few times on old cases; Ben Lee; Roth, who had had contacts with Eddie McCoy; the clerics, who knew

Patrick. All of them were being moved around to put a certain king in check, but Bobby was too sleepy to unravel it all.

He felt woozy with guilt about his mother, about not spending time with Maggie while she prepared for her PSATs and tried to mend her first broken heart. He felt uneasy about the loose ends in the case and wondered if *he* was being led down a bread-crumb trail. Who was the Big Bad Wolf? Kronk? Daggart? Mayor Brady?

He went back to bed, tossed and turned, and finally slept for two more hours before Izzy Gleason arrived. Bobby went out on deck under an overcast sky. Izzy had a woman with him. She was in her late thirties, shy, dressed in a modest maroon skirt hemmed just above the knee. She wore low, plain heels, horn-rimmed glasses, and her dark hair was cut in a pageboy. She had an armful of textbooks and spiral notebooks.

"Lucinda, meet Bobby Emmet . . ."

"Lucille," she said.

"Okay, then from now until they crate you off for your dirt nap, you are my little Lulu," Izzy said.

"Good morning, Lucille," Bobby said. "Izzy, it's six-thirty . . ."

"Lulu is my new intern," Izzy said.

"*Intern?*"

"Clinton had one, didn't he? What am I, the wrong color? I'm the *president* of my law firm. I advertised in the *Voice* personals and now I have me a Lulu of an intern."

Lulu looked at Bobby and shrugged. "I want to learn to become a law secretary," Lulu said. "Izzy said he'd teach me everything there is to know."

"Oh, I just bet he did," Bobby said. "Lucille, are you recently divorced, by any chance?"

"What the hell kind of personal question is that?" Izzy asked.

"As a matter of fact I am," said Lulu. "I refused to sit at home while my husband ran around with a younger woman. I'm going to fulfill a lifelong dream and become a legal secretary. Then someday hopefully a lawyer. Izzy has enrolled me in the Katharine Gibbs School."

"Lulu, one of the first courses you gotta take to be a law secretary is Keep Your Trap Shut 101," Izzy said. "The second one is advanced Please Go Wait for Me on the Bench by the Gate. Practice your shorthand, it'll come in handy on some long night."

"I'm sorry, Izzy," she said.

"Lucille," Bobby said. "Don't mind him. It's a good school. You'll do great. He does know the law. He breaks it on the hour."

She walked off the boat and up the walkway, carrying her books in her hands. Storm clouds were moving across the sky and the wind riffled the river and made the Silverton bob in its slip.

"There will be a special room with your name on it in the sub-basement of hell," Bobby said. "That woman is in obvious pain. And you're trying to exploit her."

"I put her in a fuckin' *school,* didn't I?" Gleason

said. "That's why I'm here. I need some of Daggart's scratch to pay the tuition. I need a fuckin' secretary to do my briefs for my own case, for the plastic surgeon's case, for the Roadrunner kid. You think I'm my only fuckin' client? I'd fuckin' *starve* representing me, speaking of which, what do you know about *The People versus Israel Gleason?*"

Bobby gave him a quick fill, about his suspicions regarding Kronk and Paragon, and the gambling vote in the legislature and the upcoming meeting in Puerto Rico.

Izzy shrugged, unwrapped a Clark bar and took an airplane-size bottle of Bailey's Irish Cream from his inside jacket pocket and washed the candy bar down with the liqueur.

Bobby told Izzy that he had Patrick watching Paragon, that he'd see Ben Lee after midnight at the Golden Pagoda, and that he was going to Puerto Rico in the morning.

"I wouldn't trust this Ben Lee," Izzy said. "These people are all in the same take-out order."

Izzy opened another little Bailey's bottle and lit a cigarette.

"I need five grand for this softie's tuition," Izzy said. "She got the house from the ex-husband. A piece-of-shit wood-frame in Greenpoint worth just over a hundred large, but, hey, part of the deal is she cooks me dinner while I help her study."

"Don't you hurt her, Izzy," Bobby said, counting out six thousand, an extra thousand for himself.

"I don't mistreat women, Bobby," Izzy said. "I just love them in a very unique way. I put them on the road to self-discovery and self-improvement."

"Then how come they always hit the road?" Bobby said.

"I can't help it if I don't tie these broads down," Izzy said. "This one here, little Lulu, after six months with me, she gets a crash course in legal secretarial skills, she meets interesting people, she gets her confidence back while I throw her a wiggle here and there, she helps me through a tough time while I help her through hers. All in all, I think that's very human of me. How the fuck do you expect me to get in touch with my feminine side without a broad next to me in the sack to show me the ropes?"

"There'll be a rope around your *neck* if you don't get in touch with your *legal* side," Bobby said. "You haven't told me yet what *you* think is going on in your case."

"That's why I have you working for me," Izzy said, tossing one of the little liqueur bottles over his shoulder into the river.

"Hey!" Bobby said. "You just littered the goddamned river!"

"So what? If I put a note in it that said 'Help, I'm gettin' gang-banged by Aborigines in Borneo,' then it would be seaworthy? It's a fuckin' bottle in the water. Sea mail."

Bobby watched the bottle bob downriver under the dangerous sky.

"Bobby, you're the best investigator I ever met," Izzy said. "But maybe this time you're looking too high. You're investigating the mayor, Sam Kronk, billions in casino cash. Instead of stopping to smell the roses, set your sights lower and smell the horseshit that's fertilizin' them. The McCoys are dead, buried. Chung will pop up again. He knows they can't convict him without bodies. But he won't come up for air until some big fish goes down, see? I'm not saying the mayor, Kronk, his goons, even this asshole Daggart, might not be involved. I wouldn't trust a golden egg from Mother Goose without a fat Yid with an eye loupe to check the karat count first. Now, there *is* a big picture here, and you're right that Empire Terminal is the top prize. But what I'm saying is that the key to the big picture is little Jimmy Chung. Find that chiseling chink from the bottom shelf who signed over a dummy deed to me and not only do I walk but the whole fuckin' tower of power tumbles. And you'll also find out who whacked the brother of the lovely little rug-muncher who did this to me."

He pulled off his shades to reveal the shiner had gone down slightly and was artfully covered in makeup. "Lulu is caring for me," he said. "She's an expert on black eyes."

"You mean her husband beat her, too?" Bobby asked as he felt the first raindrops fall from the swollen clouds.

"Yeah, so by comparison I'm a real Alan fuckin' Alda," Izzy said. "I think Lulu's brave bully also hid some loot from her, and I'm gonna find it if I have to subpoena him every Thursday from now until he spends it all on carfare."

Sometimes Izzy amazed Bobby. He was representing Lulu in her divorce, pro bono. Coming from an abusive husband, Lulu would probably think Izzy was a sweetheart. Bobby knew he'd never lay a hand on any woman except in lust. Izzy was also right about his own case. In chasing the big players, Bobby had ignored a few of the smaller-fry.

"Don't mention a word to anyone about where I'm going," Bobby said. "Not even to Lulu."

"With that extra grand I'm gonna take her shopping," Izzy said, draining the second booze bottle and leaving the boat as the rain grew steadier. "I'm gonna teach her how a legal secretary is supposed to dress."

"Izzy, don't . . ."

"There's a place called the Pink Pussycat on West Fourth Street," he said, tossing the Bailey's bottle overboard. "They make thong underwear you could floss with. Keep me apprised of how close I am to the never-neverland needle. With any luck, I'll be incognito, wearing a bearded clam under my nose, but I'll have the cell phone with me if you're looking for me."

Bobby showered, dressed in black jeans and boots, put on a ginger-haired wig, mustache, beard, bushy sideburns, a white golf hat, and a reversible jacket with a zip-on rain hood. He rummaged through his

Snoop Shop boxes and strapped on the wristwatch with built-in camera and put on the rearview sunglasses.

He sprayed strategic areas of the boat with liar's powder, threw a rain slicker and a pair of high-power binoculars in the Jeep, and a half-hour later was parked on Seventy-second Street, across from the Dakota, looking at the entrance where Mark David Chapman had blasted his way into rock-and-roll history by murdering the guy who sang "Give Peace a Chance."

Zelda Savarese was another small part of the big picture that Izzy had talked about. It didn't make sense that he should have seen a photograph of her and Moe Daggart together in his office and then seen her on the arm of the man Daggart said was trying to destroy him.

It also didn't make sense that twice she had picked him out of a crowd to lock eyes with. That she should have asked him to have a drink. That she blatantly flirted with him and asked him to work for her on a problem she had with Sam Kronk. He dialed the number she had given him and heard her answer. He pretended to be an Arab looking for a guy named Fuad. She told him he had the wrong number and hung up. He knew she was home and awake. He sat for almost two more hours waiting for her to come out of the Dakota. His ass was numb. His lumbar vertebrae hurt. He was thirsty.

Finally at a little past 11:00 AM, a woman came

out of the Dakota dressed in a big floppy straw hat, sunglasses, big baggy pants, and a peasant blouse. He couldn't tell if it was Zelda, so he lifted the powerful binoculars from the seat and studied her. He saw the mole on her cheek. The best concealer makeup couldn't hide that famous birthmark in the lenses of the powerful binoculars. It was her.

He expected her to hail a cab but she didn't. Instead, she started walking west on Seventy-second Street toward Columbus. *Shit*, Bobby thought, *a foot tail*. He got out and started following her, on the opposite side of the street, as she walked up to Broadway. She turned once, twice, to look over her shoulder. She didn't check across the street. Most subjects never do.

He followed her down into the IRT subway. He bought a copy of the *Daily News* and stood leaning against a support column with his back to her, checking her out with the rearview mirror glasses. She took a book called *Management for Dummies* from her purse and started to read. A number 2 train roared into the station and Bobby waited until she climbed on. He got in the next car. She paid him no mind.

Bobby stood by the access door leading from one car to the next and watched as Zelda took a seat. He thumbed through the *Daily News* and on page 12 found a story about the gambling resolution in the legislature. Assembly Speaker Carl Pinto was supporting the bill. But in a surprise turn of events, Senate Majority Leader Lebelski was now opposing it, citing "unsavory characters that are attracted to legalized gambling." He claimed it was strictly a vote of conscience at this point and that he would listen to reasonable arguments pro and con, but he said, "As a dedicated family man with six kids, I don't think I want to see them raised in a state where mortgage money, retirement savings, and children's tuition are tossed away on a roll of the dice."

Pinto countered, arguing that Lebelski was caving in to pressure from special-interest groups, like the banking lobby from New Jersey, which had contributed heavily to his campaign. Pinto claimed that New Jersey did not want New York to legalize gambling because most of their gamblers came from New York.

"MGM, Resorts International, Bally's, and some of the other big casino owners in the country have put $6 billion of new investments in Atlantic City on hold," Pinto was quoted as saying, "awaiting the outcome of our vote in the New York State Legislature. That's $6 billion just to build casinos in New York. Right now New York residents are spending some $2.35 billion a year in out-of-state casino destinations. New York City–area residents alone make over eleven million out-of-state casino trips a year, more than the combined attendance of the Yankees and the Mets. So it's crazy not to have it here. If Atlantic City can generate $4 billion a year in revenue, New York can triple that."

Bobby thought Kronk's opposition to the New

York resolution was pure pose. Kronk knew gambling was inevitable in New York. And he wanted to position himself to be in the right place at the right time when it came to pass. So he publicly opposed it while surreptitiously putting together the land and the political connections to build Empire Island Terminal once gambling was legalized. It was a brilliant strategy. When it was passed, he would feign defeat, and then clutch victory from the jaws of that defeat.

Bobby found Lebelski's sudden turnaround suspicious. He wondered if it was another Kronk manipulation.

The train roared into Times Square and Bobby saw Zelda get up and prepare to exit. The train stopped, she got off. Bobby paused a moment and stepped off just before the doors closed. He looked around, as if disoriented, looking for directions on an overhead sign. She didn't notice him, and he followed her at a discreet distance up the stairs.

She didn't continue up to the street, however, but went down a different set of stairs and climbed aboard a waiting N train. Bobby again got in the next car. Zelda took a seat and returned to her book. He could barely see her through the graffiti etched in the surface of the shatter-proof glass of the door leading to Zelda's car. But he could easily make out the big hat. He saw her give a panhandler a buck. He kept her in view at each stop until the train rumbled into Brooklyn, stopping at DeKalb Avenue and continuing on toward Bay Ridge.

Where the hell is she going? Bobby wondered. Zelda Savarese taking a subway to Brooklyn? Again, it didn't fit.

After Fifty-ninth Street, the train veered south into the tunnel, then out onto the exterior elevated track toward Dyker Heights and Coney Island. Rain splattered the dirty windows, causing little muddy streams. Bobby looked around. The train was now mostly empty. He sat in a corner seat behind the conductor's cabin, out of view from the next car. He took off his jacket, reversed it from the red to the white side. He took off the white golf cap, shoved it into a jacket pocket, unzipped the hood, and pulled it up. He peeled the lower beard off but left the mustache on his upper lip.

As the train approached Bay Parkway, Bobby stood again, glanced through the window to the next car, and saw Zelda get up. Bobby rushed to the other end of the car, pulled open the door, and went into the next car, so that he was now two car lengths away from Zelda. When the train stopped, he stepped off. Zelda never turned as she walked to the exit of the elevated stop. Bobby hesitated, watching from a perch near the token booth to see what street Zelda would take. She walked up toward Twentieth Avenue.

Bobby bounded down the stairs and followed in the same direction, on the opposite side of the street. Suddenly it dawned on him. The last time he'd been in this neighborhood was with Herbie and it was nighttime. And everything looked a little different. But he was certain that Zelda Savarese was walking toward St. Brian's Church, where that night the basement had looked like the casino at Kronk Castle.

Zelda climbed the steps of the church, looking both ways on the block, though taking no notice of Bobby, and entered.

Bobby followed, passing a sign that read CONFESSIONS TODAY, and took a seat in the last pew of the church. His eyes searched for Zelda. Didn't see her. He knew from the way they were praying that the parishioners who had their heads buried in the pews or at the altar were doing penance.

He heard murmurs from the confessional booth. Murmurs that grew into loud but unintelligible whispers, making heads turn. Bobby knelt, put his face in his hands, but splayed his fingers so he could keep an eye on the confessional. After another minute he saw the curtain pulled aside. Zelda Savarese stormed out of the church. Bobby was about to rise when he saw Father Jack Dooley lurch out of the priest's chamber of the confessional. He looked embarrassed and worried. He genuflected, blessed himself, and followed Zelda out. The congregants all looked up, bewildered and glancing at each other before returning to their penance. Bobby rose, made the sign of the cross—which came as instinctively, even to a retired Catholic, as dotting an *i* or crossing a *t*—and cautiously pursued Zelda and Father Dooley out into the vestibule of the church. It was empty.

He heard a loud, angry exchange from the street and then he heard the screeching of tires. Bobby hurried through the outside door in time to see a battered, ten-year-old Cadillac racing down the street. He saw Father Dooley put up his hands and try to flee. But the car mounted the sidewalk and picked up speed, crushing the priest against the iron fence of the churchyard. Bobby saw Dooley's eyes bulge and then go blank in instant death as blood lapped over his lower lip and down his dark frock.

The Cadillac never stopped, kept racing, sideswiping another car as it roared down the avenue. Bobby turned and saw Zelda Savarese's floppy hat bobbing in the opposite direction, a full block away.

Bobby yanked off his hood, pulled the wig, mustache, and sideburns from his head, shoved them in his pocket.

Bobby looked at the lifeless priest, who lay twisted in the mangled railings of the fence. Screaming women came dashing out of the church, some of them dressed in widow's black and shouting in Italian, some in Spanish. More people sauntered over, in astonished slow motion, from neighboring houses, covering their mouths with their hands, turning away from the horrific sight of Father Dooley's face. One woman fainted; another became sick. More people stepped out of passing cars that stopped in the middle of the avenue. A police car pulled up. Then another.

Then an unmarked police car with a spinning cherry

light squealed to an abrupt halt at a crazy angle. Detective Noel Christmas emerged from the car amid the screaming and the tears and the shouting and the praying and the rain. He walked directly to Bobby.

"This better be good," he said.

"I can't think of one good thing to say," Bobby said.

"Did you see it happen?"

"Yeah. It was a black Caddy, maybe ten years old, needed a paint job. I didn't get the plate. I couldn't get a look at the driver."

"Why?"

"I was sort of watching the padre's life end."

"What the fuck were you doing here, Bobby?"

"What can I tell you," Bobby said. "I'm a sinner. He was hearing confessions."

"I take them, too," Christmas said. "Wanna give me one?"

Bobby looked down the block in the direction Zelda Savarese had run. She was nowhere to be seen. He pulled his hood up over his head.

"What the hell are you doing here?" Bobby asked Christmas. "This is Brooklyn, you're out of your jurisdiction."

Noel Christmas struggled to break open a three-pack of Tums. Bobby took it from him, lanced the cellophane seal with a fingernail, and returned it to Christmas, who bit two tablets out of one of the foil-wrapped rolls.

"This priest called me," Christmas said. "Said he

wanted to talk. Something about Jimmy Chung. I get plenty of crackpot leads. Priests I respond to."

"Me too," Bobby said.

Bobby saw a dark Chrysler with official U.S. federal-government plates pull up. He knew immediately the car was being driven by U.S. Attorney Sean Dunne. When Dunne saw Bobby he diverted his eyes.

"You and your client haven't tried to tamper with my witness, have you?" Christmas asked.

"Betty Wang?" Bobby said. "Why? You lose her, Noel? I told you to hold her as a material witness."

"I didn't say I lost her," he said, looking nervous as the rain beat on the brim of his hat. Christmas saw Sean Dunne motioning for him, tweaking his thumb and forefinger for information. As an ambulance and a morgue wagon pulled up, Christmas walked to Dunne's car to fill him in on what he knew.

Bobby gave details of what he'd seen to a uniformed cop. As they spoke, another uniformed cop approached them.

"They just found the driver," the second cop said. "Dead at the wheel on a dead-end street off Bay Parkway, wrapped around a lamppost."

In the commotion Bobby drifted off, and hurried back to the subway.

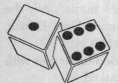

25

Bobby knew cell phones worked on the subway when the trains traveled above ground. So he called Maggie as the N train rolled over the elevated tracks of Brooklyn toward Manhattan. The borough of churches spread out under the leaden sky like a sad boyhood memory. Half a lifetime ago he had learned that his father had been killed in the line of duty on a rainy day in Brooklyn. Now the image of Father Dooley in astonished pop-eyed death was freshly stamped in his brain.

He needed to hear the voice of innocence in his ear, a shower of life to wash away the stain of death.

"Hey, kiddo," Bobby said when Maggie answered.

"Hi, Dad," she said. "Guess what?"

"You nailed your PSATs?"

"I think I did good," she said.

"Well," he corrected. *"You did well,* not *good."*

"Whatever, and I met a cute guy during the break. Name's Liam. He's from a place called Toome, in Northern Ireland."

"That ought to warm the cockles of your mother's Anglo Protestant heart," Bobby said. He paused, then asked the crucial question: "How old is he?"

"Fourteen," Maggie said, "and he's computer illiterate."

"Good, keep him that way," Bobby said. "And barefoot in the kitchen."

"Huh?"

"Nothing. Speaking of computers, what about that license plate I gave you?"

"It's a convent school in Queens," Maggie said. "Saint Maria. I think she was a martyr—Italian—raped and murdered, I think. We learned about her in religion when I went to Holy Name in Brooklyn."

"Uplifting," Bobby said. "Got an address?"

"*Have*, old man," Maggie said. "*Have*, not *got*."

"Ball-breaker," he said.

She gave him the address on Northern Boulevard in North Flushing. *Jesus Christ*, he thought. *I thought she was Amy McCoy but the nun really is a nun.*

"I'm gonna meet Liam this afternoon at Planet Hollywood," she said. "His big brother is a bouncer and we don't have to wait on line."

"Sounds like fun," Bobby said. "Listen, baby, I'm gonna be out of town tomorrow. I might be back tomorrow night. If not, the next day for sure. Okay?"

"Sure, Pop."

"Love ya, kiddo."

Bobby picked up his Jeep on Seventy-second Street, swept it for bugs. Satisfied there weren't any, he drove through the Midtown Tunnel to Queens and took the Long Island Expressway to the Clearview and exited at Northern Boulevard, continuing on surface streets toward North Flushing. The all-news radio was already reporting Father Dooley's death in a hit-and-run "accident." The reporter said that the driver of the stolen car that killed the priest was a homeless man named Ricardo Santiago, who had a long criminal record for petty crimes. They gave a brief bio of Dooley, saying he was an advocate of the poor, a champion of the city's youth, who was often at loggerheads with City Hall. Mayor Brady had issued a statement about the dead cleric. "Although Father Dooley and I didn't always see eye to eye, he was a great New Yorker who cared very deeply about the young people of this city. This is a tragedy for all of us. I will dearly miss him."

Miss him like a tumor, Bobby thought.

Nor did Bobby believe it was an accident. There were no skid marks. The car looked like its driver had picked his target, nailed him, and kept going.

Three news items later, State Senate Majority Leader Stan Lebelski came on repeating his opposition to the legalized-gambling resolution. It was the same sound bite he'd read in the *Daily News.* State Assembly Speaker Pinto countered that Lebelski was caving in to special interest groups. The reporter added that the latest Marist poll indicated that 55 percent of voters statewide now favored legalized gambling in New York.

Bobby finally saw the cross on top of St. Maria's convent school. The small, two-story building was hidden by two towering blue spruces, its solemn brick façade covered in wet green ivy. The red Dodge Durango was parked in the driveway, as blatant as a giant red fingerprint. He parked his Jeep across the street, dodged traffic across the six-lane boulevard. He passed the Durango as he squished up the soggy pathway to the door of the school. The Durango bore the same license plate. He rang the bell. After a minute an elderly Hispanic nun dressed in an all-white habit answered the door. Her white habit wrapped around her like a giant tortilla. *Sister Burrito*, he thought.

"I'm looking for the nun who was driving that car yesterday," Bobby said.

The nun looked at him with a wizened smile. "*Sí?*"

"I need to talk to her," Bobby said.

"Wait here."

She went inside the convent. Bobby dripped for a little more than a minute before the old nun returned. "She's with a child," the nun said. "You know Sister Amaryllis, *sí?*"

"We've met, yeah," Bobby said.

"You with the police, *sí?*" she asked with a smile.

"Sort of, *sí*," he lied.

"Come in," said the old nun, leading Bobby into the dark convent. The air inside was cool and fresh. He thought of sanctified grace and shivered at the thought of his unclean soul. Holy pictures and a large crucifix adorned the walls. The nun put her finger to her lips and motioned for Bobby to follow.

"The little ones only speak to her," the old nun said.

She led Bobby to an anteroom next to a small classroom. "This where the police must watch," the nun said.

Bobby nodded at her as the old nun raised a shade on a small window that Bobby knew was a two-way mirror. Another nun sat at a small child's table with her back to the mirror. A little black girl, emotionless, with swollen eyes and lips, no more than seven, sat across from her. The nun had two dolls on the table. One had male genitalia, the other had female genitalia.

"Show me what your foster father did to you, Darla," the nun said, her back still to him but her voice confirming the suspicion he'd gotten on the Boardwalk in Atlantic City when he thought he had recognized Amy McCoy under the nun's habit.

Bobby felt like a crumb standing here watching this. He knew he didn't belong. He'd been invited in under the cover of a white lie.

Without saying a word the little girl put the face of the female doll on the genitals of the male doll. Bobby felt anger and queasiness, shame for men in general. *A dog wouldn't do that to a pup*, he thought.

"Anything else?" the nun asked, writing this down, shifting in her seat to reveal Amy's familiar profile. *Sister Amy*, he thought. *Now I know I'm going to hell . . .*

The girl nodded and lay the female doll down on its back, pulled its legs apart, and had the male doll get on top, and slammed the male doll up and down. Amy wrote this down.

"Anything else?"

The girl took the hand of the male doll and smacked it across the female doll's face repeatedly. Amy nodded.

"Did he tell you not to tell anyone or else he'd beat you again?" Amy asked.

The little girl nodded.

"Anything else?"

She shook her head no. Amy wrote this down and then held open her arms and the little girl collapsed into her embrace. Amy rocked her and said, "No one is going to hurt you anymore, okay?"

The kid in her arms did not respond, no tears, no sobbing. She just lay emotionless against Amy's breast, her head on the nun's shoulder, blinking.

Another nun came into the room and led the little girl out by the hand. Now the elderly nun led Bobby into the room and left quickly. Amy McCoy turned to Bobby full-faced for the first time.

"I've been expecting you," she said.

He held out the .25-caliber automatic. "I wanted to return this . . . *Sister.*"

She looked at it and took the gun from him. She made it disappear up her puffy sleeve. He remembered as a Catholic school kid that half the world seemed to disappear up a nun's sleeve—tissues, chalk, pens, coughdrops, prayerbooks, iron rulers that they used to beat his open palm. *What's one little .25 automatic?* he thought.

Amy walked to the wall and pulled the shade down in front of the mirror.

"My father gave it to me for my sixteenth birthday," she said. "It's never been fired."

They looked at each other for a long silent moment.

"I don't know how to thank you," she said.

"For what?"

"For not letting me kill him," she said.

"If it was my brother, I'd probably have done the same."

"I haven't even gone to confession about it yet," she said.

"The way I was taught, Baltimore catechism, temptation is not sin," Bobby said.

She flicked a small smile.

"I knew you were too good to be single," Bobby said.

"I'm not really a nun yet," she said. "I'm a novitiate."

"But you're already doing God's work. I've tried to communicate with kids who have been sexually abused. It might be the most heartbreaking part of being a cop. Most of these kids clam up."

"Or worse, fabricate terrible, dangerous lies," she said. "This one was telling the truth."

"You have a way with them."

"How much of it did you watch?"

"Just the last minute or two," Bobby said. "The demonstration. I'd like you to show me how you won her confidence."

"Another time," she said. "Anyway, thanks for coming. But I have some chores to do that I neglected when I followed you to Atlantic City. I have a class to teach, and another child to try to reach. This one is a girl who was raped by her own brother and his friends—playing doctor."

"I'm still looking for your brother," Bobby said. "I wish I had more news. Maybe soon."

"Thanks," she said. "Funny, Eddie going missing has distracted me from all this for a few days. I've been of two minds about staying or leaving the order for some time now. Now this has forced me to make a decision. I'm sorry I didn't tell you all this the other night on the boat when . . ."

"That was only temptation, too," Bobby said. "I apologize. I never did that to a *nun* before."

"I told you," she said, "I'm not a nun yet. Maybe never."

"Yeah, but . . ."

"I'm a *woman*. That night I acted like one . . . or almost did."

She took a deep breath, rolled her eyes, and as she exhaled they both broke up laughing. "I can see why sin is so popular," she said. "In the same week I almost committed murder and lost my . . . well, my *senses*."

"Not your faith?"

"My faith, no," she said. "My calling, I've almost made up my mind about that. Just a little more soul searching to do."

"If there's anything I can do . . ."

"If there is, I know where to find you," Amy said.

26

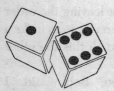

Max Roth was small but strong for his size and Bobby watched him scale the rock-climbing wall at Chelsea Piers like a mountain goat. He had to be the most physically fit reporter in New York. Bobby had already mounted the wall five times, working his shoulders and upper arms, his calves and his thighs.

Climbing was a great workout in a climate-controlled atmosphere, with a safety belt and cushioned drop. But he had no delusions. Bobby told Roth he had no plans of ever scaling a real mountain. "If anyone ever asks why I didn't scale Everest, I'll answer, 'Because it's there—way up there—and I'm here, way down here. Where I belong.' I'll leave the real thing for the loonies and their morticians."

"You'll stick to safer pastimes like murder," Roth said, after they finished climbing and again power-walked the indoor track.

"Murder's a living," Bobby said. "Frostbite or falling fourteen thousand feet doesn't pay so good."

"I've been digging, and when it comes to politics our old pal Ben Lee does a high-wire act of his own," Roth said. "No net. He's been very involved in Asian immigrants' rights."

"What's wrong with that?"

"Nothing," Roth said. "Except you make some strange bedfellows. He supports Republicans and Democrats, liberals and conservatives, depending on who's good for his cause."

"Most lobbyists support the incumbent if he's good on a certain key issue," Bobby said. "That's politically savvy, not corruption."

"That's right," Roth said. "And you usually stick with the guy if he's good on your issues, because he has more seniority and therefore clout in the House or the Senate."

"So who did Ben Lee support lately?" Bobby asked.

"He's backed Mayor Brady all the way," Roth said. "He ran his whole grassroots operation in Brooklyn. Brady has been great on all immigrants' rights. Especially Asian. The mayor is a hero to the assimilated Asian community. As a result, in the last two elections, a lot of votes and campaign money came out of Brooklyn's Chinatown."

"How much?"

"Millions," Roth said. "In small donations from little people."

Bobby slowed his pace. "Money orders signed by little seamstresses, busboys, waiters, prep cooks, deliverymen?"

"Yeah. The campaign finance regulators questioned some of it. But it was all cleverly done with money orders. Or personal accounts that were closed as soon as the checks cleared. Untraceable. The same kind of money is coming into Brady's U.S. Senate campaign."

"Ben Lee is organizing this?"

"He was brought in and questioned about it," Roth said. "But he's slick. On this Senate campaign, which is federal, guess who would have to bring an indictment?"

"Sean Dunne," Bobby said.

He thought about Amy McCoy seeing Ben Lee getting into a car with Sean Dunne outside the Golden Pagoda a few days before.

"The one and only," Roth said.

"Where's the money really coming from? Kronk?"

"Can't prove it but that's my guess," Roth said. "Ben Lee really wants to see Brady in the Senate because he'd be a tremendous advocate for Asian immigrants in Washington."

"But Ben basically told me that Jimmy Chung was Sam Kronk's bag man to the Asian community,"

Bobby said. "Now you're telling me that Ben is actually laundering the Kronk campaign money?"

"Maybe," Roth said. "Could be an ends-justifies-the-means decision. Like supporting a candidate who doesn't reflect your political philosophy but is good on one issue. It doesn't look like Ben is pocketing any of the money. He already lives a life you'd expect of a guy with a couple of successful restaurants: a lower-echelon millionaire. He sends a lot of money home to his family in Hong Kong. Drives a Lincoln. Has a nice house on Shore Road. Dates pretty girls. And he plays politics like the ponies."

Bobby had a lot of questions for Ben Lee when he saw him later.

"What about this gambling resolution?" Bobby asked.

"As you know, Brady is against it," Roth said. "Kronk is, too, at least publicly. But funny you should ask. Lebelski, who is from Westchester, just did a one-eighty and came out against the gambling resolution yesterday, and he got a lot of contributions from those same 'little people' from Sunset Park."

"You think Ben Lee might have influenced him on his turn-around?" Bobby asked.

"Your guess is as good as mine," Roth said. "I just find it hard to believe that 'little people' from Brooklyn's Chinatown are sending money to a Polish-American state senator from the suburbs. Fucking nuts. *Unheard* of. Legal, I suppose, but such a blatant attempt to buy influence."

"Thanks, Max," Bobby said.

"Thanks?" Roth said. "Thanks is all I get? I want a byline, the wood, Bobby. Front page! I'm sure there's stuff you aren't telling me. There always is."

"It's loose ends right now. I need answers myself. I don't want to give you wrong stuff."

"I appreciate that," Roth said. "I don't want to be wrong on page one. But something's been bothering me about all of this, Bobby, and it should be bothering you, too."

"All the coincidences?"

"Yeah," Roth said, as they entered the locker room. "You're working for Izzy Gleason. His client just so happens to be the landlord of a guy I know, who I just spoke to the day before he disappeared."

"We both know a lot of people, Max," Bobby said.

"Yeah, but then you ask me to look into Ben Lee, a guy we both went to college with," Roth said.

"I didn't say Ben Lee was involved," Bobby said. "This might all be unrelated to Izzy Gleason and 22 Empire Court."

"And Noel Christmas, a guy who used to be your partner."

"Noel Christmas is an investigator for the DA's office. So it's not unusual that he's looking into a high-profile crime."

"Okay," Roth said. "How did this Jimmy Chung just happen to choose Izzy Gleason's name?"

"Izzy Gleason isn't exactly a low-profile lawyer.

He got a lot of ink in the police medical pension story last year. Matter of fact, you gave him most of it."

"Unfortunately. But whatever or whoever you're not telling me about, be careful. I wouldn't trust anyone in this. It all smells."

"Believe me, Max, sometimes I feel like someone is making chess moves, too, trying to use me to put someone else into check. That's why I'm asking you to help me watch the board."

"I will," Roth said.

"Will you let me know what Ben Lee has to say for himself tonight?" Roth said. "I've tried calling him three times. He doesn't return calls."

Bobby promised.

When he left Chelsea Piers, the rain was still pelting the city.

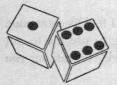 The Golden Pagoda was dark but the front door was unlocked. Bobby stood in the vestibule, looked both ways on the rain-drenched avenue to be sure he wasn't followed. It was 12:05 AM.

Bobby had parked the Jeep two blocks down and one block over, on Sixth Avenue, to be sure he wasn't being shadowed. It would be odd enough to find anyone out in the rain, never mind trying to keep a tail. He walked the three blocks through Sunset Park, the rain popping on his slicker, to keep his appointment with Ben Lee.

Soggy garbage was stacked at the curb in piles as tall as the parking meters. Rain collected in dirty puddles. Cats huddled under parked cars, their eyes shining like reflectors in the headlights of passing traffic. The cars never slowed as they whispered along the wet street. All the Asian stores along this spine of Brooklyn's Chinatown were shuttered for the night. Most of the neon signs bearing Chinese characters had been extinguished. The steady downpour had washed the heavy smell of Chinese food and composting produce from the air. Lightning sizzled in the sky.

In one fluid movement Bobby pulled open the door and stepped into the Golden Pagoda. The huge restaurant was silent except for the gurgling of the giant fish tank and the pleasant chuckling of the indoor waterfall.

"Ben," he called softly. "Ben, you here?"

Lightning flashed outside the window, followed by a rumble of thunder. The aquatic hue of the fish tank, the green underwater floodlights of the lily pond, and the red illuminated signs above the fire-exit doors provided the only light.

He called Ben Lee's name again but heard no response. He assumed Lee was upstairs in his office and walked past the cash register toward the bamboo footbridge. He froze when the big fish tank came into view. Ben Lee's bloated face was pressed against the glass, his eyes half-open. His hands and feet were hog-tied behind his back. Bobby noticed that a clear plastic bag was wrapped around his left foot, sealed at the ankle. Through the bloodied plastic he could see that the second toe of his left foot was missing.

A thick black zipper had been sewn over his mouth, heavy red thread piercing his lips. His tongue protruded through the zipper hole and the jagged metal teeth were pulled up and caught on the tongue. Like a symbol of a man caught in the act of talking. Golden carp and sea bass swam frantically around Ben Lee's face and body. Smaller fish nibbled near his bloodied tongue. A few dozen live lobsters lay on the bottom of the tank beneath him, claws bound by rubber bands, their feelers madly probing the overcrowded tank.

Bobby backed away from the aquarium in horror, looked over his shoulder, grabbed the handrail of the bamboo footbridge. He leaned over the railing, took a deep breath, and looked down into the lily pond beneath him. Betty Wang lay in the water, a zipper also sewn over her mouth. Her feet and hands were bound with duct tape, and there was a plastic bag over her bloodied left foot, through which Bobby could see that her second toe had also been severed.

Golden carp swam past her. A turtle sat on her bent knee, propping its head above water.

"Holy Jesus Christ," Bobby said.

"Bobby Emmet," he heard someone whisper and Bobby dropped to all fours, had his .38 out of his jacket pocket and pointed at the voice in one blinding reflex. His heart thumped in his chest. His eyes probed the room. Sweat beaded on his forehead. His mouth went blotter-dry. He squinted and saw George, the waiter with the fluttering eye tic, standing at a half-opened side exit door.

"We need to talk, Bobby Emmet, yeah," he said, motioning urgently for him to come. "Please, now."

Bobby heard voices from the street outside the front door and turned to see Noel Christmas and Sean Dunne tapping on the glass. They covered their eyes to see in. He looked back at George, then at the front door. He didn't want to have to explain two more dead bodies to Noel Christmas. He wondered why this cop, his ex-partner, always seemed to be right on his heels. No one had followed him.

Christmas *knew* that Bobby would be here. And he
knew that Ben Lee would be dead. Along with his
star witness against Izzy Gleason. Bobby hoped to
God that Izzy had a good alibi.

"Is it open?" he heard Dunne say.

"Yeah, it's open," said Christmas. "But I don't see
anyone."

"Fuck the warrant," Dunne said. "We have a
phone tip—probable cause. Let's go in."

Bobby looked back at George, the waiter. He
motioned for Bobby to hurry. Bobby scrambled over
the footbridge and duck-walked to the exit door and
slipped out. He stood quickly and pushed the pistol
muzzle into the soft pouch of George's neck. Rain fell
in the blackened courtyard behind the old tenements
like water rushing through a funnel. Drainpipes rattled and gurgled, lightning scribbling in the sky.

"What the fuck is going down here?" Bobby said.

"You not shoot me, yeah?" he said. "I friend of
Ben Lee's father for many years, yeah. He save me
and my family. So I love Ben Lee. Come, I show you
something."

He led Bobby down the alley, splashing through the
puddles, and lifted a metal cellar door. George took a
flashlight from his waist, gently closed the cellar door on
top of them. They descended into a huge spotless cellar
that served as a food storage area, a prep kitchen, and a
butchering area. Framed Department of Health
licenses hung on the walls. They passed boxes of
imported Asian canned foods, big sacks of rice, boxes of

noodles and fortune cookies. They hurried through a spotless stainless-steel kitchen area, past another area where cooked food was loaded onto a dumbwaiter that ran to the kitchen upstairs.

Pointing the way with his flashlight, George led Bobby into the rear of the basement, where the cellar was raw and unfinished. He took Bobby directly to a telephone junction box. George pointed to one wire amid a dozen different wires and traced with his finger. Bobby immediately spotted a mismatched splice wire—like the one he had spotted in the basement of 22 Empire Court.

"Ben Lee private office phone, yeah?" George said.

"Yeah," Bobby said, signaling for George to lower his voice.

"Come on, Bobby Emmet, yeah?" He signaled for Bobby to follow him as he ran the flashlight beam along the ceiling, through the piping and the BX cables.

Bobby trailed George as he traced the wire deeper into the cellar, which, like the restaurant, stretched the width of three full buildings. The wire extended to the very end of the cellar, where it disappeared above the wall and into the cellar of the next building.

"Where's it go?" Bobby asked.

George ran his hand and the flashlight beam along the back wall until they encountered the rusted rump of a large heating-oil tank. George reached behind the tank and located an almost imperceptible break in the wall. He beckoned Bobby closer, until he could make out a half-inch recess behind the end of the oil tank. George pushed his fingers in and slid open a relatively simple but ingenious pocket door that slid into a hollow in the receiving wall like a knife into a sheath. Here in the deep shadows and concealed by the oil tank, it was almost invisible.

Bobby followed George through the pocket door, squeezing into the next cellar, which was a corner building. George slid the door shut. This cellar was an illegal sweatshop, jammed with about sixty sewing-machine stations and tables piled high with fabric—sleeves, collars, cuffs. From a big pile Bobby picked up one of thousands of black zippers identical to the ones sewn over the mouths of Ben Lee and Betty Wang.

George shone his flashlight at the ceiling, locating the wire leading from Ben Lee's telephone junction box. It led deeper into the cellar. Bobby followed George past five huge fish tanks filled with elegant silver-bodied exotic fish with blue and orange fins, some as long as thirty-six inches. Bobby had never seen fish like them before.

"Arowana, yeah," George said. "Bring no good luck tonight, yeah."

"From Cambodia," Bobby said, nodding, remembering Ben Lee had told him that Jimmy Chung smuggled these exotic fish. "Six thousand dollars each."

"Smart, Bobby Emmet, yeah," George said.

Bobby watched George trace the telephone wire into a square room sitting on cement slabs almost identical to the one in the basement of 22 Empire Court. George opened the door. They entered. The room was furnished exactly like the one downstairs from the McCoys. Same rugs, same desk, same liquor from the same Sunset Park liquor store. And the same ten-hour Panasonic VOX tape recorder rigged to a TT Systems caller-ID box. Both bought from Hing How Electronics, down the street. The tape was gone. There were only two numbers on the ID box, the last ones it had recorded. One number belonged to Bobby. The other one was the main number for Kronk Castle in Atlantic City.

"Who owns this building?" Bobby asked.

"Jimmy Chung," George said, his eye spasming with nervous excitement. "He have my good friend Ben Lee killed, yeah?"

"What did Ben want to tell me?"

"He receive call from Hong Kong, yeah," George said. "His father say he ask postman who deliver mail to Jimmy Chung family if he deliver any mail from Jimmy Chung lately, yeah."

"Yeah, George, yeah, yeah, yeah. What did he say?"

"Say yeah," George said.

"Say yeah *what?*"

"Express Mail take three day deliver Hong Kong from New York."

"Yeah, and?"

"And Jimmy Chung mail one dated same day he disappear."

"How does he know it was from him?"

"Always use fake name but always put number eight in return address. Number eight lucky number for Chinese, yeah."

Bobby thought about the farm in New Jersey owned by Rapa Properties Inc., called Lucky Eight Farm.

"You trying to say Jimmy Chung is alive?"

"Yeah."

"That *he* killed Ben and the girl?"

They heard muffled voices from Ben Lee's cellar. George cut the light and led Bobby quietly up a flight of stairs into the hallway of the corner tenement.

"I have your number," George said. "I call you soon, yeah. I have to go now or they kill me too, yeah?"

"Wait," Bobby said. "Don't call tomorrow. The next day, yeah?"

"Yeah," George said and then slipped out of the building.

Bobby waited a full heart-pounding minute, pulled up the hood of his rain slicker, and exited onto the side street. He quickly crossed the street and splashed down toward Eighth Avenue. He saw the swirling police lights of the patrol cars outside the Golden Pagoda, where Noel Christmas was conferring with Sean Dunne under a big umbrella. Bobby put his hands in his pockets and hurried down to Sixth Avenue, where he'd parked the car. He looked up, both ways, making sure he wasn't being followed. He wasn't.

Sunset Park was one of the most magnificent vantage points in the city from which to view the Manhattan skyline and the harbor. Tonight most of that view was veiled in punishing rain. Lightning scorched the angry sky. Bobby shuddered at the bloated image of Ben Lee, who had spent much of his life fighting for immigrants' rights and wound up hog-tied with a zipper stitched over his mouth, a toe amputated—literally sleeping with the fishes.

He climbed in the Jeep, started the engine, clicked on the wipers. He called Izzy Gleason on the cell phone. Izzy, half in the bag, answered on the first ring. "Polacks Anonymous," he shouted into the phone. "What's the first and last name of the party you want?" Bobby could hear loud laughter and a comedian in the background. He asked Izzy where he was. "I'm in a Polack nightclub called The Pole Vault in Greenpoint with Lulu," Izzy said. "Been here all night. They got a Polack comedian here who looks like a fuckin' Saint Bernard telling mick jokes that would make you shit mashed potatoes. I'm in the front row and he's been breakin' my nuts all night. Okay, Bobby—how many micks does it take to get drunk? Three. One to drink the whiskey and two to spin the fuckin' room. Why did the mick cross the road? He thought it was his best fuckin' friend. If my

old man was alive he'd turn this dump into a Polack
wake."

Bobby told him about Ben Lee and Betty
Wang and advised him to take down the names of
some alibi witnesses. Izzy was too stewed to make
it register. Bobby made him put Lucille on the
phone and he explained the situation to her. She
said she would get the necessary names. In the
background Bobby could hear Izzy heckling the
comedian. "Hey, you kielbasy smuggler ya," Bobby
heard Izzy shout. "How many Polacks does it take
to clear one mick of murder?"

Bobby hung up before he heard the punchline.
He drove toward the Brooklyn Battery Tunnel.
Below him, in the rain-shrouded harbor, beyond the
abandoned expanse of Empire Island, Lady Liberty
glowed through the wet gloom like the night-light of
New York. *It's raining dead bodies,* Bobby thought.
And he knew the storm wasn't over yet.

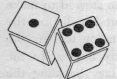 *The Fifth Amendment* swayed in the storm-rocked river as Bobby climbed on board. He heard the TV from inside the salon. He stepped in from the rain with his fist wrapped around his .38.

"You told me to come by if I needed you," Amy McCoy said.

Bobby looked at her sitting on the sofa with her legs crossed, dressed in a short black dress, high heels, wearing a little bit of lipstick and a little bit of perfume, which he could smell across the compact room. After dead bodies, ugly cops, and Izzy's bad jokes, she was a very welcome sight.

State Senator Stan Lebelski was on New York One TV news repeating his opposition to legalized gambling in a political roundtable with Assembly Speaker Carl Pinto. Lebelski looked sweaty, nervous. He droned on, about how gambling was a failure in New Orleans and that one only needed to walk two blocks from Atlantic City's glitzy Boardwalk to find urban blight. He also said that in Detroit, which was 80 percent black, the inner-city poor were flocking to the casinos, but not one of them was black-owned.

Bobby put the gun away. He switched off the tube, dissolving a close-up of Lebelski.

"What is it you need?" he asked her.

"I need you," she said.

Bobby looked at her and saw the crazed nun with the gun, and then the gentle nun working to repair the damage done to a little girl. He also saw one very sexy woman.

"Amy, don't you think you should wait . . ."

"I've been waiting all my life," she said.

His heart raced and he felt the testosterone in his body starting to surge. She walked to him. She was nervous, swallowing hard as she looked in his eyes. In a world of slick charmers and bimbos on the make, Amy McCoy was wondrously clumsy, awkward, self-conscious. She shrugged like an adolescent trying too hard to be a woman. He felt her tremble as she put her arms around his neck and kissed him on the lips.

"Show me how," she said. "Like you started to last time. This time I won't stop you. Promise."

"Amy, are you *sure?*" She smelled so good, looked even better. She held his face in her two hands. He needed a shave. She rubbed the stubble, touched his lips, grabbed his hair in her tight fists. He kissed her and her lips parted and he kissed her deeper. She got lost in the kiss, making out with him with the enthusiasm of a girl whose emotional and sexual development had been arrested as a teenager.

Her arms went around his big shoulders and she pressed herself against his body in a pliant, needy offering. He lifted her up in his arms, her bare legs cleanly shaved and warm. His fingers probed under the ruffled edges of her silk panties.

"Last chance to say no before I start praying to St. Blueballs," he said, smiling at her.

"The answer is *yes*," she whispered, her breath warm on his face. "Yes, yes, yes."

He carried her into the stateroom, laid her on the big bed, helped her off with her dress, and unhooked her bra. He watched her instinctively cover her small breasts, then uncup them, revealing their hard pink nipples. She blushed, and that alone made him fully aroused. She dropped her arms to her side, waiting for him to show her the way, and watched him undress with fidgety anticipation. Then he slid next to her in the bed and took her in his arms.

With rain on the windows and the storm rocking the boat, he was as gentle and patient as he could be. He showed her how a man used protection and taught her about foreplay. He showed her as much as he thought she could handle in one session. After ten minutes, raw instinct overtook her and nature provided everything else she needed to know. Then, one by one, as if from a checklist of things she'd seen in movies, or read in books, or imagined in a bed she shared only with her God, she tried *everything*, unleashing all the human desires and fantasies she had locked inside her.

Her innocent curiosity mixed with animal impulses made her an exceptional lover. Her beginner's enthusiasm was infectious and Bobby felt a renewed excitement. Making love to Amy McCoy was like learning a new language, discovering an unimaginably exotic cuisine. She reminded him of what young love was like. Halfway through their love-making, the student began instructing the teacher.

It scared the hell out of him. He could easily fall in love with her.

"Am I doing it right?" she asked.

"I should be asking you," he said.

"Bullshit artist," she said, laughing, and tried another item on her checklist, something brand-new for her. She started slowly and then as she fell into the rhythm, she became enthusiastic and skillful at that, too.

When they were finished, when *he* could perform no more, Bobby lay exhausted.

She, of course, was ready for more. He had to explain that men really were the inferior gender when it came to sex.

She laughed and continued to explore him as they talked.

"I wasn't a virgin," she said.

"Me either," he said. She laughed and slapped his behind.

"But you were the first man I ever did it with . . . willingly," she said.

"Something told me when I saw you working with that little girl in the convent that you had been in her chair once yourself," Bobby said.

"I wasn't that young," she said. "I was sixteen. I was with my first and only boyfriend—Michael was his name, a real macho football jock. It was his seventeenth birthday. We had his father's car and we were parked on a pier in Brooklyn, a lovers' lane. I was going to give up my virginity to him for his birthday. I never got the chance. A guy with a gun suddenly yanked open the door . . ."

"Jesus, Amy, you don't have to tell me all this," he said.

She put a finger on his lips and rested her face on his chest, speaking in a soft voice.

"Michael tried to fight him but the guy was huge and he beat Michael unmercifully with the gun. He beat me, too. Then he made Michael lie down on the backseat and handcuffed his hands to the door handle. Then he made me lie on top of Michael. He put the gun in Michael's mouth as he raped me, taunting him about how he was having his little chick. I heard Michael crying the whole time. When he was done, this monster said he was sorry, that he wished we could have met under nicer circumstances . . ."

"Oh, Jesus," he said.

"I called the cops to free Michael's hands. We both wound up in the hospital. The cops took a report. It was in the newspapers. They didn't use our names but everyone knew it was us. Michael was so humiliated he hanged himself a week later. After Michael's funeral, my father gave me the gun, and I've kept it ever since."

"Amy, you don't have to say any more."

"And then my father started to drink. My mother was sick with breast cancer. When she died a year later, my father drank even heavier. He would babble irrationally about how he was a failure as a father because he hadn't protected his little girl. He drank until his liver gave out, and then I lost him, too."

"How old were you?" Bobby asked, stroking her hair.

"By then I was eighteen. I lived with my brother for a year. I loved him. We got along great, but he was so involved in politics. Then he got married and went away to South America for a while. And I went to an all-girls' Catholic college. Eddie paid for it with the little bit of money he earned from freelancing."

"Didn't you date in college?"

"Twice," she said. "The first guy was a jerk who went around telling people he had slept with me. It wasn't true, but the story spread. I felt violated by that. All he gave me was a kiss goodnight on the cheek. The second guy was really nice. I kissed him. I liked him a lot. He said he would call me the next day. He didn't. He never told me he was engaged and he got married a month later."

"You didn't have a lot of luck with guys," Bobby said.

"Afraid not. So I just stopped dating," she said. "When I finished school last year with a degree in child psychology, I didn't know what I wanted to do. I was afraid to do anything else, so I went into the order."

"Did you really want to be a nun?"

"I wasn't sure," she said. "I wanted to find out. There's a real shortage of sisters today, and they do such great work."

"They did some number on me when I was in school."

"Well, some of them resent being there," she said. "And sometimes they sublimate that frustration the wrong way. But they're terrified of leaving. Like unhappy women who are afraid of leaving bad marriages. I didn't want to become one of them. I guess that's why I'm here."

"So this has been coming for a while—excuse the pun."

"Yeah," she said, smiling. "But with both my parents already dead, and the idea that my brother might have been murdered, I decided I owed it to myself to see what it's like to live a regular life. Before I decided if I wanted to spend the rest of my days as a nun."

"So you're still not sure?" he asked. "I mean, you're allowed to do this, to experiment, and then go back and . . ."

"Hey, didn't you ever hear of confession?"

Bobby flashed on Zelda Savarese storming out of the confessional at St. Brian's. Father Dooley chasing after her, then dying so horribly.

Amy laughed and kissed him again, making out with him, as if she were trying to get her technique down, like a teenage boy learning to unhook a bra one-handed.

"But you might go back?" he asked.

"It depends," she said. "After what we just did, I gotta tell you, it'll be an even bigger sacrifice for God if I do."

They laughed as he fondled her young, hard body.

"First, I want to help find my brother," she said, "or what happened to him. He's the only family I have left. I'll do *anything* to find what's happened to him."

Bobby thought about that for a few moments as Amy kissed him.

"Anything?" he asked.

"Except murder," she said. "I realized that after I almost did it. I went down there to Atlantic City thinking I could get him alone. Get Kronk by himself, put the gun in his face, and make him tell me about Eddie. But everywhere he goes he's surrounded by his security people. Like the president."

"Or the Pope," Bobby said.

"I even spoke to one of the young girls who work there," Amy said. "She said she was a greeter. A 'Kronkette' she called herself. I said it must be awful for a man like Sam Kronk never to have any privacy. She said even when he's alone, he's not alone. That there are always cameras on him."

Bobby told her all about the Kronkettes, about how Dum Dum Dunne recruited them on Wednesdays in the back room of the Straight Flush Saloon, how the girls had to be twenty-five or under, how they had to sign a confidentiality clause, how they had to take two blood tests six weeks apart before Kronk would sleep with them, how they got their $75,000, a thirteenth-floor room for a year, sometimes served as escorts for rich friends of Kronk's, and after a year received a letter of recommendation but not even so much as a goodbye.

"If I were pretty enough I'd become one just to get close enough to Kronk to find something out about Eddie," Amy said.

Bobby propped himself up on the pillow and looked at her, at this mesmerizing young lady with the gee-whiz innocence of a teenager and the intelligence of a woman. He also knew a killer lived inside her. That excited him, too, because he had killed people—and would again, if necessary. The killer in him could relate to the darker parishes of Amy McCoy's soul.

"You're prettier than any of them," Bobby said.

"Get lost," she said. "I saw some of those girls, I mean, they're like magazine models. Absolutely gorgeous."

The best looking women are always the ones who don't know, he thought. *Modesty gives their beauty dimension.*

She kissed his neck and started to suckle it.

"No hickeys, for Christ sakes," he said.

"Why not? It's been a long time since I gave one."

"You're twenty years too late for my hickey days," he said. "How would I explain a hickey to my fourteen-year-old daughter?"

"You could say it's a kiss from God."

So she kissed him other places, all of them new for her, which made them heaven-sent for him. Being the first man she had ever made love to swelled his ego, raced his blood, the physical sensation quickly translating into emotion. *Control,* he told himself. *Control your feelings. It would be too easy to fall in love with this one. Enjoy it. But remember, control is crucial here.*

And soon they were at it again as the rain continued to fall through the night.

29

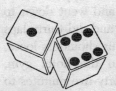

AUGUST 3

In the morning she was gone.

Bobby had slept like he'd been drugged. Amy McCoy had known no limits. She spent most of the night making up for a lifetime of self-denial.

Her note thanked him for a "glorious night" and said she would call him as soon as she took care of some family business. He couldn't remember the last time a woman had thanked him for going to bed with him. She was dangerous. It would be too easy to fall in love with a lady such as Amy McCoy.

He checked his watch. It was 6:19 AM. His plane for San Juan was leaving JFK at eight. He'd never make it in time through the morning traffic. He called an old friend who owned a waterfront saloon named Petey Maguire's in Howard Beach—on Jamaica Bay, just a few miles from JFK. Bobby asked Petey if he could dock his boat there overnight. After Maguire cursed him out for calling so early, he said sure.

He made the plane with two minutes to spare and slept most of the way down in the comfortable first-class seat.

After landing in San Juan, Bobby took a cab to the Caribe Hilton, checked into his spacious, elegantly furnished room. The king-size bed, peach-colored armchairs, glass-topped writing desk, and well-stocked mini-bar met with his approval. He pulled on a pair of swim trunks and went down to one of the three swimming pools and did thirty laps to get his wind up to speed and his shoulders loose, fluid, and strong. He went into the hotel gym, worked out on the Nautilus for forty-five minutes to put pop in his arms and brawn in his upper chest. Without a gun, he needed to oil the only weapon he'd brought along—*himself*. After ten sets of sit-ups the muscles of his sweat-slick body stood out in defined relief, endorphins exploding in his brain like jumping beans. He went up to his room on the sixth floor, showered, put on his ginger-haired disguise, dressed in jeans and a loose, flowery, summer shirt, and strolled down the white beach past the stately palms, the fronds rattling in the warm trade winds.

As he left the Hilton grounds for the property of the Kronk Caribbean Hotel he saw a gradual downscale change, as if crossing a delineated geographical border on a map. The sand seemed to be a shade darker, with little patches of litter that had not been cleaned up. The tikis on the beach were smaller than the ones on the Hilton beach, and made of synthetic straw and bamboo. *Plastic palm bark,* Bobby thought, *on a tropical island resort hotel.*

As he entered Kronk territory he became more aware of the absence of his gun. A chill pebbled his flesh even in the warm tropical zephyr. He walked to the lobby through an oceanfront bar called the Last Wave. He guessed Kronk had hired the same cockeyed workmen he used in Atlantic City to do the work here. He noticed that the glitzy design of the wallpaper didn't match at the seams. The varnish on the rattan furniture was worn away by humidity, chlorine, and sweat, leaving the tables and chairs an unappealing dirty gray.

The open-air bar looked out on prematurely balding palms and a few of the bar stools had missing straps of bamboo. The cocktail tables wobbled and waiters ran around jamming coasters and matchbooks under the legs to balance them. Even the cocktail napkins were flimsy to the touch, like cheap recycled toilet paper.

Bobby ordered a Diet Coke. They didn't have any. He didn't want to get jumpy with sugar so he ordered a club soda with lime. The drink came in a plastic cup with an annoyingly sharp lip. He heard a commotion from the casino and he carried his drink with him across the spotted carpet of the lobby to the gaming area, which had the deafening acoustics of a Coney Island arcade. A big crowd was standing around a craps table, cheering on a high-roller. Bobby took a slug of the drink, tossed the soggy cocktail napkin into a butt-jammed sand jar, and drifted over to watch the action.

Bobby was startled when he saw the familiar face of the shooter, who bet all the chips in front of him on his next roll of the dice. The shooter wore a straw hat, Hawaiian shirt, Bermuda shorts, brown sandals, outdated aviator prescription sunglasses. The people who had gathered around him became excited that he was betting fifty grand.

"Plus, I wanna lay a center bet for another twenty-five," the mad shooter announced, taking a big swig through a straw from a piña colada. He lifted out the cherry and, dangling it above his mouth, let it drop like a little red bomb.

The box guy signaled for permission from the croupier, who looked to a pit boss. The pit boss made a quick inquiry into his radio. He got his reply and nodded approval to the croupier. A tense "Ooooo" arose from the crowd. The stick chick handed the dice to the gambler, who chewed his cherry and fingered the dice in his hand, shook them, closed his eyes, rattled them next to his right ear. Right bettors and wrong bettors put down their action on the pass line. The shooter closed his eyes and led the right bettors, who believed in his streak, in a small prayer. "Lord, bless these dice and all who believe in them as they believe in you!" The right bettors said, "Amen."

The shooter's teeth and tongue were maraschino red.

And then he threw the dice. A seven. A winner! The dealer paid. A chorus of "Sís" and "Yeahs" was offered up by the onlookers.

The shooter appeared itchy with luck, sweaty with money, high on the juice of the action. He sucked a deep gulp of the piña colada through the straw, took off his sunglasses, wiped his sweaty eye sockets and his spongy brow with a hankie, tried to fasten an unfazed demeanor on his ecstatic face. He quickly put the shades back on.

He let the whole pile ride and rolled again. An eight. Then he threw a six. On the next roll he rolled an eight, made his point. The crowd cheered. The shooter licked his lips, sucked his straw.

"I'm cashing out," he said.

The crowd heaved a disappointed groan.

"A man has to know when to walk away," the gambler said. "The day is long. The night even longer. I shall return!"

Bobby took a sip of his club soda and watched New York State Assembly Speaker Carl Pinto gather his chips and walk to the cashier's cage. No one seemed to recognize Pinto here at the tourist-jammed gaming tables of San Juan. Most people wouldn't recognize their local assemblyman if he knocked on their door on election eve. That kind of political intimacy ended with machine politics when the ward heeler stopped making the rounds with Thanksgiving turkeys. But back in New York, Pinto was out front with his support of the legalized-gambling resolution that would almost certainly bring casinos to Empire Island.

At least he practices what he preaches, Bobby thought. There was one problem. A New York assemblyman makes about $60,000 a year. Pinto had just bet about two and a half times his annual salary on a single roll of the dice.

Perhaps it was no coincidence that he was here, Bobby wondered, in Kronk's hotel—winning.

Pinto had arrived early to get a jump on the action, Bobby thought. The rest of the players would be here before the sun went down.

Bobby strolled the lobby and the outside pool area to see if there was anyone else he recognized. There wasn't. He started back down to the beach to his own hotel when he saw the other half of the political equation.

From out of a private beachfront cabana mostly hidden behind a grove of palms, a large suety man with skin the color of buttermilk strode into Bobby's view. Stan Lebelski, the majority leader of the New York State Senate, wore baggy boxer-style swim trunks, old-fashioned tennis sneakers, a loose, colorful shirt bearing a map of Puerto Rico, and a floppy fishing hat. A slather of Noxzema protected his booze-veined nose from the sun. He couldn't cover the burst of spider veins in his cheeks. Lebelski checked to make sure the door to cabana number 10 was locked. It was. Bobby watched him trudge from the Spanish-tiled walkway of the yellow cabanas out across the gray sand toward the pool bar, where a bronze Adonis of a bartender served brightly colored drinks to the mostly singles crowd. In the cool shade of the bar, Jimmy Buffett's "Changes in Latitudes" played as hard-bodied chicks in string bikinis chatted with vacationing yuppies with too much disposable income for their ages.

Bobby walked to the opposite side of the pool bar and ordered a Diet Coke. They had it. He watched Lebelski order a double Johnnie Walker Black, neat, with a Becks beer back. Bobby figured that if Lebelski drank three of those in this heat they might find him doing a dead man's float in the kiddie pool before sundown.

Lebelski enacted an old-fashioned, two-fisted saloon ritual. He lifted the Scotch with his left hand and threw the double dose down his throat like someone watering a cast-iron plant. He didn't flinch as he lifted the Becks with his left hand and gulped a good third of the bottle.

Bobby noticed that Lebelski—the family man who said he was opposed to legalized gambling because he was afraid it would rip good families apart—was not wearing a wedding ring. He was out of another era, when hard drinking was a measure of your manhood. But John Wayne was dead. Leonardo DiCaprio was the new male hunk. Tom Hanks was an enduring sensitive star. The days of boilermakers had disappeared with the arrival of the designer water fad.

Still, Bobby was amused when he saw an attractive Latina in a yellow string bikini take the stool next to Lebelski. She had a wide, generous mouth, big coal-black eyes, short jet-black hair, and fierce, pronounced bones in her cheeks. She was in her early thirties, and her large breasts looked like they might even be real. She couldn't fake the egg-carton belly. Bobby made her for a babe whose full-time job was going to the gym between tricks.

"I can't remember the last time I saw a man drink like a man," she said. "Mind if I match you shot for shot?"

"I don't think you'd want to try that, honey," Lebelski said, smiling, a little nervous.

"Dinner in the Sunset Grill says I can."

"You're on," he said and smacked the bar.

The woman signaled to the bartender and said, "Tequila, *dos*."

A few of the younger people at the bar laughed as Lebelski looked at her and winked. "Give the Chiquita what she wants," he said. "Do me again."

The bartender poured them both drinks and the woman stood, displaying her hard-tooled body, lifted the lime wedge off the shot glass, rubbed it on the back of her hand, shook salt on the wet spot, parted her big painted lips, and wrapped them around her hand in a suggestive way. Lebelski watched with horny anticipation. The Latina raised the tequila and drank it down in one long gulp. Then she bit into the lime with her pretty white teeth, sucking on it as she stared directly into Lebelski's eyes. Then she wrapped two fingers around the neck of Lebelski's beer bottle, brought it to her lips, and took a long, slow drink.

"I'll be ready at eight," she said. "What's your room number."

He told her his name was Stan, gave her his cabana number, and asked her name.

"Maria," she said.

If this guy were a tuna, he'd be in a can by now, Bobby thought.

Lebelski lifted his scotch and threw it back and ordered Maria another. She shook her head, said she was going for a nap. "I want to make sure I'm up for you," she said, grabbing his hand, clutching his thick pink thumb. "See you at eight, Stan."

She walked toward the hotel. Lebelski watched her stroll past the people at poolside, watched as men half his age craned their necks to get a look at her narrow-waisted, full-hipped figure. She turned once to see if Lebelski was watching. He was. She knew he would be. She waved and he waved back as she entered the hotel through the Last Wave bar.

Lebelski turned and ordered another round.

Doomed, Bobby thought and left half his Diet Coke and strolled back to his own hotel.

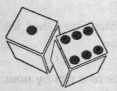

30

The first one he saw arrive was Zelda Savarese.

She carried a single suitcase and checked in without a hitch at 5:28 PM wearing white jeans and a white blouse and white sandals.

Bobby watched her from the far side of the Last Wave bar, his back to the pool area and the sea, but with a clear view of the front desk in the lobby. He was dressed in the same ginger-haired disguise, wearing dark jeans and black sneakers and a black-collared short-sleeved shirt. He sipped a club soda mixed with cranberry and watched Zelda follow a bellman to a private elevator.

Kronk's suite, Bobby thought . . .

A half-hour later Kronk arrived with his

entourage: Dum Dum Dunne and six gray-jackets, three of whom looked like Hispanic locals, probably retired *federales* who obviously had local licenses to carry guns. One was huge, six foot four with a chest that made him look like he was wearing catcher's padding under his gray jacket. *If he were a boulder, he could block a highway,* Bobby thought. He wore dark wraparound sunglasses that promoted as much menace as the tinted windows of a getaway car in a drive-by shooting.

He searched for Ralph Paragon but he was nowhere to be seen. He called Patrick on his cell phone.

"I tailed Paragon this morning to a 10 AM meeting with Noel Christmas and Sean Dunne in a strip club on the outskirts of Atlantic City," Patrick said. "I went in, they were in a booth, bullshitting. They paid no attention to the skanks on stage. They obviously chose the place because they didn't want anyone important to recognize them. I passed them on the way to the men's room and overheard a snippet of conversation. Dunne was saying, 'Take the deal from Kronk.' That's all I heard. I took pictures of the three of them together."

Patrick told Bobby that Paragon went to Kronk Castle, did his rounds, left work early, drove home, kissed his wife, took his son for pizza and to a movie. They communicated on Audiovox wireless phones that could be used from anywhere in the world and as they spoke Patrick was parked in the lot of the Bay Head Cineplex, watching Ralph Paragon's car.

"Good father," Patrick said. "His kid seems to idolize him. So does his wife, who helps support the family as a real estate agent, going to all the conventions, showing homes in the local towns, spending all her free time with the kid at the local yacht club."

He remembered "Number One" on the phone saying maybe he would and maybe he wouldn't go to Puerto Rico. Paragon had sent his stooges to do his bidding instead. *Clean.*

"He's one lucky son of a bitch," Bobby said. "And smart. He stays up there like Father of the Year while the dirty work goes on down here."

"Want me to stay on him?" Patrick asked.

"Yeah," Bobby said.

"I'll rent another car so they don't get suspicious. But I gotta tell ya, watching Ralph Paragon is like watching C-Span."

Bobby watched two gorgeous women stroll past him, dressed in little white shorts and halters. "This is tough duty, too," he said. Then he saw someone else checking in.

She was a very attractive dark-haired woman wearing an expensive floppy hat and big dark glasses and carrying a suitcase with a first-class tag from American Airlines on the handle. She comported herself with an air of confidence that matched her designer clothes.

Something about her triggered familiarity. A nagging detail that he couldn't quite isolate. It was there in front of him, like a face in a hologram that

wouldn't focus. *Was it the way she touched her hat?*
he wondered. *Or the way she impatiently put her
fist on her hip as she waited for the clerk to process
her room? Or the way she looked around the room
like she was planning to redecorate? Or the way she
pointed at herself, telling the clerk she was someone
important?*

He couldn't figure what exactly it was about her
that sent a bulletin of recognition into his brain. It
annoyed him, the way the elusive name of some old
movie star might torment him in a game of trivia.

The desk clerk handed her a key card and Bobby
watched a chunky bellman grab the suitcase and put
it on a little cart. The bellman led the way through
the lobby and out to a Spanish-tiled walkway that led
down to the row of yellow cabanas overlooking the
ocean. He'd seen Stan Lebelski come out of one of
them earlier in the afternoon.

Following at a good fifty yards, Bobby watched
the woman walk with an elegant, erect gait, swinging
her arms like a runway model. They stopped in front
of cabana number 12, next door to Lebelski's, which
was cabana 10. These cabanas stood alone, shielded
behind a grove of palms, away from the steerage
tourists who lodged in the economy rooms of the big
hotel. Unlike the rest of the hotel, these top-dollar
accommodations looked like they were well
appointed and given the very best of care.

The bellman carried the bag inside and the
woman followed. After a minute the bellman

emerged and stopped when the dark-haired woman handed him a tip. *Who the hell is she?* he wondered.

This time he snapped a photograph with the wristwatch camera from the Snoop Shop.

She slammed the door with a flourish of authority and the bellman passed him on the pathway.

"She never gets any older looking, does she?" Bobby said to the bellman.

"*Qué?*" asked the chunky bellman.

"You know, what's-her-name?" Bobby said, snapping his fingers. "She looks great for her age."

"*Sí,*" the bellman said. "And if this is a spot check, *amigo*, I never give out the names of guests. If this isn't a spot check, I still don't give out the names of guests because jobs are too hard to find to break the rules. *Adiós.*"

The chunky bellman kept pushing his cart back toward the lobby.

Why can't we find guys like that to run for office? Bobby wondered.

Bobby was about to follow him to the lobby when he saw Carl Pinto step out of cabana 14. Whoever that woman was in number 12, she had Lebelski on one side of her, Pinto on the other. Instinct told him that the lady in the middle had something to do with the vote in the state legislature and the dirty, bloody maneuvering for Empire Island. But still he couldn't nail down who she was.

Bobby strolled slowly up the tiled walkway and Pinto excused himself as he hurried briskly past him, as if the numbers on the dice might change if he were late. This time Pinto was dressed in a light summer suit with open collar. Bobby watched Pinto go back into the casino.

At a little past six-thirty Bobby took a seat at the Last Wave and opened the *San Juan Star*. Stan Lebelski took a seat farther down the bar, ordered a scotch and a Becks, and sat reading the *New York Times*. Lebelski was dressed in a seersucker suit with a white shirt and pale blue tie. He had showered and shaved and gotten a quick trim. With fresh color in his droopy basset hound's face, he looked like a man ready for a big night. Bobby was amazed he was still on his feet, never mind able to read a newspaper.

At seven o'clock Dum Dum Dunne stepped off the private elevator with Sam Kronk and Zelda Savarese. Three gray-jacketed Latins flanked him, including the one Bobby had nicknamed Roadblock in his head. Dum Dum nodded for them to loosen the knot around Kronk and they fanned out, keeping their subject in clear view at all times, scoping for crackpots, drunks, and sore losers.

Zelda held tightly on to Kronk's arm, leaning up to kiss him. He pretended to be embarrassed, but he let her make a fuss over him, messing his hair, falling dramatically into his arms, posing for snapshots for working-class hotel guests who recognized them and idolized their wealth and fame. Bobby took some shots of his own with his wristwatch camera. *This broad is a fraud,* he thought. *She hardly looks like she's under duress.*

Dunne whispered into the ear of an Anglo gray-jacket Bobby recognized from New York. The gray-jacket went off on a mission into the casino. Kronk checked his watch as he conversed with Zelda. They looked like they were making arrangements to meet later. She walked off toward the late-night boutiques in the lobby. Dum Dum waited a few moments and then nodded to Roadblock and he began trailing her at a prudent distance.

Now Bobby saw the Anglo gray-jacket return from the casino with an agitated-looking Carl Pinto. He had a small stack of chips that he clicked together in his hands like he wanted to get back to those tables. Dum Dum draped an arm over his shoulder and then the same Anglo gray-jacket came into the bar where Bobby was sitting and whispered to Lebelski. He looked up from his *Times*, nodded, belted back the last of his scotch, took a swig of beer. He sprayed a blast of breath freshener into his mouth and followed the Anglo gray-jacket to the lobby area.

Kronk shook hands with Pinto and Lebelski and then Dum Dum led them all into a swanky-looking restaurant–cocktail lounge called the White Sands. Bobby waited five minutes, left a tip on the bar, and walked to the White Sands.

"Sorry, sir," the man at the door said. "We require a sports jacket in the White Sands."

Bobby looked past him at Dum Dum, Kronk, and the two politicians sitting in a booth. A waiter was opening a bottle of champagne and the men already were engrossed in animated discussion. This was no idle chitchat; there was a heavy negotiation going on.

He drifted back to the lobby, passing the chunky bellhop, who was waiting for late-night arrivals. Bobby walked in the general direction Zelda Savarese had gone moments before. He spotted her in a boutique, looking through a rack of overpriced summer dresses. Roadblock rumbled past the store like a tank moving through a city street. Bobby stopped as if admiring the women's clothes in the window. He stared in at Zelda as she browsed. Then he saw her check the reflection of a store mirror and catch his eye briefly. Bobby turned away as she turned full face to look at him.

He returned to the White Sands, glanced through the window, could see Kronk, Dum Dum, Pinto, and Lebelski still brokering some kind of deal at the booth. Then he saw Lebelski look at his watch. Bobby checked his own—7:44. He knew Lebelski had an eight-o'clock date with the Latina who called herself Maria.

Bobby returned to the lobby, exchanged a twenty-dollar bill for two rolls of quarters, and started feeding them into a slot machine just inside the door of the casino. After a few minutes he saw the four men come out of the White Sands. There still seemed to be a level of disagreement amongst them. Kronk was clearly peeved, as most rich men are when circumstances—even the weather—don't go exactly their way.

Lebelski stubbornly shook his head, examined his watch, and hurried off. Pinto sauntered into the casino.

Dum Dum and Kronk remained talking, and Kronk looked like he was in a dark mood. Dum Dum was getting his ass chewed out and took it like a proper butt-boy subordinate. Dum Dum spoke into his walkie-talkie and escorted Kronk to the front of the hotel. Bobby traipsed across the lobby toward the front desk, picking up some tourist brochures about sightseeing in Old San Juan. New guests arrived, tired and cranky from a long-delayed flight. The chunky bellhop pushed his cart to accommodate them. Bobby watched Dum Dum lead Kronk outside as a stretch limousine pulled up. One of the Latin gray-jackets opened the back door for Kronk, who climbed in, waving a finger at Dum Dum. The Latin then closed the back door and hopped into the front seat next to the driver. The limo sped off.

Dum Dum went back into the hotel and Bobby turned away, reading the brochure. Roadblock came up and murmured into Dum Dum's ear.

"For fuck sake find her!" Dum Dum said. "And don't lose her again."

Zelda had obviously given Roadblock the slip and

he trotted off to search the pool area, where diehards were swimming under the brilliant stars and a giant lemon moon.

Bobby followed Dum Dum through the casino, where he stopped long enough to see that a crowd had gathered around a craps table. Carl Pinto was again the center of attention. He was sucking on a piña colada and wagering $50,000 on a roll of the dice. The croupier had to get the okay from his pit boss, who nodded. Pinto shook the dice as the crowd gathered. Dum Dum stood out of Pinto's line of sight as he watched the assembly leader skip the little red cubes across the green felt, looking to match a six point.

"Seven," said the dealer. The crowd groaned as the box guy hauled in Pinto's stack of chips.

Pinto asked for permission to wager a $50,000 marker on a line bet. The pit boss nodded. Pinto picked up the dice and rattled them.

"It's coming back now baby, you were just sleeping, come on now, gimme a seven."

Bobby saw him mouth the words to the Hail Mary as he rolled the dice. Snake eyes. Another loser. Pinto asked for another fifty-thousand marker. The pit boss took a deep breath, turned as if talking into his radio. Got an okay. Nodded. Pinto threw the dice again on the come-out roll. Three, a loser.

The crowd fell silent, as if embarrassed for him, and some drifted away in fear of catching his bad luck. Pinto sucked on his straw, trying to maintain a look of indifference on his face, which was crumbling one tic at a time. "Again," Pinto said.

The pit boss nodded.

Dum Dum smiled, shouldered through the crowd, and key-carded his way through a door marked AUTHORIZED PERSONNEL ONLY. Bobby figured Dum Dum would go inside and let Pinto write markers all night until they owned his soul, and his vote.

Bobby looked at his watch. It was 7:53. He knew the Latina callgirl named Maria would be knocking on Lebelski's door in seven minutes. He hurried from the casino into the lobby, down the Spanish-tile pathway. He drifted out onto the beach, took a position in the thicket of palms, and watched the door to cabana number 10. His black clothing blended into the shadows cast by the trees.

At two minutes to eight he heard a pair of high heels clacking down the tile walkway. He saw Maria walking in a skintight canary yellow dress and carrying a bottle of scotch and a bottle of tequila in either hand. Her breasts were barely contained in the low-cut dress and her large dark nipples were visible through the sheer yellow fabric. She stopped in front of number 10 and Bobby saw that the backless dress went almost down to the crack of her ass. He didn't see a panty line under the skintight dress. The muscles in her calves were like sculpted marble. She tapped on the door with the bottle of scotch.

Stan Lebelski opened the door.

"Hi, Maria . . . I . . . I made the reservation," Bobby heard a nervous Lebelski say as he took pictures with his infrared mini camera.

Maria held the bottles up to Lebelski; he took them out of her hands. She stepped into the cabana and loosened Lebelski's tie. Bobby snapped a photograph as Maria pulled Lebelski to her with the two ends of his unfastened tie and kissed his lips.

"Fuck dinner," Maria said, "I brought Viagra." And she kicked closed the door.

Bobby knew Lebelski was being set up the way Frank Gifford had been stung by the supermarket tabloid. The room was probably rigged with video and sound. He also was sure Pinto was being allowed to OD on his own gambling jones. But what could he prove? These were consenting adults surrendering to human weaknesses.

He looked at cabana number 12 and still wondered about the mystery woman inside. The shutters of her window were half-open and Bobby was about to take a peek when he saw Dum Dum walking down the pathway. Bobby half-expected Dum Dum to kick down Lebelski's door and start popping pictures of him in the sack with Maria like an old-fashioned PI in a forties movie. Instead, Dum Dum passed by Lebelski's door. And knocked softly on the door of cabana number 12. After a few moments the dark-haired woman answered and she threw her arms around Dum Dum's neck and kissed him. Bobby took several quick pictures with the motor drive as the two lovers roamed their hands over each other's bodies. Then Dum Dum entered the cabana.

Bobby hurried to the half-open window and snapped some more very suggestive photographs as the woman knelt and unbuckled and unzipped Dum Dum's pants. He took some more pictures that went over the line into porno and then turned to leave.

And then the sky started to spin. He saw the full moon and the bright stars twirling, streaking into the inky sea. Saw the neon lights of the beachfront casinos in long smears of red and green and silver. He felt like someone had driven a railroad spike into the back of his skull.

He staggered, instinctively reached in his pants pocket for his gun. It wasn't there. He jammed the small camera in the pocket. He felt a kick in the chest that sent him crab-walking across the beach toward the back of the cabanas. He staggered to his feet, struck a fighter's defensive peekaboo pose. He was seeing double, swayed to keep his balance. He saw Roadblock, the massive Latin gray-jacket, coming at him, slapping a blackjack against his open palm. Then he saw the chunky little bellman pointing at Bobby.

"That's him, that's the nosy guy, watching everyone," the chunky bellman said. "Peeping Tom!"

Bobby began backing away from Roadblock, who came at him in long, slow, deliberate strides, as if he'd been waiting for a chance to use the muscles he'd worked so hard to build.

"I told you he was asking questions about the lady in

number 12," the bellman said. "He's been walking back and forth in the lobby all day, all night. Watching everyone, everything. I see, I see everything. I know my job."

Roadblock pursued Bobby, who kept backing away, trying to clear his head, gulping the good, clean Caribbean air, searching for *control*. Focus was returning.

"Gimme the fucking camera," the big Latin said.

"Fuck you," Bobby said, regaining his footing. "These pictures of your mother sucking cock will make me a fortune."

He knew that ranking on Roadblock's mother would make the guy lose control—which put *Bobby* in control. The enraged Roadblock charged Bobby. Bobby stepped to the side and hit him with a six-inch right hand in the ribs. He heard a sound like walnuts cracking. The guy dropped to one knee, wincing in pain. But he was big and strong and tough. He came out of the crouch and threw a right hand of his own. Bobby sidestepped it again but the bellman came from behind Bobby and broke a length of driftwood across his back.

Bobby spun, backhanded the bellman, sending him sprawling face first into the sand. Inert. But before Bobby could turn around, Roadblock had grabbed him in a ferocious bearhug, lifting him off the sand in an iron grip. Bobby wished he would have brought Herbie with him.

"I'm gonna put you in a fuckin' wheelchair for life for talking about my mother," the Latin said.

Bobby could feel the wind leaving his lungs as

the big man increased the pressure. He sagged his head forward, feigning unconsciousness, and then in one ferocious snap he smashed his skull against the big Latin's nose. He felt it flatten like an egg.

Roadblock screamed, loosened his grip, and buried his face in his hands, blood rushing through his fingers. Bobby planted his feet, detonated a full-bodied right hand to his temple, and watched the big man topple to the sand like a jointless statue.

Then Bobby heard the slide action of a gun.

"Turn around nice and fucking slow, fella," Dum Dum said.

Bobby turned, his ginger wig gone, his mustache dangling.

"Step over here in the light where I can see you," Dum Dum said. Bobby hesitated, clinging to the palm shadows. The thing about sand is that you can't hear someone coming from behind you. It's how Roadblock and Dum Dum had gotten the drop on Bobby. For the same reason Dum Dum didn't hear or see the slim figure approach him from the rear and bang him across the back of the head with the same blackjack that Roadblock had dropped in the struggle. Dum Dum pitched face first onto the beach.

"What the hell are you doing here?" Zelda Savarese asked Bobby as she held out her hand for him.

"I won't bother asking you the same thing," he said, taking her hand and hurrying down to the surf and trotting along the moonlit ocean toward the Caribe Hilton.

31

They entered the hotel through the rear pool and beach area and went straight up to Bobby's room.

"So you followed me here?" she asked.

"Yes," he lied. He'd come to see who else would be attending the summit. He had no idea she'd be there.

"I'm flattered," she said.

"You said you needed my help and I wind up needing yours."

She picked up the ice bucket, went down the hall, came back with it full, dumped a bunch of ice into a towel, and pressed it against the lump on the back of his head.

"Thank God the skin isn't broken," she said and laughed.

"What's so funny?"

"You, with the mustache half falling off," she said.

He chuckled. He didn't mention anything about following her to see Father Dooley or seeing her all over Kronk in the lobby.

"You think I'm a liar, don't you," she whispered as she turned his face toward her. She looked at him with her big dark-chocolate eyes. *Gorgeous,* he thought. He suddenly realized he was in a hotel room with Zelda Savarese. *Alone.*

"You saw me acting like a giddy lover with Sam, didn't you?"

"Yeah," he said. He didn't mention the pictures he'd taken of that or the ones he'd snapped of her with Father Dooley.

"It's part of the deal," she said. "That's what he wants. For me to look like his little adoring queen in public. Dressed in white. Sam insists I must always wear white. He says he wants to marry me for real now. I can't live with that, Bobby . . ."

She bit her lower lip, her eyes welling with tears. *Female machismo again,* he thought. *Tears instead of spears.*

"What's he got on you?" Bobby asked.

She brushed the sand off his face and his hair, looked him in the eye as if studying a gem for flaws.

"Come with me," she said. "Please."

She took him by the hand and led him into the bathroom. She turned on the shower and started to undress.

"You want the dirt on me," she said, looking him hot in the eyes. "I want you to see me clean first. No more secrets."

"Just like that?"

"Actually, when I first saw you in the lobby in Atlantic City I thought you were absolutely gorgeous. Then, when I saw you on the Boardwalk, I was even more attracted to you. Even Sam noticed that I couldn't keep my eyes off you. And when we sat alone together over a drink, I wanted to jump your bones and kiss you so bad it made my lips hurt. And watching you beat the shit out of that big ape that Donald Dunne had following me around, it turned me on."

The flattery was working wonders on his libido. So was watching Zelda Savarese undress. He thought of Amy McCoy. Fleetingly. He'd been with her a grand total of one night and she'd left in the morning. No commitment there. She was a mixed-up woman-child with whom there might never be a second time.

And here was Zelda Savarese—*the* Zelda Savarese—totally naked. *Unbuckling my pants,* he thought. *What the hell. A little naked truth never hurt anyone.*

In the shower she lathered and scrubbed and kneaded him, everywhere, shampooing his hair and massaging his scalp with strong, small fingers, kissing his mouth under the hot, hard spray, gliding the soap over every inch of his muscled body. He became fully aroused and she knelt and sampled him as the warm water ran down his spine.

Then he washed her, running his fingers with the soap into all the privileged places of her body, secret magic spots that millions of adoring fans dreamed of in desperate fantasies, watching her respond with involuntary spasmic moans. As he washed her strong shoulders he felt the minuscule stitches of an old surgery at the top of her right arm. The plastic surgeons had been extremely skillful because the scars were not visible to the eye. She self-consciously guided his hand from her shoulder to somewhere softer.

She did not behave like a woman in love with Sam Kronk.

By the time they fell, scoured clean, onto the crisp sheets of the king-size bed she acted even less like a woman ready to marry another man. Her body lived up to the fantasy, an athlete's perfect machine, not an ounce of body fat, all firm muscle and sinew but soft in the right places and as feminine in her lovemaking as any woman he'd known.

She was as trained, experienced, and skillful in bed as she was on a tennis court. Zelda Savarese was the opposite of the awkward, virginal, exuberant Amy McCoy.

Afterwards, as they lay naked, she told him what Sam Kronk had on her.

"Two years ago, at the U.S. Open . . ."

"It wasn't one of your shining moments," Bobby said. "The innuendos in the press, the rumors . . ."

"I threw the match."

There was a long silence as Bobby considered this. She'd promised the truth and she delivered it like one of her serves—straight, direct, blazing, 100 mph. He could almost hear the reverberating *thwack* of the racquet and the furry whiz of the ball.

"So how does Kronk fit in?"

"I was broke," she said. "I had an accountant who

convinced me to invest most of my money in Asian stocks. They went down the drain. I also invested in a fast-food chain in Europe. It was about as successful as New Coke. Then I found out my accountant had been robbing me for years. He filed fraudulent returns with the IRS. When I confronted him, he blew his brains out. The IRS didn't give a shit about him. They were still dunning me. Accusing me of tax evasion. Threatening jail. I was desperate."

"So you went to Kronk?"

"I'd known him for years," she said. "He was always trying to get in my pants, since when I was a kid. Before I even turned pro, he would come down to see me when I played in tournaments like Sport Goofy in Disney World. Or the Orange Bowl. He visited me when I was in the Bolletieri Tennis Academy in Bradenton, Florida."

"That's where Agassi, Seles, Courier all trained, wasn't it?" Bobby asked.

"Yeah," she said.

"But you were a kid. What? Like fifteen?"

"Uh-huh."

"Is he a pedophile?"

"No," she said. "He never tried anything overt. He was planting seeds for when I turned eighteen. Sam is too smart to get caught doing anything that foolish and illegal. He was trying to make a young girl develop a crush. It didn't work. Not that I wasn't vulnerable. I was a little girl who was raised without a father. I had no father figure in my life, only coaches.

My mom was great, traveled with me everywhere. It was very sad. And awkward. Mom developed a crush on Sam. But he wanted *me*. Sick. He tried to get to me through Mom, gave her gifts, maybe even money, I'm not sure. But I didn't need some middle-aged millionaire with a wig to take the place of the father I never had. Yes, I had an emptiness in my life, a hunger, an insatiable void that only ferociously competitive tennis could fill. On a court, facing a top player, the fans, the nerves, the tension, the press, the pressure, the savagery of tennis gave me an *identity*, filled that hole in my soul. I didn't need Sam Kronk. I had *The Game*. I loved tennis and it loved me back. Besides, I always thought Sam was gross."

"But he's stayed on your trail since?"

"He would follow me on the circuit," she said. "Australian Open, Canadian Open, French Open, Italian Open, Wimbledon, Washington, D.C., the Virginia Slims in Dallas, at Madison Square Garden, in Hawaii. I'd walk on the court, whether it was supreme, grass, or clay, and I'd look up in the stands to find my mother and there was Sam Kronk, winking, smiling, waving. No matter what hotel I stayed in, he was in the same one, on the same floor. He always seemed to know what restaurant I was dining in. When I went dancing, he was in the same club."

"Creepy."

"When I turned eighteen I asked him why he followed me around the world," Zelda said. "He said, and I quote, 'I love a woman with a killer instinct that can match mine.' I told him to fuck off and leave me alone. He laughed and said someday I would need him and I would come to him." She shrugged sheepishly and said, "He was right."

"He suggested you throw the Open match two years ago?"

"No," she said. "What he said was, 'What will you do for me?' I thought he meant he wanted me in bed. I even considered it. That's how desperate I was. I asked if that's what he wanted. Well, he really knew how to make a fading girl athlete feel great: he told me I was too *old* for him. He just wanted me, like a possession."

"So you still don't sleep with him?"

"No, I really don't," she said. "Thank God for small mercies."

"So what happened?"

"He told me to think about what else I could do for a man in his line of work," she said. "He owns casinos. He promotes boxing matches. I know people bet on tennis, especially rich people, like him and his jet-set, globe-trotting friends. Two years ago I was a favorite at the U.S. Open. I knew immediately what he wanted me to do. More than winning money, he wanted to be *right*. The one who *knows*. The all-knowing, inside-trader, never wrong, infallible Sam Kronk, Mister Right."

"So you approached him?"

"I went to him and told him in no uncertain terms that I planned to bet against myself and throw

the match," she said. "I gave him the details of how
I would do it. Blow a serve here, fail to make a
backhand there, keep it close but dump it. And
that's how I did it."

"And you didn't know he was videotaping the
conversation?"

"No," she said.

"Wouldn't it implicate him, too?"

"No," she said. "I came to him like it was a confession. He's very clever on the tape in not saying a
word. There is no indication of who I am even talking
to. The camera is just on me as I say I plan to throw
the match. A plain white wall behind me. There's no
talk of money changing hands. But that tape, coupled
with the rumors and the terrible press I got after that
game, could get me banned from the game, blow any
chance of ever working as an announcer, and, worst
of all, get me arrested for fraud. I'd lose what few
endorsements I have left. My place in tennis history
would be tarnished. The statute of limitations doesn't
run out for another four years."

"For this, he paid your back taxes?"

"Well, he had someone else do it," she said. "One
day I wake up and, voilà, I'm in the clear with the tax
man. It can never be traced to him. The IRS would
take a check from Saddam Hussein."

"Now he's using the tape and you want me to get
it back?"

"Yes, and find out if there are any more around,"
she said. "I don't think there are, because he'd be

afraid they'd leak out and then he'd lose his hold on me. He likes having the only one of anything, be it a Picasso, a vintage car, a rare coin, an incriminating tape. *Me*. He's using this tape to make me marry him. A trophy in white. I'll have to sign a pre-nup that says I get nothing when he decides to dump me. It's what you do when you have too much money, after you've bought and collected everything else. You collect people."

"I hear he buys them dead or alive," Bobby said.

"You mean his skull and bones collection? I've never seen it but I've heard all about it."

"Yeah," Bobby said. "What's that all about?"

"It's the new fad amongst the bored idle rich. Like rare cigars and wine from Thomas Jefferson's collection. I hear people talk about the greatest bone trophy they could own. Most want JFK's skull. Lee Harvey Oswald's trigger finger. Someday Muhammad Ali's fist. Pelé's foot. Elvis's pelvis. Maybe my elbow. Any part of the skeletal anatomy, from head to toe."

Bobby thought of the toe fragments in the McCoy bedroom and Izzy's office, and the missing toes on the floating corpses of Ben Lee and Betty Wang. *Trophies*, he thought.

"When are the nuptials?"

"Next month."

"Doesn't give us much time," he said.

She looked at her watch. "Speaking of which," she said. "I have to meet Sam by eleven. He doesn't like it when I'm late."

She jumped out of the bed and Bobby watched her pull on the tight white dress, which made him aroused again as he lay naked on the big bed. She walked to him, bent, and kissed him where it made matters worse.

"I wish I could stay for more," she said. "I'll find a way to see you back in New York."

He watched her unlock the door.

"By the way," he said. "What were you doing in Brooklyn yesterday with Father Dooley?"

She stiffened, looked like she'd been shot between the shoulder blades. She turned, frightened, lower lip trembling.

"You saw that?"

"I followed you, Zelda," he said, pulling on his underpants.

She shook her head and took a breath.

"I got a call from a man who said his name was Father Dooley," she said. "He said he knew about the tape that Sam Kronk had. I had never heard of him in my life. But he said he thought he knew a way to get it back."

"So you went there?"

"Yes," she said. "I went there. In the rain. On the subway, where I didn't think I could be followed by Sam's people."

"So what happened?" Bobby said.

"I went into the confessional booth like he said I should," she said. "I asked if he was Father Dooley. He said yes. I asked about the tape Sam Kronk had.

He said he knew a man named Morris Daggart who might be able to get it back for me if I agreed to work with him to help expose Sam Kronk for some murder—or murders. I'd heard Sam rant about this Daggart guy before. But it all felt like a setup to me. Like one of Sam's tests. I didn't believe this Dooley was even a priest. So I told him to go fuck himself and I ran out of the church. Next thing I know I see this car speeding down the street and this so-called priest gets killed. I just kept running."

"You don't know Morris Daggart?"

"The priest said the same thing," Zelda said. "He said Daggart had a picture of me and him together."

"I've seen it," Bobby said.

"Bobby, do you know how many people I've posed with over the years?" she asked. "Fans, friends of sponsors, people on the circuit?"

"This one is signed, 'Love always,'" Bobby said.

"And you think it's my handwriting?" she said. "Christ almighty, Bobby, do you know how many bogus Zelda Savarese autographed tennis racquets people have sold? Tennis balls? Photos?"

Bobby nodded. Autograph forgery was big business; he'd investigated it himself as a DA cop. *Christ,* he thought, *she might really be telling the truth.*

"I'm sorry," she said. "But I have to go before he shows up. He wants me to do a walk through the casino with him. Some British tabloid is doing a photo shoot."

He walked to the door. She looked at him with the brown eyes again and kissed him.

"Help me, Bobby, please."

And then she was gone, taking the stairs down six flights.

As Bobby finished dressing, he looked out his oceanfront window. He watched her lone ghostly figure in white jogging along the slick shore against the black sea under a big yellow moon.

He had seen enough. He was going to leave in the morning, whether he found out who the lady in cabana 12 was or not. She was probably just some anonymous piece of ass that Dum Dum was knocking off.

He took the elevator down to the lobby and as he stepped off adrenaline shot through him.

He saw three men leaving a fancy restaurant called the Ocean Grille. Sam Kronk, Mayor Tom Brady, and Sean Dunne all shook hands as they left, picking at their teeth with toothpicks. Two Latin gray-jackets stood nearby. Bobby turned his face away from the three men and studied the menu in the restaurant window.

In the reflection in the glass Bobby saw Kronk look at his watch. "I think we have most of it all ironed out, then," Kronk said.

"Thanks, Sam," Brady said. "For everything. Again. As always."

"I still have some snags to fix up back home," Sean Dunne said.

"My jet is gassed up and waiting for you guys," Kronk said. "Go. I better go, too. Zelda will be waiting."

* * *

Bobby ate chicken, rice and beans with plantains, washing it down with ginger ale. He didn't want to venture back to the Kronk Caribbean, because there would be an alert out. He went back up to his room, where the smell of Zelda Savarese lingered on the sheets as he slept soundly through the night.

In the morning he showered and caught the first flight out of San Juan for New York.

32

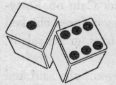

AUGUST 4

Back in New York, Bobby collected *The Fifth Amendment* at Petey Maguire's dock, motored it back to the Seventy-ninth Street Boat Basin. He hopped in the Jeep and dropped off all the film he'd shot at a color lab on Forty-fourth Street.

He met Max Roth in the lobby of the *Daily News* on West Thirty-third Street and gave him the faxed pages showing that Ralph Paragon, Sam Kronk's head of security, was the real landlord of 22 Empire Court.

"I'm gonna go with this for tomorrow," Roth said.

"I hope you know this links Kronk to the disappearance of the McCoys."

"I'm aware of that," Bobby said.

"And because he's so active in the Brady campaign, it touches the mayor too," Roth said.

"I know that, too," Bobby said. "Max, off the record, I just came back from San Juan. Kronk was down there. So was Brady, Lebelski, Pinto, Sean and Donald Dunne. I think it was a summit to influence the legislature's vote on legalizing gambling."

"Father Dooley's death is tied to all this, too, isn't it?"

"I think so," Bobby said. "One more thing, Max. Those documents show that Paragon also put his wife and kid's names on the deeds. I don't think you have to drag them through the mud in print."

"I agree. I better get started. I'll call you later."

He met Maggie in the West Bank Cafe on Forty-second Street for lunch, where they ordered chicken sandwiches with fresh shoestring fries, green salads, and icy pints of soda.

"I got that file on Ralph Paragon," she said and showed Bobby a printout. "I don't understand it."

Bobby did. It said Paragon had a totally clean if unremarkable record in the Bureau. Nothing very heroic, but no major fumbles in a twenty-year career. *A very careful, cunning operator,* Bobby thought. But in the section concerning his time in the Idaho office, he saw that Dum Dum Dunne worked under him for six months.

Maggie took a sip of soda and an impish smile spread on her face. "So, who are you dating, Pop?"

"I'm not *dating* anyone. I'm *talking* to a few chicks."

"Cool. Names?"

"So how's Liam?"

"He's cool," she said. "But he's not the only guy I'm talking to. I'm just gonna talk to guys, not see any for a while."

"That's good," Bobby said. "You ever hear of Zelda Savarese?"

"The tennis player?" Maggie said. "Pretty. Wears nice clothes. You talking to *her*, old man?"

"I've met her," Bobby said, telling her as much as he thought necessary. "I'd like to find out some things about her."

"Like what?"

"I dunno," Bobby said. "Who her parents were. Where she's really from. The magazine stories all say she was raised by her mother. That her father abandoned her mother before she was even born. I'd like to see medical records. Her financial stuff."

"If I had a Social Security number I could tell you what she bought on her credit cards for the last seven years," Maggie said. "If you get me her mother's maiden name, I can tell you everything there is to know about her."

"I'll work on that," Bobby said. "Meanwhile, find what you can. What else is going on?"

"My history teacher gave me my mark early."

Bobby's heart raced. He hoped for the best, expected the worst.

"And?"

"I got a ninety-five," she said.

"YES!" he shouted in the crowded restaurant, slapping the table. Heads turned and Maggie hung hers.

"You're getting like Mom," she mumbled, putting down her fork and folding her arms. "Public humiliation. Now I won't be able to eat with everyone looking over. I'd be better off if I failed."

"Sorry," Bobby said, smiling with exuberance.

She sat blushing, arms folded. Bobby started spearing her fries and she grabbed her fork, jabbed the back of his hand.

"I didn't say I wouldn't eat the fries, old-timer," she said.

Bobby sat in the basement office of Kings County Hospital listening to Brooklyn Medical Examiner William Franz. They had both donned protective gowns and surgical gloves to shield themselves from airborne germs when they had walked through the morgue lab. Their face masks now dangled around their necks in the filtered air of Franz's office. Through the half-drawn blinds on the office window Bobby could see out into the lab of stainless-steel sinks, linen hampers, and scattered gurneys. Medical students worked at the autopsy tables using scalpels, probers, Stryker saws, and Luma-Lite lamps, speaking into dangling microphones as they worked on the dead.

Franz had once given Bobby information that convinced him his girlfriend, whom he was accused of killing, was still alive. He'd told Bobby that the teeth of the cremated woman in question showed she was a smoker, and probably a New Yorker because of the unique fluoride found in her teeth. Bobby's girlfriend was from the Ukraine and did not smoke.

With details like those, Franz had a way of turning a roomful of silent corpses into a chorus.

He was a small, round-faced man with glasses as thick as ashtrays who spent too much time underground with dead people to have a normal sense of humor. But when Franz held a file folder in his small hands, it commanded the respect and attention of a loaded pistol.

". . . so forget whether or not it was the car that killed Father Dooley," he was saying. "Of course it killed him. But if the police are saying this Ricardo Santiago fellow was driving, he must have been some stunt man."

"Why?"

"Because blood rusts."

"Huh?"

"Santiago was dead at least forty-eight hours before Father Dooley was killed," Franz said. "Rigor mortis had already set in when we got him. His hair was wet when he died. Come here, look."

Bobby walked around and looked at a color photograph of Santiago, the man accused of driving the car that killed Father Dooley. "See this wound here?" He pointed to a deep contusion on the back of the head. "There, on the edges, you can see the early traces of rust around it," Franz said.

"Rust?"

"Blood rusts," Franz said. "Blood is filled with iron. So if it dries and the body lies in the rain, the blood rusts. Rust takes at least forty-eight hours to start forming. Plus the rigor mortis. This wound killed Santiago. A blunt instrument hit him from behind. He didn't die crashing the Cadillac."

"You saying someone killed this poor bum a couple of days before, then put him behind the wheel of the Cadillac that killed Father Dooley and ran the car into a wall?"

"I'm saying blood rusts," Franz said, smiling behind glasses that made him look bulletproof. "Sun shines, flowers bloom, blood rusts, cadavers talk. And this is all off the record. For now."

"Then Santiago, this poor helpless wino, couldn't have been the one who ran over Father Dooley?"

Franz slammed closed the file folder. "If he died during that rainstorm a few days before the one when Father Dooley died, it would account for the blood rusting. I'll release my report in a few more days."

Bobby nodded and leaned on the desk toward Franz.

"I also asked you if you could review the evidence from Manhattan on the blood and flesh matter they found in Izzy Gleason's office," Bobby said. "Supposed to be from Jimmy Chung."

The corners of Franz's mouth rose in a devilish smile and he sang, "Jimmy crack corn and I don't care."

"What?"

"It's either a horny callosity of the epidermis," Franz said, "or an inflammation of a synovial bursa. I'm not sure yet without doing my own tests. But Manhattan's preliminary tests show that the flesh matter found in Gleason's office was either from a corn or a bunion, which usually means a toe. The bone fragments tend to suggest they are not from the great toe, or big toe, so I would guess it's from the second toe of the left foot, which would lean more toward a corn than a bunion."

"A toe?" Bobby said, flashing on Ben Lee and Betty Wang, their corpses each missing the second toe of the left foot.

"Remember the nursery rhyme?" Franz said. "Well, that little piggy went to market while your little piggy got none."

"Is it possible all that blood came from a guy just getting his toe amputated?" Bobby asked.

"Absolutely," said Dr. Franz. "Like feces, blood runs downhill."

The drive to Bay Head took Bobby seventy-two minutes.

On the way, he called Ralph Paragon at Kronk

Castle to make sure he was working. When he heard him answer, Bobby knew he was there and hung up.

He then drove directly to Paragon's house. He wanted to warn his wife that a story about her husband that might embarrass her and her son would be running in the next day's New York *Daily News*, and that it would probably be picked up by the wires, radio, TV, and Jersey papers. He rang her bell several times. There was no answer. Both the Lumina and the Mercedes were absent from the driveway.

Patrick had said that except when she was working in her small real estate office in town, or traveling on business, Toni Paragon spent a lot of time with her son, George, on the small private beach of the local yacht club.

Using his old NYPD police shield, Bobby bluffed his way past a teenage security guard at the yacht club. He found Toni Paragon on the private beach, building a sand castle. He saw little George pouring water from an orange bucket into a mud hole next to the castle and then go splashing back into the surf with a bunch of other kids his age.

Toni Paragon was wrist deep in the mud hole of wet sand, skillfully adding turrets to the elaborate castle. She wore a baby-blue one-piece bathing suit over an athletically trim figure. Her curly blond hair sparkled in the hot sun. Bobby thought she looked terrific for a woman of thirty with a son who looked about ten. *Too damn good for a bastard like Ralph Paragon*, he thought.

"Mrs. Paragon?" he said.

She looked up, shielded her eyes, and smiled politely. "Yes?"

Bobby squatted, told her who he was, that he was a private investigator working for a client involved with 22 Empire Court in Manhattan.

"I've read a little about that," she said. "Awful story. But what does it have to do with me?"

"Your husband secretly owns the building," Bobby said.

She laughed and then saw that Bobby wasn't laughing. "That's ridiculous," she said. "We just about make the mortgage on our own house, plus the dues here, two cars, boat fuel. Ralph doesn't own any other property. I'd know it if he did. I balance the checkbook."

"Your name and your son's name are also listed as corporate officers," Bobby said. He showed her a copy of the fax Maggie had sent him. She held it in one trembling hand, held the other hand to her mouth.

Sunbathers roasted on beach chairs all over the small beach, boomboxes blaring music or broadcasting the Yankees game. Her son, George Paragon, ran up from the water with the orange bucket filled with water and plopped it next to his mother. She forced a worry-creased smile.

"Here ya go, Mom," he said, looking at Bobby.

"This is an old friend of your father's," she lied. "Go ahead back in the water."

"Hi," he said to Bobby and ran back to join his

pals. She turned to Bobby, handing him back the paper.

"This must be some kind of mistake."

"I just wanted to warn you before it appears in case you want to leave town for a few days with your boy," Bobby said. "I have a kid of my own. I know what public humiliation can do to a kid. Your name won't be in the story, or your son's. Your husband's will be."

"You're saying Ralph is involved in those people being missing?"

"My guess, and I'm not the law, is that he's fronting for his boss, Sam Kronk. If he's being used as a patsy, or a fall guy, maybe you should warn him, have him come clean. But once this comes out, the cops are gonna start looking into him—big time."

Bobby watched her dig a moat around the sand castle, a deep jagged ravine to keep out all imaginary intruders. Her fingers dug furiously, almost violently, as if to protect her nest.

"Do you believe Ralph's involved?"

"I think he works for a bad guy," Bobby said. "I think there's lots at stake, and maybe a few people are dead. I think maybe you should think about packing a bag."

She dug deeper into the wet sand, her hands like little backhoes. She looked like a woman on a mission.

"No, I couldn't do that," she said. "Ralph married me when I was alone with my son. My son calls him

Daddy. His real father died when he was a baby. Ralph at least put some sort of father figure in his life. And I took a vow. 'In good times and in bad.' If Ralph's in trouble, he'll need me. Now more than ever."

"It could get very nasty," Bobby said, "for you and your kid."

She stopped digging for a moment, looked down at her son splashing in the water, then into Bobby's eyes.

"Mister, I don't know who you are," she said. "I guess I should appreciate you coming to warn me. I might not look like much of a fighter, but if my family is under siege, I won't run. I'll fight."

This shit-bum Ralph Paragon has a helluva wife, Bobby thought.

She dug her hands deeper into the moat surrounding the castle, as if for emphasis, and said, "Like I said, thanks for the tip, but now, if you don't leave I'll call a fucking security guard and have you removed. Because if you're my husband's enemy, you're also an enemy of mine."

She stared straight into Bobby's eyes. A scared but loyal wife protecting the man her son called Daddy. He admired her. As pretty as she already was, it made her all the more attractive.

Some bums have all the luck, he thought.

"I'm sorry."

"Leave," she said, staring him dead in the eye as she poured the bucket of water into the moat surrounding the sand castle.

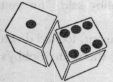

33

The wake was mobbed.

And now the mourners were leaving after reposing hours had finished at nine PM. All the people whose lives Father Jack Dooley had touched in his busy days in the city streets seemed to have come out of the New York night to be there at the funeral home on Bay Parkway. Young people of every stripe from places like Bensonhurst, Park Slope, Sunset Park, Bay Ridge, Coney Island, Crown Heights, Red Hook, Fort Greene, Bedford Stuyvesant, East New York, and Flatbush had been in attendance and still lingered outside on the street. Whites mixed with blacks, Hispanics with Asians. A lot of them weren't even Catholic. Some were dressed in suits and ties. Others in street clothes. Some boasted the colors of various rival youth gangs. A truce had been called on all beefs between the gangs until after the funeral in the morning.

Grown men and women Father Dooley had counseled when they were teenagers were there with their kids, some of them openly weeping as they exited the funeral parlor after paying their final respects to one of the most popular clergymen in the city.

Politicians paid their respects—judges, council-men, assemblymen—posing for TV news crews and giving quotes to print reporters. Max Roth worked the crowd like a lone wolf, avoiding running with the press herd, instead accumulating quotes from anonymous people, noting keen observations, searching for the small image that might tell the big story.

Bobby listened as Max Roth found one guy in his senior year at Boston University. He had a pair of old sneakers draped around his neck. He told Roth that when he was a kid in junior high, his mother had bought crack with the money she was supposed to give him for new sneakers to wear in a championship bas-ketball game. Dooley bought him the sneakers. He was high scorer in that championship game, and that helped win him a scholarship to a terrific high school, which led to a scholarship to Boston University. When his mother died a year later, Dooley raised the money for a proper burial. Now he'd grown up and here he was at Dooley's wake with those very sneakers—worn and battered, but which he had saved—draped around his neck.

"I came to thank Father Dooley for giving me a life," he told Max Roth. The sneakers would be in the lead and the kicker of his column.

Bobby saw Noel Christmas walking his way, imprisoned in his own muscle mass, like a man hooped with rubber tires. There were times Bobby actually felt sorry for Christmas. This wasn't one of them.

"Remember anything more about Dooley dying?" Christmas asked, belching trapped poison into his fist.

"Noel, take a hike, will ya," Bobby said. "Not tonight."

Bobby drifted away from Christmas and Roth when he saw Assembly Leader Carl Pinto exit the funeral home, his eyes skittering back and forth in his head like the reckless dice he'd used in San Juan to wager his soul. Other religious leaders left the wake, Hasidim from Crown Heights, priests and bishops from the diocese, Rabbi Simon Berg, and Reverend Gaston Greene.

Morris Daggart came out of the funeral parlor and nodded to Bobby. Bobby ignored his glance, especially with Noel Christmas around. Willie, Daggart's preppie bodyguard, walked with him. He didn't nod to Bobby.

Bobby stopped and straightened his brother Patrick's tie. His kid brother had worked closely with Father Dooley over the years and was deeply saddened by his death. "The whole city loses," he said. "It isn't corny to say that some people can make a difference. I watched this guy turn around kids who teethed on jail bars. That goddamned car crashed into the whole city."

In a loud flourish a wall of cops arrived with Mayor Tom Brady, who pulled up in his Ford Explorer. He was whisked into the funeral home after everyone was gone to say a prayer at the coffin as a photo-op for an AP pool photographer.

Brady was out in five minutes, professionally somber, offering more sound bites. "The diverse group of New Yorkers he has brought together tonight in harmony in honor of his death speaks volumes about the remarkable life Father Dooley led," the mayor said, and then he was gone, off to his race for the Senate, flush with Sam Kronk's money.

"Dooley was no accident," Bobby said to Patrick.

"You're sure?"

"Yeah," Bobby said.

"Well, I can tell you Ralph Paragon was nowhere near Brooklyn while you were away," Patrick said. "My sore ass can attest that he put in the whole time babysitting."

"Of course," Bobby said. "He sends his goons while he hides in his little cocoon as daddy and Kronk Security Chief, secretly taking orders from Number One."

"Who's Number One?"

"I'm not sure," Bobby said. "Kronk, most likely. But maybe Brady. Or it could be Sean Dunne. They were all in San Juan."

"Whoever it is, you're saying Number One is orchestrating this whole show?" Patrick said.

"Yeah," Bobby said.

"Well, I can tell you that if Paragon is Number Two, he's damned good," Patrick said. "Because after following him, he looks as clean as the Pope's feet."

"Jesus, they'd be big on Kronk's trophy shelf," Bobby said.

"Huh?"

"Sick freak collects bones," Bobby said. "I'll tell you later."

Reverend Greene and Rabbi Berg made their way through the crowd toward Bobby. "Got a minute?" Greene asked.

Patrick nodded and Bobby walked off to the side.

"There's people here I don't want knowing my business," Bobby said, pretending he was exchanging small talk.

"Okay, but we gotta talk," Greene said. "Father Dooley called and left a message before he died. I was out but he was upset about something he'd discovered. We can feel something big coming down. We gotta move the money."

"Moe hears that Kronk and the mayor know how much we've raised," Rabbi Berg said. "They don't intend to let us use it."

"We've called for an emergency meeting," Greene said. "Father Dooley asked for it himself before he was . . ."

"Murdered," Bobby said. "I was there. It wasn't an accident."

There was a solemn silence as the two clerics stared at Bobby.

"Moe is going to tell us where to meet tonight," Greene said.

"We'd really like you to be there," Berg said.

"Move it from where?" Bobby said.

"Coney Island Aquarium," Berg said. "Midnight."

The lights outside the funeral parlor were extinguished and the big crowd began to disperse. Moe Daggart moved through the crowd and fell in next to Bobby as everyone made for the parking lot.

"Things are getting ugly," Daggart whispered.

"Do I know you?" Bobby asked, warning Daggart that he didn't want to talk to him in public.

Daggart nodded and dropped back behind Bobby, who walked with Reverend Greene.

"What did Dooley say to you exactly?" Bobby asked.

"He said he'd found something out about someone who might jeopardize the operation," Greene said.

"Who?"

"I'm not positive but I have an idea," Greene said. "Let's discuss it at the meeting tonight."

Then Bobby heard the screeching of tires, loud cursing, shouting from passing cars. Women in the crowd screamed. The cars careened and crashed. One Chevy convertible was packed with Hispanic gangbangers flying Latin Kings colors; the other car was filled with blacks boasting the red garb of the Bloods.

"Nigger *maricons*," shouted one Hispanic.

"Spic motherfuckers," came the reply from the carload of black gangbangers.

Then came the machine-gun fire. Mourners screamed and dove for cover. Bobby saw Reverend Greene, the seasoned military veteran, instinctively push Rabbi Berg to the ground out of harm's way. Someone tackled Bobby from behind. As he fell, Bobby heard Reverend Greene moan and saw him get spun as the bullets ripped into him. Clumps of his bloody flesh tore away and splattered on the sidewalk like overripe tomato pulp. Car windows burst into storms of glass. Bobby looked up from the ground and saw the muzzle of an Uzi from one car blazing as the two cars crossed paths. The cars sped away in opposite directions and Patrick was quickly on his feet firing after the one with the Hispanic occupants. Noel Christmas, moving like a human glacier, raised his gun to fire, but it was too late. The cars had disappeared into the vast dark netherworld of Brooklyn, one toward Coney Island, the other downtown.

Bobby shrugged for whoever it was on his back to get off. Moe Daggart rolled away, got up to one knee. Bobby looked at him and nodded. Then he and Bobby scrambled to Reverend Greene.

Women sat screaming and grown men rocked back and forth, holding their ears, babbling, some weeping. People stared at the gang members in the crowd with hostility.

"Wu'nt us," said one Hispanic gang leader who also got up from behind a parked car. "This is bullshit, man. We all chillin' till we bury the padre. Wu'nt us. We had nu'in' to do wi' dis shit. Uh-uh."

A black gangbanger concurred: "Fuckin' wannabes, man. No way we involve. Nuffin' to do wif this shit, man."

There was no pulse in Reverend Greene's body. No breath came from his mouth. Blood leaked from a half-dozen holes in his black suit. Members of Reverend Greene's flock now knelt around him, praying, weeping, cursing, begging him to open his eyes for the Lord. He did not. The starched white collar of his ministry was quickly running red as it blotted up his lifeblood. The proud Vietnam veteran, who had survived the Tet Offensive and brought his God, dignity, and a little hope to his people of the streets, had finally died in the war at home.

Within minutes police cars with lights and sirens going squealed to the scene. An ambulance arrived right after them. Remarkably no one else was hurt. Already a reporter from New York One was doing a live remote, broadcasting that warring gangbangers had opened fire from two cars following the wake of Father Dooley. The other reporters already on hand to cover the wake were going with the same story.

Bobby was confused. He didn't believe the gang-bangers were shooting at each other. It looked to him like one shooter was firing directly at Reverend Greene. Windows were smashed for effect, but Bobby didn't think it was an accident that no other people were hit.

"When I saw the guns come out, I jumped on you," Daggart said.

Bobby looked at him, then at Patrick, who nodded that he was telling it as it happened.

"Thanks," Bobby said softly.

Bobby pulled Patrick to the side. "How many guns were firing?"

"A few came out the windows," he said. "Only one fired."

"That's what I thought," Bobby said.

"Funny how they didn't hit each other," Patrick said.

Through the pandemonium Bobby noticed a dark Lumina drive slowly down the side street, crossing Bay Parkway, which the cops now had blocked to traffic as the morgue attendants covered Gaston Greene's body with a heavy sheet and the uniformed cops pushed the crowd back.

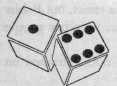

34

The hammerhead shark swam right at him, the one visible black eye like a vortex to hell, its teeth as menacing as anything Bobby had ever seen. Since he was a kid the shark tank at the Coney Island Aquarium had always been the great spook house of Bobby's life. Forget the make-believe devils, witches, and hobgoblins of Dante's Inferno over at the Astroland amusement park. Here in the Aquarium there were real-life monsters that could eat a human being for lunch like a Nathan's Famous hot dog.

The hammerhead made the turn in the tank, swimming past a big, old-fashioned rusty safe. Years ago salvage hunters had taken the safe from the sunken wreck of the *Andrea Doria*, placed it in the saltwater shark tank to preserve its contents when it was opened on a live TV special. The old, waterlogged bills inside didn't bring as much revenue as that generated by the TV show. Afterward, the safe was left at the Aquarium as a haunting addition to the shark exhibit.

A tiger shark, smaller and cockier, came right behind the hammerhead, like a novice hit man trying to impress the big guys. It was tough enough to make Bobby step back and grip the handle of the .38 revolver in the left-hand pocket of his windbreaker and the 9-mm Glock auto in his right pocket.

After seeing the black Lumina, Bobby had sent Patrick back to Paragon's house in New Jersey with instructions to ring the bell, then run away and hide—to see if he came to the door, to make sure he was home.

After watching Dooley and Greene die in front of him, Bobby came prepared for a two-gun night to meet Rabbi Simon Berg and Moe Daggart and his preppie bodyguards for a tête-à-tête.

He'd called to make sure Herbie would be there,

too. He knew if there were any unscheduled shenanigans, Herbie would be in his corner, because the bottom line was still Izzy Gleason's freedom, and Izzy was Herbie's blood.

The Coney Island Aquarium was the second-largest one in the nation, and as a fundraising source it now rented out its space at night for private parties. Weddings, birthday parties, anniversaries, corporate functions were held here, under the stars of the twenty-acre outdoor park grounds, or inside, amid the oceanic fauna and flora in exotic seascape exhibits. A rent-a-cop hired by the New York Zoological Society, an elderly black man, was on hand to make sure no one walked off with a pet penguin or the office machines, as well as to prevent some delirious drunk from going in search of Pinocchio in the belly of a white beluga whale.

Moe Daggart had rented the Aquarium for the night.

Bobby got there early to get the lay of the land. The Aquarium was protected by a twelve-foot fence running along the Boardwalk. The only other access was from the big street-side parking lot where Bobby had left his Jeep. He saw the black security guard, more interested in the Mets game on the TV in the office than in the scheduled midnight party. Bobby checked out the exits and each exhibit. Everything seemed copacetic.

He ended up at the shark exhibit, which was the planned meeting place.

At 11:55 PM Bobby heard a truck and several cars roll from the parking lot onto the grounds and pull up outside the shark exhibit. A three-quarters moon dangled in a starry sky like a theater prop. The image of Zelda Savarese, running along the San Juan shore under the yellow moon, dressed in ghostly white, flashed in his mind.

Herbie arrived from the parking lot with Rabbi Berg in a Chevy station wagon.

"Are we expecting more trouble?" a shaken Rabbi Berg asked.

"These days I'm always expecting trouble," Bobby said. The rabbi had not wanted to come to the meeting. Bobby convinced him he had to be there. He was the last of the three clerics with a claim to the money. He needed to be there for the two who could not. The rabbi had reluctantly agreed.

"Tell me who to waste and he goes in the sewer system," Herbie said. Bobby asked if Herbie had his gun. He nodded.

Daggart's Mercedes limousine rolled through the gates, passing the dolphin amphitheater, and parked by the shark exhibit.

Now the armored truck that Bobby had seen collecting the gambling cash from the various houses of worship rolled into the area outside the shark tank.

Moe Daggart got out of the backseat of the Mercedes with a pretty blonde, whom Bobby recognized immediately as Cindy, Daggart's receptionist from NuCent Ventures Inc. She was dressed in a diver's wet suit that nicely showed off her shapely figure.

Willie also stepped out, glared at Bobby, and

then went to chat with the Aquarium guard, handing him some cash. The guard nodded, jumped into a scooter, and took off.

"I've sent him on his lunch break," Daggart explained. "You remember Cindy, don't you, Bobby?"

"Sure," Bobby said.

"Cindy's a lady of many talents, as you're about to see," Daggart said. She walked to the back of the limo and the driver popped the trunk and climbed out of the car. Two more preppie goons emerged from the front seat on the passenger side.

The two armed guards climbed down from the truck.

Cindy reached in the trunk and took out a harpoon and a big white plastic barrel with a sealed lid. She also took out a scuba tank and a face mask and a pair of flippers.

"Go ahead, darling," Daggart said. "Be careful."

"Piece of cake," she said and walked into the shark exhibit.

"So, we're supposed to talk business," Rabbi Berg said.

Daggart nodded and signaled to his preppie help, who were all dressed in light-colored sports jackets, cuffed blue jeans, and topsiders with no socks.

"Are they on a little league polo team?" Bobby asked.

Willie shot him a look and murmured to his colleagues as they entered the shark exhibit. The armored-car guards followed them in.

"When we got involved in all this, I never thought people would die," Rabbi Berg said. "I'm sick in my heart and soul."

"Someone is talking to the other side," Daggart said.

"Who are you talking about?" Bobby asked.

"Kronk and his people," Daggart said. "The mayor is about to crack down on our Vegas nights. He knows that if the clerics build the First Stop social services center to fill the void he's left, it'll embarrass him when he runs for the Senate. I think he knows you're tightening the noose on him, Bobby. He also knows that if Kronk winds up being investigated for the Empire Court murders and if I have money to bid on the Empire Island Terminal, he'll lose his golden goose."

"I've been thinking about that," Bobby said. "I think getting yourself in that position might be motive enough for you to whack out a couple of business partners."

"You think I'd have Father Dooley and Reverend Greene killed?" Daggart said.

"I think they were both clearly targets. Not accidents."

"Hey, you were there, too," Daggart said. "Both times. I could draw assumptions from that about you, too."

Rabbi Berg looked from one to the other, intrigued.

"I suppose you could," Bobby said, nodding.

Daggart smiled and shook his head. "Look, I called for this meeting before anything happened to Father Dooley or Reverend Greene. Because I knew the other side was getting desperate."

"But they were killed right after it was called," a suspicious Rabbi Berg said.

"I'll tell you what, Rabbi Berg," Daggart said. "Since there are only two of us left in this business arrangement, and since you don't trust me, I suggest that *you* take charge of the money—tonight. We'll load it into the truck and your friend Emmet here can drive it wherever you want. I trust you implicitly."

Rabbi Berg looked momentarily taken aback. He glanced at Bobby, who shrugged. "I didn't say I didn't trust you," Berg said. "We're all thinking out loud here. My good friends are dead. I'm upset . . ."

"Kronk and his cohorts are using the old-fashioned divide-and-conquer tactic," Daggart said. "But rather than us splitting, I insist you take the money. You sit on it. Surely you know a place where you can safely stash it for *two* days until the legislature passes the gambling resolution."

Berg looked flustered. "No, I trust you to handle it."

"Where were *you* thinking of hiding it?" Bobby asked Daggart.

"I thought just the three of us would bring it there so there could be no more leaks," Daggart said. "I'd rather show you than tell you."

Berg nodded to Bobby. He looked at his watch: 12:13 AM.

"Let's do it," Bobby said.

They entered the shark exhibit. Bobby asked Herbie to wait outside, to watch the parking lot for new arrivals.

Cindy had the stepladder rigged to the top of the shark tank and adjusted a winch, which was attached to a big nylon net that was used to lift sick or injured sharks from the big tanks to an adjoining smaller recovery tank.

"It's the same winch they used to put the safe in," Daggart said. "Cindy was working her way through college here then. It's where I found her. She's a wizard with sharks."

Willie handed her up the white bucket and she popped off the lid and pulled out a crab cage filled with live flapping fish. She tossed some of the live fish into the far end of the tank. The sharks instantly swam in pursuit of the fish. Cindy slipped lithely into the tank carrying the crab cage and a harpoon for safety, and swam directly to the safe. She turned the dial several times, opened the heavy iron door, and pulled out the dozens of blue-colored, waterproof packages that were sealed against seepage the way Bobby had often seen boat-smuggled cocaine and heroin packaged.

She quickly tumbled the packages into the waiting net, pulled the webbing securely up around them, and signaled for Willie to activate the winch.

"Each of the forty-two packages is exactly forty pounds," Daggart said. "A total of sixteen hundred and eighty pounds of one-hundred-dollar bills. In case you're ever a contestant on *Jeopardy*, that's how much seventy million dollars weighs."

"Some school, that Harvard," Bobby said.

Bobby tightened the grip on his 9-mm Glock in his right jacket pocket. The .38 was sweaty in his left hand. As the money rose through the shark tank, Bobby saw a hammerhead make a hairpin turn and torpedo toward Cindy.

She turned and faced it, fumbled with the harpoon. Dropped it. Looked up and faced the shark, motionless. Bobby felt an ugly bile rise from his stomach. Then he watched Cindy nonchalantly reach into the crab cage and pull out another live fish. She set it loose just as the hammerhead was upon her. The fish wiggled frantically away. The hammerhead made an abrupt turn, its mad black eye gleaming through the bubbles, and lashed after the doomed fish.

More sharks swam at her and she set loose all the remaining fish, and soon the shark tank was a boiling feeding frenzy.

Cindy grabbed on to the bottom of the rising net just as it broke the surface with the $70 million.

Bobby watched the hammerhead turn back to where Cindy had been, its teeth poised for slaughter.

"I told you she had many talents," Daggart said.

The winch lowered the net to the ground in the

viewing area. Bobby watched as the three preppies and two guards loaded the bags onto a hand truck.

They wheeled the cart out of the exhibit.

Bobby left last, lingering as he had as a child, to take one last look at the sharks.

Then he saw the five ski-masked men in black with the compact Uzis. One of them had his gun under Herbie's chin. Another had his to the back of Rabbi Berg's head.

"I was watching the parking lot from the street," Herbie said. "They came from the Boardwalk side."

Bobby hadn't thought of that. He looked around and saw the five machine guns trained on them. He knew if he tried anything Herbie would certainly die. Rabbi Berg would be the last of the Three Wise Men to die. Then they'd kill the rest of them. Sometimes you had to admit there was no fight; only surrender. Like now.

"Everybody, feed your guns and your car keys to the penguins and then put your fucking thumbs in your mouths," said the head gunman, in a raspy whisper. "Do that, nobody dies."

Because it was a whisper, Bobby couldn't place the voice. As he slowly removed the guns from his pockets, he checked out the footwear of the rest of the gunmen, saw the thick soft-soled black shoes the Kronk gray-jackets all wore.

Ralph Paragon's goons, he thought.

He saw the others throw their guns over the fence into the penguin exhibit. The goofy-looking birds who claimed a single mate for life dispersed in unsteady waddling pairs.

A small, plain, black van now rolled down the ramp from the Boardwalk entrance to the Aquarium. Three of the five ski-masked gunmen rapidly loaded the forty-two bundles of money into the back of the van.

The head gunman walked over to Daggart.

"You don't have a fuckin' gun, asshole?" he said.

Daggart shook his head. The gunman frisked him and found a little .25 in an ankle holster. He smacked the broad side of the little gun across Daggart's head and knocked him down. A small trickle of blood spilled from a head wound.

"On your fucking knees, Daggart," he said.

Daggart knelt, trembling, head bent as the gunman pointed the small pistol at his head. "Let's see if it's loaded," the gunman said.

"Please, no, please, I beg you . . ."

"I hate it when they beg," the masked gunman said. "Do I have to frisk the woman, too? C'mere, lady . . ."

"No," Daggart said. "She's got no gun."

Bobby stood watching, his thumbs jammed in his mouth, as the gunman approached him. The masked man nodded, turned to walk away, then spun and threw a vicious punch deep into Bobby's midsection. Bobby doubled over, gasping for air.

"Nice party," the head gunman said, climbing into the front passenger seat of the plain black van, as the others hopped in the back. "Great party favors."

The black van sped across the Aquarium grounds

and up the ramp to the now deserted Boardwalk. Herbie and Bobby chased after it and watched it speed a half-mile along the wooden planks to the newly refurbished Steeplechase Pier, where it made a left-hand turn toward the ocean end of the pier.

Bobby slowed and watched from the railing as the van stopped. The money was quickly lowered from the pier in a net to a waiting boat in the blackened waters off Coney Island below. Then the men rappelled on ropes the thirty feet down one side of the pier into the boat.

The boat then sped out to deep water and veered west, toward the Narrows, lost in the New York night.

Moe Daggart sat on a bench in the Aquarium as a tearful Cindy blotted his head wound with a pink hankie.

"They got it all," Daggart said, staring into middle-space in a dumbfounded daze. "Kronk won. I've lost. It's over."

"They stole the dream," said Rabbi Berg. "They killed two of the best men in the city, and then they stole the dream."

"Should I call a cop?" asked an Aquarium security guard.

"No cops," said Daggart, shooing the guard away.

What would they tell the cops? Bobby thought. *That five masked men came and stole seventy mil in illegal gambling money?*

He also thought it was all too neat.

Bobby searched the slope of the outdoor penguin exhibit. He had located both guns but was still looking for his car keys.

"The great fucking detective," said Willie as Bobby scattered a few cranky penguin couples. "So great he didn't even think of them coming by boat."

Bobby didn't even look up, just decked Willie with a single punch to the chest. Willie flapped in the water amid the squawking penguins.

Bobby finally found his keys.

35

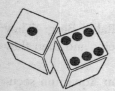

When Bobby got back to *The Fifth Amendment* Zelda Savarese was sitting on a deck chair, shivering in the night river wind. But her trembling appeared to be coming from within.

"I've been waiting for hours," she said.

"You could have gone inside and waited," he said. "Everyone else does."

"I wouldn't pry," she said. "I'm not like everyone else."

"No," Bobby said. "No, you're not. That your red Lexus parked up on the rotunda?"

"Yeah," she said.

"You have two tickets on it," he said. "You're not allowed to park there."

"I'm cold," she said.

He took her inside and opened a cupboard and searched for the tea bags. He must have put the box in a different place. He found it pushed into the next cupboard. He took one tea bag and put it in a cup, then filled it with tap water, placed it in the microwave, and punched in 2:12.

"Same as my area code," he said. "It makes perfect tea."

She placed her pocketbook on the table and rubbed her hands together. He lifted a throw blanket from the nearby sofa and wrapped it over her shoulders.

"Gotta pee," she said. "Then we have to talk."

While she was in the head he rummaged her pocketbook, found her medical insurance card in her wallet. He knew the ID number would be the same as her Social Security number. He jotted it down and put the wallet back in her purse.

The microwave oven beeped and he took out the cup of tea, dipped the bag a few times, and opened the fridge. He saw that the orange juice was in front of the milk. When you live alone in confined spaces, you know where you put things. It had been rearranged. "Milk or lemon?" Bobby asked.

"Milk," she said. "No sugar."

He poured it for her and handed her the cup. She took it from him and warmed her hands with the cup, then reached up and grabbed his lower lip between both her lips and sucked on it.

She took a sip of the tea and placed it down on the countertop and held out her arms. "Hold me, Bobby."

This damsel-in-distress routine is too hokey, he thought. But he took her in his arms anyway. She shivered in his warm embrace.

"I'm scared," she said.

"Of what?"

"Take me to bed and make me stop shaking," she said.

"I'm not in a loving mood," he said. "I watched a good man die bad tonight."

"Please," she said.

He thought about someday being on a rocker in a nursing home talking with the other horny old gents and having to admit that one night, long ago, when he was younger, and could still get it up without Viagra, he had said no when *Zelda Savarese* asked him to make love to her.

He took her into the bedroom, turned off the light, and they made love until her trembling was replaced by another kind of quivering. When he could make love no more, they lay in the pitch dark. She was silent for a long minute, as if listening to the night sounds of the old river, the dings and swooshes, far-away hollow moans, faint cries in the wind, haunted echoes, and the ebb and flow of the universe.

"On the plane home Sam thought I was sleeping," she said, her voice low and tremulous. "I heard him talking on the phone. He mentioned that he didn't care who got in his way. He said the McCoys got in his way and they were now trophies."

"Trophies?"

"That's the word he used," she said. "He mentioned that he planned to have something called Empire Terminal in his hands right after the election."

"Who was he talking to?"

"I'm not sure," she said.

"Where was Donald Dunne?"

"Sleeping in the back of the plane," she said.

"Did he mention anything else?"

"Yeah," she said. "That's why I'm here. He kept asking whoever it was on the phone if everything was all right with 'the rap,' like maybe a rap star?"

Bobby thought of Rapa Properties but didn't mention it.

"What else?"

"He listened for a long time and then he said, 'If this fucking Emmet gets in the way, make him into a trophy, too. Like the McCoys and the Chinks.' He was talking about having you killed, Bobby, wasn't he?"

"It sure sounds that way," he said.

He reached into the drawer of his night table, took out the portable ultraviolet light from the Snoop Store, and switched it on.

"What's this, the sixties?" she said. "Black lights? Plug in your Jimi Hendrix eight-track!"

Bobby smiled and then saw that her fingers glowed in the UV rays. So did his. His were supposed to. Hers weren't. She had used the bathroom, only where he hadn't sprayed liar's powder. She had said she hadn't gone into his cabin. If that were true she would never have gotten the liar's powder on her hands. She had been rummaging in his refrigerator, kitchen cabinets, bedroom drawers and closets. Searching for something. Anything. Information about what he knew.

"Look at our hands," she said and laughed.

"The salt air does that," he said, concocting a quick lie.

She half-chuckled, then said, "Sam's threat isn't funny."

"No, it isn't."

They heard someone enter the boat through the cabin door. Bobby put his hand over Zelda's mouth and rolled out of bed silently. He grabbed his .38 from his jacket pocket as he heard the intruder fumble in the salon. Bobby saw Zelda grope for her panties in the ultraviolet light.

Bobby stalked naked to the bedroom door, the gun held high. The door slid open and Bobby reached out for the intruder with his free hand, ready to fire with the pistol in his right hand. He grabbed a handful of hair and twisted.

"Bobby?" Amy McCoy said.

Zelda Savarese fell to the floor, pulling the sheet over her naked body.

"Oh," Amy whispered, wide-eyed and astonished. "Sorry . . ."

Bobby ushered her out into the salon, sliding closed the door to the stateroom.

"Amy, what the hell are you doing here?"

Amy pointed to the bedroom door and said, "There's a . . . a *naked woman* in there."

"I noticed," Bobby said and walked her out of the salon onto the deck of *The Fifth Amendment*.

"But I thought . . ."

"Thought what, Amy? That we were going *steady?*"

"I gave you my . . ."

"Oh, Jesus," he said.

"Don't you dare bring His Holy and Sacred Name into this."

"This is not going very well, Amy," Bobby said. "I think maybe you should leave. We'll talk tomorrow. Please call me."

"Up yours," she said. "You bastard! God forgive me. I don't need your help. I'll find out what happened to my brother without you. You and your . . ."

She looked down at his penis and he realized he was standing naked, holding the gun, with Zelda Savarese in his bedroom.

Amy stormed off the boat and Bobby saw Pam and Dot, the two women from the *Armitage*, peeking out the back door as he stood there naked. Pam had the little calico kitten in her hands, petting it.

"Hi, Bobby," she said. "Don't forget I still have your pussy cat."

"Feel free to come over and pet it, anytime," said Dot.

"Thanks," he said. "Maybe tomorrow."

When he went back inside, Zelda Savarese was fully dressed. Bobby pulled on dungarees, sneakers, and a sweatshirt. He walked her outside to the deck.

"I'll be right back," he told her and hurried back inside, where he rummaged in his Snoop Shop boxes and picked up a magnetized FM tracker bug.

He walked Zelda up the winding ramp to the rotunda overlooking the river.

"What time do you have?" she asked.

"Three-thirty."

"I better get home, get some sleep," she said. "I have to get back to see Sam early or he'll go nuts."

"I'm sorry about the interruption."

"Hey, a guy like you, I figure there has to be a parade of chicks," she said.

"That's not really true."

"I didn't get to see her but I'll bet she's a doll," she said. "She your main squeeze?"

"I only met her this week."

"Oh," she said. "Then we're in competition. I don't like losing."

"That's too flattering," he said. And thought, *Even from a liar whose hands glow in the dark.*

"I'm worried about you," she said, kissing his lips.

"I worry about you," he said.

She didn't know how to take it. "I'll be okay," she said. "But I still need your help."

"I'm working on it," he said.

"Help me and I'll do *anything* for you."

She climbed in the car and rolled down the window. He bent to kiss her goodnight and magnetized the FM tracker bug underneath the frame of her front door. She drove off and he went back down to the boat.

His bed still smelled of Zelda Savarese, but he couldn't stop thinking about Amy McCoy.

36

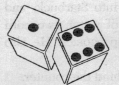

AUGUST 5

He slept for four hours, awoke, swallowed his vitamins for breakfast, did his push-ups and sit-ups, took a three-minute shower, dressed in jeans and a T-shirt, and drove over to Avis on the West Side and rented a drab gray Plymouth Breeze with tinted windows. It wasn't the kind of car you chose to pick up chicks but in a surveillance tail it would be as anonymous as a quarter in a laundromat.

He left the Jeep parked on the street and loaded his Wackenhut microwave-beeper surveillance computer into the console between the Plymouth's bucket seats. Orange letters zippered across an illuminated grid on a bright-green nine-inch screen. A flashing blip on the screen pinpointed the beep coming from the FM bug Bobby had planted on Zelda's Lexus. He programmed the computer and called up an illuminated digital map of Manhattan. The beep immediately located the target within a three-mile radius.

Bobby programmed for a pinpoint of Zelda's car and the computer gurgled and the blip began flashing on a street next to her apartment building. Across the bottom of the screen digital letters spelled out the exact location: *Seventy-second Street west of Central Park West.*

Bobby knew she hadn't left yet, so he picked up a *Daily News* from a newsstand with the headline REV SLAIN AT PRIEST WAKE. He went into Starbucks and bought a small coffee, a bottle of water, two corn muffins, and some chocolate chip cookies. He also asked for two large empty cups.

"For what?" asked the guy behind the counter.

"To piss in," Bobby said.

"Oh," the guy said. "I gotta charge, but . . ."

"You get me coming and going, pal," Bobby said as he paid.

He sat watching the Dakota for over an hour, glancing at the *Daily News*. The headline story said Reverend Gaston Greene was killed in a gang cross-fire outside the wake of Father Jack Dooley. A sky-line box above the logo on page one read: KRONK AIDE TIED TO MISSING MCCOYS, *see page 3*. Bobby turned to page 3 and read the Max Roth column about Ralph Paragon, Sam Kronk's head of security, being the secret owner of 22 Empire Court.

The lead read: *"Sam, did you make the lease too short?"*

The rest of the column was a scathing series of questions for Sam Kronk, Ralph Paragon, and Mayor Brady concerning the disappearance of Eddie and Sally McCoy.

Bobby was pleased with the coverage, even if it was buried under the headlines of the Gaston Greene killing.

He called Maggie, gave her Zelda Savarese's Social Security number. She said she would do a complete search on her.

At 9:17 AM Zelda came bounding out of the building, looking scrupulously around for familiar cars or faces this time. Satisfied she wasn't being watched, she walked to an open-air parking lot a half-block down. Bobby started the engine and studied his screen. There was no need for him to ever show up in her rearview mirror.

He waited and saw the blip starting to move on the screen. Her car headed south on Broadway, and Bobby started to tail her from a distance of about six blocks. He coasted downtown, through Columbus Circle, over to Seventh Avenue. When he hit Fortieth Street, he saw her computer blip pulse left on Thirty-fourth. He was surprised. He thought she would have taken the West Side all the way down to the Lincoln Tunnel and over to Jersey, then pick up the Garden State Parkway south to Atlantic City.

He also wanted to know who she stopped to see along the way—maybe someone like Ralph Paragon.

But she veered east and he followed at an unseen distance. She made a right on First Avenue and then began to make a left. Then her blip disappeared from the computer screen. He hit the digital printout: *Last entry Thirty-first Street and First Avenue.*

The Queens Midtown Tunnel, he thought. *She's going to Queens.*

He picked up speed because he knew he wouldn't receive transmissions from the tunnel. He reached the tunnel two minutes after she had entered it and raced through.

As soon as he reached the other side he punched in a Queens map and he picked up Zelda's blip again. She was taking the Long Island Expressway east toward Long Island.

Why? he wondered. *Where? To see whom?*

He put the car on cruise control at 55 mph. Zelda was doing 65 and 70, and occasionally he had to speed up to keep her within his three-mile radius. After about forty minutes on the LIE, Zelda's blip disappeared again as she crossed over the county line from Nassau into Suffolk. He called up a Suffolk map and found her blip, still heading east, out toward the Hamptons.

A few times, on long stretches of open flat road on eastern Long Island, where traffic became sparser and the exits farther apart, he spotted her little red Lexus in the distance.

When he did, he slowed, stayed in the center lane.

Zelda finally exited at Westhampton Beach, and Bobby fiddled with the computer until he was able to get a local map up on the screen. He found her again, heading past the small airport and into the town. She then made a series of turns, as if to be sure she wasn't being followed, and finally took Old Riverhead Road down toward the bay, passing the elegant estates of the rich and super-rich.

The blip slowed and Bobby programmed for a read-out—*Old Riverhead Road, East of Bay Street*. Bobby followed the twisting contours of the map, until he passed the sprawling estate. He saw the red Lexus in the traffic circle that led to a big colonial mansion. Zelda Savarese walked up the wide steps, nodding to a Hispanic pool man, a white man who cantered a horse on a bridle path, an Asian gardener, and two black workmen who were repairing the roof of a guest house that could accommodate a family of ten. Zelda rang the bell.

Bobby made a U-turn and cruised along the high hedges that embroidered the estate until he found a break in the foliage where a large tree towered above the grounds. He parked, took out his Nikon with tele-photo lens, and snapped photographs of Zelda as she waited. Bobby took pictures of the entire estate, which was scrimmaging with workers. An awful lot of money was being spent.

Then Bobby saw who was spending it.

Finally a black butler opened the door for Moe Daggart, who stepped out of the house and embraced Zelda Savarese, lifting her off her feet and kissing her on the mouth.

Lying, conniving bitch, he thought as he continued to snap photographs. Many of the workers—the horse trainer, the pool man, the gardener, the butler, the maid—came up and shook her hand as if they knew her for years, congratulating her. Bobby took more pictures.

And then she went inside with Moe Daggart, who the night before had sat as Cindy blotted blood from his head, moaning about having lost everything.

Moe Daggart didn't look like a man who had lost so much as a night's sleep, never mind $70 million.

He'd lied to Bobby. And so had Zelda. She lied about not entering his boat. Then she had made love to him, playing the vulnerable damsel in distress, lied some more, and even made him feel sorry for her. He had probably ruined any chance he would ever have of being with Amy McCoy again. All because he fell for the celebrity, the fame, the disarming beauty, and the lies of Zelda Savarese. Who was—literally—in bed with Morris Daggart . . .

Is Daggart Number One? Bobby wondered. *In cahoots with Zelda Savarese? Or are they both taking orders from Paragon?*

Right now all he could prove was that they had both lied to him, but that was hardly against the law. He had to catch them at their bigger game: the Empire Island terminal sweepstakes, and all the money and murder it took to get it.

He climbed back in his car and was about to pull away when he saw a Geo Metro with rental plates enter the gates of the estate. He watched the car wind up the traffic circle. He saw the front doors of the estate open and Moe Daggart come out again and descend the stairs to the car.

Then Bobby saw a nervous State Senate Majority Leader Stan Lebelski step out. Moe Daggart led him into the mansion.

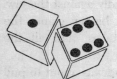

37

On the way back to the city, Bobby called Izzy Gleason and Max Roth and asked them to meet him on his boat. He checked his messages and there was one from George, the waiter from the Golden Pagoda with the eye tic. He asked Bobby to meet him in a fondue restaurant named A Taste of Sweden on Eighty-sixth Street in Brooklyn at three o'clock. If this was agreeable, he asked Bobby to beep him and leave eight number 8's on his beeper and he would know. Bobby left the 8's.

He stopped at the film lab on Forty-fourth Street to pick up the film he'd shot in Puerto Rico and drop off the new film he'd shot at Daggart's estate in Westhampton.

When he got to the Seventy-ninth Street Boat Basin, Izzy Gleason and Max Roth were already waiting on board *The Fifth Amendment.* The three of them sat in front of the TV in the salon after looking at the photographs of Lebelski with Maria in Puerto Rico.

Bobby told them most of what he knew, leaving out pieces of the story until he could check them out further. He didn't tell them about Zelda Savarese—or Amy McCoy. He did mention his suspicions concerning Ralph Paragon, about how he thought he had the

McCoys killed to get the property for the Empire Terminal scheme, then had Ben Lee and Betty Wang killed because they knew something about Jimmy Chung. And that he suspected Paragon had the clerics killed and, finally, robbed all the money they had raised with Moe Daggart.

He also told them about finding both Pinto and Lebelski in Kronk's hotel in Puerto Rico, and that he had seen Lebelski at Daggart's house in the Hamptons that morning. "I'm convinced they had Lebelski's cabana rigged for video," Bobby said.

He didn't show them the rest of the photographs, the ones of Dum Dum with the mystery woman in cabana 12. Or the ones of Zelda Savarese and Sam Kronk—or the ones of Zelda with Father Dooley. If she really was a victim of Kronk's treachery, there was no need for anyone else to know her secrets. Other than throwing a tennis match to pay off debts, he wanted her to be clean, the way she was when they showered together before falling into his big hotel bed in Puerto Rico. But by now he was almost certain she was dirty. He just needed to ask her why—in person.

The three men looked through the photographs of Lebelski and Maria and then watched a breaking TV news report from an Albany reporter who was saying that State Senator Lebelski, who only a few days ago had come out adamantly against the legalized-gambling resolution in the legislature, was now wavering.

The New York One broadcaster said Lebelski had spoken to reporters in the past hour by phone from an unknown location.

"Here's the statement Lebelski gave just an hour ago," the reporter said, reading from his notebook, looking occasionally into the camera. "Quote: 'I am listening to the will of the people instead of my own prejudices on this issue. Because as I travel around the state, more and more of the people I meet tell me they want gambling in New York. The polls show that they want it. My mail shows they want it. Phone calls and telegrams to my office indicate the people want it. For this reason I am at least going to reevaluate my previous opposition to this resolution. With a new century coming, perhaps legalized gambling is an idea whose time has come. After all, we in the legislature are supposed to reflect the will of the people. So my vote is not yet carved in stone.'"

Bobby looked toward Izzy and Roth for reactions.

"I can't believe it," Roth said. "He blinked. A complete flip-flop. Political blackmail. Why would he do it?"

"After consulting with his dick," Izzy said, "which his babushka wife would cut off with a fuckin' sickle and boil with cabbage if I know Polack broads, Lebelski decided to change his fuckin' vote before they show the wife the video of him burying his burrito in that Porto bimbo in Old San Juan-o. Hey, I don't blame him one bit. What's the fuckin' difference? You've heard the expression, 'The law is an ass.' Wrong. The law is a *piece* of ass. Jurors—guys *and* bims—change their votes all the time for a piece of ass and, hey, the republic survives."

Izzy opened a Hershey's Krackle and stuffed it in his mouth, devouring it in three chomps. He then peeled the cellophane from a Slim Jim and gobbled the processed pepper sausage as he popped the cork out of a bottle of Roederer Cristal champagne. Took a foaming gulp. Opened another Slim Jim and sipped his champagne with it.

Max Roth watched in galvanized horror. "Bobby, do I have to subject myself to this?" Roth asked. "In one outburst he derided two races, one gender, and the entire American judicial system. Plus, watching him eat—if you can call it that—is like witnessing a crime against humanity."

"Hey, Max, what'd you wake up on the wrong side of your fuckin' exercise mat?" Izzy said. "Maybe if you rolled on the treadmill with Lois Lane's daughter you wouldn't be so uptight. Take off the fuckin' press card, pull on a condom, and join the human race, will ya? Get a hump and maybe you'll stop being one."

"I'm leaving," Roth said.

Bobby put up a hand. "Izzy, lighten up," Bobby said.

"The guy has a personality about as excitin' as a fuckin' Yule log," Izzy said.

"Yours is like germ warfare," Roth said.

"Max, you're a columnist, get a sense of humor," Izzy said. "Call a fuckin' cab and tell the Habib driver to take you to Bellevue to watch the screwballs rock back and forth in their straitjackets like fuckin' human bowlin' pins. Those are 'serious journalists' who didn't have a sense of humor, pally. Laugh, Max. Get laid. Eat a fuckin' hot dog. Then maybe you'll understand why a guy like Lebelski sells his vote for a piece of heiny. Because it feels fuckin' *good*. Remember that? Feeling good? In a health food store it has a skull and crossbones on it."

"Bobby, this is pointless," Roth said. "That he's an officer of the court is one of the great mysteries of the ages. But I really do have better things to do."

"Listen to me, Max," Izzy said. "Good homicide cops have to think like criminals to nail them. Imagine yourself into Lebelski's life for a fuckin' nanosecond, will ya? Has a wife who looks like fuckin' Walter Matthau. Before he goes on the trip his doctor writes him a scrip for Viagra, first boner in twenny years, in the tropics, and along comes a sizzling hot Rican mama, tits like mangoes, ass like a couple of honeydews in a spandex bag, and you wanna know why he'd be compromised into changing his vote? Because he wants to feel alive once more before he fuckin' dies from advanced nonliving in a shithole like Albany, where the most exciting event of the stultifying day is watching the Amtrak arrive late."

Max Roth sat staring at Izzy, blinking. "Bobby, I

came to discuss strategy and instead I get Dutch Shultz's dying words."

"Basically Izzy's right, Max," Bobby said. "They found an aging pol's weakness and they're exploiting it."

"Then I'll write it," Roth said.

"Good," Izzy said. "I'd love to see you get sued for libel. Even I couldn't defend you and I'm the fuckin' beboppin' best. By the way, Max, would you like to testify as a character witness for a guy who kills the fuckin' Roadrunner on a First Amendment case?"

"What the fuck is he talking about?"

"He said 'fuck,' Bobby," Izzy said. "There's hope for him yet. Now we gotta get him to practice what he preaches."

"We don't have the evidence yet, Max," Bobby said. "But let's try to figure out what's going on. Lebelski and Pinto will assure that the resolution passes. Then the terminal gets built in the last days of Mayor Brady's term. Kronk gets even richer . . ."

"But where does Daggart fit in?" Max asked.

"I'm trying to figure that out myself," Bobby said. "That's why I asked you both to be here."

"I don't know what you expect to get out of the human toxic waste dump here," Roth said, nodding toward Izzy. "But I just don't see where it works to Kronk's advantage to bring Lebelski down to his hotel, get him in a compromising position, videotape it, and then have him change his vote in *favor* of legalization when Kronk is *against* it."

"The fuckin' tofu is clogging your brain, Max," Izzy said. "You guys are missing the point here . . ."

"Try this on," Bobby said, cutting Izzy off. "Kronk can't go back to the banks in New Jersey for more money, right?"

"Right," Roth said. "He's already overextended with them. And they'll call in their notes if he supports legalized gambling in New York, because they'd see it as a threat to their investment in his Atlantic City casinos."

"Right," Bobby said. "Try this. That's why he has to put on the public position of being against the legalized-gambling resolution in New York. Meanwhile he uses Moe Daggart to raise illegal money in the church Vegas nights and the enormously lucrative sports book, creates a dummy corporation under Ralph Paragon's name to acquire the land needed to build the Empire Terminal. Then after gambling is voted in by the voters, he'll simply do a friendly merger with Paragon, whom he already owns."

"This sounds great," Roth said. "But how do we prove it all?"

"Nah," Izzy said, chewing a Rice Krispies bar now. "Something smells like shit in a new car here. You guys are forgetting that they tried to frame me for a murder."

"They needed a fall guy," Roth said.

"Yeah, but why me?" Izzy said, pacing the salon. "For a while there, I sort of liked thinking this Jimmy

Chung called me because I was the best lawyer in New York. But now I think he called me just to frame me. Because he knew Bobby would investigate and because they knew Bobby had a direct pipeline to you, Max."

"The chess moves we talked about, Max," Bobby said. "He's making sense."

"I'm listening," Roth said.

"I think one set of guys is definitely trying to use the three of us to help frame someone else," Izzy said. "This ain't two assholes on a street corner, killing each other over dope turf. These are people with a very intricate, well thought out agenda. Major money. And so I don't buy the Kronk-Daggart marriage. I think Daggart wants us to think Kronk killed the McCoys. But maybe Daggart actually had them whacked."

"And used Jimmy Chung to set it up?" Roth said.

"Maybe," Bobby said, as he realized that Daggart might also have used Zelda Savarese to seduce him, to persuade him to go after Kronk, knowing most men would do anything for a woman like her. But what kind of man shares a woman like Zelda—for *any* reason?

"Which brings us back to the Chinaman," Izzy said.

"How do you deal with this asshole?" Roth asked. "Polacks, broads, hebes, Chinamen . . ."

"Because I'm one smart mick, that's why," Izzy said. "I'm smart enough to recognize an even smarter mick when I meet one. That's what you get when you throw the Star of David into the blender with a few jiggers of Saint Patrick—you come up with me, Izzy McYid, Esquire."

"Chinese," Bobby said. "The word is *Chinese*."

"Okay," Izzy said. "Then the bottom line is we can sit here and scratch our balls until the fleas hop home but we ain't gettin' any real answers until we find this yellow peril who set me up. I know the prick is alive. Bobby, I may not know much, but if you find Jimmy Chung, put him in a room for five minutes with Cousin Herbie, this guy sings."

"Now he's talking *torture*," Roth said.

"Torture's boring," Izzy said. "It's the threat of mutilation is what usually makes people talk. Remember, he has CIA training."

"CIA?" Roth said.

"Culinary Institute of America," Bobby said.

"*What?*"

"I've seen Herbie tie a guy naked to a chair in a stainless-steel kitchen and just make the guy watch him prepare a surf-and-turf with his special set of cutlery," Izzy said. "Watching him clean and fillet a swordfish, shuck a few oysters, and trim a few sirloins. They watch all the blood run down the drain, listen as the garbage disposal grinds up the trimmings. If the main course don't get the guy talking, then prepping the appetizer, which he always saves for last, usually does. When they watch Herbie devein the jumbo shrimps while he looks at the guy's

pecker, the naked guy usually gets pretty fuckin'
chatty to the point where he sounds like a cage full of
mynah birds on meth."

"Is there a point to all this fascism?" Roth asked.

"Yeah," Izzy said. "Bobby, you find Jimmy Chung
and the speculation about who killed the McCoys,
this Ben Lee guy, Becky Wang, and the two holy
rollers becomes fact—and I *walk*, which is all I give a
fuck about anyway."

"Afraid he's right, Max," Bobby said.

38

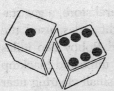

Bobby picked up the photos of
Zelda Savarese embracing Moe
Daggart and then drove to
Brooklyn to meet George the
Chinese waiter at A Taste of
Sweden, on Eighty-sixth Street, the busiest shopping
street in Bay Ridge. George was sitting alone at the
small bar, drinking a Heineken, munching crackers.
He didn't touch the cheese crock.

"Thank you for coming, yeah," George said.

"Why'd you pick this place?"

"No Chinese see us here," George said. "Chinese never come here. Chinese don't eat cheese, yeah."

"Chinese don't eat cheese?" Bobby said. "I didn't know that. No wonder they never landed on the moon. What did you want to see me about?"

"You brought car, yeah?"

"Yeah," Bobby said.

"You follow me," George said. "I show you something. Meet someone, yeah."

They picked a spot on Fourth Avenue to rendezvous, and from there Bobby tailed George, who was driving a brown Toyota. From the Verrazano Bridge, they proceeded to the Staten Island Expressway, to the Outerbridge Crossing bridge into New Jersey, and on to the Garden State Parkway. Fifteen minutes later George exited and soon they were driving back roads across the rolling farmland of Middlesex County.

They stopped in a tiny hamlet called Glover, which consisted of one small general store, a gas station, and a bus stop. They bought sodas, used the men's room, and then George led Bobby two miles down the road to a turnoff on an unposted blacktop road. They parked their cars in a small clearing near an apple orchard. The sun was softening to a midafternoon gold, falling on the farmland like a celestial blessing.

"Walk on feet now, yeah," George said.

"Yeah," Bobby said. "I don't walk so good on my hands."

George smiled and his eye clicked like a taxi meter. "We meet family now?"

"Your family?"

"Betty Wang family."

Bobby nodded, intrigued. They crunched up the dirt road until they came upon the tall rear gates of a farm that was ringed with a high hurricane fence topped with razor wire. Beyond the fence he saw the neat even rows of cultivation—squash, cauliflower, sweet corn, broccoli, assorted other late-summer vegetables. Asian workers, many of them women and children, wearing conical hats, toiled in the fields. He saw a big refinery with heavy steam gushing from an aluminum stack and could smell the overwhelming aroma of fish wafting on the summer air. He heard the *chugga-chugga-chugga* of machinery from within the refinery and saw men transferring plastic packages to an adjoining icehouse staffed by men wearing snow boots, winter coats, and heavy gloves. Juxtaposed against the sweating field workers, these men looked incongruously spooky as their frosty breath instantly evaporated in the August sun.

"Shrimp, yeah," George said. "Farm the shrimp and the veggable. Make lots fresh farm food for lot of Chinatown restaurant, grocery store, yeah."

Bobby saw rows of prefab barracks buildings where young children rocked babies in prams as old people sat in wheelchairs sewing fabrics or darning.

A sign on the gate read LUCKY 8 FARM. PRI-

VATE PROPERTY. NO TRESPASSING. This was another of Ralph Paragon's holdings.

"People live in those barracks?" Bobby asked.

"Yeah," George said. "Many family. Me, I did once, too. Ben Lee, he bought me out. I love Ben Lee like son."

"Bought you out?"

"I owe for my trip from Canton, pay off with work here," George said. "Three year. You owe money, you work for passage."

"Indentured servitude is illegal."

"So are workers, yeah? No green card, so you work here, yeah. But they charge you for bed, yeah, for food, for clothes, so debt go up, yeah? So you work longer. Never win. Three year become five year. Called Lucky Eight Farm but workers call it Number Four."

"Why number four?"

"Number four most unlucky number for Chinese," he said. "Like slave work. In Brooklyn over five hundred sweatshop. Half of them filled with women pay off passage from China, sixteen hour a day. Children, too. Most from Fujian. They make young girls like Betty Wang work in massage parlor to pay off for brother and sister and mother and father. They all here, also work, on farm."

George checked his watch and then from behind a row of hedges appeared a small, sun-browned man in his early fifties, but he might have been younger. He stared at Bobby with unblinking eyes that looked like drops of shiny hot tar.

George spoke to the man in Chinese but the man's eyes never left Bobby's eyes, as if Bobby were the microcosm of the America he dreamed of before he discovered the nightmare. He answered George in harsh Chinese sentences as he kept staring at Bobby through the slitted eyes set between sharp cheekbones.

"He says now that his daughter Betty is dead his other daughter, Helen, sixteen year old, yeah, she must go take her place in massage parlor to pay for family," George said.

"Ask him how long he's worked here," Bobby said.

George asked and Betty Wang's father answered, still staring at Bobby. "He says three years," George said. "Still owes two years."

Mr. Wang rattled off an angry burst of words. George seemed embarrassed. "He wants to know if you know how many men his daughter had to *service* in that time," George said.

"Tell him I said one was too many," Bobby said, trying to hold Mr. Wang's stare but looking away at the workers in the fields and the icehouse. Then back at Mr. Wang, who was still staring.

George relayed the answer and the older Chinese spoke again, more softly this time. George told Bobby he wanted to know if he was one of the men who slept with her. Bobby shook his head no.

The man dropped to a splay-footed crouch, talking and looking at George now, closing his eyes, relating a story. When he was finished he looked back at Bobby as George translated.

"He say daughter Betty came to him at fence here last week, yeah," George said. "She say she doing something for round-eye that would get enough money for whole family to get out of farm, pay off the debt, yeah. When they say Betty younger sister must also go work in massage parlor, Betty don't want that. She make deal with them to testify in court against your lawyer friend. If she do that, that pay off whole family debt. She no want her sister work in massage parlor like her. She want family out of farm, free of debt. So she say yeah, yeah?"

"So what happened?" Bobby asked.

"All my fault," George said. "I know whole family and Betty from when I was in here. I know she work in massage parlor. Then I see you come see Ben Lee and ask about Jimmy Chung. When I hear what Betty doing I tell Ben Lee. He agree to pay off Betty family debt. But she say they won't take money. They want her to testify in the court. Then Ben Lee tell her that if she testify against Izzy Gleason, Bobby Emmet will prove she lying. Then she get sent to jail, maybe for life. And her sister definitely go to work in massage parlor. Maybe family never get off farm. Maybe they kill them. Ben convince Betty to talk to you. Maybe you help her get her and whole family asylum if she tell whole truth. But then Ben Lee talk to you on tap phone. They afraid Ben Lee and Betty will tell police what going on so they kill them. Now Wang family still in here and Betty sister now must go work for massage parlor soon. Never win."

Mr. Wang waved to a young woman who was working in the field. She walked over and stood by the gate, a skinny girl with the same pretty features as her dead sister. But her face was as empty and mournful as a playground in the rain. She stood there like a mannequin, staring at Bobby in the same unblinking fashion as her father. She was the embodiment of the Asian immigrant nightmare, graduating from an indentured labor farm to a whorehouse in order to live under the flutter of Old Glory.

"This is Helen," George said.

"You know who killed my sister, Mister?" Helen asked in English she had probably learned from Betty.

"I'm trying to find out, honey," Bobby said.

"Betty never hurt nobody," Helen said. "Someday I find out and I kill who did it to her."

The father shooed her back to work in the field and she ran with the loping gait of an adolescent, a work still in progress, no longer a child but not yet a woman. *She runs the way Maggie runs*, Bobby thought. She was two years older than Maggie. And ready to service men to pay off a family debt.

Anger pulsated in Bobby's blood.

"Why don't they all just leave?" Bobby asked, gripping the handle of his .38 in his pants pocket. "Right now. I'll shoot the first bastard who tries to stop them."

"Can't," George said. "The enforcers only need to worry about single people without family. No one tries to stop families. Can leave when they want. But then family in China be hurt. Or killed. Snakeheads blacklist them, never get on boat, never smuggle them into America too. Plus, these people, they have nowhere to go. No home. No money. No English, no papers. No work. No car, no house. They be arrested, deported, yeah. Here they get promise of papers when they finish paying debt. Then they can bring rest of family over. Can't leave. Just way it is, yeah?"

The father looked up from his crouch, staring at Bobby with the tight, sad face, his eyes never blinking as he spoke aloud.

"What did he say?"

"I not know how to say it nice," George said.

"What did he say?"

"He ask if you know how many cock Helen now have to suck to get her family free of debt, yeah?" George said.

Bobby stared at the man and had no answer. The sun felt like it would burn a hole in the top of his head. "Ask him who runs the farm," Bobby said.

George asked and the man answered. "He says Jimmy Chung."

"Ask him when the last time he saw him was," Bobby said. George asked, the man answered, raising his hand high and pointing to an imaginary tie on his chest.

"Yesterday," George said.

"Yesterday?" Bobby said, excited.

"He was here with white guy, one who want Betty to testify in court. The one who have two English letter on his tie."

"Tell him to draw the letter on the ground," Bobby said. The man bent, breaking his stare with Bobby for the first time, and drew the letters *KC* in the soil.

"Ask him when he thinks Jimmy Chung will be back again." George relayed the question and Bobby saw the man answer with a shrug. "Doesn't know," George said. "He said he was limping, his foot was bandaged, like he been hurt."

"Tell him I said thank you," Bobby said. "Tell him we'll get him and his family out of here. Tell him his daughter won't have to . . . service any man."

George told him and the man kept staring. Then he went back to work in the fields.

39

 Bobby called Herbie and told him to drive straight to the Kronk Castle in Atlantic City.

When Bobby arrived he parked in the regular lot and then circled on foot to the employee lot. He saw Zelda Savarese's red Lexus parked under an awning, next to Kronk's Jaguar stretch limousine. *She's here,* he thought. *Straight from Bobby's bed, to the bed of Moe Daggart, to the satin sheets of Sam Kronk. In tennis they called that a volley,* he thought.

He checked out the tennis courts and the lobby to see if she was around. She wasn't. The whole place was abuzz with talk of the big boxing match that night in the Kronk Auditorium.

He spotted a group of paparazzi standing by the front doors of the hotel and asked one of them if Zelda and Sam were expected. The paparazzi said word had come down that they'd be dining in the Atlantic Antic at seven, before the big fight, stopping for a photo-op at 6:45 PM.

Bobby checked his watch. It was 6:08 PM. He zigzagged across the casino which was crackling with the high rollers of the boxing world, current champions and former champions, promoters and sports writers, sports groupies and celebrities who always flocked to the big fights. Bobby took a stool at the bar of the Straight Flush Saloon and ordered a club soda and cranberry from Gerry the bartender.

"Hey, how's it going?" Gerry said.

"Cold dice and slow horses," Bobby said, placing a twenty-dollar bill on the bar. "How's it been here today after that story?"

"Just missed your friend Ralph," Gerry said, flicking his eyebrows. "Smoke coming out of his ears today about that story. But Mr. Dunne is back there, interviewing a Kronkette."

"That a fact?"

"Cute as a button, too, man," Gerry said. "Wholesome. I'll tell ya, don't know where he finds them. Like they were hatched."

"What's with that story about Ralph and Kronk?"

"You missed it," Gerry said, looking around, leaning closer, whispering. "I was just coming in this morning—in front of the elevators, Sam and Ralph went at it, toe to toe, screaming in each other's face. I never saw anyone talk to Sam Kronk like that before. I was shocked he didn't fire him on the spot. Ralph was saying he wasn't taking a fall for anybody. Kronk was screaming that he was trying to destroy him. Donald Dunne had to get between them. I hear they went upstairs and powwowed all afternoon with the lawyers. The whole thing is under investigation. A special meeting of the staff was called. No talking to reporters. We're supposed to put a happy face on it with customers but I smell trouble. I'm worried about my job. I got a mortgage. Two girls in college."

Gerry walked off to serve some newly arrived patrons who were loud with the adrenaline of gambling and booze. Bobby took the photographs from San Juan from his inside jacket pocket and shuffled through the lurid pictures of Dum Dum and the mystery woman. There was still something familiar about her that eluded him. Her face was hidden behind the big dark glasses and the veil of long dark hair, worn Veronica Lake style. This time she looked more familiar than before . . .

He flicked through the pictures of Zelda climbing all over Kronk in the Kronk Caribbean lobby. Then fanned out the sequence of photos of Zelda kissing Moe Daggart at the Hamptons estate in front of all the hired help who stood around him like a league of nations. *Moe Daggart, equal opportunity bandit,* he thought.

He glanced again at the pictures of Lebelski with Daggart. Bobby was going to have a few private words with Daggart—very soon.

But he didn't want him to know what he knew. Yet. First he was determined to confront Zelda Savarese.

At 6:30 PM Bobby put away all the photographs and looked across the casino toward the front doors, where the paparazzi were preparing for the Sam and Zelda Show.

Herbie still hadn't arrived from New York. Bobby crossed the casino when he saw the crush of photographers rush toward Kronk's private elevator. Bobby watched the faces of the adoring fans, holding autograph books and positioning for handshakes. And then popping out of the collage of anonymous faces he saw a dark-haired woman who looked an awful lot like the mystery woman from cabana number 12. Same dark glasses. Same Veronica Lake hairdo. Same elegant, erect, runway model's gait as she hurried across the lobby toward the front doors. He watched her wave for a bellman to get her a taxi.

Bobby made a move to go after her, to confront her, when in the wiggly reflection of a cheap mirror he saw Dum Dum Dunne escorting a red-headed Kronkette recruit toward the black door that led to the private elevator to the thirteenth floor. He instinctively spun and was startled to see Amy McCoy on Dum Dum's arm, stepping through the black door. Bobby made a move in that direction but the black door quickly slammed. He turned back to the mystery woman and saw a taxi door close behind her as she was whisked away into the dying day.

He turned again and there was Ralph Paragon, barking orders into a hand radio. The gray-jackets took positions all around the private elevator. Business as usual. As if there had been no story. A buzz went through the lobby. The crowd began to swell and grow edgier as the minutes ticked by. The gray-jackets formed their flying wedge in front of the elevator door. Anticipation bubbled in the crowd.

Working people, most of them losers at the tables, jockeying for position for a glimpse of the man to whom they had lost their hard-earned money. A man the papers said might even be connected to a double murder. And still they idolized him.

After fifteen minutes Sam Kronk and Zelda Savarese finally stepped off the elevator. Zelda, dressed in a snugly tailored white pants suit, hung on the arm of Sam Kronk, who wore a white suit with black tie. Bobby watched Zelda smile for the cameras, white daisies dotting her gleaming dark hair. Bobby looked at the front door, where the mystery woman had vanished. He checked his watch. It had been about twenty minutes since he'd seen her. She had been about the same height, same frame as Zelda Savarese.

Down in San Juan he had seen the mystery woman with Dum Dum Dunne in cabana 12. This was after Zelda had given her bodyguard the slip. *She could have gone to meet Dum Dum,* he thought. Then when Dum Dum was holding a pistol on him on the beach, Zelda had suddenly appeared and hit Dum Dum over the head. She could have slipped out of cabana 12, it could all have been a setup.

Was Zelda Savarese the mystery woman from cabana 12? he wondered. *Could the one in charge of all of this treachery be a woman? Could Zelda Savarese be the elusive Number One?*

He watched the photographers take a blaze of photographs as Zelda and Kronk posed in front of the entrance to the Atlantic Antic restaurant. A reporter shouted to Kronk, "How about a response to the story in today's *Daily News*, Sam."

"It's a load of bull," Kronk said. "Unfortunately my lawyers won't let me elaborate. Yet."

"But what about . . ."

Before the reporter could finish the sentence two gray-jackets had him by either arm and were leading him out of the hotel.

Through the mayhem Zelda's eyes found Bobby's, as if she had been searching for him. *Trying to manipulate me a little more,* he thought. As the ejected reporter protested, Zelda stared at Bobby. He saw her mouth the words *"Help me."*

He watched Sam Kronk follow Zelda's gaze directly to him. Bobby stared Kronk dead in the eye, like an assassin fixing the crosshairs on his target. Kronk leaned to a sweaty Ralph Paragon and whispered in his ear, nodded in Bobby's direction. Bobby kept staring at Zelda. Kronk nudged Zelda through the doors of the Atlantic Antic restaurant. She gave one last glance at Bobby over her shoulder and then the maitre d' closed the door to the public.

Bobby stared at the black door leading to Kronk's private harem. Amy McCoy was up there, a lamb being trussed for slaughter.

"Excuse me, sir," Bobby heard the voice behind him say.

He turned and faced Ralph Paragon, who was standing with a posture of authority. Two gray-jackets stood a dozen feet away, hands clasped in front of them, watching.

"Howdy," Bobby said.

"Are you a guest at the hotel, sir?"

"Didn't know it was a private party," Bobby said, staring deep into Paragon's eyes. When he'd boxed for the NYPD team he always scoured an opponent's eyes during the prefight instructions, searching for the scared lost kid who still lives somewhere in the private, terror-filled shadows of every grown man. He used to search for the same spooked kid in the eyes of adult suspects during interrogations. Everyone had that private corner he ran to, to tremble when he was alone. Bobby located that hiding place in Paragon's uncertain eyes, saw Paragon flinch and take a baby step back before replanting his feet, refocusing his eyes.

"It's just that you've been hanging around the lobby and . . ."

"Who are you?" Bobby asked. "You look familiar."

Paragon flashed him an ID badge and a casino security card issued by the gaming commission bearing his name and title.

"Chief of Security," Bobby said, reading his card. "That would make you *number two*—under Sam Kronk. Maybe I should bet that number in roulette."

He was hoping the reference to "Number Two" would register some spasm of concern in Paragon's face, but it didn't, and that worried Bobby.

"We never suggest bets to customers, but if you're gambling, maybe you'd like to show me some ID so I can get you rated," Paragon said with a smile. "Could mean a comped room, fight tickets, a few shows, a nice meal."

Bobby smiled and shook his head. "I never show anyone my cards," Bobby said. "The less anyone knows about me the harder it is to beat me. You do understand. But haven't I seen you somewhere? On TV maybe. The newspapers?"

He saw a shadow of shame pass over Paragon's face.

"You're mistaken," he said.

Bobby took out a wad of cash and walked toward a cashier booth. Paragon walked with him, casually.

"Do you know Miss Savarese?" he asked.

"Who doesn't?"

Bobby pushed some bills under the cashier's slot.

"Mixed chips, please," he said.

"I meant *personally*," Paragon said.

"If I did, that would be personal, now wouldn't it?"

"Why are you being so evasive?"

The cashier pushed the chips into the well and Bobby scooped them out and looked Paragon deep in the eyes again, finding that little boy in the dark corner.

"Why are you being so inquisitive?" Bobby asked. "I'm sober. I'm not disturbing the peace. I have money. I'm comporting myself like a gentleman. I don't count cards, pick pockets, solicit hookers, or steal ashtrays. I'd say you have better people to scrutinize, Chief Paragon."

A flustered Paragon nodded. "Enjoy yourself at Kronk Castle, sir," he said. "Sorry for any inconvenience."

Paragon turned and hurried across the lobby, nodding to one crewcut, broad-shouldered gray-jacket as he left. Crewcut remained behind, like a man with a sandwich board that read: I'M YOUR TAIL.

Bobby walked into the casino, picked out a roulette table, and put a hundred-dollar chip on the number two. He lost. He turned and saw Crewcut had him in sight. Bobby moved to a blackjack table and bet one hand and won three hundred dollars. He bought a few rolls of silver dollars, walked to a slot machine, and put on his rearview mirror glasses.

As he played the silver-dollar slot, he saw Dum Dum emerge through the black door with a dozen Kronkettes all dressed in sexy evening gowns. Amy wasn't one of them. Meaning she was still up on the thirteenth floor, signing papers and taking blood and urine tests. Other gray-jackets arrived to escort the Kronkettes to the boxing arena.

Dum Dum joined Paragon, who began speaking to him. Bobby scanned the front doors, looking for Herbie, but he didn't see him. He knew Herbie should be arriving any time now in the public parking lot.

After they'd been in the Atlantic Antic restaurant for half an hour, Bobby decided to get Zelda out for a few answers to some big questions.

Bobby approached the men's room, and before he entered he checked in the rearview mirror in his shades and saw Crewcut taking up a position beside a pillar. Bobby went in and locked himself in a stall, then dialed the main number of Kronk Castle on his cell phone, and had the call transferred to the Atlantic Antic. The maitre d' answered and Bobby said, "Tell Mr. Kronk that the mayor wants to see him in his car in the employees lot. ASAP. Urgent."

"I'm sorry, but I can't disturb Mr. Kronk during dinner . . ."

"You don't tell him, I doubt you'll have a job by the time he orders dessert," Bobby said. "If you're afraid to talk to the guy, slip him a note. Tell him it's about the story in the papers. Do it or chew it, fella."

Bobby exited the stall, checked to be sure no one was in the men's room, took out a book of matches from the Golden Pagoda, and dropped lit matches into the two litter bins. The fire would be contained but smoky because of the dampness of the hand towels in the aluminum bins. He watched the fires lick to life and returned to the lobby.

He sauntered to the same silver-dollar slot machine and watched Crewcut in the mirror. He also watched the front door of the Atlantic Antic restaurant.

Kronk emerged from the restaurant in an animated flourish, looking pissed off, flanked by Paragon and two gray-jackets as he strode toward the rear exit, which led to the employees parking lot. Then Bobby saw a man push open the door to the men's room and saw a cloud of smoke billow out.

"Fire!" shouted the man.

A small commotion rumbled through the lobby. The gray-jacket assigned to Bobby was the nearest one to the men's room. Bobby saw him look his way and then hurry toward the men's room, yanking a fire extinguisher from the wall. Bobby took the opportunity to hurry to the front door of the Atlantic Antic as a shower of silver dollars rattled into the steel tray of his slot machine. Other gamblers saw him hurrying away and three women scrambled to collect his coins amid the pandemonium caused by the single shout of "Fire."

Bobby entered the restaurant and brushed past the maitre d'.

"Can I help you, sir?"

"Nah," Bobby said and strode straight to Zelda Savarese.

"Bobby, thank God . . ."

He took her by the hand and pulled her out of the booth toward the back of the restaurant, into the loud clattering kitchen, which smelled like a glutton's heaven.

"You can't come in here!" shouted a prep chef.

"I have CIA training," Bobby said, passing men who were sautéing shrimp and veal and chicken in small individual pans. Others were stirring soups and tossing salads as dishwashers stacked glasses, plates, and silverware and harried waiters ran in and out screaming for orders.

"Where are we going?" Zelda asked as Bobby dragged her along.

"Every kitchen has a fire exit," he said.

He found it at the far end of the kitchen, hit the panic bar that opened the door to the public parking lot. A tired breeze blew in from the direction of the crowded Boardwalk. Bobby ushered Zelda by her muscled left arm to a rear truck port where food, liquor, and other hotel staples were delivered. The big green Dumpsters for soiled linen, organic trash, and meat scraps were also located here. Bobby saw a swarm of flies buzzing around the meat Dumpster in the candle-lit sun that was quickly guttering toward twilight.

Bobby dragged Zelda into an empty truck bay and leaned her against a wall like a common perp.

"Bobby, I need help," she said.

"No," he said. "The horseshit stories stop here. You're a liar and worse, and I want answers."

He reached into his inside jacket pocket and pulled out the pictures of Zelda embracing Moe Daggart out in the Hamptons.

"Oh," she said, suddenly frightened.

"*Oh?*" Bobby shouted, grabbing both her arms and staring in her face. "*Oh? Oh say can you see what a fucking asshole I am? You come to me, fuck my brains out, make me feel sorry for you, maybe even fall a little head over heels for you. But when I ask you if you know this asshole Moe Daggart, you say no. Then I find you kissing the face off him out in Westhampton. Then, the same day, I find you back here with this loathsome sleazeball Kronk. Hey, I've been two-timed before, baby, but this is the first time I can remember being sloppy thirds."

Tears bulged from her eyes like tiny prisms, the magenta sun bursting small rainbows on her wet lashes. She looked like someone you'd take home and ask to stay a lifetime. And then watch her kill you a little every day.

"I'm sorry," she said.

"Not as sorry as I am, lady," he said.

"I didn't know if I could trust you," she said. "After Daggart, I didn't know if I could trust anyone."

"Talk to me," he said. He wanted to see if she said anything about Dum Dum Dunne and cabana 12.

"Daggart knows about the tape," she said. "He knows I threw the match. He claims he has evidence to prove it. Somehow he recites almost word for word what I said on that tape that Kronk played for me. So he's either seen it or has a copy."

"And what?" Bobby said. "He wants you to dress in milkmaid white and marry him, too? Trapped like a modern-day Rapunzel in his Westhampton tower?"

"No," she said. "What you see in those photographs is just for the benefit of Daggart's staff. To make us look like, well, *close.* It keeps them from talking. But Daggart doesn't want to marry me. No, he wants me to help him destroy Kronk from the inside. Wants me to go along with his program and then sabotage him. But if he can help me hurt Sam Kronk, I almost welcome his help, even if he is black-mailing me, too. I know it's all my fault, but I'm trapped, Bobby. I'm drowning."

Bobby knew how badly Daggart wanted to topple Kronk, so the story she was telling had a faint sniff of truth. But he couldn't entirely believe anything she told him again.

"So you're telling me you're caught in a squeeze between these two guys?" he said.

"Yes," she said. "You can believe it or not believe it. I have nothing more to lose if you think I'm lying. I'm sorry I lied to you. What wasn't a lie was how I feel about you. You're the kind of guy a woman always falls for because you're the kind of guy you can turn to for help."

"I'm tired of the sob-sister routine, too."

"You hate me," she said. "I don't blame you."

"I don't know you well enough to hate you, Zelda," he said. "But I don't like liars. You never tell me the truth. You say you want me to nail Kronk, but you don't even help me get close enough to him to do it."

"Okay, I'll tell you what I learned from one of his security guards," she said.

"From who? Dunne? Something he told you in

cabana 12 in San Juan?" He was giving her the opportunity to come clean on that count. But she just frowned.

"I don't know anything about Dunne, or 'cabana number twelve,'" she said, wiping her muddy eyes on her white sleeve. "But I overheard Ralph Paragon telling Sam about those trophies we talked about. He said they're in his private collection. Toes from the dead people, the McCoys and two Chinese people. Sounds far-fetched, but that's what Paragon said."

"Where will Kronk be tonight?"

"We'll be at the big fight," she said. "All his little Kronkettes will be working as escorts for Sam's friends and high rollers. I'll probably leave about five AM."

"Do you have a way to get into the thirteenth floor?"

"They change the security codes every day," she said. "They issue new key cards all the time. But when he's not up there they only have one security guy on duty to escort one of the girls if they want to leave the floor or to call for additional guards in case more than one wants to leave."

"You better get back to his table," he said.

"I'm sorry," she said. "I wish I could be more help."

She began to walk away and then turned and hurried back to him and kissed him on the mouth.

"I just want you to know that if you walk away from all this, from my problems, I understand," she said. "I got myself into this mess. I have to pay the price. I just wanted to say thanks and kiss you good-bye in case you do."

She kissed him again, her body pressed against him as darkness fell on Atlantic City and the neon began to blaze along the Boardwalk. She backed away and circled toward the front of the hotel.

Bobby waited a minute to give her time to get inside and then followed. As he passed the kitchen fire exit he had used earlier, Crewcut, the gray-jacket, stepped out.

"Fucking comedian," Crewcut said, throwing a wild right hand. Bobby managed to duck far enough down to catch the punch high on the top of his head. Crewcut howled in pain and Bobby delivered a left hook to the liver and lower ribs that dropped him, twisting him into a pretzel of agony. Another gray-jacket rushed out of the noisy kitchen and slammed into Bobby as if he were a tackle dummy. Bobby hurtled backward and rammed against the fender of a Lincoln.

He slumped to the asphalt, the wind blown out of his lungs. He felt an elbow smash down on his solar plexus. Then a gasping Crewcut grabbed Bobby by the ears and lifted his head and smacked it against the hot asphalt. The impact went through his head like a baseball bat hitting a melon. The orange sky went suddenly dark and he felt a big hand grabbing a hank of his hair. But he was certain his head belonged to someone else, the pain becoming an out-of-body experience. It was a dream now, and the clashing voices belonged to the stampeding crowd in his head. Human voices in a panic—screaming, shouting, banshee wails he was sure were blaring on a soundtrack from the next dimension. Or was it real? He felt himself trapped in the zombie zone between sleep and consciousness, a limbo of delirium in which he felt paralyzed, helpless, doomed.

"Keep your big nose out of this, Jewboy," he heard someone say.

"*Jewboy?*" he heard Herbie shout. "*Nose? Say fuckin' nose?*"

Bobby heard a body slamming onto a car hood, heard grunts and fists on bone, war whoops and finally a roar that came from a very angry belly.

"Shoot the big kike if you gotta," someone shouted.

Bobby rose from the black hole in stop-action, as if climbing a rope ladder from a deep well. He realized that no one was beating on him any longer, and as he pulled himself higher out of the well he saw an all-black sky turn suddenly brilliant with twinkling stars and he felt himself climbing to his feet.

"Get Goebbels, Bobby," Herbie said.

Bobby was upright again. He saw Crewcut getting to his feet and Bobby landed a single right hand to his jaw that toppled him like a hat stand with one too many coats.

Herbie had his gray-jacket belly down on the ground, his right heel on his spine. Crewcut lay belly down alongside him. Herbie dragged him closer and lifted his head by an ear. He picked up the head of the other one by the hair. He swung their heads back and forth, nose to nose, building momentum, and finally detonated one face against the other, noses crunching in a mixed spurt of blood.

"Mazel-tov, motherfuckers," Herbie said.

Herbie shook them as if for signs of life. He looked ready to bang them together again.

"Jesus, don't kill 'em, Herbie," Bobby said.

"Why the fuck not?"

"Too many forms to fill out."

"Douche bags tried to kill you, bro," Herbie said. "Called me a Jewboy and a kike. Shovels were invented for swine like this."

Bobby waved a finger and Herbie dropped them to the ground. Bobby checked Crewcut's wrist for a pulse, found one, and looked at his watch: 7:28.

"What the hell took you so long?" he asked.

"I stopped at OTB," Herbie said. "I bet a nag in the seventh, but I think I just saw a cop riding it on the Boardwalk."

"We got a piece of work to do," Bobby said. "Fast. I need some stuff from my car."

They dragged the two gray-jackets to the rear of the hotel and deposited them into one of the big green Dumpsters, the one used to store animal bones and fat that the kitchen discarded after butchering their own meat.

Herbie slammed shut the metal lid and fastened

it with some chicken crate wire. There was ample air for them to breathe but it was unlikely anyone would hear them before morning.

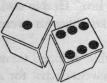 After stepping off the service elevator, Bobby and Herbie hurried down the corridor of the fourteenth floor. Herbie broke the glass emergency panel with his elbow, grabbed the fire ax from the wall mount, and chopped open the door to the linen supply room.

Bobby wasted no time. He looped a black nylon rope he'd collected from his Jeep around the terrace railing. He laced the rope through his climber's belt the way he'd learned from Max Roth at the Chelsea Piers rock-climbing wall. The belt was also equipped with a glass cutter, suction cup, and other tools.

Bobby looked down the fourteen floors to the darkened parking lot. A swoon of vertigo seized him. He pulled on a pair of tight black gloves and made sure the laces on his climbing boots were double tied.

Bobby and Herbie synchronized watches and then Bobby climbed over the railing. Herbie held the other end of the rope and was going to feed it to Bobby as he descended.

"If you drop me I'll kill ya," Bobby said.

Herbie thought about that for a brief moment, then smiled and said, "No you won't, because you'll be . . ."

"Don't say the word," Bobby said, checking his watch against Herbie's. It was exactly 7:35 PM. "Ready?" Bobby asked.

"You're gonna be in there exactly ten minutes," Herbie said. "Then I'm gonna meet you downstairs in front of that black door. You don't come out, I'm taking a key card from one of those gray-jackets and I'm going through that door to get ya."

Bobby nodded. Herbie gripped the rope and Bobby rappelled off the side of the terrace above the public parking lot. He sailed outward, Herbie watching the line. Bobby saw the moon and the stars spin by like faces on a merry-go-round, and then glided himself inward toward the big corner window on floor number 13. His ripple-soled climbing boots caught the ledge and Herbie pulled the rope taut, giving Bobby the leverage to find the window washer's handholds on the windowframe.

He teetered on the ledge, his stomach a witch's brew of fear, then steadied himself and felt a surge of relief. He peeked through the window and saw that the drapes were parted and the big, dimly lit room was empty. He tried the window but it was locked. He was going to use the suction cup and glass cutter but first he tried with his Swiss Army knife to unfasten the simple snap-lock. It worked on the second try. He slid the window open. If it was alarmed, it was a silent one.

He entered the room and disengaged himself from the rope.

He stopped and studied the room, which was about forty by thirty feet, with a huge four-poster bed in the middle, surrounded by antique standing mirrors set up at strategic angles. Mirrors also lined the ceiling over the bed. The deep-pile Iranian rugs, ruby-red sofas, overstuffed chairs, and matching ottomans were strategically placed around the room. Bobby scanned the room for cameras but didn't see any. They were obviously hidden in the cornice work.

The walls were lined with teak display cabinets with gleaming glass doors. On the polished shelves sat skulls of various animals—giraffes, tigers, monkeys. One whole cabinet was filled with human skulls. Another cabinet displayed human leg bones. Another displayed arms and elbows. Another, hands and fingers. Finally he found one that held the remains of human feet and individual toes.

He tried to open the door but it was locked. He popped the little lock with the Swiss Army knife. Under each piece was a little display card indicating its origin. Some were toes found in archeological digs in Egypt, Nepal, South America, Africa, Alaska, the Himalayas. Some were thousands of years old and other of more recent times, the cards reflecting dates from BC to AD. These were relics of history, bearing understandable value and worthy of collection and fascination. *Not really so weird,* after all, Bobby thought.

The room was like a private natural history museum. No one thought it particularly weird to admire the dinosaur skeletons in the great museum on Manhattan's Central Park West. And just as some people collected art privately and turned their homes into mini-museums, Kronk collected these specimens of the ages.

Then Bobby spotted some bones that were too new to be called history, too fresh to be called anything but evidence in a series of homicides.

Two of the five skeletal toes on a middle shelf had display cards that read: 22EC. Two others had cards that read GP, which he knew meant Golden Pagoda. The final one was labeled ESB, or Empire State Building, where Izzy Gleason's office was located.

Bobby figured all of them had been soaked in acid to strip away the flesh. If he was right, two of the toes belonged to Eddie and Sally McCoy; two to Ben Lee and Betty Wang. The fifth one belonged to Jimmy Chung, whom Betty Wang's father had said was still very much alive. Kronk had them displayed right here in a cabinet, like exhibits in a murder trial.

Either Kronk has the biggest set of balls since King Kong or he has the big ape's brains, Bobby thought.

He snapped shut the cabinet.

He couldn't take them with him. He could hardly present as evidence what he'd discovered during a breaking and entering. If Kronk was going to be arrested for his participation in these murders, an authorized cop would have to come in here with a search warrant. But how could they get the probable cause for the warrant?

Something bothered Bobby about the find. It had been too easy. He'd been steered there by Zelda Savarese. It was too convenient, too pat, just like there were too many coincidences in this whole case.

These bones in Kronk's display case smelled of a plant, a frame, something concocted by Daggart and carried out by Zelda. He checked his watch and realized he'd found physical evidence tying Sam Kronk to multiple murders in three and a half minutes.

"You work fast," said Amy McCoy, who stood in the doorway of the bedroom. "It took me fifteen minutes to find them. You can take off the silly mask, Bobby, the cameras only go on when Kronk's here."

Bobby was momentarily startled when he turned to see Amy with the .25 in her right hand. She was dressed in a skimpy little Kronkette outfit—red high heels, red mini-skirt, red vest—looking hot in a vulgar kind of way, like an angel in a cathouse. He took off his ski mask and approached her.

"Whose ID did you use to apply for the Kronkette gig? Another novitiate's?"

"God provides," she said.

"So does the FBI," Bobby said. "By morning these guys would have run your fingerprints, come up with your name, Social Security number, a complete dossier. You charged right in. You switch gears faster than me."

"That's pretty fast," she said. "Your sheets weren't even cold from me when you had that bimbo toasting them for you. That make you feel like a big man, Bobby Emmet? Taking me and then doing the famous Zelda Savarese? The fiancée of the man who had my brother killed. That put extra lead in your pencil, Bobby? Huh?"

"Amy, put the gun away."

"I was hoping you were Sam Kronk," she said. "I was going to kill him this time for sure. Now I have the evidence."

"The evidence smells, Amy," Bobby said. "It's contrived, planted, too easy. Sam Kronk isn't this stupid."

She pushed her gun into her panties under the mini-skirt and led Bobby out to the office.

"Who else is here?" Bobby asked.

"The other girls are all down at the fight," she said. "There's still a guard out by the elevator. The only ones up here are me and the attorney, Mr. Polo, and he's indisposed."

She led Bobby to the office where the attorney was stripped to his boxer shorts, handcuffed, blindfolded and gagged. "I took the handcuffs off Kronk's bedpost," she said. "Before I gagged him he told me the combination to the safe, and a few other things."

"Of course," Bobby said. "But first you made him take off his pants and threatened to blow his balls off. No?"

"Like I said, the Good Shepherd leads the way."

She led Bobby to the next room, where there was a Mosler walk-in vault with a heavy steel door opened wide. Bobby stepped inside the vault. On one shelf there were stacks of cash, maybe a half million dollars, probably skim money. On another shelf were boxes of financial files. On another he found the collection of videotapes and various legal documents. He also found an envelope with the markers Assembly Speaker Carl Pinto had signed in Puerto Rico.

"Those are the tapes of him with all the Kronkettes," Amy said. "There must be three hundred girls on those tapes. I told the lawyer I wanted the names of all the girls so I could give them back the tapes. He called them up on the computer, printed out the list with the current addresses of all of them, including all their confidentiality documents. Then I deleted the file from the computer. I also found the back-up disk here in the vault."

Amy had carried two duffel bags into the vault and Bobby began packing the videotapes into them, checking each one for Zelda's name. He didn't find it. Bobby thoroughly searched the vault for the incriminating match-dumping videotape Zelda had sobbed about. If there was such a tape, it wasn't in this vault.

Bobby scanned through the corresponding list of Kronkette names to see if Zelda's was on it. It wasn't.

Just the names of pretty, ambitious, once-young girls who had passed through Kronk's bed in the pursuit of big dreams that never materialized. But he did find the names and addresses of Giselle, Marjorie, and Priscilla, who had first told him about the Kronkettes.

He paged through the list, back to front, and finally his eyes fixed on one name—*Smith, Antoinette*. He remembered that Giselle, who worked for Connie now, had said the original Kronkette was named Smith or Jones.

He checked his watch. Eight minutes had elapsed. "We gotta go," Bobby said.

"I have to get back to the convent, too," she said, shoving a folded sheath of papers into his breast pocket. "But here's something else you might want to look at later, lover boy."

Bobby grabbed Amy by the hand, reached down into her warm panties, and grabbed the .25. She smacked his face.

"Smacked by a nun," he said, pulling out the small pistol. "Again."

She half-smiled. "You walk out to the guard first," he told her.

"I know what to do," she said.

Bobby waited as Amy stepped through the door to the private elevator outside the living quarters of the thirteenth floor. He heard her talking to the gray-jacket.

"Come on, big guy, take a lady for a drink," she said.

"Mr. Dunne says you're not allowed to go out tonight," the grayjacket said. "Unless I get his clearance on the radio . . ."

He never got to finish the sentence as Bobby spun him and coldcocked him with a quick right hand. Amy searched his jacket, found the elevator card, and pushed it into the slot. The elevator door popped open.

Bobby checked his watch. The ten minutes were up. He knew Herbie was probably already causing mayhem in the lobby.

As the elevator descended Bobby looked at Amy in the vulgar little Kronkette outfit.

"What's black and white and red all over?" he asked.

"A newspaper?"

"No, a wounded nun," he said. "Grammar school joke. How did you know which guy to approach for this gig, anyway?"

"I recognized Donald from the day he left the Golden Pagoda with your friend Ben Lee," she said.

"No, that was his brother, Sean, the U.S. attorney," Bobby said.

"Not unless they both smoke big cigars."

"No, Sean hates smoke," Bobby said.

"This one smokes a big cigar. So did the guy who left the Chinese restaurant with Ben Lee that day."

"You sure?" he said, handing her back her gun.

"Positive. I only saw Sean once, at my brother's crime scene. He seemed reserved. This one is more arrogant, swaggers more, smokes the big cigar."

This revelation turned several things upside down in Bobby's mind. Ben Lee had probably been tricked by Dum Dum into thinking he was Sean Dunne. He might have told him some of what he had spoken to Bobby about. It made him wonder if Sean Dunne might not be clean, after all. It made him rethink Dum Dum's stature in the chain of command of the whole operation. It threw Bobby for a loop.

"You done me wrong, Bobby Emmet," she said, her injured blue eyes looking up at him. "I gave myself to you and . . ."

"Amy," Bobby said. "Will you go to the prom with me?"

"I hate you," she said and lifted her hand to smack him again. He caught it in mid-swing and pulled her to him and kissed her. She felt small but lethal in his arms.

The elevator came to rest and the doors opened. Herbie stood with the key card in his hand, staring at them kissing. A gray-jacket lay slumped on the floor next to him.

"We better go," Herbie said, dragging the gray-jacket into the elevator and pushing button 13. "He called some asshole on the radio. They're all at the fights but they'll be coming pronto."

Bobby asked Amy to call him the next day. She said she would. They kissed once more.

When they got to the lobby they split up and made for different exits.

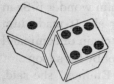

They left Atlantic City in separate cars.

Bobby stopped for gas at a rest stop and as the attendant filled his tank he unfolded the papers that Amy had shoved into his shirt pocket. The papers consisted of several successive drafts of a prenuptial agreement between Sam Kronk and Zelda Savarese. A quick perusal told him that Kronk was offering her three million bucks if they divorced within three years, five million for five or over, and ten million if they divorced after ten years. Zelda's attorney had made a counter-proposal of three times those amounts. Bobby shuffled through the papers. The negotiation seemed to be ongoing, with Kronk claiming he was in financial straits.

It was hardly the kind of horse trading that suggested Zelda Savarese was being blackmailed, a Rapunzel trapped in the tower of Kronk Castle.

Another lie, he thought.

He paid the attendant and drove north toward New York.

He was almost convinced that Kronk was being set up for the murders of the McCoys and Ben Lee and Betty Wang. Zelda Savarese had come to his bed, tried to win his confidence with sex and tears and a hard-luck story of blackmail and coercion, and then he'd found her with Moe Daggart in a fully staffed Hamptons mansion the day after he was "robbed" of $70 million. When he confronted her with that she'd steered him toward the "trophies" in Kronk's bone collection.

What she hadn't counted on was Amy McCoy penetrating the thirteenth-floor lair and digging up the pre-nup. He wasn't supposed to find that. Or the Kronkette list with the name Antoinette Smith on it. His cell phone rang and he recognized the number on the readout.

"Maggie, my love, how are you?"

"Hey, Pappy," she said.

"I think I like 'old man' better than 'Pappy,'" he said.

"I have the stuff you wanted on the tennis chick, Pop."

"Zelda Savarese," Bobby said. "Good."

"Her medical records say she's had surgery three times in the past four years for a torn right rotator cuff. Looks serious."

"Was that in any of the newspapers?"

"Couldn't find it in the clips," Maggie said. "But she still takes painkillers."

"It must be why she hasn't been appearing in any matches. When was the last surgery?"

"Two years ago, just three months before she lost the big match at Forest Hills. She went into a hospital in Florida under another name, but her insurance company was billed under her medical ID number, which is her Social Security number."

"What was the name she used?"

"D'Aguardia," Maggie said. "Z. D'Aguardia."

Bobby knew this was Moe Daggart's real name.

"What about her finances?" Bobby asked.

"No offense, but you have more in the bank, Pop," she said. "Well, almost. Before the surgeries, she had like ten million dollars. Then she invested half of it in an import-export company based in Hong Kong. But the government in Hong Kong along with American INS agents stepped in and closed them down for some kind of violations. It says here that the company filed for bankruptcy in less than a year."

"What was the name of the company?" Bobby asked.

"Zel-Dag Inc," she said. "She was the CEO. The president was Morris Daggart. The treasurer was Jimmy Chung."

"Are you sure?"

"I downloaded it, Pop," she said.

"What did they export?"

"Exotic fish, plants, gourmet Chinese food, stuff like that."

"And probably people," Bobby said. "Illegals."

He knew now that Zelda Savarese was broke and couldn't play tennis anymore and had been hooked up with Jimmy Chung and Moe Daggart for at least three years.

"Anything else?"

"Not really," Maggie said. "Just career bio stuff. Seven years ago, after she won Wimbledon and the U.S. Open in the same year, she made a fortune from endorsements. She thought of becoming an actress. Studied at the HB Studio in Manhattan. Went to Hollywood. Did some guest appearances on some sitcoms. She actually shot three pilots that never got picked up by the networks."

An actress, he thought, *who was able to turn her tears on and off and spin lies like a black widow.*

"What kind of pilots?" Bobby asked.

"One was called 'Charging the Net,' about a tennis pro who after her career slides teaches the spoiled children of the rich," she said. "Never aired. Then there was one called 'The Circuit,' about an international tennis star who becomes an amateur sleuth. Then there was one called 'Lady in White,' about a lady who is blackmailed into marrying a really rich guy, and forced to live in his mansion. It's described here as a modern Rapunzel. That never got picked up either. None of them became a series. Even the commercials have dried up. She does some European ones, but most of her American sponsors didn't renew their contracts after that U.S. Open match. She's what you'd call 'cold' in the biz."

"Maggie, you're amazing," Bobby said.

"I told you with a Social Security number I could find out some stuff," Maggie said. "Anything else?"

"Yeah," he said. "I need some information on a

woman named Antoinette Smith. She used to work for Kronk Castle."

A call-waiting beep sounded on the line.

"Who is she?" Maggie asked.

"I'm not sure," Bobby said. "But I have a hunch. Try New Jersey and New York DMV databases. Can we have breakfast together at Starbucks on Broadway. Nine? Tell your mom I also need to talk to her friend Giselle."

The beep sounded again.

"Okay, and I'll find out whatever stuff there is," Maggie said. "You have another call, you better take it. Love ya. See ya in the AM."

Bobby hit the flash button and switched over to the incoming call. It was Rabbi Berg. "Bobby, we need to talk," the rabbi said with urgency. "I have something I have to show you. Something Father Dooley mailed to me before he was . . . *murdered.*"

"Can you come by my boat tonight? I'm on my way there now."

"Tell me where it is and I'll be waiting when you get there," Rabbi Berg said.

Bobby gave Berg directions and then called Izzy, got his machine, left a message asking him to meet him on the boat in the morning. Next he called Max Roth and asked him to meet at the same time.

Then he called Patrick and asked him to stake out Ralph Paragon again.

"I'd rather put a stake in my heart," Patrick said. "But I'm leaving right now."

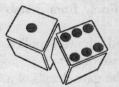 He saw them rushing out of his cabin door as he walked down the wooden walkway to the slip. Four men—wearing black masks and dressed like the ones from the Aquarium—scattered under the half-moon. Then he heard the desperate moans of an injured man. Bobby began to run toward the boat, reaching for his .38.

"Hey!" he shouted, firing at the dispersing figures.

He saw the intruders scramble overboard, on the river side of the Silverton. He heard the low rumble of an idling engine and noticed a small boat that looked like a twenty-foot Regal lolling in the water alongside *The Fifth Amendment*. The intruders had obviously arrived by boat and boarded from the dark river.

By the time he got aboard *The Fifth Amendment* the smaller boat was roaring away, speeding south with the current, the wind at its back. There was no way to catch it.

He spotted Rabbi Berg in a twisted heap on the floor of the salon. He had been beaten severely and methodically, as if by someone who had tried to extract some vital information before leaving him for dead. His clothes were torn, his pockets pulled inside out, the contents of his wallet strewn across the floor. His face was a pulpy bleeding splat, three fingers on his right hand were broken and stood up at right angles, and he was bleeding profusely from a stab wound in the abdomen.

The boat had been ransacked, drawers pulled out, cushions overturned, closets tossed.

Bobby quickly dialed 911. As he gave details of a stabbing and beating victim to the operator, he grabbed a clean towel from the linen closet and pressed it against the stab wound. The dispatcher said an ambulance was on the way.

Bobby knelt and watched Rabbi Berg try to speak through his broken teeth but the blood was clogging his throat.

"Rabbi, it's me, Bobby Emmet," Bobby whispered.

"Dooley . . . McCoy . . . Zelda . . . Rapa . . . Number One . . ."

Bobby saw the blood pulsing through his white shirt, saw the glazed, cold, departing look of the dying in the rabbi's eyes.

"You're going to live," Bobby told him. "But you have to work at it. Stay awake. Try to talk. Don't slip away. Work for me, Rabbi. Work for you. You have to fight, fight for your life. Come on, now. Fight."

"Father Dooley . . . Eddie McCoy . . . Paragon . . . Number One . . ."

He began to choke on the blood. Bobby

twisted the rabbi's head, to let the blood spill out before he drowned in it. Anger built in Bobby like an energy mass he could no longer contain. He tried to control it. He had learned that only *control* had saved his life as a cop in the can. Now as another good man lay dying, on Bobby's boat, where he lived, where he brought his kid, his lovers, he had to summon that same control to keep him from doing something stupid.

Control yourself, he thought. *Anger will make you lose to these people. Control will bring you victory. And vengeance.*

"Don't say any more," Bobby said. "It's choking you. Just breathe. Get air. Just blink once for yes, twice for no. Okay?"

The rabbi blinked once.

"Are you saying that before he disappeared Eddie McCoy came to Father Dooley and told him that Number One was Paragon?"

Rabbi Berg blinked once—and then, just as quickly, blinked twice. He shook his head, frustrated. *What did he mean?*

Bobby wondered why Father Dooley had never told anyone.

"But Father Dooley didn't believe him, so he didn't tell anyone until he checked it out, is that right?"

Rabbi Berg blinked once as he sucked for air. As he exhaled he groaned, "Woman . . ."

Did he mean Zelda Savarese was Number One and

Paragon was Number Two? That must be it. Bobby was going to ask him that and some more questions but Noel Christmas arrived with the ambulance. The attendants immediately pushed an oxygen mask over Rabbi Berg's face and administered emergency trauma treatment. Bobby stood and faced Christmas.

"Three for a quarter," Christmas said.

"Since when does a DA investigator answer a nine-one-one?"

"I was monitoring," Christmas said.

"The police band or my phones? Another illegal tap? Like the ones on Eddie McCoy's phone and Ben Lee's?"

"How'd you know about those taps, Bobby?"

"I was monitoring."

"I can pinch you for tampering."

"Go ahead," Bobby said.

"What did the rabbi say?"

"Shalom," Bobby said.

"This one *is* in my jurisdiction," Christmas said. "So you better start answering some fucking questions or else our old boss is gonna want you down in the bullpen with the skells."

"The rabbi called and said he had something to talk to me about. I told him to meet me here. When I got here four guys were scrambling overboard into a small boat and I found him like this."

"What did he say to you?"

"He's incoherent."

Noel Christmas smirked as the EMS attendants

and paramedics rushed the rabbi on a gurney to the ambulance, a plasma IV already running into his arm, oxygen tubes in his nose.

"You'll be happy to know your client, Izzy Gleason, has been under surveillance," Christmas said. "He was at a party in the Tisch Building at NYU where they were all watching Roadrunner cartoons. Is he like a little fucking mentally retarded, maybe? On drugs?"

"He has a fast metabolism. Just like you're always fast on the scene when someone in this case ends up dead. Or in this case, half-dead. Almost like you have a crystal ball—or an itinerary."

"I keep my eyes and ears open," Christmas said.

The ambulance screamed away. Bobby was waiting for the right time to drop a piece of information on Christmas.

"I do too," Bobby said. "So what did Ralph Paragon have to say when he met with you and Sean Dunne in the titty bar outside Atlantic City?"

Christmas was stunned. He pulled out his roll of Tums, bit two into his mouth, spat out the foil.

"I have no fucking idea what you're talking about."

"No?" Bobby said, reaching into his inside jacket pocket and taking out the photographs Patrick had taken in the strip bar. "Place called The Community Chest? Cute. Like on the Monopoly board? Maybe these will jiggle your memory."

Christmas shuffled through the pictures of himself sitting in the booth with Ralph Paragon and Sean Dunne, some of them shot through the legs of a half-naked dancer. "Who the fuck are you to follow me?"

"Someday you might have to explain what you were doing there, with the U.S. attorney for the Eastern District and the head of security at Kronk Castle."

"Not to you I won't," he said.

A forensic crew of criminalists arrived and started taking photographs and dusting the boat for fingerprints.

"This is gonna take most of the night," Christmas said.

"That's okay," Bobby said. "I have somewhere to go."

43

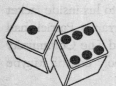

Bobby drove straight through the Lincoln Tunnel to New Jersey. After an hour on the road Bobby called Mount Sinai Hospital, where Rabbi Berg had been taken, and learned he was in the operating room, in extremely critical condition. A white-hot rage ignited behind Bobby's eyes. It affected his night vision as he drove on the Parkway south, like the afterglow of a welder's torch.

The rage glowed brighter the longer he drove. Sweat broke on his brow and soaked his armpits as emotion boiled his blood. He thought about the deceitful manipulations of this bug-eyed little man, this Ralph Paragon. Behind the scenes he was pulling all the strings, working with Moe Daggart and Zelda Savarese. All for money. Killing good people along the way. He thought of poor Eddie and Sally McCoy, almost certainly dead. He thought of poor Amy McCoy, who had lost her innocence to rape, her parents to disease, and her brother to murder. She was torn between God and vengeance, a woman trapped in a mortal struggle for physical and metaphysical answers. He thought of his buddy Ben Lee, murdered while trying to help a family out of a labor camp and a girl out of a life as a whore. He thought of Dooley and Greene, cut down before they could finish saving the lives of kids the city had turned its back on.

And now Rabbi Berg.

All in the name of money, money, and more dirty money.

The flame in his head burned hotter, whiter, out of control.

At a little past one AM Bobby banged on Ralph Paragon's front door. His brother, Patrick, who had been dozing on stakeout duty in a rented red Jeep, came running down the quiet street when he heard

Bobby screech to a halt at a mad angle, engine still running. Ralph Paragon pushed open the front door in an outraged fury.

"Who the fuck do you . . . wait a minute, I've seen you . . ."

Bobby grabbed Ralph Paragon by the front of his T-shirt and hauled him out the door. A startled Paragon pulled an automatic from his back waistband. Bobby wrenched Paragon's gun hand until he dropped the weapon.

"Bobby, what the fuck!" Patrick shouted.

Bobby backhanded Paragon across the face, knocking him to the lawn in a daze.

Patrick ran to his brother, shouting, "Bobby, he's been home all night, man!"

"He did it, he killed them all, and he took all the money," Bobby said as Paragon struggled to his feet. "Now Rabbi Berg . . ."

"Kick his butt, Pop," shouted Paragon's son, George.

Neighbors switched on porch lights and leaned from second-story windows. Dogs barked behind suburban doors.

Bobby looked at Paragon, whose manhood was on the line in front of his wife and kid. The skinnier, older man put up his hands.

"Come on, asshole," Paragon said. "I'll fight you. I'm not afraid of you, you sick fuck."

Patrick got between them, walked to Paragon.

"You don't want to do that, pal," he said. "Believe me."

"Fuck you, too," Paragon said. "I'll fight both of youse. I'll . . ."

Ralph Paragon abruptly fell quiet as his wife appeared from the house.

"Inside, George," Toni Paragon commanded her son in a firm, measured voice, methodically tying a silk robe about her thin waist.

Bobby turned and saw Toni Paragon pointing her son into the house, raising her steady hand just a fraction. The boy cowered and ran inside. Patrick tried to pull Bobby down the hillock to his car, which was idling at the curb. Neighbors stood in dumbfounded astonishment.

Toni Paragon walked to her husband, her stride elegant and erect, her arms swinging like a runway model. Bobby watched her, silently, as she glared at her older husband. "Get in the house," she said in a low, icy command. Ralph Paragon looked at her as if he'd just been caught in an act of infidelity. He was about to speak when she widened her eyes—wordlessly. Ralph Paragon broke her stare and without turning to look at Bobby or Patrick, his wife or the neighbors, he walked quickly into the house.

Bobby's fury seemed to sputter and die like a fire robbed of its oxygen supply.

Toni Paragon turned to Bobby, stared into his eyes without blinking. "Leave," she said.

Bobby again watched her stride in the familiar

elegant gait across the lush lawn and into her house, slamming the door with complete authority, the same way as the mystery woman in cabana 12.

"What the hell is going on?" Patrick asked.

"Ralph Paragon had nothing to do with it," Bobby said.

"I told you he was home all night," Patrick said.

"I mean, I don't think *Ralph* Paragon had anything at all to do with any of it," Bobby said. "I think *Toni* Paragon might be Number One."

"Are you serious or delirious?"

"I'm not sure," Bobby said. "I'll know better tomorrow. And if I'm right, the question is . . . *why?*"

44

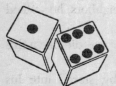

AUGUST 6

At nine AM Bobby met Maggie for coffee at a Starbucks on Broadway. She ordered an iced tea and a corn muffin and Bobby showed her some of the photographs he'd taken over the past week, editing out the more lurid shots of the mystery woman from cabana 12. He asked her to scan them into her AGT Foto Editor computer, which could enhance, edit, enlarge, superimpose, and reconfigure the photos on a display monitor.

"I got some basic information on that woman Antoinette Smith," Maggie said. "But I'm having a hard time getting early birth and hospital records of Zelda Savarese. It's weird. It's like she wasn't born anywhere. But I'll keep trying. I have a few more ideas on where to look."

Bobby said he'd drop by her apartment later to get any new information and to look at the enhanced photos on the big screen.

Maggie had arrived in Trevor's Rolls-Royce Silver Cloud, and after Maggie kissed Bobby good-bye and climbed back into the Rolls, Connie stepped out with Giselle. Connie wore small expensive sunglasses and was dressed in white bell-bottom hip-huggers, a midriff-baring blue and white striped shirt, and high-heeled sandals. Giselle wore tight jeans, a loose T-shirt, and low-cut tennis sneakers. Two men passing on the street made a comment and Connie gave them the finger as nonchalantly as if she were testing the air for wind direction. The two of them entered the Starbucks in a flourish of attention and sat at Bobby's table. *I wouldn't want to do a stakeout with these two,* Bobby thought. Something about the sudden smell of perfume and all those good looks at one table made Bobby gulp his coffee more quickly.

"Hi, Bobby," Giselle said with her spicy voice. "Connie told me you wanted to see me. I wanted to come alone but she wouldn't let me. So wazzup, honey?"

Bobby explained why he was there. He handed her the videotape and the file he'd taken from the thirteenth floor of Kronk Castle. As she took it, tears welled in the beautiful Latina's eyes.

"I . . . I don't know how to thank you," Giselle said.

"Get in the car before he thinks of a way," Connie said.

"One thing," Bobby said.

"It better be rated G," Connie said.

"You remember anything more about the very first Kronkette you told me about?"

"Yeah," Giselle said. "They say she fell in love with Sam. Fell hard. They say she got pregnant. She wanted him to marry her. He refused. I think they found out the kid wasn't his. The lawyers and the security people gave her marching papers, some shit like that. She left, kicking and screaming, swearing she'd get her revenge. That's when Sam started all the confidentiality stuff, the security, the blood tests, the one-year limit. All because of the first one. That's what they say. But no one knows the whole story."

"They say what her name was?"

"Jones, Smith, Jane Doe, some shit like that," she said. "Probably an alias. Everyone always just calls her Number One. When you sign up they warn you

not to make the same mistakes as Number One. I
heard a few years later she tried to get a bunch of
other girls to help her get even with Sam. But everyone was too afraid. They took the marching money
and moved on with their lives. They say Number One
finally did too, took her money, went away, met
somebody else, got over it. That's the way the story
goes. Like I say, I never met her."

"You sure they called her Number One?"

"Sure I'm sure," Giselle said.

Bobby thanked her. She thanked Bobby again
and kissed him on the cheek, leaving a lipstick print.

"In the car, toots," Connie said, and wiped
Bobby's face with a napkin. Giselle walked off toward
the Rolls, clutching the envelope with the videotape
and file. Every guy in the store studied her exit.

"That was nice of you," Connie said, chewing a
coffee stirrer. "You have any dirty pictures of you and
me I can have?"

Bobby tapped his head and said, "They're all in
here, and I wouldn't part with one of them."

"Why the hell did we ever get divorced, anyway?"

"We didn't get along," he said. "You wanted me
to live the way you live. But I like driving my own car,
and I don't like the way butlers butter toast."

"Oh, yeah," she said. "Now I remember. And
you wanted me to live in a little house in *Brooklyn*
with a clothesline in the yard. Truly irreconcilable
differences."

"We went together like oil wells and tap water."

"But couldn't we amend the agreement so that we just get together once a month for an afternoon matinee? I'll have the lawyers work it out. Who would know?"

"We would," Bobby said.

"You never even cheated on me, did you?" she asked.

"Nope," he said, sipping his coffee and picking at some of Maggie's half-eaten corn muffin.

"I never did on you, either," she said. "But not because I was Mrs. Virtue. It was because sex with you was the best I ever had. So by being faithful to you, I was really just being faithful to me. I do like the *best*—of everything—and you *were* the best. I'm not ashamed to say I'd like some more."

He handed her two more envelopes. "Those are for Priscilla and Marjorie," he said. "I'm contacting the rest of the girls on Kronk's list, to return what's rightfully theirs."

"Why couldn't you have married me for money like every other asshole who ever tried to get in my pants?"

"The price was too high," Bobby said. "Besides, I got two things money can't buy: great memories— and Maggie. I couldn't ask for more, Con."

"How about just one more tumble? I'll fly us to Monaco, Hawaii, anywhere you want. Jesus, I'll even go to *Brooklyn*. I'll buy a brownstone for the occasion. Near the River Cafe. Cheating with you isn't really cheating. You're Catholic. In the eyes of your church we're still married forever, or some silly shit like that, right? I'll convert for a day. I'll send a check to Pope Whatsizface to have his hat cleaned and blocked."

"If I were married I wouldn't want another guy to do that to me," Bobby said. "I especially couldn't do that to Trevor. I like him too much."

"Then maybe you should bang *him*," she said, angrily.

She picked up the other two envelopes and prepared to leave. "Speaking of Trevor, he asked me to give you a message," she said. "He wants you to meet him at ten-thirty at his office on Madison. He said he has someone he wants you to meet. Something about your case."

"Thanks," Bobby said.

"You're welcome," she said. "Someday you'll come to your senses."

He watched her walk back to the Rolls in the tight hip-huggers and took a deep breath. Sometimes doing the honorable thing goes against human nature. After saying no to his ex-wife, he went to see her current husband.

45

"I'm glad you came," Trevor said when Bobby entered his big office overlooking Madison Avenue and a sprawling downtown cityscape. The office was a giant glass and steel box, the walls decorated with light boxes displaying Scavullo portraits of famous models wearing Sawyer lipstick, eyeliner, and blush. His desk was an inch-thick sheet of glass resting on two silver sawhorses. The furniture was all polished chrome and leather. The room was a testament to success and promoted about as much warmth as a peak in the Alps.

"I don't have much time," Bobby said. "Connie said there was someone you wanted me to see."

"Connie looks hot in those white hip-huggers, doesn't she?"

"Oh, is that what she was wearing?" Bobby said.

Trevor smirked knowingly, walked to a plain black door and opened it. Sam Kronk stepped into his office, wearing polished loafers, no socks, creased Levi's 501 jeans, a tight white T-shirt under a denim sports jacket. His hair looked like it had just come back from the dry cleaners.

Bobby looked at Kronk and then at Trevor.

"Like I told you, Bobby," Trevor said, lighting a

big Havana cigar. "I think Sam here is a piece of shit. A swindler, a liar, a thief, a scoundrel, a cad, and a fake—but I don't think he had anyone murdered. And he couldn't do *anything* without help."

"Oh, he has plenty of that," Bobby said. "In fact, this is the first time I've seen him without a body-guard or a bimbo on his arm."

Kronk held out his hand for Bobby to shake. "I thought it was time we actually met," he said.

Bobby looked at his hand and then at his own reflection in Kronk's tinted glasses.

"If you want to talk to me, take off the lie cos-tume."

"The what?"

"Take off the fancy shades, the fucking rug, the girdle, and the elevator shoes and stand in front of me as the man you really are."

Kronk slowly removed his sunglasses, looked at Bobby in shock, then over at Trevor, who just shrugged and shifted the big cigar from one side of his mouth to the other. "Is there a point to all this?" Kronk asked.

"If you want to talk to me, I wanna see who's doing the talking," Bobby said.

Kronk hesitated a moment, then slowly removed the toupee, revealing the bald dome bordered by natu-ral hair on the sides. Without the hair he looked like he'd shrunk an inch and a half. He pulled off the jacket and the T-shirt with the Magic V abdomen fingers that held in a soft white potbelly. The belly seemed to pull him even further toward the center of the earth. When he removed the two-inch elevator shoes and stood in his stocking feet, he looked like he'd stepped into a hole. The real Sam Kronk now stared up at Bobby. Bobby looked down into the small, frightened man's eyes and found the neglected little boy raised by nannies and butlers right away. He was easy, like the flimsy lock on a teenager's secret diary.

Now Bobby put his own hand out to shake. Kronk shook and Bobby squeezed—hard. Kronk looked at Bobby's hand as Bobby continued to crush the rich man's soft hand until he began to sag in pain.

"Please," he said.

"S'matter, don't like being squeezed, pal?" Bobby said. "The way you like to squeeze little people with smaller bank accounts than you, huh? The way you squeeze little girls out of their drawers with promises of the big time?"

Kronk was halfway to his knees when he appealed to Trevor.

"Trevor, please, make him stop," Kronk said.

"He writes checks with that hand, Bobby," Trevor said. "He said he'd write me one for what he stole from me if I set up a meeting with you. I might never have this chance again. Even if it bounces, which I suspect it might, I can at least have the sucker framed."

Bobby let go and Kronk collapsed into a leather chair, placed his hand under the pit of his left arm to soothe it.

"Talk," Bobby said.

"I know you were on the thirteenth floor of my hotel," he said. "You're all over the security tape. The girl you were with was mistaken. The cameras are on twenty-four hours a day. We just tell them it's only on at certain times."

"Like when you're making private little fuck movies with girls just out of high school," Bobby said.

"I'd never use one of those tapes as anything but a defense," he said. "Look at me." Bobby did. He looked like a ruined cake after someone slammed the oven door. "Do you think I'd want anyone to see *me* in a porn film? They were just security against anyone speaking to the tabloids or cheap-Charlie biography writers. They were all I had to prove everything I did with any of those girls—of-age, adult women— was consensual. Maybe people don't like my lifestyle, but what I did was legal. None of those girls was ever kept against her will. All of them came to my bed of their own choosing."

"Filled with promises of fame and fortune," Bobby said.

"They all meet highly influential people," Kronk said, his voice like a computer-generated telephone operator's. "After we sever relations, any one of them is free to stay in touch with any of them. A few do. Most wind up married to nice guys. I never hurt a single one of them."

"What about Number One?"

"Who?"

"The first one? The first Kronkette."

"Antoinette Smith?" Kronk said. "That's ten years ago, for Chrissakes. She was a beauty contestant, Miss New York. She came on to me. I told her I was a confirmed bachelor. That I slept with lots of chicks. She said that was okay with her. She said her only family had died in a fire when she was sixteen. She needed a job and a place to stay. I set her up in a room. I bought her clothes. I paid her a lot of money. I told her that as long as I was paying I expected her to be faithful to me. Was it a double standard? Sure. Was it legal? Absolutely. Did I treat her well? Yes. Sure, she was a kept woman, but she could have left anytime she wanted. She didn't. Then a few months later she announces she's knocked up. I knew it couldn't have been mine because I'd had a vasectomy and put my sperm in a bank for a rainy day."

"High-interest-bearing account, I'm sure," Bobby said.

"She didn't believe me and took me to court. She lost. I still felt sorry for her and gave her fifty grand to get on her feet."

"You mean you had your lawyers do it for you," Bobby said.

"I didn't have to give her a dime," Kronk said. "Is this what all of this is about? Are you working for her?"

"No," Bobby said.

"Who was the little chick you were with?"

"None of your business."

"All right, then let me guess," Kronk said. "It's the sister of Eddie McCoy. The guy you think I had killed, along with his wife. Well, I'm here, properly humiliated, to tell you that I never killed anyone in my fucking life—never. Why the hell would I ever risk everything to have someone *killed* when I can have them *ruined* instead? Legally. And watch them die a little every day?"

Bobby stared at Kronk and said, "Because you like to play God."

"No, I like playing the rich bigshot. Big staff, big fancy homes, big fancy yacht, big fancy cars, big stable of gorgeous women. Who the fuck wouldn't want all that? That makes me a big bullshit artist. Maybe even a big prick. But it doesn't make me a big killer. Or even a little one. On the security tape I saw you examining some bones from my collection. Then, I checked them out myself. I never saw them before. I presume the toes came from the McCoys and a few others. Someone obviously wants you to think I killed them. Or had them killed. Well, that's bullshit. And I certainly did not put them there. Conveniently, a portion of the videotape has been erased, the portion when the stuff was planted. Someone close to me is trying to destroy me. You see, Bobby . . ."

"Mr. Emmet to you, asshole."

"You see, *Mister Emmet*, someone is trying to frame me, just like they're framing your lawyer friend."

"Or you're trying to make it look that way, so I'll look at someone else," Bobby said.

"Believe me, I'm not that smart," Kronk said.

"Sure you are. First you use Zelda to get close to me . . ."

Bobby saw Kronk's eyes widen, his facial muscles erupting in spasms like popping corn denting aluminum foil.

"I've seen Zelda staring at you," he said, swallowing with dread. "It *upsets* me. I told her that. I asked her who you were. She said she didn't know. But I found out. I know you're investigating me. I found out you used to be married to Trevor's wife. I know you're a friend of this Max Roth at the *Daily News* who has been a hemorrhoid in my ass for years and now suggests I'm a fucking *murderer!* And I saw the way you looked at my Zelda, too. I don't like it. I need to know . . ."

"Stop the horseshit, Kronk," Bobby said. "She told me how you had a tape of her, too, admitting that she dumped the match at Forest Hills. That you knew in advance that she was going in the tank and that you cashed in on that information."

"Knew in advance?" Kronk said, standing up, incredulous, looking from Bobby to Trevor and back to Bobby. "Cashed in? I bet her to *win.* I lost millions on a dozen bets with friends who are still laughing at me."

"One of them to me," Trevor said.

Bobby turned to Trevor, who nodded and took a puff on his fat cigar. Bobby looked back at a sweaty, animated Kronk, shoved him down into the leather chair, and leaned over him, talking into his face. "She told me you were blackmailing her into marrying you. That you always made her dress in white. That she was nothing more than a prop. That you didn't even sleep with her because she was too old for you because you only like girls half your age or younger . . ."

"None of that is true," Kronk said. "I asked Zelda Savarese to marry me because, because, well, because I'm in love with her. Have been for ten years. She agreed to marry me, too. Until she demanded to see the numbers, which showed that I'm virtually broke. All I have is a sea of red ink and paper. I'm holding my life together with smoke, mirrors, helium balloons, loans, and public relations. I'm trying to unload the casinos and go back to real estate. If I get indicted for *murder*, all my notes will come due. My mortgages will be foreclosed. I wouldn't be able to get new credit. Even if I beat the charge, the stigma would follow me."

"You told Zelda all this?"

"No. Who wants to admit to the woman you love that you're an empty suit?" Kronk asked. "I told her I was in a transitional period. I promised to put a few million into an escrow account for her for a pre-nup, but she says it isn't enough. She thinks I'm hiding my real assets."

Bobby looked at Trevor for a reaction to all of this.

"He showed me his books and he *is* basically a

busted valise," Trevor said. "He has some property, houses, boats, a few office towers. Some art. His bone collection. He'll be able to live the illusion for another few years. Maybe by then the casinos will start making money again. But if new ones open in New York to compete with his Atlantic City casinos, he's dead. I've looked at his books, Bobby. He's telling the truth."

Bobby paced the office, stopped and stared out the window at the big brawny city, flexing all its noon muscles as people stormed out into the hungry streets for lunch.

"You met the mayor and Sean Dunne in San Juan two nights ago," Bobby said, turning back to Kronk.

"How the hell did you know that?" Kronk asked, looking at Trevor, who blew a big smoke ring.

"I told you he was good," Trevor said to Kronk.

"Yeah," Kronk said. "We met down there to get away from the press. Not even at my own hotel, so no one would see us together. I knew someone was trying to connect me to the McCoy disappearance. I wanted the mayor to promise me he would oppose legalized gambling in the city because it would kill me. I also wanted to warn him to steer clear of me as he ran for the Senate in case I did get indicted. I also wanted to talk to Dunne, to let him know I'd answer any and all questions from his office or the office of the U.S. attorney in Manhattan about what I know about the McCoys—which is zero. I flew him in because I trust him. His brother Donald even works for me. Not that they get along, but he respects that I gave his brother a job. I needed to get some people in my corner in case someone tried to frame me."

"What do you know about Eddie McCoy?" Bobby asked.

"McCoy tortured me in print for years, but I kind of respected him. I even offered him money to leave me alone. I tried to hire him to do PR for me. I even bought some of his wife's crummy paintings, as charity. He turned me down. But for Chrissakes, I didn't kill the poor Commie bastard. And why would I hurt his poor wife?"

Bobby was beginning to believe him.

"What about Pinto and Lebelski being down there in San Juan?"

"I was lobbying Pinto, sure," Kronk said. "Sure, I wanted him there, to try to convince him to vote against the gambling resolution. I didn't bribe him. I flew him down, gave him a room, same as any high roller gets. He claimed it was a fact-finding trip. He lost money. I expect him to pay. As for Lebelski, that Polack prick, he took the trip, got his knob varnished, came home, and flip-flopped on me. Now he's on the fence."

"Did you videotape him with the bimbo?" Bobby asked.

"Good idea. But I didn't do that. I was convinced I already had him in my corner, against the gambling resolution. I was just bringing him there to say thanks and to see if he could help change Pinto's mind. If he met a broad, more power to him. I'm in enough trouble without trying to blackmail the fucking Senate majority leader of New York. Jesus Christ, give me a break! This was politics, an attempt to stay alive, not commit suicide."

Bobby thought he was certainly telling a convincing version of the truth. He was trying to influence legislative votes. It was called lobbying and it was awful and underhanded, but it was legal. Hell, over $10 million was spent the year before by lobbyists trying to influence Mayor Brady, and two of the biggest lobbyist firms were partly owned by guys in his own administration. Unethical but legal.

"So you wanted to meet me, to convince me you're innocent."

"Yes," Kronk said. "When I saw you on that videotape looking at those bones someone planted in my collection I knew someone sent you sniffing my trail. Probably hoping you'd run to Max Roth. So, yeah, I want to set you straight. I didn't kill anyone. But that's just one reason I wanted to see you." Kronk stood up, holding his shirt and his toupee and shades. "Can I get dressed now?"

He looked like a school kid asking for permission to go to the boys' room. Bobby waved in a disinterested way. Kronk pulled on the special belly-bulge shirt and adjusted the perfect toupee in the reflection of the glass of a signed Picasso *Don Quixote* lithograph. Bobby watched Kronk step into the elevator shoes like an actor climbing onto a stage and assuming a role. The man was a walking fiction. But something about seeing him stripped to his essence had made Bobby believe him.

"Actually, I came here particularly to ask you about Zelda," Kronk said, putting on his tinted glasses. "I can live with almost anything, but I need to know if she . . . if you ever . . ."

"You want to know if I'm banging the woman you love?"

"Yeah," Kronk said. "I *really* need to know."

Bobby leaned in close, lifted Kronk's shades, looked in his pleading eyes. He thought of all the Kronkettes he'd ever exploited with money, all his smug, prearranged, megalomaniacal photographs with famous women in the gossip columns, all the good little people he'd stepped on in a long and repugnant public performance as one of America's most eligible bachelors. He thought of telling him, *No, I didn't fuck her. She fucked me. And later she told me that Sam Kronk was revolting.* But that would be too easy.

Instead, he said, "Yeah, that would be nice to know, wouldn't it."

"No, no, you don't understand," Kronk said. "I really *need* to know. I'll pay whatever you want. I must know the truth . . ."

Bobby walked toward the door, waving to Trevor, who sat grinning in a cloud of pale blue smoke. As Bobby left, Kronk stood imprisoned in a millionaire's poverty of uncertainty.

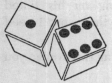

46

Maggie sat at the keyboard of the AGT Foto Editor computer and clicked the mouse several times. Bobby stood over her with Izzy Gleason looking on.

Izzy bit the ends off a strawberry Twizzler and dropped it, like a straw, into the hole of a beverage can that he held, wrapped in a small brown paper bag, in his left hand.

"Any luck getting that DMV photograph I asked you about?" Bobby asked.

"Working on it, old man," Maggie said. "Getting text information is easy. Getting an actual graphical duplicate of a driver's license—with the photograph—is a little harder. I ordered new software that should arrive this afternoon that will access it."

"Good, Mag," Bobby said. "It could be the key to the identity of the person they call Number One."

"The one in charge of the whole operation?" she asked.

"Yeah," Bobby said. "I have a serious hunch on this one."

"In the meantime I wanted to talk to you guys about Jimmy Chung," Maggie said. "That's why I asked you to come here with Mr. Gleason, because he's seen him in person and I thought he could ID him."

"I could pick Jimmy Chung out of a crowd scene in a kung-fu movie," Izzy said. "He's just a player in all this but he's still the key. He sings and the whole operation cracks open like an egg."

Maggie clicked the mouse again and brought an image onto the screen. "I saw his photograph in the newspaper and it stuck with me, Pop. And then when I started going through the other photographs you took, something caught my eye . . ."

Connie Matthews Sawyer appeared in the doorway of Maggie's room, frozen in disbelief as she pointed an elegant finger at Izzy Gleason. "Bobby Emmet, you brought *that* into my home?" she said.

"Wasn't easy, babe," Izzy said, taking a sip through the strawberry licorice stick. "I had to cancel a few intern interviews to fit it into my schedule."

"Beyond the incredible!" Connie said.

"You ain't half-bad yourself," Izzy said. "Bobby got better taste in exes than I do, tell you that. If my ex-wife ever tried to wear hip-huggers like that, somebody'd call the cops."

"Izzy, shut up," Bobby said and turned to Connie. "We have to look at some photographs, Con. We won't be long."

"Matter fact, I was thinking of branching out into a little corporate law, so you don't mind me asking, hon, how much you and the old man worth as a tag team now?" Izzy asked, making rattling noises as he sucked up the last of the drink.

"I can figure it out on my computer, Mom," Maggie said, laughing.

"Maggie, don't you dare!" Connie shouted.

"Just joshing, Mom," Maggie said as she made several complicated moves on the computer. "I don't have enough memory to count all the zeros, anyway."

Izzy took the can of premixed Bloody Mary from the bag, shook it for last drops, and drained the last of it from the can, then ate the Twizzler straw.

"So, Bobby tells me you run a stable of hot model chicks from your clown-paint factory," Izzy said. "Any of them wanna learn about the law, up close and personal, like? I'm offering free internships and a training program . . ."

"Bobby, if this fungus isn't removed from my home in the next ten minutes I'm calling the cops," she said.

As Connie stormed off, Maggie said, "You guys are looking for this Jimmy Chung, no?"

"Yeah," Izzy said. "We find him and this is a bunt."

"Take a look," Maggie said, leaning back in her chair.

Bobby and Izzy leaned closer to the screen where Maggie had displayed the INS file photo of Jimmy Chung that ran with the various news stories about his disappearance. Juxtaposed with that picture was a close-up of an Asian gardener in a conical hat tending some shrubbery.

"Am I nuts or is that him?" Maggie asked.

"Enlarge it, and let's lose the hat," Bobby said.

Maggie made the appropriate alterations and now the INS photo and the photo of the gardener were side by side. It was the same man.

"That's Jimmy Chung," Izzy said.

"Where's the second picture from?" Bobby asked.

Maggie made several clicks and kept widening the photograph until it blossomed out to a full shot of Zelda Savarese hugging Moe Daggart on the steps of Daggart's Westhampton Beach estate. Jimmy Chung was the anonymous Asian gardener tending the shrubbery, one of a crowd of workers on the estate.

"Jesus Christ!" Bobby said.

Maggie blew up Jimmy Chung's image in several other pictures Bobby had taken the day he followed Zelda Savarese to Westhampton.

"Maggie, you're a genius," Bobby said.

"Talk about hide in plain sight," Izzy said. "This guy's been a roach in the fried rice all along."

Bobby picked up the phone and dialed his brother Patrick and said, "I need you. Right away. And I want you to pick up someone else along the way."

47

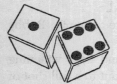

Patrick carried the clipboard in his hand as he walked across Moe Daggart's estate. He saw two black men fitting new windows into the attic of the guest house, watched a Hispanic man mow the lush Kentucky bluegrass lawns, and a lanky young white guy adding chemicals to the Olympic-sized pool.

He spotted an Asian gardener wearing a conical hat, white socks, and hemp sandals, limping as he clipped the shrubbery, favoring the left foot. Patrick approached him, pointing at the clipboard and the electrical wires up above.

"Hey, buddy, I'm from Lilco and we have a problem with our Schenectady rods in the overhead frammis cables," Patrick said.

"No English," the Asian said and went back to tending his shrubs.

Patrick turned and set the clipboard on the ground, and in a single motion he spun, flashing his NYPD badge and pulling a 9-mm Glock automatic from his jacket pocket.

"Jimmy Chung, you're under arrest in connection with the disappearance of Eddie and Sally McCoy," Patrick said.

Bobby plowed the rented red Jeep through the wooden gates of the estate.

"Patrick!" Bobby screamed. "Behind you!"

Too late. The pool man came running and whacked Patrick across his back with a long aluminum pole. Patrick fell, momentarily dazed. Jimmy Chung yanked the gun from his hand.

Chung looked as if he considered firing but changed his mind when he saw Bobby speeding his way. Chung ran with a hobble toward the garage at the rear of the main house.

Patrick managed to get to one knee in time to deflect the second swing from the pool man with his right forearm. He buried a left hook into the lanky man's ribs, and he collapsed like a cheap ironing board.

The two black workers hurried down a ladder from the guest house and rushed to the scene, carrying hammers.

"Yo, man, wassup?" said the first guy.

Bobby skidded to a stop, ejected himself from the Jeep, and brandished his .38. A figure in the backseat ducked down low.

"This ain't your beef, fellas," Bobby said.

"No beef, baby," said the second black worker and the two of them backed away, holstering their hammers in their tool belts, holding their hands up in front of them. After ten yards they turned and ran for the gates.

The Hispanic groundskeeper abandoned his lawnmower and sprinted after the black guys.

Bobby helped Patrick to his feet. He held his .38 in his right hand and handed Patrick a .357 Magnum and they each circled the house from different directions, searching for Jimmy Chung.

They heard the motor before they saw him. Then Chung came zipping past Bobby on a yellow dune buggy, the large-tread tires spinning past the pool and down a gravel path toward the beach.

Bobby and Patrick ran to the rented Jeep, hopped in. George, the Chinese waiter from the Golden Pagoda, was in the backseat, excited, his eye tic aflutter.

"Jimmy Chung, yeah!" he shouted.

Bobby engaged the four-wheel-drive and followed Chung, past the pool, down toward the road to the beach.

Patrick said, "He has my Glock and . . ."

He didn't get to finish the sentence as Chung turned and fired at them from the yellow dune buggy. The bullets flew high over the Jeep.

"Jesus Christ," Patrick said.

"He's purposefully firing over us," Bobby said. "Just trying to scare us off. Don't for Christ sake kill him."

George dropped from view once more in the backseat.

Bobby and Patrick watched Chung mount a hillock of sand and Bobby pushed the red Jeep faster along Dune Road in a parallel chase, until he found a flatter access to the beach. Then he spotted the dune buggy heading straight toward him. Chung aimed the Glock. Chung fired twice and missed. Patrick returned fire. His shot was lost in a fog of sand as a gust of wind blew inland off the sea. An explosion of gulls suddenly flapped loudly in front of the Jeep.

A few sunbathers shielded their eyes to watch, oddly intrigued by the spectacle of the red Jeep chasing the yellow dune buggy, and kept looking around as if for the camera crew that was filming this movie.

When they realized there wasn't one, they fell flat on the hot sand.

Chung skidded and spun the dune buggy so that it faced the onrushing Jeep. Bobby hit the brakes and his vehicle slid sideways in the loose sand. He and Patrick ducked. Chung tore off a burst of automatic fire. The bullets stitched the windshield, one of them sending a web of cracks across the passenger side like long silver veins.

Bobby rolled out the driver's door to the beach and fired three shots at Jimmy Chung. One punctured the near fuel tank, making the gasoline spill out into the sand, and Chung spun away again, trailing fuel.

"Make him fire again," Patrick said. "He's already blown ten outta thirteen."

The dune buggy veered toward the surf and Bobby followed. He knew he could make good time on the hard-packed shore. He began to gain on the dune buggy. Chung heard his engine begin to sputter from loss of fuel. He steered inland to the beach again and turned to fire. He ripped off three shots— *pop, pop, pop*. And then Chung turned and saw his buggy was piling into a blanket filled with oiled sunbathers who screamed and dove for cover.

A big orange and blue beach umbrella came down on top of the yellow dune buggy. The wheels ground into a cooler and the blanket got sucked up and tangled in the rear axle. The dune buggy toppled, pinning Jimmy Chung's right leg beneath it.

The frantic sunbathers ran for a nearby house.

Bobby and Patrick rushed from the Jeep. Patrick pulled Jimmy Chung's hands behind his back and snapped on a pair of handcuffs. Then they freed his leg from under the dune buggy. Chung never uttered a word.

Blood had saturated his left sock as the wound from his recently amputated toe opened up in the chase. The left leg was also probably now fractured. They lifted Chung under the arms and quickly carried him to the rented Jeep and pushed him onto the backseat.

Chung's eyes opened wide in horror when he looked directly at George, who put a knife to his throat and began screaming in Chinese.

"George, don't lay a hand on him!" Bobby said. "Not yet."

They had come prepared.

Bobby knew that if local cops got involved, there

would be yet another jurisdiction to deal with. He wanted to get Jimmy Chung back to the city as quickly as possible and into the Manhattan DA's office to clear Izzy Gleason.

He drove to the Westhampton Marina, where he had docked *The Fifth Amendment*. Patrick, who had driven the red rental Jeep out from the city, parked it in the lot behind the marina bait shop.

Then they loaded Jimmy Chung onto the Silverton and steered west for the city.

48

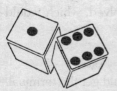

As *The Fifth Amendment* sped the length of Long Island Sound, Izzy Gleason stepped out of the stateroom carrying a piña colada and a bag of Cheez Doodles. He looked at Jimmy Chung and said, "Confucius say, this time you really do need a fuckin' lawyer, and you ain't gettin' a better one than me, babaloo."

"This is no time for ambulance chasing, Izzy," Bobby said.

Jimmy Chung, still handcuffed, started blabbing

in Chinese. George answered him, took out his knife, and dragged him toward the outside deck.

"Hey, man, make this mad fucker stop," Chung said in perfect English that was inflected with a mild British accent, an imperial hangover from colonial Hong Kong. "He says he's gonna cut me."

"Bring him back to Lucky Eight Farm. Let workers have him, yeah," George said.

"Great idea, George," Bobby said. "Enough foolin' around."

Bobby stepped outside onto the deck, cupped his hands, and shouted to Patrick, who was piloting the boat from the fly deck.

"Patrick, steer this sucker toward Jersey. This boy is going to buy the farm—literally."

Izzy dipped a Cheez Doodle into his piña colada, took a soggy bite, and leaned close to Jimmy Chung. "My best advice is: Sing or swing."

"I didn't kill anyone," Chung told Izzy. "I was just part of the setup. To get you involved, which would get him involved."

He nodded toward Bobby.

"To frame Kronk, right?" Bobby said.

"Yeah," Chung said. "So we could get the terminal. They figured you'd get your newspaper mate, Max Roth, to start pointing the finger at Kronk and the mayor. And while they were busy defending themselves, we'd get the terminal after the vote to legalize gambling. I was just in for a piece of the take, right? I never thought they were going to actually *kill* anyone."

"Then you'll have to turn state's on your co-mutts," Izzy said.

"You'll still represent me?" Chung asked.

"I know 22 Empire Court ain't really yours," Izzy said. "But I read in the papers that the building in Brooklyn next to the Golden Pagoda belongs to you. You really own that one?"

"Yeah, it's mine," said Chung.

"How much is it worth?" Izzy asked.

"Half a million," Chung said.

"Any liens?" Izzy asked, sipping the piña colada.

"No," Chung said.

"Of course I'll represent you, Mr. Chung," Izzy said. "But like I said, you turn state's evidence or the state is gonna give you a bye-bye booster."

"You can work out a deal?" Chung asked.

"You flip and I can keep you from dying," Izzy said. "Maybe get you off with a facilitation-to-murder, or maybe even conspiracy and a slow boat back to China. Then we might have to defend you on the slave-labor laws, if they can find anyone to testify against you. But that's another matter. You gotta own two houses I can attach for that. After all, the lower the crime, the higher the price."

"Lump them all together," Chung said. "Because whoever he is, Number One owns Lucky Eight Farm, not me. I'm just the manager."

"Okay," Izzy said. "Start from the jump. How'd it start?"

"I was involved in a company with Moe Daggart

and Zelda Savarese," Chung said. "We imported silk, trinkets, Chinese foods, rice wine. But we were losing money so we started smuggling other stuff in. Rare fish, Arowana. Then we got even bolder and started smuggling in people, illegals. They pay a fortune, life savings, and if they don't have the full shilling they work off their passage . . ."

"In fucking slave labor camps," Bobby said.

"Yeah," George said, cleaning his nails with his knife.

"Keep that mad fucking Cyclops away from me!" Chung said. "And they aren't slave camps. They weren't dragged here. They all knew the deal before they left."

Bobby said, "Izzy, advise your snakehead client that I am going to throw him and his bloody foot overboard to the sharks, with the cuffs on, unless he starts showing some fucking remorse."

"Explain how the terminal scam works," Izzy said.

"The one in charge is called Number One," Chung said.

"Who is it?"

"Don't know," Chung said. "Never met him. Starting four years ago, he originally negotiated the deal for 22 Empire Court and all the other buildings that would someday become the Empire Island Terminal. A real estate whiz, putting other people's names on the deeds. People connected to Kronk. He even made sure he rented to Eddie McCoy, an enemy of Kronk's. So that one day he could stage a revenge murder. And make Kronk look responsible. I don't know who he is, but I do know that he was in cahoots with Donald Dunne, who got in touch with Zelda Savarese, because Number One knew Zelda Savarese had been Kronk's dream girl since she was a teenage tennis star. Zelda agreed to get involved from the inside. She enlisted Daggart's help to set up Kronk—who would by association implicate the mayor. Kronk and the mayor were the only ones in the way of all of us getting the zoning for the terminal. We already had the votes in the City Council from financing local campaigns, but we still couldn't get this mayor to agree to it because of Kronk."

"What is Daggart and Savarese's relationship?" Bobby asked.

"I could never figure it out," Chung said. "But they go back a long way. He obviously doesn't care if she fools around. He doesn't sleep alone often either. Zelda doesn't seem to care."

"My kinda broad," Izzy said. "Legs in the air and open-minded."

"But Number One wanted more than money," Chung said. "The way it looks to me now, whoever he is, he wants personal revenge on Kronk. Wants to ruin him financially, and frame him for murder, get even for something. Number One knew every-thing about him, about his harem of young birds, his weakness for ladies in white, his wig, his shoe lifts, that he wore a girdle, his collection of rare bones."

"Which is where they got the idea for cutting off the toes," Bobby said.

"Hey, I didn't know about that part of the deal until Gleason here left me alone in his office," Chung said. "I was just supposed to play the Hop-Sing-no-speak-English Chinaman. The landlord who gets pinched on suspicion when the last two rent-control tenants disappear from the building. I'm listed as the front for a dummy corporation. I know they can never make a murder charge stick because there wasn't gonna be any killings. I call Gleason here to defend me. We knew you were a steady customer of Betty Wang's."

"Chronic back problem," Izzy said, tilting backward, pushing his fist into his lower back.

"We arranged it so that Betty would offer you a free massage that night," Chung said, looking at Izzy. "When I called you and pretended I couldn't speak English I knew you'd bring Betty Wang to translate. After both of you arrive, the cops spring me. I go back to your office. I sign over the deed to 22 Empire Court to you. You go to get your friend Bobby Emmet here, as Moe and Zelda figured you would, to do the investigating."

"I should shave points and let you get convicted, ya know," Izzy said. "But I wouldn't do that to my reputation. Go on."

"After you leave," Chung said, "Donald Dunne comes in."

"You're sure it was Donald Dunne and not Sean?" Bobby said.

"Yeah, by the big cigar, and because I know what a fucking wack-job he is," Chung said. "He comes in, with a gun and a pair of cable cutters and says I have to give up a toe to make it look like I'd been murdered, too. I think he's putting me on. I never agreed to give up a fucking toe. But I'm there in the office and he tells me the McCoys are dead and I have a choice: I can die, too, or give up a toe and make it look like I'm dead, make it look like Izzy Gleason wasted me. He tells me I'm now part of a murder conspiracy. They told me this was just going to be a scam, a dirty trick, a ruse. They told me the McCoys had agreed to take a bundle of money to disappear, down to South America for six months. But make it look like they were murdered. And have fingers pointing at Kronk, which would embarrass the mayor long enough for us to pull off the Empire Island Terminal deal. I had no idea they were actually going to *murder* the poor sods."

"Then the McCoys were supposed to resurface but by that time the terminal would be a done deal, is that right?" Bobby asked.

"Yeah," Chung said. "I went along because they were throwing around figures in the billions once casinos arrived in New York. I'm a gambler, always have been, so I rolled the dice."

"You chased a point and threw a seven," Bobby said. Chung nodded.

"Then Donald Dunne frames my adorable ass?" Izzy asked.

"First, he tells me the McCoys are *dead*," Chung said. "He shows me two of their toes, one with nail polish on it, so I knew it was a woman's. He scares the shit out of me. He says that I'm the fuckin' prime suspect. But since no one will ever find the bodies, I'll never get indicted. Hey, this is more than I bargained for. Now he says he can kill me and make it look like Izzy Gleason did it, or he can take a toe of *mine* and still make it *look* like a murder and I can still be part of the terminal scam. Hey, I'd rather have nine toes above ground than ten six feet under, so I let him take the fucking toe."

"And he spread the blood and little pieces of your toe around the office to make it look like you were slaughtered," Bobby said.

"Yeah," Chung said. "Then they took me out to Westhampton, where a doctor friend of Daggart's took care of me."

"They figured when I got accused of wasting you, Bobby would start digging and it would lead him to Kronk," Izzy said.

"Yeah, that was their thinking."

"You really think they were keeping you alive to be generous?" Bobby asked. "They were keeping you around to use you as another fall guy later, asshole— or as a plant. You would have wound up dead somewhere at just the right time. To frame Kronk, or me, or some politician, or anyone else who got in their way. You were kept around as a living corpse waiting to be planted. They knew you couldn't go anywhere.

Meanwhile, they still used you to run the Lucky Eight Farm, and I bet they also used you to threaten Betty Wang into testifying against Izzy."

Chung said, "I told her that if she testified against Izzy the whole family would be let out of Lucky Eight with papers, their debts erased. If she didn't, the kid sister was probably gonna have to go to work in a massage parlor to get the family out."

"Then George here got to Betty," Bobby said.

"I told her Ben Lee would help her," George said. "Ben Lee say something on phone to Bobby. But it was tap and they kill him and Betty Wang."

"Wasn't me," Chung said. "Sure, I told Donald Dunne about the secret wall in the cellar which we used to escape from INS raids. Dunne figured it was a good way to tap Ben Lee's phone. See, Emmet, he saw you there with Lee the day I disappeared. He knew you were Lee's college buddy, so he tapped his phone to see what he was telling you. When he heard Ben Lee talking to you about Betty Wang, he killed him and Betty. Then he took their toes, too. Later I found out they were going to plant all the toes in Sam Kronk's bone collection—to frame him. Dunne had the access. That part of the plan was all his. He is one crazy wanker."

A silence fell on the boat as they rode the waves toward the city. "What about the clergymen?" Bobby asked.

"That was pure greed," Chung said. "That part gave me chills. I don't care if it's a monk, a swami, a priest, a mullah, or a rabbi, I don't like messing with holy men. But Daggart said that Father Dooley suspected something was fishy. Dooley found out something about Zelda and Moe and somehow realized they were connected to me. He thought they might have been involved in murder. And so Daggart had Zelda try to talk sense into him, but he wouldn't listen. So Dunne ran him over and put some poor dead rummy behind the wheel when he abandoned the car."

"Reverend Gaston Greene?"

"Greene grilled Daggart about the hit-and-run," Chung said. "He received a call from Dooley before he died saying he had to talk to him about someone he suspected had another agenda. That there might be murder involved. After Dooley was killed, Greene was beginning to have second thoughts about the whole operation. Daggart called Number One, who had Dunne take care of it. He used guys from Kronk's San Juan hotel security staff to pose as Latin gangbangers and some of Daggart's NuCent Ventures crew to pose as rival black gangstas, and they took out Greene in the phony crossfire at Dooley's wake."

"Then Daggart had his own money robbed," Bobby said.

"Yeah. Hey, I need a doctor, my toe won't stop bleeding."

"Who'd he use?"

"Dunne and his gray-jackets from Atlantic City," Chung said.

"Where's the money stashed," Bobby asked.

Chung looked up at Bobby and then at Izzy. "Same place as the McCoys but I gotta save something for my trade."

"You can tell me," Izzy said. "Lawyer-client privilege."

"No way, Izzy," Bobby said.

"You keep it confidential till we get a deal?" Chung said.

"Of course," Izzy said. "I'm bound by ethics."

Bobby rolled his eyes as Chung whispered in Izzy's ear.

Patrick steered the boat toward Manhattan.

49

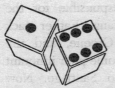

Noel Christmas looked nervous. He watched Patrick leading Jimmy Chung into the squad room, followed by Bobby and Izzy Gleason. George had gone back to Brooklyn, where he was arranging to have the body of Ben Lee—which was finally released by the medical examiner—shipped to his family in Hong Kong.

"Cop shops all over the world make me nervous," Jimmy Chung said. "I gotta take a leak, man."

Bobby had wrapped Chung's bad foot in a towel and tied a plastic Gristedes grocery store bag over it. Chung was walking with a very bad limp, still handcuffed as they approached Christmas, who stood in the middle of the squad room.

"How's it hangin', Chanukah?" Izzy said. "Got a little gift-wrapped present for you, boy. For the record, Israel Gleason, Esquire, the lawyer, not the fuckin' magazine, representing. And my client has a mother-humper of a tale to tell—but preferably to someone a little higher on the evolutionary scale, someone ennobled with a high school equivalency diploma maybe. Because in exchange for certain promises of immunity and a few other small amenities—a hot meal, immediate medical attention, protective custody until trial, and a court stenographer with blond hair, black roots, and grape lipstick—he will deliver to you on a dim sum platter those responsible for the disappearances of Edward and Sally McCoy, the perpetrators also responsible for the murders of Ben Lee, Betty Wang, Father Jack Dooley, and Reverend Gaston Greene, and the assault of Rabbi Simon Berg, and some poor itinerant Goya-brand-dipso named Ricardo Santiago. Now how does all that grab ya, Captain Kwanza?"

"By the balls," Christmas said, trying to keep a tough façade.

"This man's very presence exculpates me of all

charges of any wrongdoing in the matter of the disappearance or murder of himself, James Chung, and therefore any affiliation with the disappearance or murder of anyone else," Izzy said.

"Guys, please, I really have to piss," Chung said.

"All of a sudden he talks fuckin' English?" Christmas said.

"Took a crash course from a cab driver," Izzy said.

"Hey, I'm gonna piss in my pants," Chung said.

Christmas looked at Chung, taking short breaths. Bobby thought there was a glint of familiarity between the two men that exceeded one single previous interrogation.

"Come on," Christmas said, leading a limping Chung to the men's room on the other side of the squad room.

"I'm coming with you," Izzy said.

"No you're not," Christmas said, putting a hand on Izzy's chest.

"Don't answer any questions, Jimmy," Izzy instructed. "Watch out for plungers . . ."

Christmas led Chung, still handcuffed, to the men's room. Bobby looked around his old squad room, the place where he once ruled as the top investigator before he had been framed for the murder of his own fiancée, Dorothea Dubrow. A few old friends nodded begrudging hellos. A few others saw him standing with Izzy Gleason, whom they detested, and smirked and wisecracked among themselves.

A bunch of new DTs who Bobby didn't know had been added. The place smelled like a musty piece of his past, and as he looked around he was glad he resigned. After he was cleared of his charges he turned down an offer of reinstatement. The scandal would have followed him around like a dirty shadow.

Instead, he turned in his gold shield, took his measly pension, and kept walking. The security was gone, and so was the bittersweet authority, but he was free of the bureaucracy, the office politics, the grubby deal-making with mutts like Jimmy Chung.

"You okay?" Patrick asked.

"Yeah," Bobby said.

"Bad memories?"

"And premonitions," Bobby said. "Place gives me the willies."

For a brief time after resigning, Bobby had missed the camaraderie of the job, the private club of good guys who chased bad guys. But he'd learned when he was on the other side of the law that the good guys didn't always wear white hats.

He was thinking all of that when he heard the scream from the men's room—loud, terrified, almost unbearably desperate. Then came the muffled crack of a gunshot. As he ran toward the men's room Bobby heard the scream trailing off as if lost in a deep tunnel.

He smashed into the door shoulder first and saw Christmas standing at the open window, gun at He looked like he had just been caught a school test.

"He did it to himself . . . he was trying to bolt out the window . . . drainpipe . . . grabbed the gun . . . it was a good shooting . . ."

Bobby rushed to the window and looked down four stories to a roof abutment where Jimmy Chung lay lifeless, his arms and legs bent at crazy angles, a crimson pool forming on the hot black tar.

Three more DA detectives piled into the room and started pushing Izzy, Bobby, and Patrick out.

"I took off the cuffs," Christmas said, licking his lips, his eyes darting from Bobby to Izzy to Patrick. "No way I was gonna hold his dick for him. He stood at the urinal and then he made a beeline for the window. He grabbed the drainpipe like he was gonna shimmy down. I tried to stop him. He grabbed at my gun. We wrestled for it. It went off and he, he . . . just went out."

"He wrestled with *you?*" Bobby said. "He's about a hundred and thirty fucking pounds."

"You take shits bigger than him," Izzy said.

"He had a really bad limp," Patrick said. "He couldn't run, or climb."

"I'm telling you how it went down," Christmas said.

"You made a paper airplane outta my client and sailed him out the window, Christmas," Izzy shouted. "You're gonna go down for it."

"I'm making my own report," Patrick said. "He was my prisoner."

"You surrendered him to me," Christmas shouted

as the other detectives pushed past Bobby and Patrick and Izzy, putting fingers to their lips, telling Christmas to be quiet.

"Wait for a delegate to Jew you up, Noel," one detective yelled, advising him to wait for a union rep to get him a lawyer.

"Dummy up, Noel, take the forty-eight," another detective said, referring to the NYPD rule that a cop does not have to give an account of a shooting until forty-eight hours after the event. The union had won the provision in collective bargaining, claiming a cop needs that time to recover from his trauma after a shooting before giving a statement. Most people understood it was really a cushion of time for cops to get their stories in sync.

Now several uniformed cops were summoned to usher Bobby, Patrick, and Izzy out of the men's room, across the squad room, into the elevator, and out of the building.

Bobby knew that once word of Chung's being found and dying went out, all the Empire Island Terminal players would rally around the one salvageable part of the hemorrhaging operation: the money, all $70 million of it.

Bobby's cell phone rang. It was Max Roth, who said he should come right over to Mount Sinai. Rabbi Berg was out of his coma, and talking. Bobby said he'd be right there.

"Iz, Chung is dead," Bobby said. "Now where's the fucking money?"

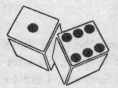

50

In the hallway, Bobby got a call from Trevor, who gave him some information about Moe Daggart. Bobby thanked him, hung up, and went into the hospital room to join Max Roth at the bedside of Rabbi Berg, who lay with tubes running into his arms and his nose. A nurse asked them to wait outside while she dressed the rabbi's wounds; she said they could talk to him afterward—for five minutes.

They walked to the solarium at the end of the hall and Max Roth took out an envelope addressed to Rabbi Berg. There was no return address.

"It's all in this letter," Roth said. "Father Dooley knew Hebrew. He sent Berg a copy of what he knew in case something happened to him. The dummies who tried to kill him ignored it."

"I also have something for you," Bobby said, handing him a videotape. "On my boat Jimmy Chung confessed to the whole operation. I secretly video-taped it. I don't know how admissible it would be in a court of law, but it would make some damned good TV after you break the contents in the paper."

"Is this exclusive?"

"Of course it's exclusive. Look, I just got wind from my buddy Trevor that Moe Daggart is having lunch at a certain Midtown eatery. I'd like to join him for a small repast. So let's make this quick."

"There's someone else gonna meet us here in two minutes, completely off the record and under the hat," Roth said.

"Okay, who?"

"You'll see," Roth said. "Anyway, the great thing about you Catholics is the record keeping. So after talking to you about Daggart and Savarese, I got to thinking. What an unlikely pair. They have an open relationship. That to me defies imagination when it comes to the Italians I've known in my life."

"Max," Bobby said, checking his watch. "You're starting to sound like Izzy. But your point is well taken. Open marriages certainly aren't big in Brooklyn Italian neighborhoods. So tell me what you have?"

"So I know that the best place to do a background search for Italian-Americans is the church," Roth said. "They almost always use their real names instead of aliases or the Anglicized ones some WASP asshole gave them on Ellis Island. What they tell a parish priest is sometimes different from what they tell the county clerk, the Social Security office, the IRS, the cops, the courts, or a hospital."

"It comes from confession," Bobby said. "For us, lying to a priest is like lying to your diary. I mean, what's the point in waiting on line and telling another man your sins if you're gonna lie about it?"

"That's what I counted on," Roth said. "The same thing came up in a paternity suit I covered once as a young reporter. A bastard kid who tried to claim she was an heir to a family fortune couldn't prove she was a legitimate heir. This was before DNA testing was recognized. She finally proved it by digging up an old baptismal certificate with her name on it, signed by the father who had sired her, while married to someone else. The mother was Jewish but the father was Catholic enough to have secretly taken the infant one day to have her baptized. He signed his name as the father on the baptismal certificate, admitting his fatherhood in the eyes of the church, figuring it would be stashed in some musty church basement for God's eyes only. He never signed the *birth* certificate and officially he denied it for years in order to save his marriage. When he died, the daughter found the baptismal certificate and she won the case."

"Get to the point," Bobby said, checking his watch again.

"So after you told me about Zelda Savarese going to see Father Dooley, I went over to the main Brooklyn diocese office. I have some contacts in there because I've done columns about them over the years. Anyway they have duplicates of all baptisms in the borough for the past century. I asked for the file on St. Brian's. I found Moe Daggart's date of birth from DMV. I checked the St. Brian's file from the same month and found that Morris D'Aguardia was baptized at St. Brian's. Then I got Zelda Savarese's DOB, checked her month, and sure as shit, there was the same signature listed as father."

"Alfonse D'Aguardia is Zelda Savarese's father, too?"

"Yep," Roth said.

"Daggart and Savarese are brother and sister?"

"Yep," Roth said. "Half-brother and sister, anyway. When I asked for copies of both baptismal certificates, a young seminarian shook his head, said it was funny—someone had asked for those same baptismal certificates only a week ago. A priest . . ."

"Father Dooley?"

"You got it. He was starting to put two and two together."

"That's why Zelda Savarese went to see him in Brooklyn the day he died," Bobby said. "The priest realized these two were up to something more than church gambling."

"Father Dooley started asking some of the oldtimers in the parish about old man D'Aguardia," Roth said. "It seems the father sired Zelda with a mistress named Carmella Savarese. So after she was born, the gangster sent the mistress and his daughter to live in Italy. But when she was a teenager, the mistress told Zelda who her real father was. She contacted Moe and they established a brother-sister relationship. Seeing each other on holidays, writing, calling. Daggart would meet her on the tennis circuit."

The nurse walked out of Rabbi Berg's room and said they could see him for five minutes. When they went in, the rabbi was propped up on fresh pillows, looking gaunt but defiantly alive. Bobby said hello, complimented him on how tough he was, and in broad strokes quickly filled him in on what was going on. Then Roth filled him in on what he had told Bobby so far, and then the rabbi picked up the story.

"In the letter Dooley said he asked some of the old Italian women in the neighborhood about Zelda and Morris," Rabbi Berg said. "He found out that one day Moe's mother, D'Aguardia's wife, had found a letter from Zelda in her son's jacket pocket when he was home on Christmas vacation from Harvard. The whole secret about the bastard daughter was revealed. The wife went crazy. She shot her husband to death in his sleep with his own gun. To cover the shame and to keep the mother from going to prison, the family made it look like the father had died in a mob hit. And had the mother committed."

"The mother's still alive?"

"No," Berg said. "She died about five years ago. But after she killed Moe's father, he naturally wanted to follow in his father's footsteps in the mob. But the old-timers wouldn't let him in. They said the old man had always wanted him to go legit, a Harvard man. They felt bad enough about what had happened, so they wouldn't let him in. He vowed to them he would be back one day and they would want him in their organization."

"And what? That's what happened? He came back to assume his father's old mantle?"

The nurse came back in and said they had to leave now.

"Max knows," Rabbi Berg said. "It's all in Dooley's letter."

As they walked back to the solarium, passing nurses and interns and orderlies pushing food carts, Max Roth continued the story.

"After his father died, Moe and Zelda continued their relationship as brother and sister," Max said. "Then his mother died, and three years ago her mother died, and they had no one but each other in the world. They became closer. But they never let on publicly that they were related. They never wanted Zelda to be tainted with the D'Aguardia mob connection, especially since she was a big star in professional tennis. So they often traveled as if they were a couple. Or good friends."

"And they went into business together," Bobby said.

"More than that," Roth said, as they stepped into the solarium. Bobby saw a man in a light trench coat standing staring out into the city streets. He turned. It was U.S. Attorney Sean Dunne.

Bobby looked at Max Roth in surprise.

"I think you should listen to him," Max said. "This is all off the record. For now."

"When Max called to say he was doing a story on all of this I knew it was time I brought you guys into the loop," Sean Dunne said.

"I promised not to print anything," Max said. "Yet."

"Okay, we've been investigating Daggart, big time," he said. "We suspect that now that the mob families have been so badly damaged by our RICO indictments and rats like Sammy 'the Bull' Gravano, that D'Aguardia has stepped up to take his father's old position, but as a newfangled Harvard-educated don for the twenty-first century. We knew about the church casinos and the sports book, but we had no idea how goddamned big the money was until we picked it up on a wiretap. Daggart told you he got permission to run these rackets from what's left of the old mob bosses, but that's bullshit. Moe Daggart *is* the mob, the *new* boss. The old mustache Petes are letting him have his shot, to see if he can get the terminal and establish a few casinos on Empire Island."

"You mean all of this has been a plan for a new Ivy League mob to take over casino gambling in New York before it even starts?" Bobby asked, laughing. "Moe Daggart as the new Godfather?"

"Hey, the Cosa Nostra of yesteryear is gone," Sean Dunne said. "Gotti, Gotti's son, Gotti's brother, Vincent 'The Chin' Gigante, Sammy the Bull . . . all history. Max will tell you. His own paper and the *Times* ran big stories about how the mob as we all knew it is now a shell. All the old gangsters are either dead, doing life, or in the witness program. Rats have gone from *omerta* to Oprah, selling tell-all books. Dressing dapper for the camera like Gotti didn't work. Gigante's bathrobe finally wore thin. If it's gonna survive, the mob must reinvent itself for a new century. So the new godfather will wear a Brooks Brothers suit, a white shirt, red tie, cordovan shoes, and carry a briefcase instead of a gun."

"And hold court in the Water Club instead of a social club on Mulberry or Thompson Street," Max said.

"And do sit-downs in the Harvard Club and keep an office on Wall Street or in Metro Tech in Brooklyn," Bobby said. "Like Daggart. So Daggart is Number One in the Empire Terminal operation?"

"No," Sean Dunne said. "In the operation to seize control, to frame Kronk, get the terminal land, he is Number Two. After the operation is completed, the terminal is built, the casinos are built, you can be sure Number One, whoever it is, will disappear like the McCoys. Then Daggart will take control—with his sister. My guess is that whoever Number One is, he doesn't know who and what Daggart really is."

"But Daggart needs that seventy million to pull it off, doesn't he?" Bobby said.

"He sure does," Sean Dunne said. "The old mob is broke. All their money has either been seized or spent on lawyers, and no one is earning any more. These guys get caught pitching pennies, we indict them on RICO."

"So if we stop the money, we stop the whole she-bang," Bobby said.

"I think so. The other old hoods are waiting, watching. If Daggart fails, they'll probably whack him, and they'll go back to their old ways, and the mob as we know it will simply sputter away in the next century."

"What about your brother?" Bobby said. "He looks like he's hip deep in the whole mess."

"He made his choices," Sean Dunne said. "I

warned him a long time ago. I'm torn, like Ted Kaczynski's brother. Like that poor FBI agent in the Midwest who had to testify against his own son in a murder trial. I have a choice, too: Do I let my brother run wild in a game of murder and racketeering, influence-peddling and conspiracy? Or do I stop him and plead for the government to spare his life later? I'm not happy in this position but these are the cards I've been dealt. If I step down, my brother would get suspicious, know something was up. In the end I'm doing what I was hired to do, locking up bad guys."

"Is he Number One?"

"I hope not," Sean Dunne said. "But this investigation is now bigger than my office. We're working with Manhattan and Jersey bureaus now in a joint task force."

"Why are you telling me all this?" Bobby asked.

"Because we think you know more than we know," Sean Dunne said. "Because we didn't want Max to go to print before we end all this madness. Because you're a terrific investigator, on the inside, and we need your help."

Bobby looked in Sean Dunne's eyes and saw the cold, monolithic insignias of the federal government stamped in them. He still didn't trust him. *How can you trust a guy so cold-blooded that he would bust his own brother?* he wondered. He wasn't convinced that Sean Dunne wasn't dirty himself. But this was no time to test him.

"What do you want to know?" Bobby asked.

"Where the hell is all the money?" Sean Dunne asked.

"Don't know," Bobby lied.

Sean Dunne gave him a card with a special number to his cell phone. "If you need me, just call me."

"Sure," Bobby said.

"You'll keep all of this information confidential?" he asked.

"Sure," Bobby said.

"What are your plans?"

"I don't know yet," Bobby lied. For he'd already set them in motion.

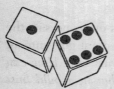

51

Bobby entered the Harvard Club, an oak and leather sanctuary for Harvard University alumni in the dumb-downed heart of Midtown Manhattan. At the door, the maitre d' said, "Sorry, sir, but you can't come in without a jacket and tie . . ."

Bobby flashed his father's old shield and said,

"Sheepskin Squad, checking IDs. Got to make sure no CUNY graduates are being served."

"Huh?"

Bobby gently moved the maitre d' to the side and strode into the busy lunchtime din of the Harvard Club and scanned the dining room. He spotted Morris Daggart at a large center table, sitting with Dum Dum Dunne and two other men in business suits who Bobby recognized as prominent Wall Street investors who had publicly expressed interest in casino gambling in the past.

A bald preppie bodyguard and another muscular Ivy League goon sat at a table-for-two next to them, munching breadsticks.

Daggart was squeezing lemon on clams casino as Bobby moved through the best-educated lunch crowd in New York straight to Daggart's table.

"Hey, Moe, Chung sang like a subway beggar before he died," Bobby said. "He said you had the McCoys whacked."

Other lunchtime diners stared curiously at the man wearing a zipper jacket, jeans, and work boots.

The bald preppie stood, scraping his chair back, and said, "Maybe you'd like to join him in the fucking grave."

Bobby grabbed him by the back of his neck and with a ferocious downward thrust slammed Baldie's face into a steaming bowl of New England clam chowder. A gasp went up from the dining room.

Bobby held Baldie's head in the steaming soup bowl as he addressed Daggart in a soft flat voice. The investors sat in lockjawed silence.

"Hey, Moe, do me a favor, will ya, tell your sister it was a real search, but I finally found something rarer than the Hope Diamond," Bobby said. "A guy she didn't fuck for money yet."

Baldie was still gurgling in the soup bowl, vainly flailing and squirming to free himself from Bobby's dominating grip.

The second preppie guard moved toward Bobby. Bobby let him get close before ripping a short left hook onto his chin which sent him reeling across Daggart's table, scattering clams, salads, wine, soup, flowers. He twisted Baldie's head in the soup bowl to let one blistered nostril surface for air.

The investors got up and hurried away. Other patrons screamed for the maitre d' to call the cops.

"And as for you, Dum Dum . . ." Bobby said, wagging a finger.

"Your life is about to end," Dum Dum said in a low seethe.

". . . you just can't help leaving messes everywhere you go. Being the dumb fuck in the family sure must have been tough. Dad liked Seanny better than Donnie, didn't he, Dum Dum? *He* had no trouble telling you two apart. You were the dumb twin with the 'duh' look on your face, wearing the dunce cap at school while Seanny made the honor roll. Second best, Dum Dum?"

"I'm gonna kill ya," Dum Dum said.

"What happened, Dum Dum? I hear you were born last, Mom saw you were doomed to a lifetime of dumbness, and did a mercy-sit on your face to put you out of your misery. But as luck would have it, you were too dumb to die. So you lived, happily dum dum after."

Bobby wanted these guys to lose control, act stupid, use emotions instead of intellect. He knew the mother remark would bring Dum Dum to his feet. It never failed. Bobby let go of Baldie, who got up gasping, screaming for ice. Dum Dum came at Bobby like a Kodiak bear on its hind legs. Bobby jabbed four straight fingers into his throat, gagging him, then kneed him in the groin. As Dum Dum doubled over, Bobby lifted him and body-surfed him across the table at Daggart, who calmly sat with his hands folded on the table.

"You better start putting your affairs in order, Moe," Bobby said. "Because when the wise guys who gave you this one shot see that a lone-wolf mick like me stopped you from pulling it off, they're gonna drop you in a hole alongside your old man, who was put there by your own mother. They'll dump your sister in the same miserable hole, too. You couldn't be the don of a chop shop."

"I believe this club is for Harvard grads only," Daggart said.

Bobby smiled and began to stroll away. He stopped and turned. "Oh, almost forgot, I have Chung's entire confession on videotape. Time to roll the dice, Moe."

52

On Maggie's computer screen was the image of a New Jersey driver's license bearing the photograph and identifying information of a pretty blond woman named Antoinette Smith.

"This was ten years ago," said Maggie.

Bobby leaned in close and studied the picture. She looked very familiar. Just as he had suspected.

Patrick said, "Jeez, she looks like . . ."

"Here's a more recent license," Maggie said and clicked the mouse again. A current New Jersey license appeared on the screen. Same woman, still very pretty, but ten years older, and with a new name—Toni S. Paragon.

"She looks better in person," Patrick said.

"Yeah," Bobby said. "She sure does."

"So what's with her?"

"She was also Kronk's very first Kronkette—as in Number One."

"You mean you think she's Number One?" Patrick asked.

"She's been planning this for ten years, bro. Kronk treated her like a bimbo. She's been plotting her revenge ever since."

"But I thought you said this Paragon had all the properties set up so that if anyone asked questions his wife would take the fall."

"Yeah," Bobby said. "But I never looked at it from the other point of view. The properties list both their names as officers of the corporations that own them. If Paragon happens to die, guess who inherits the rights to all the land earmarked for Empire Island Terminal?"

"The wife. And she can always claim she was an innocent in the conspiracy. You think once the gambling bill is approved they'll have this poor sap Paragon whacked? Her own husband?"

"Let's see just how faithful Mrs. Paragon is to her husband," Bobby said. "Maggie, go through the pictures from San Juan, call up the one I grease-penciled 'DD,' for Dum Dum Dunne."

Maggie clicked through the photos.

"Is this the picture you want, old man?" Maggie asked as a tame shot of Dum Dum with the mystery woman appeared on the screen.

"That's the one, Mag," Bobby said. "Do me a favor, make that woman's dark hair blond."

Maggie computer-rendered the dark-haired woman blond.

"Good," Bobby said. "Now make her lose the shades . . ."

Maggie eliminated the sunglasses.

". . . and take the eyes from the photo on the

most recent driver's license and give them to the woman in this picture with Dunne."

Maggie made all the moves and Bobby asked her to enlarge the photo of the woman with Dunne and the license photo of Toni Paragon and arrange them side by side.

When she was finished, Maggie said, "It's the same woman, Pop."

"I'll be damned," Patrick said. "I saw her leaving with a suitcase and a plane ticket, kissing hubby Ralph goodbye that day, but she was supposed to be going to a realtors' convention."

"She went to San Juan instead and spent the night with Donald Dum Dum Dunne," Bobby said.

"So much for the faithful little missus who helps the family make ends meet as a part-time real estate broker in Bay Head, New Jersey."

"She knows real estate, all right," Bobby said. "Like 22 Empire Court—and most of those surrounding buildings."

"She's behind the whole thing, Pop?" Maggie asked. "The Waterfront Holdings and Rapa Properties. Everything? This woman?"

"Her nickname is Number One," Bobby said. "She's the one who followed me around in that dark Lumina, knowing it would lead me to her husband, hoping I'd guess he was acting on Sam Kronk's orders. She knew all of Kronk's moves, all his weaknesses. She picked her poor husband's brain. She used him, set him up to take the fall along with Kronk."

"You figure she might have him whacked," Patrick said. "Then she innocently inherits the properties for the terminal?"

"Yeah. And to be built with the Brooklyn gambling money. All of them are in it together—Daggart, Savarese, Dum Dum Dunne, all working for Toni S. Paragon, Number One."

"Why did she do all this, Pop?"

"Your mother's friend Giselle told me Kronk was sued by a woman once for paternity."

"I wish I had Giselle's hair," Maggie said.

"Yours is perfect," Bobby said. "Do me a favor, use what's under it and do one of those computer legal searches using Antoinette Smith's and Sam Kronk's names, maybe ten years ago."

"Is it criminal or civil?"

"Civil," Bobby said.

"Then I'll use the *Computerized Guide to Background Investigations* program already loaded on my hard drive," Maggie said, making her mouse clicks on a different keyboard. "It lists every county-level criminal record file in the entire country. What county are we talking about?"

"Atlantic County, New Jersey."

Maggie typed in "Kronk," "Smith," and "Atlantic County." The computer began its search as a PLEASE WAIT pulsated on the screen. Then the machine blinked and a series of numbers and codes appeared.

"We have a hit," Maggie said.

"Let me sit there," Bobby said as the screen filled with a legal caption: *Smith v. Kronk*.

Bobby used the down-arrow key to scroll through the charges brought by the former Antoinette Smith against Samuel Kronk nine and a half years before.

"Maggie, get us a couple of Cokes, will ya, please?" Bobby said.

"I get it," she said. "It's about lurid sex and the depraved shenanigans of the super-rich and bastard kids and millions of dollars. Sounds like the evening news, old man."

"The sodas, kid," Bobby said.

Maggie left the room and Patrick sat beside Bobby at the computer. Together they read through the court transcript.

"Basically she's saying here that she had an affair with Kronk," Bobby said. "Listen to her own testimony: 'Sam Kronk gave me a place to stay in his hotel. We started having regular sexual relations. Then one day, a month after I moved in, he took me on a cruise to St. Barts on his 150-foot yacht. Sam invited along a half-dozen of his guy friends for a party. We set sail. I was twenty years old, a former Miss New York State. I was also the only woman on the boat that day . . .'"

"With six other guys," Patrick said. "I can imagine what happened. In Brooklyn they call it a 'hump or jump cruise.'"

"In her Examination Before Trial by Kronk's attorneys she claims she was young, impressionable, and manipulated," Bobby said. "Listen to her testimony again: 'I was drinking, champagne cocktails, the men kept giving me drugs—cocaine, Quaaludes, marijuana. I was in a haze. Sam kept telling me to be *nice* to his friends. They started kissing me. Touching me. They took me into the main stateroom. I have memories of being *nice* to many of Sam's friends. I didn't have much of a choice. They were always just . . . there—on top of me, all over me, drugs, sex, sex, drugs. At least three or four had me—maybe more, maybe all of Sam's friends over the weekend. It seemed like one long night. I was under the impression that was what Sam wanted me to do. I was afraid not to. I was in love with him. I pleased them to please Sam. I don't remember having any clothes on or leaving the stateroom for most of the trip. I don't remember eating. Just drinking and snorting and swallowing pills and smoking pot and being *nice* to Sam's friends . . .'"

"She was manipulated by the older, wealthy man she was in love with and eager to please," Patrick said. "So one after another, over the weekend, most of these guys took turns with the party girl—the young beauty queen."

"She *was* the party," Bobby said. "The party really ended a few weeks later when she found out she was pregnant."

"I can see where all this could sort of piss a woman off," Patrick said. "Make her want a little bit of revenge."

"All these guys, Europeans mostly, took off and went back to wherever they were from," Bobby said, still scrolling through the court transcript. "Probably to their wives and kids. But Kronk claimed the incident never happened. Said no such party ever took place. She had no witnesses. She couldn't recall the names of any of the men. The judge said that even if such an incident took place, she appeared to have been a willing participant, a consenting adult. If it was rape, it should have been reported as a crime to local authorities in St. Barts at the time. But it never was. The judge was right. *Legally*, she had no case."

"What about her paternity suit against Kronk?"

"It was thrown out of court," Bobby said, scrolling the document. "As soon as Kronk produced medical evidence that he'd had a vasectomy two years before the alleged incident. His attorney painted her as a slut who had an affair with Kronk but obviously was unfaithful to him, using drugs and sleeping around with so many other guys she couldn't figure out which one was the actual father. So she concocted this cock-and-bull story and picked the man with the most money, Sam Kronk, claiming he was the father. Problem was, she didn't know Kronk had had a vasectomy a couple of years before."

"So she was left barefoot and pregnant and on her own."

"Kronk gave her fifty grand to hit the road. Probably to clear his guilty conscience. And she had the baby, went to school, studied real estate, and has been plotting her revenge ever since. She came back six years later, found out Kronk's new head of security was a bug-eyed, dumpy-looking guy named Ralph Paragon. This attractive dame had no problem getting him to marry her and to buy a house forty miles away from Atlantic City. She knew an elitist social butterfly like Kronk would never socialize with the help. He'd never meet Paragon's wife. So all she'd need was a new hairdo, a little plastic surgery, and Kronk wouldn't even recognize a photo of her on Paragon's desk. In fact, I doubt he's ever been in the security office to see Paragon's desk."

"Then using her real estate skills," Patrick said, "Toni set poor Ralph up as a fall guy in the Rapa Properties scam, listing his name as chief corporate officer, picking his brain about Kronk, his itinerary, his political affiliations, all the inside dope."

"Then she started an affair with her new husband's subordinate, Dum Dum Dunne, who became like a human Rottweiler for her. She probably promised him that once he set up her husband as a fall guy and helped frame Kronk for murder, the two of them could get rich together and live happily ever after."

"The woman who had been used by men for their selfish pleasure was now using men, any men, to exact her revenge," Patrick said. "This is one very damaged and dangerous lady."

"She knew from way back," Bobby said, "when she was the first Kronkette, that Sam Kronk was fix-

ated by Zelda Savarese, so she had Dum Dum enlist
her into the scheme. Zelda brought in her brother,
Moe Daggart, to raise all the seed money in the
church Vegas nights—and to orchestrate the murder
frame on Sam Kronk. But you just *know* she intends
to have Dum Dum whack Zelda and Moe, too. This
crazy chick wants to have Kronk on death row for
murder while she runs the Empire Island Terminal,
with a foothold to build the first casino in New York
City. Talk about turning the tables."

"Success is the ultimate revenge," Patrick said.

Maggie brought the two Cokes into the room.

"Is it safe again for my virgin ears?" she asked.

Bobby kissed Maggie goodbye. He pocketed the
more graphic photographs of Toni S. Paragon with
Dum Dum Dunne in cabana 12.

"I think we should tell the husband, no?" Patrick
said. "Before they waste the poor guy."

"Yeah," Bobby said. "Try to track him down.
Then let me know where he is. Let me tell him.
Meanwhile, I have to go see another guy who's on a
bad losing streak."

53

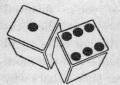

Bobby met Max Roth in the lobby of the Twin Towers, where Assembly Speaker Carl Pinto was scheduled to hold a final press conference before leaving for an all-night session in Albany on the gambling resolution.

Reporters from all the media were gathered in the lobby, downstairs from the speaker's New York City office. Outside the skies were leaden and the forecast was threatening heavy night rain.

Max Roth had arranged an informal, off-the-record chat with Pinto before the press conference. He brought Bobby upstairs with him. Roth shook Pinto's hand, introduced Bobby. A young aide stood by like a prop.

"So what do you want to talk about, Max?" Pinto asked. "I'll lay two-to-one it's about my vote on the gambling bill."

"We should talk alone," Bobby said, nodding toward the aide.

"Mel sits in on all my meetings," Pinto said.

Bobby handed Pinto a manila envelope containing photographs of him in San Juan, pictures of him schmoozing with Sam Kronk, and copies of his signed markers totaling $230,000, which he had gotten from the safe of Kronk's thirteenth-floor lair.

Pinto's face locked, as if he'd been shot with too much novocaine. He nodded for his aide to leave. He did.

"What the fuck is this?" Pinto said.

"These are bad-news people you're involved with," Bobby said. "Your pictures are tame. The flicks they have of poor Lebelski with the hot babe could cost him his seat in the State Senate—and the more important one at his family's dinner table. That's why he's flip-flopped."

"You saying Lebelski blinked because of black-mail?" Pinto said.

"Yeah," Max Roth said. "Have they contacted you?"

Pinto fell quiet for a few moments, looking from Bobby to Max. "This completely off the record?"

Max and Bobby assured him it was.

"I was told as long as I maintained my original position, the debts would be taken care of," Pinto said.

"What did you say?" Bobby asked.

"I said fuck you," Pinto said. "I've already applied for a second mortgage on my house to pay part of the debt. My wife is ready to divorce me. She and my kids did what's called an intervention about my gambling jones. I've agreed to go into Gamblers Anonymous. GA says they'll work out a payment plan for the rest. But no way am I gonna ever hock my vote for money. Or blackmail. Never. The one thing I won't wager is my pride, my integrity. It's all I have left. So I'm gonna pay my debt and vote in favor of the gambling resolution anyway, because I think we need it. It'll create revenue, jobs, help schools, social programs. Besides, New Jersey, Las Vegas, Canada, and the mob are making all this money from New Yorkers who want to gamble anyway."

"I think gambling in New York should be legalized, too," Bobby said. "But not this year. And I'm gonna tell you why."

For the next fifteen minutes Bobby told Pinto most of what was going on, about the McCoys being murdered, how Daggart and Savarese and others with personal vendettas had tried to frame Izzy Gleason and Sam Kronk. He told them that Daggart, who wanted to be the new Ivy League Godfather for the new century, would control Empire Island Terminal and probably build the first casino there. He told him all the grimy details about the murders of the two clerics, and Ben Lee and Betty Wang, and the connection to sweatshops in Brooklyn. And a slave-labor farm in Jersey. Pinto kept looking to Max Roth for assurance that Bobby was telling the truth. Max kept nodding and Pinto grew increasingly astonished. And outraged.

"This is beyond fucking belief," Pinto said. "Have you approached Lebelski yet?"

"And do what?" Bobby asked. "Blackmail an alcoholic with pictures of his infidelities, like they're doing? Threaten to expose him in the press? If this poor bastard gets squeezed from them to vote *for* the bill and me to vote *against* it, I'm afraid he'll guzzle a bottle of Jack Daniel's and jump under a train."

"What do you suggest I do?" Pinto asked, looking pained.

"A vote for the resolution this time could be a vote for these people to run it," Max Roth said. "Or you could stop it cold by opposing it before it ever comes to a public vote this year."

"You're holding the cards, Assemblyman," Bobby said.

54

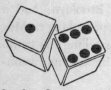

When Bobby got back to *The Fifth Amendment*, his brother Patrick was waiting for him with Ralph Paragon—who was holding a 9-mm automatic to his head.

"Just take it easy, Ralph," Bobby said.

"I tracked him down and told him what was going on," Patrick said as Paragon stood behind him in the salon of *The Fifth Amendment*, his gun nestled in the base of Patrick's skull. "He didn't believe me. I told him you had proof."

"I'll blow his fucking head off," Paragon said, the

boat tilting in the irritated river as the skies crowded with swollen summer rain clouds.

"I don't think you'll want your kid to see both his parents going down for murder," Bobby said. "Your wife is already a lethal injection waiting to plunge."

"What the fuck is this all about?" Paragon said.

"I'm gonna take out my gun, nice and slow, and throw it across the room to you," Bobby said. "Then I want you to take that gun away from my brother's head. Then I'll show you a few things about your wife I wouldn't be thrilled to have to show to any husband."

"Move nice and fucking easy, Emmet, or I'll do both of youse."

Bobby took his .38 out of his jacket pocket and slid it across the room. Paragon stepped on it and told Bobby to raise his pants legs, so he could see if he was wearing an ankle holster. He wasn't. He made Bobby remove his jacket and turn around to make sure there wasn't a gun in his back belt. There wasn't. Paragon slowly stepped away from Patrick, bent, picked up Bobby's gun, and lowered his own. He now held a gun in either hand.

Bobby lifted the plastic liner bag out of the trash bin and hidden between the bag and the bottom of the bin was a manila envelope. He lifted it out and sorted through a collection of eight-by-ten photographs, including printouts Maggie had made on her Foto Editor machine. He spread the photographs out on the table and countertops, graphic photographs of Dum

Dum Dunne and the mystery woman in cabana 12. One photo showed her bejeweled hands on Dum Dum's penis.

"Recognize the rings on the woman's hands?" Bobby asked.

Paragon stared at the photograph without blinking and softly said, "I was never happier than the day I bought her that wedding ring . . ."

Bobby saw Paragon's angry face collapse the way he'd seen the hardest of criminals' faces fall when a judge handed down a life sentence. Paragon saw all that he was, all that he had ever worked for, all that he'd built and loved suddenly destroyed in one frozen frame of time.

"I computer-enhanced the pictures in case there was any doubt," Bobby said, pushing forward the photos he'd done himself because they were too graphic for Maggie's eyes. "Got rid of the dark wig, the shades, and there's your wife. I'm sorry."

Paragon looked at them and swallowed the dry knot in his throat. He shuffled through more photos and when he got to the more lurid ones, he just couldn't bear to look at them anymore.

Paragon sunk to the floor, his back against the wall, the pistols dangling. Bobby took them from him as Paragon began to weep.

"Tell me everything," he said.

"You sure you can handle it?" Bobby said.

"Look, that kid calls me *Daddy*," he said. "He has no other family. Someone has to raise him. I might hate Toni for what she's done. I won't stop loving that little boy. So, I have to know exactly what's going on. Everything."

Bobby told him. He showed Paragon the Kronkette list from the thirteenth-floor safe. Explained how Antoinette Smith was the very first Kronkette, who had been seduced at age nineteen, deflowered, passed around to rich friends on a yacht, knocked up, and unceremoniously dumped by Sam Kronk with a $50,000 going-away present to a life as an unwed mother with no idea who the father was.

She blamed Kronk and vowed revenge. And became known as Number One in a carefully orchestrated conspiracy to frame Kronk for murder while she got even richer than he.

"She almost pulled it off," Bobby said.

Paragon looked nauseated. "She used me the way they used her," he said. "I feel like I've been raped."

Bobby showed Paragon the evidence about the property holdings for the proposed Empire Island Terminal. Told him how eventually his name would have come up when the murders of the McCoys were thoroughly investigated and finally prosecuted. About how his name was also connected to the Lucky Eight Farm. How his name was probably traceable to millions of dollars in illegal campaign contributions to key city councilmen who would vote to okay zoning for the Empire Island Terminal. How he would be implicated in the blackmailing of certain politicians to influence the legalized-gambling vote in the New York Legislature.

"You were set up as the patsy," Bobby said.

"She had to know I'd figure out she was behind all this," Paragon said.

"Not if you weren't around," Patrick said.

Paragon narrowed his eyes, looked from one brother to the other, in horror.

"See, you were supposed to look like Sam Kronk's bag man on all of this," Bobby said. "When he finally got indicted, you'd turn up missing, just like the McCoys, and it would look like Kronk had you whacked to silence you. Then they'd hang him."

"You think she actually intended to kill me?" Paragon asked, bug-eyed and astonished.

"Not personally," Bobby said. "Loverboy Dum Dum would do that for her. He killed all the others. And then she would look like the poor, innocent, exploited widow with a kid to raise. Kronk would be on his way to jail, and she'd inherit all the holdings and would control the terminal, maybe a casino, and untold kazillions."

Paragon sat stunned for a long silent time as the boat rocked in its slip, staring into middle space with wounded eyes. The afternoon grew dark as clouds tumbled downriver, promising heavy rain. Bobby looked at his watch and walked to the TV. He turned on New York One, which was carrying Assembly Speaker Carl Pinto's press conference from the lobby of the World Trade Center.

". . . and so after a long and thorough review of my own conscience, and taking into consideration everything that this vote means, I stand here today as the speaker of the Assembly to say that I am reversing my position on the legalized-gambling resolution currently before the Assembly," he said. "While gambling might be a positive idea in the future as a source of revenue and jobs, we must not seek to enhance the state economy by means that are at best marginally productive at this time. There have been many studies that indicate that casino gambling actually has an increased cost for the public sector as a result of its social and economic impact on families. Lest anyone call me a hypocrite or point to my personal life, I openly admit here today that I have personally wrestled with the octopus of gambling addiction and have sought counseling.

"Other information that has come my way indicates that the only ones who can really benefit from casino gambling at this juncture in this state are certain very wealthy private entrepreneurs and organized crime, which these days comes in fancy new packaging but is still the old ruthless mob in my eyes. So, today I am rolling a seven, 'crapping out' on the gambling resolution, and I urge my fellow Assembly members to join me in this vote."

A rumpus went up in the lobby as reporters shouted questions at Pinto. Bobby lowered the sound and turned to Patrick and Paragon.

"The rats will be scurrying," Bobby said. "The only thing left is the money."

"I'll do whatever you want me to do," Paragon said. "I have to stop her."

"We can use your help," Bobby said. "Go home, go along with whatever she suggests, let us know what's happening, call me. And take your gun."

"I owe you another thank-you," Paragon said. "That other night, when you could have beat the shit out of me in front of my son—you didn't."

Bobby looked at him and realized that that kid, who was sired by some lousy rich stranger he'd never know, was lucky to have a guy like Paragon to call Daddy.

"Let's just make sure that kid doesn't lose his father tonight," Bobby said.

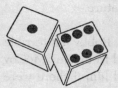

Three boats headed for Empire Island, in the middle of the great harbor, as rain began to fall.

Right after receiving the call from Ralph Paragon saying the meeting on the island was set for nine PM, Bobby piloted *The Fifth Amendment* from the Seventy-ninth Street Boat Basin downriver toward the $70 million that Izzy Gleason had told him was buried somewhere on the island, in the grave of Eddie and Sally McCoy.

Aboard Toni Smith Paragon's Mainship 47 motor yacht, Dum Dum Dunne sipped champagne in the salon with Ralph and Toni. Upstairs two Kronk Castle gray-jackets—along for added protection—steered from the New Jersey side of the harbor. Paragon watched the eye contact between Dum Dum and his wife. It wasn't subtle. Dum Dum wore a smirk that seemed to say, "That's right, I'm banging your wife, asshole, and what the fuck are you gonna do about it?"

From Brooklyn came Morris Daggart and Zelda Savarese, accompanied by two NuCent Ventures Ivy

League goons. All four of them were unaware of the stowaway under the rubber dinghy on board the forty-foot cabin cruiser. The boat cut through the rain-roiled waters toward more than enough money to reclaim a family's once proud stature.

As he sailed south on the Hudson, Bobby felt terrible about the phone call he'd received from Amy McCoy in the late afternoon. She'd asked him if there were any new developments in the search for her missing brother and sister-in-law. Bobby had lied and said nothing was new. Amy said she knew that Assemblyman Carl Pinto reversing his vote meant that certain people would become suddenly desperate, and that there was no more time to delay. She knew that her brother's investigation into that proposed terminal had led to his disappearance. Or death. But the terminal would be moot now that the vote in the legislature was going against legal gambling in the state.

"I might be inexperienced in all this cloak-and-dagger stuff," she'd said, "but I'm not an idiot. I know something must be going down—tonight. Are you going to clue me in?"

"There's nothing going on," Bobby had said.

"Fine," Amy said, "then I'll find out on my own," and hung up.

Bobby couldn't let her get involved and wind up on Empire Island, where everything would come to a head that night. With so much money at stake, bullets were almost certainly going to fly.

Bobby wished he could have just called the cops to tell them that he thought the McCoys were buried somewhere on Empire Island. He would've told them that the bad guys were meeting tonight to divide $70 million raised in illegal church-casino gambling and a yearlong sports book.

But after Jimmy Chung went out the window, Bobby certainly didn't trust Noel Christmas. And with Mayor Tom Brady running the NYPD like a private political army, he would be afraid they'd storm the island like Navy SEALs to vindicate Sam Kronk and blow any chance of making an arrest that could stick on anyone else. Bobby was also concerned that once the information was passed to NYPD brass, some greedy asshole in Moe Daggart's or Toni Paragon's pocket would tip the conspirators off, scare them away.

The same with the FBI: Dum Dum Dunne still had enough contacts inside the Bureau to get advance warning of such an operation.

He didn't yet trust Sean Dunne enough to bring him completely into the loop. Even if he was honest, Bobby was afraid he'd come roaring in with a joint task-force invasion of boats, helicopters, and spotlights. It would just scare the conspirators away before they were caught in the act, before they led Bobby to the money and the bodies of the McCoys. Plus, Bobby still didn't believe Sean Dunne could take such a straight-arrow, law-and-order stance when it came to his own twin brother.

So Bobby wasn't going to trust any other cop but

his brother Patrick, an NYPD sergeant, to sort this
one out. He wanted Patrick to get the collars instead
of some last-minute hotshot member of the brass.
Patrick was with him, carrying a legitimate gun and
shield, aboard *The Fifth Amendment*.

Patrick was the only cop he needed.

Bobby knew they needed to see the conspirators retrieve the money at the same place where
the bodies of the McCoys were buried and let
Patrick make the arrests. Most important, Patrick
could also look the other way while three quarters
of the loot was loaded onto *The Fifth Amendment*
to be given to Rabbi Berg for his First Stop social-
services and sports complex, which would be a last-
ing monument to Father Dooley and Reverend
Greene. The rest of the money could be used as
evidence against the conspirators.

Herbie was already stashed on the island for
backup. After Jimmy Chung went out the window
with one of Noel Christmas's slugs, Izzy told Bobby
that the bodies and the money were stashed somewhere on Empire Island and Bobby immediately
called Herbie and told him to pack a few of his
favorite guns and a pair of night-scope binoculars.
Herbie took a rented boat right out to Empire
Island, picked a strategic spot on the high ground,
where he could see arriving boats.

As the three boats converged on Empire Island, Max
Roth was having dinner with Sean Dunne in the

River Cafe on the Brooklyn waterfront, overlooking Empire Island. He asked the U.S. attorney to have a squad of joint task-force police on standby alert, telling him he'd gotten a tip that something big might go down that night somewhere in the city involving all the players in the conspiracy that began with the disappearance of Eddie and Sally McCoy. Bobby had told Max that if he didn't hear from him by 9:25 PM, he was to tell Sean Dunne where he was and why he was there and to send in the joint task force.

It was all the preparation Bobby could think of.

The rest would play out on its own.

When he neared a buoy a few hundred yards from Empire Island, Bobby checked his watch before tying off *The Fifth Amendment*. It was 8:45 PM. He and Patrick would motor to shore in the small rubber dinghy he kept on board, big enough for five people, or two plus the bulk of $70 million in cash.

More than anyone else, Bobby was worried about Ralph Paragon. Ralph had a kid to go home and raise.

On the phone earlier, Paragon told Bobby that Toni wanted him to accompany her to a nine PM real estate closing for which she could not be late. "She said she wanted me to come because the deal was so big it could change our lives forever," Paragon told Bobby. "She said she wanted to take the boat because it would be on Empire Island."

"Just be careful," Bobby had said. "Remember, I

think your wife and Dunne are planning to kill you or else they wouldn't have brought you in the loop."

"I have a gun down my pants," Paragon said. "I never fired a shot in my entire career at the Bureau. But I'm not planning on taking one now either."

"Who else is going?" Bobby asked.

"She comes on to me all kissy-face, all dolled up, says this time she wants me to be there as protection," Paragon said. "She also asks me to bring my *friend* Donald Dunne and a few gray-jackets for extra security because this could be a cash transaction. Sure. All along I felt so proud of her for bringing money into the house, working late, winning the boat as Broker of the Year, telling me she was out at night showing people houses. Meanwhile all she was ever showing was the A-frame between her legs to Dum Dum Dunne. What a fool I've been. What a fucking asshole chump. I want to kill her, Bobby, I want to put one in her brain. His too."

"Remember," Bobby told him, "someone has to be around for the kid."

"I know," Paragon said. "I'm not leaving him an orphan."

As they neared Empire Island in the dinghy, Bobby reminded Patrick that keeping Paragon alive was a priority.

The Emmet brothers arrived on shore, dressed in black, their faces also blackened. Bobby was armed with a Browning Auto-5 12-gauge shotgun, his .38, and a seventeen-shot 9-mm Glock. Patrick carried his 9-mm Glock—with a thirteen-shot capacity—and a .38.

They pulled the dinghy up on the shore and hid it among the wild reeds as the rain fell in a loud spiraling whoosh. Terrified rats scurried in the dark underbrush. The steady rain was the only sound. Otherwise, the silence in the center of the harbor of the loudest city on earth was eerie. Far away a foghorn moaned.

As they moved in a low crouch across the island toward the abandoned construction site—where a cement-mixer truck, a backhoe, and a crane stood idle—Bobby stopped to get his compass bearings. To the north was the Manhattan skyline, a ghostly mountain of light in the foggy gloom. Brooklyn was a sleepy black walrus to the east, dotted with thousands of blinking lights. To the west, Lady Liberty stood bravely before New Jersey, which looked like the darkened end of the earth.

"What a place to die," Patrick said.

"Then let's not," Bobby said.

From the New Jersey side Bobby heard the low rumble of an approaching boat beneath the wash of the rain. When the engine was cut, human voices became audible, men and a woman, all of them at first unintelligible and weak in the growling wind. The voices grew louder when the boat docked.

"Ralph, you go first," he finally heard a woman say.

"What the hell are we doing on Empire Island at night?" Ralph Paragon asked. "In the rain? What kind of real estate deal is this supposed to be, Tone?"

"The last one we'll ever have to do, baby," said Antoinette Smith Paragon.

Through the spooky green hue of his night-scope binoculars, Bobby and Patrick watched Ralph help his wife off the boat, followed by Dum Dum and the two gray-jackets.

"Number One and Dum Dum," Bobby said. "Sounds like a seventies band."

And then came the sound of another approaching boat from the Brooklyn side.

"Tie the fucking thing off," Moe Daggart yelled. "Come on guys, don't be afraid to get your topsiders wet, for chrissakes! Lets do this and get the fuck out of here."

"This sucks a big one," Bobby heard Zelda Savarese say. "Promise me I'll never have to go through this again, Moe. Promise."

"I promise, sis," he said. "We're going to live like royalty again, one way or the other."

They climbed from the bank, wearing yellow rain slickers and carrying flashlights, sloshing through the weeds, closer to the rendezvous point, which was the cement pit at the center of the construction site.

"Wait till they dig up the money, doing the split," Bobby whispered to Patrick. "I'll yell 'busted,' and when Ralph separates, we come in from each side."

"You got it," Patrick said.

Bobby took a flattened position in the reeds behind the cement mixer, clutching the shotgun. Patrick split off and hid in the high thistles and weeds growing up around the base of the abandoned crane. The steady barrage of rain turned the island into a giant mud pie.

Both of the arriving groups carried high-powered flashlights from either direction, long needles of silver rain visible in their piercing beams.

"Someday, Moe, we'll own this," Zelda Savarese said.

Bobby turned his attention to the group approaching the construction site from the Jersey side, dressed in dark, hooded rain ponchos. He heard Toni Paragon say, "Get the money and do it."

"Do what?" Ralph said.

"We give them twenny-four dollars' worth of wampum, we get Manhattan Island, Ralph," Dum Dum said.

"Fuck you, Donald," Paragon said.

"Relax, Ralph," Toni Smith Paragon said. "It's a simple transaction. Nothing will go wrong."

They all congregated at the cement pit, standing on top of the remains of Eddie and Sally McCoy. Rain splattered on the concrete surface and popped on the rain slickers of the gathered. Bobby counted nine in all. Four players, four goons, one victim. Then, out the corner of his eye he thought he saw another fast-moving figure. Then, just as quickly, it was gone. *Too small to be Herbie,* he thought. *Maybe an animal. Or a bird. Or a ghost.*

"What a goddamned mess," said Toni S. Paragon.

"Hey, who the fuck knew that Pinto would flip-flop," Daggart said. "We have Lebelski. Never figured on Pinto blinking. This guy would bet on rain in the Gobi."

"If he bet on *you* he'd lose," Dum Dum said.

"What is all this?" asked Ralph Paragon.

"Dummy up," Dum Dum said.

"Up yours," Ralph said.

"I already do that with your wife," Dum Dum said.

"Knock it off," Toni Paragon shouted. "Where's the money?"

Daggart threw Dum Dum the keys to the crane and walked over to the corner of the concrete slab. He took a small ball peen hammer from his back pocket and chipped away at some surface cement. An inch down he revealed a heavy metal ring, which he pried up with a pinch bar.

"What's he mean by that, Toni?" Paragon said. "That he already does it with my wife?"

"Quiet, Ralph," she said.

"Lower the crane hook," Daggart said.

Dum Dum walked past Patrick, who lay flat in the reeds, and climbed up into the crane cab. He switched on the engine, worked the levers, and lowered a hook on a long cable. Daggart guided the hook to the ring in the concrete slab and attached it. He motioned for Dum Dum to hoist it up.

As the hook ascended, a section of the concrete slab lifted loose from the ground, and with it rose two attached fifty-gallon oil drums. The concrete was simply a ten-inch lid sitting on top of the barrels. Dum Dum lowered the barrels to the ground. Daggart walked to them, toppled them, and pried open the metal hasps that sealed the bottom lids to the drums.

When he popped the lids, the 42 blue packages of cash Bobby had seen rise from the shark tank in Coney Island tumbled out.

"Lovely," said Toni S. Paragon as she raised her .380-caliber automatic from under her rain slicker and pointed it directly at Moe Daggart. "Bye-bye, asshole."

But Ralph Paragon, anticipating such an action, deflected her shot. Daggart hit the ground and scrambled into the wet weeds.

Bobby was on his feet and fired two blasts of the shotgun into the air. "BUSTED!" he shouted, and Patrick came tearing out of the tall thistles.

Then everything happened fast.

"You fucking asshole!" Toni screamed and shot

Ralph once in the chest. He fell to one knee, astonished, grasped his chest, got up and stumbled away and fell into the overgrown grass.

Zelda Savarese produced her own gun and aimed it at Toni.

"You back-stabbing cunt!" she yelled. She fired and missed. Toni ran toward the abandoned Coast Guard barracks beyond the construction site. Zelda chased her with an athlete's speed.

The crewcut gray-jacket fired at Bobby, hitting him square in the chest. Bobby fell and got right back up. The astounded man fired again and once more Bobby went down and got up, the bullets bouncing dully on the five-by-eight-inch steel sternum plate built into the Zepel-treated American Body Armor vest from the Snoop Shop. Patrick was wearing identical armor. When Crewcut aimed to fire a third time, Bobby took out his legs with a shotgun blast, sending him into an agonized, boneless twirl.

Zelda chased Toni into the reeds, firing wildly.

Bobby ran to see if Ralph Paragon was alive. He felt for a pulse. There was one. He realized the wise old fed was wearing a Teflon vest. He had just been knocked out by the close range of the impact. "Stay down," Bobby said.

Before Bobby could stand, one of the Ivy League goons ran up behind him in the driving rain and took aim at his head.

Patrick dropped him with a single bullet through the throat.

The other gray-jacket now dashed out of the weeds, aiming at Patrick and Bobby. Herbie appeared out of the storm, silhouetted by a scribble of lightning, firing two guns. The gray-jacket started to fall to the left, but another blast sent him whipping to the right before he dropped with a soft splash.

Herbie stalked the edges of the construction site, both guns waving, looking around as he passed the big backhoe. "Okay, who the fuck's next!" he screamed.

Dum Dum cocked a pistol behind him, set the gun on Herbie's spine, and softly said, "Recite your Talmud, Jewboy—and, please, no begging like the oven-stuffers in the kike camps. You're my ticket off this rock. Move."

Herbie lowered both guns to his side and without turning, fired both of them at the ground behind him. He heard Dum Dum scream and when he turned he was hobbling away on one and a half feet. The bloody stump of his right foot slashed a crimson stripe through the mud of the construction site. "Say 'Jewboy'? Something about fuckin' 'ovens'?"

Herbie fired again but Dum Dum dove behind a mountain of gravel and sand, Herbie's bullets landing like spongeballs.

"Herbie, get the money into the dinghy!" Bobby shouted as he ran deeper into the island, where he'd seen Daggart and Zelda chasing after Toni Paragon.

Bobby saw all three disappear into an old military barracks, out of the punishing rain. Bobby approached with caution. There was a long moment of silence followed by a fusillade of shooting from inside. Single shots followed by bursts of semiautomatic fire.

Then more silence.

Bobby waited. He wasn't about to charge in after them. He'd wait for whoever survived to emerge.

Finally Zelda Savarese appeared in a doorway surrounded by a halo of gunsmoke. Through the downpour, even with her hair matted to her head and her makeup running down her high cheekbones, she was stunning, the mole on her cheek like a thumbprint from God saying she was special. She stood leaning against the doorframe, flashing the big beautiful smile, her legs casually crossed, elbow bent, with one hand on her hip, still holding her pistol. *Gorgeous*, he thought.

"Match," she hissed.

And then a geyser of blood erupted from her mouth as if from a mythical figure in a Bernini fountain. Her eyes rolled back in her head and she pitched face-first into the mud. She had been shot twice in the back, and blood leaked through the back of the yellow rain slicker.

Daggart came running out of the barracks in a discombobulated, tearful panic, holding his pistol.

"Zelda . . ."

He fell to his knees and lifted his sister into his arms.

"Zelda . . . Zelda . . ."

Bobby again thought he saw a slight figure appear out of the rain in a stand of trees to his left.

He spun, lowered his Glock.

But there was no one there. Just the steady chatter of the rain. He heard a muffled shot from behind him. When he turned back that way, Toni Paragon had her pistol pointed directly in his face.

Moe Daggart was now slumped in death with a dark hole in his temple, still in a seated position, holding his sister in his arms, the two of them grotesquely entangled as the rain drummed on their slickers.

"Thanks for your help," Toni Smith Paragon said. "I was gonna kill them all anyway."

"I'm not alone."

"Yeah, but if I'm smarter than you, I'll have no trouble with the other two," she said.

"You had reasons to hate Kronk. But why, why did you have to kill all these people?"

"Simple," she said. "Because I'm a greedy bitch. I also wanted the money so that no one could ever hurt me again. And I wanted to show that fucking bastard Kronk not only that I could kill him, but that I could *beat* him, that I was smarter, and more ruthless, and richer, and *better* than him or any of his rich fucking swine friends who used me up and spit me out. And I would have pulled it off, too, except that dumb fuck Daggart picked you to try to frame Kronk. Rule number one—never hire anyone smarter than you. They always bury you. Like I'm gonna bury Kronk and all the rest of these assholes. Even Dum Dum, once he carries the money to the boat for me, he's fish food."

"But why innocent people, like the McCoys?" Bobby asked.

"Hey, I hand-picked them. So it wasn't like they died in vain. They died in an attempt to put an end to Sam Kronk. That's what McCoy wanted for as long as I can remember, writing all his exposés that no one ever read. In life he was a fringe joke. In death I made him *famous*. I validated his existence. I made people finally pay attention to what Eddie McCoy was saying about Sam Kronk for years. It was no coincidence that he lived in 22 Empire Court. I rented McCoy the fucking apartment! I put him there. And then when it was useful, I gave the okay to his last byline and his first headline. Now it's your turn, Bobby Emmet. See you in the funny papers . . ."

Bobby braced for the bullet as she cocked the pistol to fire.

"No, lady, you're going straight to hell," said Amy McCoy, who appeared out of the pouring rain with her little .25 outstretched.

Toni Paragon laughed, spun to fire at her. But Amy squeezed her own trigger first. The bullet entered Toni Paragon's right eye and didn't exit. Bobby knew that meant it had mushroomed in her brain. She fell soundlessly.

"Oh, my God, I am heartily sorry for having offended thee," Amy McCoy said as she fell to her knees in a stoic act of contrition. Bobby took the little gun from her hand and let her finish her prayer in the rain. Herbie ran to the clearing outside the barracks with both pistols ready to fire.

"Cops," he said. "Real ones. Let's go. I got the money loaded on the dinghy. Just hope it don't sink it."

Bobby took Herbie's guns and stuffed them inside his body armor. He looked at his watch. It was 9:38.

By the time he got to the abandoned construction site, Max Roth had arrived with Sean Dunne and a half-dozen joint FBI-NYPD task-force cops. Dead bodies were scattered around like tattered throw pillows. A few of the young goons were moaning in wounded agony.

Herbie said Ralph Paragon had awakened and had gone after Dum Dum Dunne. Dunne had managed to take him hostage in a standoff behind the hillock of gravel. Bobby signalled for Herbie to leave with the money. He did.

Sean Dunne was trying to talk his twin brother out.

"Don, let the guy go, man," Sean said. "It's over."

"She's dead, Dum Dum!" Bobby shouted. "Toni is dead!"

"Bullshit," Dum Dum said.

Dum Dum's head appeared above the gravel. He pushed Ralph Paragon to his feet and walked him in front of him. Sean Dunne had his hands behind his back, a 9-mm Glock in his right hand. Two brothers in an almost biblical confrontation.

"Let him go, Donnie," Sean said.

"Don't call me that," Dum Dum said, pushing Ralph Paragon to the side. "That's what the old man called me. *Donnie*. What am I? A fucking Osmond brother?"

The two brothers had their guns pointed at each other now.

"Come on, Donald," Sean said. "Time to come in from the rain."

Dum Dum looked around and saw the other cops aiming at him, Bobby and Patrick also aiming at him.

Dum Dum shrugged and said, "I guess they got us, huh, Seanny?"

He waved his gun in a way Bobby was certain was a gesture of surrender. "Now they'll know everything about us, bro . . ."

Sean Dunne fired three quick shots and Dum Dum staggered back and fell in a bewildered heap. Bobby just blinked and swallowed. Everyone else froze in amazement. Sean Dunne turned and looked at the crowd of cops and then at Bobby.

"You all saw it, he made a move with his gun," Sean Dunne said with the bloodless pitch of a bureaucrat. "I had no choice. It was a judgment call, a good shooting."

Bobby looked at Patrick. Theirs was a different kind of brotherhood. There was rain and death and money on Empire Island. There was nothing left to say.

Amy McCoy wandered through the tall grass, and when she reached the place where her brother was buried, Bobby put his arms around her shoulder.

"It's over," he said.

EPILOGUE

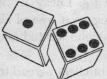

SEPTEMBER 1

As he sat in his Jeep on Northern Boulevard, Bobby knew he should be feeling happy.

After all the death, good things had started to happen. The legalized-gambling resolution was defeated in the assembly—this time. A new referendum would be introduced the following year. Legal gambling would come to New York, and soon, sometime in the twenty-first century.

But it would not come to Empire Island.

After Max Roth's front-page exposés of the entire conspiracy, the island was quickly designated by the city to be used as an extension campus for the city's university system.

Out in Coney Island, preliminary work was under way on First Stop House, a social services complex for poor kids and senior citizens. It was dedicated to the memories of Father Jack Dooley and Reverend Gaston Greene. No one dared question where Rabbi Simon Berg had come up with the money to build it. He called it a gift from God.

Bobby made sure a nice little piece of change from the church gambling money was put aside for a college fund for a kid named George Paragon, whose father had resigned as head of security for Kronk Industries and was now working for MGM in Las

Vegas. Paragon also abandoned any claim to the real estate owned by Rapa Properties. His first order of business had been to enlist the help of George from the Golden Pagoda to help close the Lucky Eight Farm and declare everyone working on it free of all indenture claims and to get anyone who wanted one an immigration lawyer.

Izzy Gleason's NYU film-student client agreed to cease and desist with his Roadrunner ripoff as soon as the publicity he received landed him a job with a noted animation house. The client had agreed to pay Izzy half of his signing bonus. Naturally, Izzy got stiffed. But he was able to locate a hundred-thousand-dollar stash Lulu's estranged husband was hiding in an off-shore account. After recovering it, Lulu offered Izzy a third. "I'd rather get it in trade," Izzy said.

Lulu agreed to continue working for him until she was finished with her first semester at Katharine Gibbs. Part of her deal was that she no longer had to eat in public with Izzy.

Maggie scored a 1,320 on her PSATs, which meant Connie was off Bobby's back. Bobby, Maggie, and Patrick were ready to fly down to visit his mother in Florida that afternoon.

So Bobby should have been happy.

But he had a sinking feeling in his gut as he turned to Amy McCoy, who was sitting next to him in the front seat of the Jeep. She was dressed in jeans, sneakers, a loose T-shirt, and they were parked across the street from St. Maria's Convent. Had Amy not followed Zelda Savarese from Atlantic City and stowed away on Moe Daggart's boat from Brooklyn to Empire Island on that terrible rainy night, Bobby would not have survived.

A very special lady had saved his life.

Now Amy McCoy was walking out of his life, for a higher calling.

"You're sure about this?" he asked.

"Yeah," she said. "It's where I belong. It's what I need. I feel like I can do what I do best in there."

"For what it's worth, I was falling head over heels for you."

"Bull-oney," she said. "With women like Zelda Savarese to compete with out there, I'm much better off in here."

"She was no match for you."

"In what way?"

He smiled. "In every way."

"Really mean that?" She seemed almost sinfully proud of that.

"Swear to Jesus."

"The Lord's name in vain . . ." She raised her hand to mock-smack him. He caught her wrist and looked into her eyes, which were bluer than the sky over New York.

"Ah, Bobby . . ."

He pulled her close and kissed her. Softly on the lips. Then she kissed him, more passionately. Soon they were making out like a pair of schoolkids across the street from the convent.

"God," she said, catching her breath. "Sin is so much easier than salvation."

"If you ever change your mind and want to commit a few mortal ones, you know where to find me."

"I love you, Bobby Emmet," she whispered.

"I love you, too, but there are some competitors I'm not willing to take on," he said, nodding toward the bright sky. "He's one lucky dude."

She climbed out of the passenger door and walked around to the driver's side. She reached down her pants and pulled the little .25 Pocket Sauer out of her panties. She handed it to him. It felt hot in his hand.

"I won't be needing this anymore," she said.

"I'll hold it for you," he said. "You never know."

There were tears in her eyes now but she wouldn't let them fall. She kissed him one last time, burying her face in his neck for what felt like an eternity.

She finally broke away and said, "God bless."

She turned and walked briskly across the avenue to the convent. Bobby watched her go.

Gorgeous, he thought.

When she was inside he looked in the rearview mirror before backing out of the parking spot—and noticed the hickey she'd left on his neck. He started to laugh even in his emptiness.

He drove back to the boat basin, where Maggie and Patrick were waiting on board *The Fifth Amendment*, all packed for the trip to Florida. He was going to dock the Silverton at Petey Maguire's dock and catch a noon flight. They'd be eating dinner with Maggie's granny under a palm tree.

Bobby started the engine, backed out of slip 99A, passing Pam and Dot, who had agreed to mind the kitten that Maggie had named Outlaw. The Emmet brothers sailed in silence for a few minutes.

"I was in Atlantic City this morning," Patrick said, breaking the silence, "to give Ralph Paragon that check for his kid from Rabbi Berg."

"Good," Bobby said. "Everything okay?"

"Guess who was hired yesterday to fill his old job at Kronk Castle?"

"Who cares . . ."

"Sean Dunne," Patrick said. "Noel Christmas is his number two."

Bobby looked at him for a long beat and then turned away as they passed Empire Island, a tranquil green thumbprint in the sparkling harbor.

"What do you think it means?" Patrick said.

Bobby smiled and said, "It means it's time for a rest before we come back for more."

Maggie joined them on the fly deck, gave her father a kiss on the cheek.

"Hey, old-timer, what's that on your neck?" Maggie asked, her eyes wide in disbelief.

"That," Bobby said, pulling his collar up, "that's just a kiss from God . . ."

ACKNOWLEDGMENTS

I'd like to thank Prof. Peter Kwong of the Asian American Studies Program at Hunter College for sharing his expertise on the Asian immigrant smuggling rackets.

I'd also like to thank Downtown Ronnie for explaining his unique variation on the separation of state and church.

Special gratitude to Mitchell Ivers for his smart ideas, keen eye, and great notes.

And as always, thanks to Esther Newberg, for simply being the best.

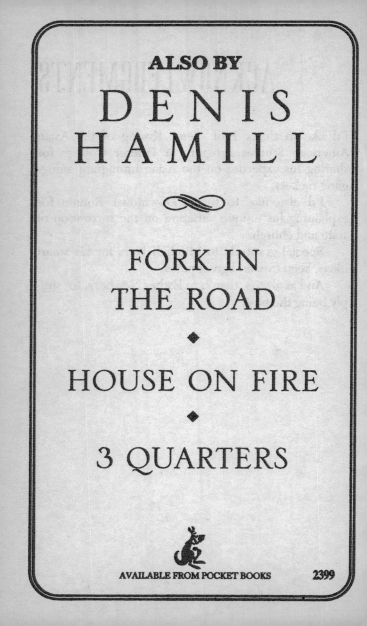

**POCKET BOOKS
PROUDLY PRESENTS**

Fork in the Road

Denis Hamill

**Coming soon in hardcover
from Pocket Books**

**The following is a preview of
Fork in the Road. . . .**

THE HOUSE WAS A ONE-STORY COTTAGE, WITH A BATH-room to the left off the foyer. To the right was the master bedroom and straight ahead was a cozy living room. The living room was big enough for a settee, a small Danish lounge chair, a padded armchair that sat by the small coal fire, and a dining-room table surrounded by six wooden chairs. The smell of cooking meat and cabbage wafted from a small kitchenette next to the living room. The kitchenette was equipped with a small two-burner stove, a tiny sink, and a waist-high fridge, and was only big enough for two, maybe three, average-size adults, but when Granny was in it there was no room for anyone else. Another small bedroom faced the back garden.

Colin plopped in an overstuffed chair in the immaculate sitting room as Gina and the cousins crammed the couch with the children on their laps. The old man sat in the low-slung Danish chair next to Colin, pouring bottles of Guinness into sparkling glasses, handing them out. Gina took one.

"For the babby," the old man said. Colin reached in his sport jacket pocket and furtively pressed the record button on his small tape recorder. *Gotta get this shit down,* he thought. *Evidence of life on another galaxy.*

"Ta, Granda," Gina said, taking the glass of Guinness.

The old man then handed Colin a glass for himself and soon everyone in the sitting room had a glass of Guinness. Paul stood by the hearth, staring into the fire, which was beginning to expire.

"None of yiz thought to go borry some feckin' coal

with a Yank coming into the house and all, wha'?" said Granny, stomping from the steam-shrouded kitchen. She bent and lifted the edge of the linoleum and tore a piece off matter-of-factly. None of the others reacted as she ripped up one linoleum hunk after another and tossed each hunk onto the fire.

"That poor Yank'll catch his death," the fat woman said, and made her way back into the kitchen as the flames roared.

Colin looked at the gaping hole left on the floor and thought, *You can't make this shit up. None of them thinks this is at all strange.*

Paul gleefully poked the torn linoleum into the blue flame. The smell of burning linoleum quickly overwhelmed the aroma of food.

"Magic, Granny," Paul said.

"We need a bit o' wood on that fire," Granny shouted.

Granda passed around a pack of cigarettes and each of the women took one—including Gina. Paul lifted out a piece of burning linoleum and lit Gina's cigarette.

"Gina, for chrissakes," Colin said.

"Go way outta dat," Gina said. "Next you'll be tellin' me to cut out me bottle of stout."

"Not a bad idea," Colin said.

"I will in me arse give up me fags and me bottle of stout because I'm with child," Gina said, her voice dropping to a low register as she spoke through the puff of smoke. "Every mother I know drinks and smokes. All this worry is a bunch of shite yous Americans cooked up. Doctors in Ireland says the bottle of stout is good for the babbies, isn't that right, Granny?"

"Aye," Granny shouted, as she stirred several pots on a small stove. "'Tis true. Lots of yer iron and ministrels in porter. But I'd switch to a fag with a cork tip all the same, Gina."

"I can't smoke a filtered fag," Gina said. "And I'll not

go nine feckin' months without an oul smoke all the same."

The old man flicked an ash behind his chair and threw his wooden match on the floor at his feet. Colin instinctively grabbed an ashtray from an end table, picked up the match, and placed it next to the assorted dead butts in the tray. He handed it to Granda. The old man shook his head and dumped the dead butts, matchsticks, and ashes onto the floor. Colin looked at the others for reactions. There were none. He saw Granda put the ashtray into his bathrobe pocket and flick another ash on the floor. *Could be a great bit of filmed business,* Colin thought. *Without a lick of dialogue.*

"Do yiz young wans have broken legs or do yiz want broken arms?" shouted Granny from the kitchen.

Gina and the cousins put their children down on the floor and sprung to action like soldiers responding to a command. Gina went directly into the kitchen, tying an apron around her waist and grabbing a serving platter. The other women began setting the table with delft, silverware, and condiments in preparation for a meal.

"See that there," the old man whispered to Colin, pointing to the butts and ashes he'd dumped on the floor. "That'll give the behemoth something to do later, so." Motioning to Granny standing outside the kitchen, he said, "And when the behemoth's busy with that, she stays off this," tapping himself on the back.

"How come I never thought of that?" Colin said.

"Wisdom comes with age, son," Granda said.

The room smelled faintly of shit and piss and burning linoleum and cabbage and Colin watched the saggy-diapered toddlers crisscross the floor in quest of their mothers.

"I hates a child what whinges," Granda said. *There's a word I have to have these people use,* Colin thought. *Whinge.*

Granda removed the pacifier from the mouth of the

whinging baby, dipped it into his stout, and plugged it back in the child's mouth.

"Shut yeh up," he said. The child shut up.

"If yer gonna have a child with that young wan, Gina," Granda said to Colin, "yeh better learn a few rare oul rules of the road. Come outside wi' me a wee minute while the wimmins set the tay."

Colin followed the old man into the chilly hallway. Granda stopped in the bathroom on the way out and urinated loudly without closing the bathroom door. Colin noticed that he intentionally pissed all over the toilet seat.

"Never lift the seat," he said. "Don't make it comfortable for the wimmims in there or they'll stay in there hours, so."

He reached up and unscrewed the lightbulb from the overhead socket, placing it in his bathrobe pocket. "Same with them diabolical feckin' light bulbs, or else they'll read in the tub or on the bowl and you'll be paying the ESB until yer own lights is shut on Judgment Day."

He rapped on the mirrorless medicine cabinet. "Another t'ing, never keeps a feckin' looking glass in a jacks in a house of wimmins or you'll never get yer dinner or yer hole."

Colin laughed, thinking: *The man is a fucking genius in his own way.*

He followed the old man outside to the cluttered front garden, where the goat was napping and the horse stood idle. The cold Dublin sky was growing overcast.

"You're trouble, boyo," the old man said, now out of earshot of the women.

"Beg your pardon?" Colin said.

"Beggin's for the wimmins," he said. "So feck off wi' tha', righ'? But you, y'iv brought more trouble on this family, yeh have. Get somethin' straight. That young wan, Gina, is a traveler. Her mammy was a traveler, God rest her soul. And no matter what she did, Gina's one of us."

"I don't think I'm following you," Colin said.

"The babby in Gina's belly is also a traveler, no matter wha' yeh say or do," Granda said, jabbing a finger into Colin's chest. "But you, Yank, y'ill never be a traveler. Are we clear on tha'?"

"That part I get," Colin said, grabbing the old man's finger. "But my kid will always be *my* kid, too. No matter fuckin' what."

"See? Tha's trouble on the way already. Tha' babby will be a traveler. With cousins and uncles who'll see to tha'."

Colin had no intention of fighting a custody battle with a crazy old man here in Ballytara. He'd get Gina to the States, with an ocean between these lunatics and his unborn baby.

"What did you mean when you said that Gina was a traveler no matter what her mammy did? What did her mother do?"

"Did Gina not tell you about her father?" the old man asked.

"She said her mother and father were killed," Colin said. "She didn't say how or why."

"Which father was she talkin' about?" the old man said as he made his move to go back inside. "The Irish one or the Eyetalian?"

"Italian? What Italian?" Colin asked.

"That bit o' business cost me a son to jail for life," said the old man. "His brothers are not too happy about it, either."

"Rory and Derek."

"Aye," the old man said. "They don't come in the house when Gina's around, except a course for the Furey Christmas hooley. Bad blood betwixt Gina and me sons, but they're still Fureys. And they won't mess with their mother."

"They talked about an Italian, too," Colin said. "What's with the Italian?"

"Time for our tay, sure," Granda said. "I'll say no more. My advice to you is, feck off to America and don't look back."

Inside, Granda plopped down in his chair and collapsed right through the cushion onto the floor. The women and the children laughed uproariously as he remained there in a comical heap. His great-grandchildren began climbing all over him and he tickled them until they writhed and squealed. Now the old man pointed to the fire, where wooden slats, which until minutes ago had held up the chair cushions, were burning.

"I knew I should have nailed them feckin' slats in," Granda said. "If it isn't nailed, she burns it. That woman of mine would burn the lid off my coffin and Christ's cross with Him on it."

"I needed the wood for the fire so that poor Yank won't catch his death," Granny said as she carried out a plate of food piled high with meat, vegetables, and potatoes and placed it at the head of the table. Gina pushed Colin into a chair in front of the food.

"Eat up, Patrick," Granny said.

"His name is Colin, Granny," Gina corrected.

"I knew a Patrick once what looked like a Colin and that's why I get confused," Granny said. "He was a bit mental, the poor crayture."

Colin noticed that Paul sat on the chair closest the fire, his dinner on his lap, feeding pieces of linoleum into the fire. He also fed the fire with spoons full of sugar, which made the flames leap.

Colin looked down at his own plate—mashed potatoes and roasted potatoes, lamb cooked until it was gray, brussels sprouts, cabbage, carrots, and peas. He waited for the others to sit. Then Granda blessed himself and said, "Thanks for the oul grub, dear Lord."

The kids ate from bowls on the floor as the adults dug in at the table. Colin made a mental note of how the Irish ate with both knife and fork in either hand at the same time, using the blade of the knife as a backstop for the fork.

Colin was swallowing a mouthful of meat and potato when he began to gag. He reached in and pulled a long bright red hair through his lips and it kept coming from his throat like a magician's endless scarf. He looked across at the sweating fat granny, her bright red hair exploding from under her greasy head scarf as she leaned across Granda's plate and cut his meat into bite-size pieces.

"Eat it all, yeh rake-thin ghet, or I'll bleedin' clatter yeh," she told him, as if he were a child.

"Feck off, and bu'er me bread," he said.

"Which teeth do yeh have in?" she asked. "I hope you're wearin' your good ones with company in the house, wha'?"

"The good ones, aye," he said. "From the Galway dentist."

"Oh, aye, all right, then. Then use them for more than smilin' at your fancy women."

"Don't start," the old man said. "Leave it out, righ'?"

"Don't mind them, Colin," Gina said. "Mad as hatters but madly in love."

"I do not love this dirty oul chancer," Granny said. "There's a difference between love and a curse. God chose me to be cursed with this scrubber. Him and his fancy women. I'm wide to him . . ."

Granda looked at Colin, rolled his eyes as he chewed, and blew out a stream of air in frustration.

"Catch the next boat home, son," he said.

As Colin tried to settle his stomach, he looked more closely at his plate and saw other sprigs of bright red hair coiled in the butter of the potatoes, mired in a bog of shiny brown gravy, clashing with the green of the brussels sprouts. His stomach bucked and rolled as the others ate.

"'Scuse me," Colin mumbled, bolting for the bathroom. He groped in the dark, leaned over, and clutched the toilet seat that was slick with Granda's piss. And vomited.

After dinner, a loud knock came upon the door. Gina answered it and Luke Furey, covered in grease and coal dust, his Elvis hairdo in full collapse, walked in with a sack of coal on his shoulder and plopped it down in front of Colin.

"This is for you, cowboy, righ'," Luke said. "I traded three crates of milk for this. Payback for the pack of fags the last time. Someday I might come knockin' on yer door in America and I didn't want yeh to think I was inhospitable."

"Feck off outta dat, you," the old man said. "Brings us some milk as well."

"Me ma would kill me if she knew I brought yiz anythin' atall," said Luke.

"Tell me daughter Tesey to ask me arse," said Granny.

Paul snatched up the bag of coal and fed the fire as if it were a famished family pet.

Now the old man passed around glasses of poitin. He poured one for Luke Furey, one for Paul, one for himself, and then one for Colin. Colin tossed it straight back, John Wayne style. It tasted like lighter fluid and he was certain it had melted his esophagus on the way down. "Holy fuck!" Colin shouted.

"Yeh know it's the best poitin when the rats go mad for it, so," Granda said. "They found six big dead ones in the vat at the still where this is from in Roscommon. Hungry feckers chews their way in, drinks it, and the oul rats gets so pissed drunk they drowns in it. When the rats die happy, yeh know it's proper poitin."

Colin said, "You're fuckin' kiddin' me, right?"

"Not atall," Granda said, swallowing another gulp.

Paul took tiny sips and spit it through his front teeth into the fire, watching the flames leap in a white-and-blue dance.

"The men always need a shot of poitin first to prepare themselves for what it does to the wimmins," Granda explained.

"Don't be fillin' that young lad's head with an old mon's shite," Granny shouted as the four granddaughters did the washing up in four separate ceramic washing basins—one for the dishes, one for the silverware, one for the glasses, and one to rinse.

The women finished the kitchen chores and the old man now poured shots of poitin for the women, who belted them back as if it were Ovaltine. Granny took three quick double shots with no initial visible effect.

"My Jaysus, we're in for a night of holy feckin' terror," the old man said. "Not to worry, music calms the married beast, wha'."

"I'll feckin' beast ya," Granny said.

The old man took a pennywhistle from his robe pocket and began to blow a lovely tune. Gina went into a bedroom and returned with a guitar and began to strum.

"A wee song called 'The Emigrant's Letter,' written by a bloke named Percy French in nineteen hundred and ten," Gina said to Colin. "Granda taught me it when I was about ten, didn't yeh, Granda?"

"Did, indeed," Granda said. "Sing it, lass."

Dear Daddy, I'm taking the pen in my hand,
To tell you we're just out of sight of the land,

> *On a grand ocean liner, we're sailing in style*
> *And we're sailing away from the Emerald Isle.*
>
> *And a queer sort of hush came over us all,*
> *As the waves hid the last part of oul Donegal.*
> *And it's well to be you that is taking your tay*
> *Where they're cutting the corn in Creeshla today.*

Several sad verses later, Gina was finished. No one clapped, but everyone drank more poitin. Soon all the women were weeping and hugging each other, which made the babies begin to whinge. The children were put to bed in the back bedroom and more songs were sung. The cousins told some funny stories about life on the road, of weddings and fairs they'd attended all over the country as kids. More tears flowed. Feeling quite drunk, Colin realized he'd drunk six bottles of Guinness and three or four shots of poitin. By night's end, he was also sagging from all the travel. Gina was kissing her Granny and telling her how much she was going to miss her, making her promise to come visit her in America.

Through it all, Granda sat nodding in a kitchen chair, watching the women embrace, nodding his head. Finally, the cousins pulled presents out for Gina. Granny went into the kitchen and stood looking out the window at a stucco wall, smoking a cigarette and crying, her big body heaving.

Colin went back to the bathroom, groping in the dark. As he stood relieving himself, he thought, *If Jack was here he'd throw a net over me and haul me off to a fucking asylum.*

He heard sudden screaming, breaking glass, and a loud commotion coming from the sitting room. He zipped up and hurried out. Granny, roaring drunk, was beating Granda over his head with a picture frame. Blood leaked from his scalp, down over his leathery, white-stubbled face, and splinters of glass covered the floor. Gina and the cousins were trying to restrain Granny, as Paul and Luke sat by the fire, laughing, sipping poitin, passing a blunt of hashish.

"You durty diabolical feckin' tomcat, yeh," Granny shouted, continuing to beat Granda, who cowered, covering his head from additional blows. "Showin' off a picture of yer fancy country woman. I'm wide to yeh, yeh filthy bollocks, yeh. I'll cut if off yeh, I will, and burn it in the fire . . ."

"Granny, for Jaysus sakes," Bridie shouted. "I'm only after buyin' that frame in town today, for Gina, to send us back a picture of the new babby."

"Lamb of Jaysus, woman," shouted Granda, his arms covering his bloodied face. "Yer after drawing feckin' blood, yeh are. This time I'm sendin' yeh in for a good long rest in the mental."

"Don't threaten me with the feckin' mental," Granny bellowed, pointing to the bloodied commercial photograph in the shattered frame. "I'd know this fancy trollop anywhere."

"Jaysus, Granny, it's a picture of a model," Gina said. "The picture comes with the frame, for the love of God in heaven. She's about fifty year younger than me poor Granda."

"He loves them young wans, so he does," Granny shouted. "That's why he stays with me."

Now all three women started laughing and were able to force Granny to sit in a kitchen chair. Luke and Paul were bent in half laughing in front of the fire as the old man dabbed at his skull and face with a snotty hankie, looking at the blood. Shaking his head. He took his teeth out of his mouth and put them in his bathrobe pocket, where they clanked against the ashtray, the lightbulb, and the pennywhistle. He looked up at Colin.

"I'm tellin yeh, boyo," Granda said, bleary with drink. "When yeh get to America, slam the feckin' gate."

The cousins' teary good-byes took half an hour. After they were gone, Colin felt exhausted, drunk, and ready for bed. Granda was asleep on the settee and Granny was snoring in the bedroom. Brianna was asleep in the small back bedroom.

"Your bags packed?" Colin whispered. Their flight was leaving at nine the next morning.

"Aye," Gina said. "I love a trip but this one is terrible sad. I'll miss them all, as mad as they are."

"Where do we sleep?" Colin asked.

"Granda is giving us his bed," Gina said.

"Which room?"

Gina took Colin by the hand and led him out the front door into the cold damp night, across the lawn, and climbed the back steps of the covered caravan.

"You're shitting me," Colin said.

"It's only pure lovely inside," she said, and he followed her in. "I'll light the oul Tilley lamp low and turn on his wireless for a bit o' music. These oul caravans is almost all gone. Hardly no one uses them anymore. All the families is borryin' money from the traveler kings in the Wards and Joyces and O'Briens clans to buy motor trailers like in America. But I love these oul caravans. I was born in this one."

He watched her light the small kerosene lamp, and it offered what little illumination they needed in the eight-by-five-foot living quarters. *This will look bizarre on film*, he thought. He had to bend to move around, but the barrel-top wagon was as neat as an army barracks during inspection. He imagined the camera doing a slow pan of the interior. The rear of the wagon provided a seating area and a small kitchen, filled with dangling pots, pans, and utensils. Canned provisions were stacked next to a hot plate. In the front of the wagon, closest to the driver's seat, was the sleeping area, where a full-size mattress lay on a platform like a captain's bed, with storage drawers underneath. All of Granda's clothes were tidily folded and stacked in a small press directly next to the bed. His shaving gear was on top of the press, next to mason jars filled with nuts, bolts, screws, nails, gizmos. Pieces of uilleann pipes clogged a small wooden barrel.

Framed pictures of the Sacred Heart and Mary with baby Jesus were jammed into the squares of the front wall of the wagon's circular wooden armature. Just over the headboard, a shotgun was wedged into a rack between a framed photo of the pope and a blue delft platter depicting the Last Supper. The overhead squares displayed reproductions of Michelangelo's Sistine Chapel. Many of the other squares on the walls of the wagon featured cracked and faded photographs of the family in different parts of the countryside over the years.

Several fishing poles and tackle boxes were stacked at the foot of the bed, along with some rabbit snares. Dozens of tin whistles, a few mandolins, a couple of fiddles, and three sets of uillean pipes hung from an overhead beam.

"Neat," Colin said.

"Granny disinfects the wagon every day with bleach and Jeyes fluid," Gina said. "Cleanest sheets you ever seen, nary a flea or louse in here."

She pulled back the bedspread on the small bed to reveal snowy white sheets, stenciled with the legend TEMPLE BAR HOTEL. She sat for a moment, looked Colin in the eye.

"Are yeh ready for a babby, Colin Coyne?"

"It scares the shit out of me."

"At least yer honest."

It sounded funny coming from a thief. But he didn't laugh.

"I'll be the best father I can be," he said, shrugging.

"I want yeh to undress me like I was yer woman," she said. "Pretend we're out on the road in the west of Ireland, just us, alone. And then I want yeh in bed beside me and I want yeh to hold me in yer big arms."

Sometimes she spoke to him as if she were narrating a tale, another part of the fiction she created for herself. *She lives a fiction while I'm imagining one*, he thought.

Then, in the tinker's caravan, on the front lawn of a house in Ballytara, where no one acted normal, Colin made love to the real-life Gina Furey, who was carrying his soon-to-be-real-life child.

When he was with Gina, making love, he understood how a woman could make a man like Kieran feel more alive than he'd ever felt before in his life.

Look for
Fork in the Road
Wherever Books Are Sold

Coming Soon
in Hardcover from
Pocket Books